CW00673418

THE HOUSE OF ECHOES

ALEXANDRA WALSH

Boldwood

First published in Great Britain in 2025 by Boldwood Books Ltd.

Cover Design by Alice Moore Design

Cover Images: iStock and Shutterstock

A CIP catalogue record for this book is available from the British Library.

Paperback ISBN 978-1-80415-965-1

Large Print ISBN 978-1-80415-963-7

Hardback ISBN 978-1-80415-964-4

Ebook ISBN 978-1-80415-961-3

Kindle ISBN 978-1-80415-962-0

Audio CD ISBN 978-1-80415-970-5

MP3 CD ISBN 978-1-80415-969-9

Digital audio download ISBN 978-1-80415-967-5

This book is printed on certified sustainable paper. Boldwood Books is dedicated to putting sustainability at the heart of our business. For more information please visit https://www.boldwoodbooks.com/about-us/sustainability/

Boldwood Books Ltd, 23 Bowerdean Street, London, SW6 3TN

www.boldwoodbooks.com

For Dad

xxx

Lie – noun

An intentionally false statement. Used with reference to a situation involving deception or founded on a mistaken impression.

Origin: Old English *lyge* (noun), *leogan* (verb) of Germanic origin, related to Dutch *liegen* and Germen *lügen*.

— OXFORD ENGLISH DICTIONARY

Bread gained by deceit is sweet
to a man but afterwards his mouth will
be full of gravel...

— PROVERBS 20:17

DRAMATIS PERSONAE

PRESENT DAY

Present Day

Caroline Harvey – granddaughter and public face of world-famous reclusive author, Dexter Blake
Dexter Blake – irascible writer who shuns the world
Gideon Morris – Caroline's long-lost teenage love
Margot Bullington – Gideon's soon-to-be-ex wife
Ben Hastings – Gideon's best friend and an ex-boyfriend of Caroline's
Flavia Montgomery – Caroline's elder sister
Steve Montgomery – Flavia's husband
Finn and Logan Montgomery – Flavia and Steve's sons
Linda Drover – Caroline's mother
Alan Drover – Caroline's father
Blanche Fellowes – Caroline's agent
Travis Hibbert – Caroline's ex-fiancé
Bella Arnold – Travis's new girlfriend
Lee Arnold – Bella's father
Eve Darnell – Caroline's friend

Robbie – Eve's husband
Suzannah – Eve's sister
Mark Llewellyn – head of The Dairy
Stacey Jones – manager of the Ten-to-Midnight Bookshop
Kenneth Aloysius Morris – Gideon's golden retriever

Ether Heracles – Characters and Actors

Ether Heracles played by Joe Newman
Allegra Cadwallader played by Connie Wells (Margot Bullington's sister)
Captain Lucifer Transmere played by Sky Baxter
Luna played by Geraldine Leaf
Beau Ferris played by Simon Keystone
Bylgja Opus played by Tegan Morris
Taranis Locomute played by Justin Stein
Ken played by Soozie Restwell
Young Ether played by Jonah Stoppard
Young Bylgja played by Maddie Wells

Tudor Characters

Anne Brandon, Lady Powis – daughter of Charles Brandon, Duke of Suffolk and Anne Browne
Randall Hanworth – Anne's lover
Charles Brandon, Duke of Suffolk – Tudor lothario and best friend of Henry VIII
Princess Mary, Duchess of Suffolk, Dowager Queen of France – youngest sister of Henry VIII and wife of Charles Brandon
Henry VIII – unpredictable monarch
Edward VI – son of Henry VIII and his third wife, Jane Seymour

Mary I – daughter of Henry VIII and his first wife, Katherine of Aragon
Elizabeth I – daughter of Henry VIII and his second wife, Anne Boleyn
Henry Fitzroy – illegitimate son of Henry VIII and Bessie Blount
Katherine of Aragon – first wife of Henry VIII
Anne Boleyn – childhood friend of Anne Brandon and second wife of Henry VIII
Jane Seymour – third wife of Henry VIII
Anne of Cleves – fourth wife of Henry VIII
Catherine Howard – fifth wife of Henry VIII
Katheryn Parr – sixth wife of Henry VIII
Edward Grey, 3rd Baron of Powis – husband of Anne Brandon
Jane Orwell – Edward Grey's lover
Mary Brandon, Lady Monteagle – sister of Anne Brandon
Thomas Stanley, 2nd Baron Monteagle – husband of Mary Brandon
Lady Frances Brandon – daughter of Charles Brandon and Princess Mary, mother of Lady Jane Grey
Henry Grey, Marquess of Dorset – husband of Lady Frances Brandon
Lady Eleanor Brandon – daughter of Charles Brandon and Princess Mary, mother of Lady Margaret Clifford
Henry Clifford, Earl of Cumberland – husband of Lady Eleanor Brandon
John Beaumont – friend of Anne and Edward, a lawyer with a slippery take on the law
Isabelle Dutton – first wife of John Beaumont and friend of Anne Brandon
Elizabeth Hastings – second wife of John Beaumont
Margaret (Meg) Roper née More – daughter of Sir Thomas More and wife of William Roper, friend of Anne Brandon

Margaret Giggs – cousin of Meg More, friend of Anne Brandon

PROLOGUE

HANWORTH MANOR, PEMBROKESHIRE, AUGUST 1545

My father is dead. His laughter will never reverberate around a room again, his wise counsel is no longer available, his passion, his power, his love of life has departed in a golden arc with his mortal soul. All that remains are his worldly goods.

His worldly goods. His houses, his tapestries, his money, his horses…

There is so much, thousands and thousands of pounds worth of treasure, yet none of it is for me. My name is not in his will. In death, he has disowned me. All his effects have been split between my half-sisters and half-brothers. My sister Mary has already left me and is no doubt greeting my father at the Gates of Heaven, while I am alone.

My mother is dead. My sister is dead. My father is dead. There is no one left to comment or judge my behaviour. I am free of their disapproval. In my heart, I promise that those who have stolen from me, those who have thwarted me and those who tried to take my father's affections will soon under-

stand what it means to cross me. The Brandon blood is dark with hidden crimes, with lies and treachery and as it flows through my heart, my vow is this: they will all pay.

— FROM THE LETTERS OF ANNE BRANDON,
BARONESS GREY OF POWIS

1

APPROACHING HEATHROW AIRPORT, JANUARY, PRESENT DAY

'...and the weather in London is drizzly with gusty winds.'

The end of the announcement was greeted with muffled laughter from her fellow passengers.

Rain, she thought, as she slotted her seat belt together, tightening it to give herself the illusion of security, *I'm definitely home.*

The aeroplane banked towards Heathrow Airport and Caroline watched as west London unfurled beneath her. A hotchpotch of coloured dots became clearer, shaping themselves into buildings. The grey strips of road teemed with vehicles weaving insect-like from lane to lane as each car or lorry, intent on its own journey, disappeared towards the horizon. In among these rippling tides of housing and concrete were incongruous stretches of green: fields, urban farms and a patchwork of gardens, all softened by the lowering skies and misty rain.

It was a far cry from the view that had been her constant companion for the past six months: the glittering sun and glowing Pacific Ocean framed by the huge windows of her beachside apartment in Los Angeles. Caroline glanced at her watch, calculating the seven-hour time difference. *Filming will have begun*, she thought. She felt a small lurch of apprehension in her stomach as she imagined the bustling set, the heat of the lights and the wild colours of the scenery. *Everything is fine*, she promised herself, but the whiteness of her knuckles on the armrests of her seat were not simply from her dislike of landing.

The flight attendant walked past, her eyes roving over the first-class cabin as she completed the final checks. Caroline smiled and shook her head in acknowledgement of the woman's murmured request as to whether she needed anything and as she did, she noticed the man in the opposite aisle was reading *Ether Heracles and The Space Sirens* by Dexter Blake. It was the ninth book in the world-wide bestselling *Ether Heracles* series written by Caroline's grandfather.

With a swooping feeling of sadness she looked away but not before the man reading her grandfather's book had noticed Caroline watching him. He grinned and held up the book.

'Have you read it?' he asked.

'Yes,' she replied. 'Several times.'

'Another fan,' he declared, and she could feel the smile in his American vowels as he thought he addressed a kindred spirit. 'This is his best yet, don't you think? It's astonishing how he juggles the story across so many books. The man's a genius. One more to go and then we'll know everything. What are your thoughts on the prophecy?'

The woman behind Caroline leaned forward, her face eager as she joined the conversation uninvited.

'It must mean Ether,' she said, her voice breathy and excitable as, to Caroline's astonishment, the woman quoted from the first book in the series, *Ether Heracles and Andromeda's Sphere*: '"When the darkness is a heavy blight, binding all souls and all stars in fright. One will emerge to save the upper places of air beyond the clouds...".'

'The second line is a reference to the meaning of the word "ether", it's the dictionary definition and later on there is the word "tasks" which is a clue to his second name – Heracles – who in Greek mythology was set a number of tasks—'

'Madam, sir, my apologies for interrupting,' said the flight attendant with a smile, 'but would you straighten your reclined seats, please?'

Caroline took the opportunity to look away and disengage with the discussion, staring out of the window again. She had no desire to discuss her grandfather's books. As his assistant she lived with them day-in, day-out and the endless discussions of fans about the complicated plots had long ago lost their charm. She knew how the series ended and she was wary she might accidentally give away clues if she spoke for too long about the stories to strangers. She was glad she had decided to travel in disguise. Her highlighted hair pulled into a ponytail, her glasses instead of her contact lenses and minimum make-up; it was a very different look from her glamorous media persona when she represented her grandfather at literary and film events.

Dexter Blake, the world-renowned author. A bitter and reclusive man, reluctantly famous and angry with the world for everything. Yet, millions of people read and adored his books, the science-fiction series recounting the adventures of Captain Ether Heracles and his crew of rebels aboard the spaceship, *The Oisin*. Caroline had long been his link to the outside world and he was the reason she was returning from her sojourn abroad. She wondered how his fans would receive the news she would soon be delivering.

There's nothing you can do to change this, she told herself. *Everything must end and Dexter is an old man.*

Her mind wandered away from her grandfather and towards her ex-fiancé, Travis Hibbert. They had separated a month before she had fled to the US and part of the reason for the demise of their relationship was her grandfather with his increasing and unreasonable demands on her time and her life. She had messaged Travis to say she would soon be back in the UK but had received no response.

Another battle yet to fight, she thought as the captain called for the cabin crew to take their seats. Caroline took a deep breath, bracing herself for the landing, her least favourite part of any flight. With her eyes squeezed shut, she waited for the thud of wheels on Tarmac, followed by her whoosh of relief as the roaring stopped and the plane taxied to a halt.

As she pushed her trolley through the arrivals gate, tears filled her eyes. Her parents, Alan and Linda Drover were waiting and when they saw her, they opened their arms. A moment later, she felt her elder sister, Flavia, encircling them all in a hug.

'This is so kind—' Caroline began as her mother hushed her.

'We've missed you,' she said. 'Anyway, you're staying with us for a few days before you head to Dexter's Place, we weren't going to leave you to find your own way home.'

Her grandfather lived in the village of St Ishmaels in Pembrokeshire. The name of the house had begun as a family joke but had somehow stuck.

'Thanks, Mum,' she said as Flavia took Caroline's trolley bearing her two large suitcases.

A few days with her family to recover from her jet lag was what she needed. She knew when she returned to Pembrokeshire, things would be gruelling. Dexter's legions of fans around the world were unaware their literary hero had been given a terminal diagnosis – the reason Caroline had returned. In Los Angeles she had been Dexter's representative on set for the filming of Book Seven: *Ether Heracles and Nareau's*

Curse but with the completion of the manuscript for the tenth and final book in the series, *Ether Heracles and Ishtar's Legacy*, Dexter's health had taken a turn for the worse.

'How's Gramps?' asked Flavia.

'Not great,' she replied. 'There isn't much time left. He says he's mentally prepared for it.'

'Are you sure though?' asked Flavia, as though in denial. 'He's teetered on the brink before but he's always recovered.'

'Not this time.' Caroline sighed, pushing a few stray strands of honey-blonde hair away from her face, her blue eyes sad. 'We have to brace ourselves for goodbye.'

'Oh, Caro,' said her father. 'You'll miss him so much.'

'We all will,' said her mother.

'Will he agree to see us?' asked her father with a wry smile.

'I'm not sure,' Caroline replied. 'Let me see how things are when I get back.'

'Whatever is easiest for you,' said her mother. Flavia scowled and Caroline nudged her sister so they could push the trolley together.

'How are Steve, Logan and Finn?' she asked, referring to her brother-in-law and two nephews.

'Steve's been promoted and the boys are excited to see Auntie Caro.'

'Really?' asked Caroline. 'Is it because they want presents?'

'Mostly,' Flavia admitted, and the shared family moment of impending grief was absorbed into chatter around Flavia's young family.

As they exited the terminal into the light, pattering rain walking towards the car park, Caroline felt a rush of gratitude to be home, even if there were dark days ahead.

2

DEXTER'S PLACE, ST ISHMAELS, PEMBROKESHIRE, MARCH, PRESENT DAY

Caroline stared at the headline:

Novelist, Dexter Blake, dies aged 89

Each of the newspapers spread across the table carried variations of this announcement. From broadsheets to tabloids to the radio to the endless scrolling TV news, the world was mourning the loss of her reclusive grandfather.

His picture flashed across the television screen, followed by a shot of her own face, before cutting to an interview with actor, Joe Newman, who played the eponymous hero, Ether Heracles, in the film series of the books. Caroline was unsure whether the tears in his eyes were genuine or skilful acting. The channel broke to adverts and the face of actor, Margot Bullington, filled the screen.

'Not today,' she muttered turning off the television before returning her gaze to the newspapers strewn in front of her.

Blanche Fellowes, the agent who represented both Caroline

and her grandfather, had warned Caroline to leave her phone off and to avoid the media as much as possible.

'Once it's been announced, Dexter's death will be an enormous story,' she had said. 'My advice is to stay at Dexter's Place until things quieten down.'

'Will they want a statement?' she had asked.

'I'll coordinate with Tanya, the new head of marketing at Antrobus Publishing, and we'll deal with it,' Blanche had replied.

From the moment Caroline had phoned and said, 'He's gone,' her voice tearful, Blanche had swung into action. They had agreed to hold the announcement for a week in order to give the family time to visit Caroline, to adjust, to grieve and to carry out Dexter's final wishes, then with her parents and sister back in London, Caroline had bolted the door of Dexter's Place and waited for the news to break. She had informed Blanche that the funeral had been a small family service with a cremation, which Blanche included in her statement to the media networks.

When Dexter's death was reported the previous afternoon, the extensive coverage and huge emotional outpouring from fans had astonished Caroline and Blanche. Despite Blanche's suggestion to avoid the newspapers, Caroline was curious to read the comments and deciding to minimise the risk of potential scandalous or unkind revelations, she picked up *The Times*. After reading the short piece underneath the one publicity headshot her grandfather had allowed his publisher to use, she turned to the obituaries.

Reclusive novelist, Dexter Blake, 89, has died after a short illness. He was with his granddaughter, Caroline Harvey, who has asked for privacy at this difficult time.

Dexter Blake is the author of the international bestselling novel series, *The Ether Heracles Adventures* which have been described as a literary mix of J R R Tolkien, Arthur C Clarke and Walter Scott. The novels cover a vast historical world combining real events with a mystical science-fiction universe created by Blake.

Born in 1935 in London, Blake was the only child of academic parents, Hugo and Elsie Blake. He was orphaned at the age of seventeen when they drowned in a yachting accident off the Welsh coast. He read Philosophy and English at Christ Church, Oxford University, which is where it was rumoured he was recruited as a spy. There were reports suggesting he worked in espionage throughout the Cold War but these are unconfirmed.

During the 1960s, Blake travelled widely in the US and attended a series of lectures at the Massachusetts Institute of Technology given by writer, Aldous Huxley, entitled *What a Piece of Work is Man*. These lectures were the beginning of the Human Potential Movement, which was formed around the concept that an extraordinary potential lies untapped in all people.

Upon returning to the UK, Blake was inspired to write the first two *Ether Heracles* books. His early attempts were rejected, causing him to question his own talent, sowing the seeds of his later reclusiveness and bitterness towards the world of publishing. However, he believed in his work and, undaunted, penned five more *Ether Heracles* manuscripts, with a detailed outline for the rest of the ten-book series. In typical Blake style he believed there were only two possible publishers for *Ether Heracles,* neither of which are still in existence. He was rejected by both and in a fit of fury, he packed away his manuscripts and threw himself into his other passion: cars. His days were spent tinkering with his fleet of beloved vintage automobiles, which he hired out for weddings and films.

In 1964, Blake married Muriel Silverlock and a year later their only child, Linda, was born. After an unconventional upbringing, in 1990, Linda, gave birth to Blake's granddaughter, Caroline Harvey. Linda Blake never revealed the name of the child's father, the one hint towards his identity being Caroline's surname. The entire family lived in the wilds of Pembrokeshire in the remote house Blake had inherited from his parents. Muriel died from breast cancer in 2005 and it was while Linda was sorting through her mother's belongings, she discovered the box containing her father's manuscripts hidden at the back of their shared wardrobe.

His daughter persuaded him to let her show them to a friend in the publishing industry and the first of the series *Ether Heracles and Andromeda's Sphere* was published by independent publisher Antrobus Publishing in 2009. Six months later, Linda died in a hang-gliding crash.

Blake's editorial debut was an unexpected hit across the world and was translated into sixty-seven languages. By the time the third book, *Ether Heracles and Lugh's Hands (2012),* was published, bookshops were forced to employ extra security staff to control eager fans. Blake went on to sign one of the largest franchise deals the film world has ever seen. However, it was at this point, the already reclusive writer disappeared from view entirely, refusing to take part in any further publicity. Rumours and conspiracy theories abounded suggesting Blake was dead. To allay these stories he issued a new photograph and through his agent announced in future his representative would be his only living relative, his granddaughter, Caroline Harvey…

Caroline stopped reading. The story about her mother's 'death' was one she had long argued with Blanche about but it had been concocted to protect Linda after she and Dexter had argued one Christmas. Dexter refused to speak to her again and this was a stance that never wavered. He also cut Linda's husband, Alan, from his life. After several years, he reconnected with Flavia and she worked alongside Caroline dealing with Dexter's social media and online profile. Although, as far as the world was concerned Caroline was Dexter's sole family.

He would never explain why he adored Caroline but she suspected it was because he knew she harboured writing ambitions of her own. When he decided to step back from his public life, he had hoped that pushing her forward would help her establish her own career, instead she had been subsumed by her grandfather's work.

But now, she thought, closing the newspaper, Dexter is dead and his legacy means I can pursue my own research.

Caroline shuffled the newspapers together and dropped them into the recycling box near the back door before flicking on the kettle. Dexter's Place was hers and she loved it.

* * *

The house had been extensively rebuilt during the Georgian period and more alterations had been made to embrace the Arts and Crafts movement that followed. It was three storeys, although the attic rooms were not visible from the front. A white stone porch with a large wooden front door sat between two vast windows, while at the far end, an extension had been added giving it a charmingly lopsided feel. Above the porch, matching original windows were framed by pointed eaves. It reminded Caroline of a child's drawing of a house but with added grandeur. The building was old, with several walls built during the Tudor period. When she had discovered this she had been very excited.

'They're only walls,' Dexter had murmured. 'You can't even see them.'

He had been correct, the walls had been added to over the years and were hidden within the core of the house. For Caroline, this was unimportant, she knew they were nestled there, their stories adding to the beauty of the old property. When a flood from the bathroom above these ancient walls had caused the plaster to flake away, Caroline had contacted an architect who would be sympathetic about repairs.

His team was all trained in the upkeep of heritage properties and were gentle in their restoration. At one point, Caroline had been able to examine the walls to see if there were any historical markings but to her and the team's disappointment an enterprising carpenter in the near past had smoothed away any anomalies. Likewise, the remains of the old cellar that had been part of the original Tudor property had been plastered many decades earlier and served as a small utility space.

Creeper covered the front of the house, mellowing its granite walls, and to either side were stone arches leading to the gardens at the rear. A large courtyard at the front was surrounded by more beautiful landscaping and a vast garage, once a barn, that had been home to Dexter's beloved cars before he sold them. In the distance on the lawn it was possible to glimpse the wooden summer house where Dexter had worked.

What Caroline loved about Dexter's Place was the way it sat so comfortably in the landscape. Fields surrounded it, gently rolling into the distance towards the village in one direction. The other way led to an ancient woodland that abutted the edge of the garden while a high wall blocked potential intrusions.

Beyond this was the Celtic Sea, where a picket fence allowed the house to enjoy the spectacular view.

Daffodils bounced their heads in the chilly breeze as Caroline picked up her mug of tea and carried it to her office. This was a large square room lined with bookshelves that enjoyed the same sea views as the kitchen. It was Caroline's favourite place in the house and she could gaze for hours at the changing tides. She placed her mug on her desk, smiling at the framed photographs of her parents, Flavia and her husband, Steve, and another of three boys: Logan and Finn with their cousin, Jonah. She had told Dexter he might have argued with the family but she had not and no matter how much he sulked she had refused to remove the photographs.

Caroline spun around in her leather office chair to contemplate the room. Framed artwork of the *Ether Heracles* book covers adorned the walls. It might be her grandfather's name on the cover but she had worked hard on these stories too. There had been many hours of historical research finding inspiration for Dexter. Despite what the world thought, Dexter's 'genius' had not always lasted through each tale and he would often become bored with a story, abandoning it halfway through, leaving her to make sense of his half-completed manuscripts. She had also created vast spreadsheets to keep track of the multiple storylines that were woven through all ten books.

With a sigh, she wondered whether the loyal readers around the world would be satisfied with the ending she and Dexter had created for his characters. Each member of *The Oisin's* crew had a conclusion to their story that fitted with the way they had developed over the books but with plenty of unexpected twists to keep people guessing.

Caroline addressed the portraits of the characters that had been presented to her on behalf of Dexter from the publishing company. 'Whoever expected you to become such household names.'

She walked over to the bookcase, running her finger over the well-thumbed books of mythology, folklore and history. The Greek myths and Arthurian legends had been a huge inspiration to Dexter.

'The old tales are mostly love stories,' he had said to her one day as they discussed plot twists.

'They're about battles and bloodshed,' she had contradicted and Dexter had nodded before one of his rare smiles lit up his face and he'd replied.

'But even among the terrible things, there is always love. It's like life, if you look hard enough, you'll see love is at the heart of everything.'

'Even *Ether Heracles?*'

'Especially *Ether Heracles*.'

The echo of the conversation made her smile as she pulled a battered book of plays from the shelf. It was one she had not looked at for years but there was a quotation inside that she felt might be suitable as an epitaph for her grandfather. As she returned to her desk, flicking through the pages, a photograph fell to the floor. Bending down, she scooped it up. An image of seven young people in 1940s style costumes laughed into the camera. She stared at it in surprise.

'The Seven,' she said. 'Gid, Ben, Nadine, Saz, Jules and Lizzie.'

She was the seventh, standing between Gideon Morris and her then-boyfriend, Ben Hastings. Caroline remembered the day it had been taken so clearly. They were students at Ashdon College and the reason they were all grinning like maniacs was because they had just finished performing the play they had written for the practical section of their drama A-level. It had been a success and it was also the last of their exams, which was a huge milestone in all their lives.

Caroline ran her finger over the faces. She had not seen any of them for years. Back then, they had been inseparable but, as so often happened, they had drifted in different directions. She looked at her own sparkling eyes, her arms around the waists of Gideon and Ben, the two best friends. Gideon had been going out with Nadine Keating, Jules – Julian Thrupp – was unsure of his sexuality at that point, Saz – Sara Longford – was dating a boy in a band and the others thought she was the height of cool, and Lizzie – Elizabeth Grey – had sworn off romance until she arrived at university when she was determined to find herself a man with a title.

'Happy days,' sighed Caroline.

Although they had not stayed in touch in person, social media had given them a vague connection and she was aware Lizzie had indeed found a man with a title but not quite the heady heights of the aristocracy as she had planned. Instead, she had married a vicar. She lived in a country parish where she spent a great deal of her time raising money for local charities. Jules and his husband, Greg, lived in Glasgow with their two sons where Julian worked in marketing. Saz had ditched the guitar-playing boyfriend a few months after they had left college but, using the contacts she had made during their relationship, had found a job in the music industry as an A&R talent scout signing a variety of influential and successful bands. Caroline had lost track of her a few years earlier but she hoped Saz continued to stride around gigs in her skinny jeans and boots with vast numbers of buckles.

She had never found Nadine Keating on any social media and after Ben had dumped her by text when he went away to university after their A-levels, she had not tried too hard to find him, although she had long ago forgiven his teenage behaviour. Gideon's life she had discovered by accident. She pushed the thought away. Even after all these years, she could not think about Gideon without a pang of regret.

'It was a long time ago,' she muttered, looking at the photograph. As she did, she could not help but stare at her own hair in the image. Back then, it was its natural rich copper colour. Over the years, she had added highlights until it was a warm honey-blonde.

A wave of nostalgia and longing overwhelmed her and on impulse she reached for her phone, switching it on and ignoring the beeping as hundreds of messages were delivered. Instead, she scrolled through her contacts and hit a number.

'Hiya, Jade, how's things? Do you have any hair appointments available? I want to go back to my real hair colour.'

3

THE PALACE OF WHITEHALL, LONDON, DECEMBER 1521

'Anne, are you awake?'

Fourteen-year-old Anne Brandon looked up from her copy of *Utopia* by Sir Thomas More. The book had been a present from her stepmother, Mary Tudor, Dowager Queen of France and sister of the king, Henry VIII – and she was now rapping on the door. Her melodic voice made Anne think of snowflakes and honey – sweet but edged with ice towards those she did not like, Anne was relieved to fall into the category of being loved.

'Yes, Mama,' Anne called, marking her place with the silken embroidered bookmark her younger sister Mary had made for her. She placed the book on the cushion beside her and stood, smoothing her skirts as the door to her bedchamber opened.

Mary, now Duchess of Suffolk since her marriage to Anne's father, Charles Brandon, Duke of Suffolk, six years earlier, entered and Anne dropped into a deep obeisance.

'Up you get, sweet child,' said Mary, touching Anne's head with a blessing. 'We have much to do...'

Mary turned away, directing the procession of people in her wake.

'Put the copper bath in front of the fire with the screens around it, stoke up the fire and place the box of perfumes on the table there.'

Anne watched in bemusement as her room filled with livery clad servants, including a stream of pages each buckling under the weight of copper jugs filled with steaming water. The duchess instructed one of her own women to line the bath with thick linen sheets before it was filled with water to which was added an array of oils and petals until the room smelled like an English country garden. The fire roared as more logs were added and screens with embroidered patterns were arranged around the bath. When the duchess was satisfied, she gave a nod and the entourage filed out leaving Anne, her stepmother and two of Mary's senior maids.

'My dear,' said Mary, smiling at Anne's bemused expression, 'tomorrow is Christmas Eve and, while we observe the fast, as is traditional, things will become busier as the days pass, which is why it's important we take care of such matters as cleanliness. There will not be time for full arrangements once the festivities begin.' Her hand swept towards the bath, 'In fact, we'll be lucky to be able to arrange this again in time for New Year.'

'A bowl of hot water will usually suffice—' began Anne but her stepmother interrupted.

'Quite right if we were celebrating at home,' she agreed, 'but you will be taking part in your first masque on Christmas night and it is essential your hair, in particular, is gleaming. You are the beloved stepdaughter of a princess and a queen and you will be carrying my train during the entertainments. We must both look exquisite in order to honour your father and my dear husband, the Duke of Suffolk.'

'Of course,' said Anne, the butterflies in her stomach, which she had been suppressing for days at the thought of her part in the masque, returning with flutters and leaps. Miniscule though her involvement would be: fleeting seconds as she processed on behind her stepmother holding her train before curtsying to the king and queen, then stepping back into the shadows and allowing the ladies and gentlemen of the court to present their elaborate tale.

'Bridget and Joan will help you bathe and will wash your hair,' her stepmother said, indicating the two smiling women who were adjusting the temperature of the water, 'then you will remain in your chamber until tomorrow while it dries. The water will be topped up for your sister Mary to use when you have finished. She will remain with you and your supper shall be sent on a tray. Be sure to eat well as tomorrow there will be nothing until after the noontide bell has rung.'

'Yes, Mama,' said Anne, and the duchess grinned, her face almost childlike in her excitement.

'This will be a wonderful Christmas,' she said, hugging Anne, who breathed in her stepmother's scent of amber and musk, a perfume she had begun wearing when she was Queen of France. 'It's always so exciting to be at court for the festive season. Now, my dear, I must hurry to attend to Queen Katherine, who is also beginning her preparations for Yuletide.'

With a final squeeze, Mary issued a few more orders then disappeared in a whirl of skirts and laughter.

* * *

'Now Annie,' said Bridget, the elder of the two women, 'let me help you undress.'

Anne gulped. After six years of being the stepdaughter of a dowager queen, she had become more accustomed to these unexpected displays of lavishness but they had always been centred on her father, Charles Brandon, and her stepmother, Mary Rose Tudor, the youngest daughter of Henry VII and Elizabeth of York. She had never before found herself with the adult-sized bath and women ready to bestow such extravagances upon her. It was both daunting and thrilling.

For the next hour, Anne luxuriated in the scented water, breathing in the heady aroma of honey soap perfumed with lavender, enjoying the sensation of Joan's gentle fingers as she massaged a concoction of rosemary and rose petals into Anne's hair. Anne lost track of time as Joan combed and rinsed before lifting a small jug containing water scented with camomile and apples.

'Is there vinegar in there too?' asked Anne in surprise as the tangy scent cut through the sweetness of the herbs.

'Yes,' said Joan. 'It's to make your hair shine. It's the dowager queen's own special recipe.'

'Thank you,' was all Anne could reply. She was finding this level of attention overwhelming.

When Bridget and Joan finally helped her from the water, they wrapped her in warmed linen sheets before giving her a pot of pink unguent.

'This is made from mallow and will soften your skin,' said Bridget. 'Rub it everywhere, from your toes to your chin.'

Anne scurried behind one of the screens, trying to ignore the gentle laughter of the women.

'No need to hide from us, my dear,' chuckled Bridget. 'We all have the same parts.'

Anne ignored their teasing and remained out of sight as she applied a small blob of the cream onto her arm. It felt like a cloud had landed on her skin and as she rubbed it in, she could not believe the soothing sensation. She smothered it all over herself as Bridget had advised, then called out: 'Do you have a robe, please?'

'Of course,' came Joan's voice, and a brand-new embroidered wrap, similar to the kind her stepmother wore, was passed over the screen. 'This is a present from the dowager queen. Her words were: "at the age of fourteen, you are no longer a child and it's time your wardrobe reflected your years."'

Anne gaped at the heavy silken robe and as she slipped it on it shimmered against her skin. At first, it was as cool as ice, then as it took her body heat, it became warm, supple and unnerving in the adult feel of it.

'Here are the matching slippers,' said Bridget, moving the screen. 'Joan will prepare the water for your sister, Mary, and as she bathes, you and I will create a masterpiece with your hair.'

Bridget led Anne to a low stool where she indicated she should sit, then seated herself on a chair behind her and began the laborious task of gathering tiny sections of Anne's hair and plaiting each one, securing the ends with a ribbon.

'This will take a long time as you have an abundance of hair and it must all be styled. When we release these braids in the morning, you will have a headful of curls to rival the duchess,' said Bridget.

A few moments later, Joan ushered in Anne's eleven-year-old sister, Mary Brandon, whose brown eyes were wide with excitement.

'Mama has told me I am to use her special soap...' she began, then stared agog at Anne's hair. 'What are you doing?'

'Into the bath with you, young lady,' laughed Bridget, nodding to Joan to lead the younger girl to the steaming copper bath, 'and we'll explain, but if you stand about gawping, the water will be cold.'

* * *

It was another two hours before Anne and Mary were left alone in their bedchamber with a vast tray of their favourite foods.

'Will we always live like this?' asked Mary as she bit into the golden crust of a savoury pie.

'If we make good marriages,' Anne replied, sipping her hot, spiced wine. 'Then we can have beautiful homes and luxuries like these.'

'Papa will ensure we're well taken care of, won't he?' said Mary, but there was a hint of uncertainty in her voice.

'Of course,' said Anne, 'why do you think he buys so many wardships? It's to ensure there are plenty of young, titled men in our household for him to inspect. I overheard Mama laughing as she teased him about assessing the wards as they grow up so he can see which will make suitable husbands.'

'Do you think he would let us marry for love, as he and our stepmother did?'

'Perhaps, if the suitor in question is wealthy and titled,' said Anne, but she was unsure.

After the ensuing scandal and potential ruin her father and stepmother had faced when they had secretly married, she wondered whether her father would behave in such a rash manner again.

'I forgot to tell you,' said Mary as Anne pushed aside the plate of food and settled into the wide chair beside the fire, snuggling into the cushions and embroidered throws provided by her stepmother, 'there is a great deal of gossip...'

'We're at court, there is always gossip.' Anne laughed.

'This was new though,' said Mary, joining Anne and tucking a blanket around herself. 'Your friend Anne Boleyn is returned from France where she's been living in the court of Queen Claude. I heard Papa telling Mama.'

'Why would Papa be interested?' asked Anne. 'He's never had much time for the Boleyns.'

'She's to marry James Butler, son of Piers Butler, Earl of Ormond,' said Mary, 'but her father is angry about the suggestion as it means he'll lose out on the chance to gain the title for himself...' Her voice tailed away. 'At least, I think that's what Papa said.'

Anne grinned at her sister.

'You're not very good at gossip, are you?' she teased. 'You forget to listen which is the most important part. Instead you drift away to your imagination.'

'True,' said Mary. 'The conversation became quite boring, so my attention turned to the new dresses we shall wear when we go to court tomorrow. Mama said you will be allowed to attend banquet this year and I might be permitted to watch the masques. She said we are young ladies of importance and it's time the courtiers began to recognise us.'

'When did she tell you this?' asked Anne.

'This morning when we were in the stables looking at the new hunter Papa bought for Mama.'

'No wonder she insisted Papa buy us so many new dresses and why she wanted to show us her jewels,' said Anne, her eyes sparkling in delight. 'In that case, I'm very interested to hear that Anne Boleyn is back because when we were girls together at the court of Margaret of Austria, Duchess of Savoy, she was always such fun.'

The two sisters gripped each other's hands in anticipation. It was a far cry from the days when, as the motherless daughters of Charles Brandon, they had been shunted from one group of relatives to another. Everyone had always been kind but it was not the same as having a family of their own. This had changed when their father had married Princess Mary, the Dowager Queen of France.

* * *

When news of the marriage had reached King Henry there had been a furore. He could not ignore the fact that to marry into the royal family without permission could be construed as treason but as their father was the king's best friend and their new stepmother was his favourite sister, the consensus at court was that it was a matter of time before they were forgiven. The king's anger abated but he imposed a vast fine. This debt remained hanging over them like a threat and was a constant concern to Anne and Mary's father.

Once the couple was settled, Mary had insisted Brandon's two daughters live with them at the family home of Westhorpe Hall in Suffolk. This had meant Anne's return from her position in the court of Margaret of Austria, Duchess of Savoy, where she had been sent when she was seven years old to learn the skills of a court lady. Mary had been with their mother's Browne relatives.

'We're a family,' their new stepmother had told them when they arrived at Westhorpe Hall. 'Your mother, Anne Browne, died when you were four years old, Anne, and you, Mary, were a baby. My mother, Queen Elizabeth, died when I was seven years old. My heart understands how painful it can be to grow up without a mother. I am your mama now and I shall ensure we live a happy life here and at court.'

Her new stepmother had been true to her promise ever

since, and the house had been full of fun and laughter. The sisters were soon joined by a number of young men and women, wards of her father. As the years passed there were also their younger half-siblings: Lord Henry Brandon, Lady Frances Brandon and Lady Eleanor Brandon.

'Shall I tell you a story I overheard once?' Anne asked Mary. 'To demonstrate the correct way to listen to gossip?'

'Oh yes,' said her sister. 'You always tell the best tales.'

'It's about a jewel called the Mirror of Naples,' said Anne. 'I heard Papa discussing it with Uncle Henry and laughing.' Anne paused. Even though her father had been married to Mary for six years, referring to the king in such an informal manner continued to feel irreverent.

'About a mirror?' said Mary in confusion.

'No, that was its name; it's a diamond brooch with a large pearl attached to it,' said Anne. 'When our stepmama was married to King Louis XII of France, he showered her with presents but when he died, Papa and Mama married without Uncle Henry's permission—'

'Everybody knows this story,' said Mary impatiently.

'Not many people know about the Mirror of Naples,' said Anne. 'When Papa and Mama realised how angry they had made Uncle Henry, they tried to appease him by offering to return Mama's dowry. The new monarch, Francis, was furious and demanded she give back all the French royal jewels, which she did, except for the items she said had been gifts given to her personally. This included the Mirror of Naples and it was worth thousands and thousands of pounds.'

'What did she do with it?'

'When Papa and Mama were allowed to return home, Mama smuggled the diamond back to England hidden in the lining of her bodice and gave it to Uncle Henry to appease him. King Francis claimed it was not Mama's to give but part of the jewels of the Queen of France. No matter how much he insisted upon its return, Uncle Henry refused. Papa said King Francis was "sore displeased".'

'Does Uncle Henry have the jewel?'

'Yes, Papa said that when they travelled to France for the Field of the Cloth of Gold last year, Uncle Henry wore the Mirror of Naples on his hat whenever he met the French king.'

Anne laughed at her sister's expression of awe. When she had first heard the story, her initial reaction had been one of shock but the more she had considered it, she could not help but admire the determination of her stepmother as she tried to make things up with her brother.

'Mama was very brave,' said Mary.

'She was,' replied Anne, 'and we must follow her example. There will always be people who try to manipulate us for their own ends, especially as we are so close to the crown. We must remember women can protect themselves if they are wise and careful, Mama has proved it.'

'We are such sophisticated ladies of the court,' said Mary, yawning widely.

Anne grinned.

'You're quite correct, Mary,' she said, 'and to ensure we don't ruin our image of sophistication by falling asleep at the banquet tomorrow, it's time for bed.'

Anne tucked Mary into the large curtained double bed they shared. As Mary fell asleep, Anne sat in the twinkling candle-light with her copy of *Utopia*. She read a few more pages but the news of her friend's return was like a bee buzzing in her mind and she could not concentrate on the words. Instead, she blew out the candle and snuggled down next to her sister, reliving the days in the Duchess of Savoy's court when she and Anne Boleyn had exchanged secrets. Would her friend have changed? She could not wait until the morning to see her again. Life lay like a shimmering pool before her and she could not wait to dive in.

4

'Annie!'

The young woman's voice called through the crowd and Anne Brandon turned from where she was standing beside a table heavily laden with an assortment of evergreen branches to see her friend Margaret More – known to all as Meg – pushing her way towards her.

'Meg,' she exclaimed and the two young women hugged. 'It's good to see you again, I hoped you'd be here for the garlanding.'

Seated behind her, Lady Elizabeth Marsh, her chaperone, murmured, 'Decorum, girls, we are at court.'

Anne bit her lip but when she glanced towards her, Lady Marsh gave a tiny wink. She had been part of the Duchess of Suffolk's household for several years and shared a similar joy for life as Anne's stepmother, which was why Anne liked having her as a chaperone. A few of the other women were dour, repressing all hints of fun, but Lady Marsh always hovered on the line between court etiquette and placing a few toes over it. Despite the warning Anne knew no punishment would follow the mild reprimand.

But, she thought, *Lady Marsh was correct to remind me.*

As the daughter of the Duke of Suffolk and the stepdaughter of the Dowager French Queen, eyes would be upon her, judging her behaviour. It was important during the first Christmas where she had been allowed to join the adults that she proved her parents' trust in her was warranted.

They were in one of the large rooms leading to the Great Hall and all around them was laughter, enlivened by shouts of glee as the courtiers threw themselves into the task of decorating the palace for the Twelve Days of Christmas. Minstrels played lilting tunes from a balcony, fires roared in the grate and the air was filled with the scent of pine, rosemary and bay. Anne could feel the spirit of Christmas infecting even the most serious of courtiers.

The midday fast had been observed and as soon as it had been broken with solemn prayers and a meal, the festivities had begun in earnest. The first task was creating the symbolic evergreen garlands. In reality, the servants had been making the lavish decorations for weeks, keeping them cool in the barns. Teams of staff were busy decorating the areas of importance but it was tradition for the nobility to spend a few hours making their own. The king and queen would attend towards the end of the afternoon and put the finishing touches to one preprepared by the royal florists and botanists; this would be placed above the dais where the royal couple would preside over the Christmas feast the following day.

'Father was summoned to court by the king to discuss the war with France,' said Meg, standing beside Anne. 'He insisted we join him to take part in the merry-making.'

'We?'

'Father's ward, my cousin, Margaret Giggs, is here; she has brought her cousin, Randall Hanworth who is a relative from her mother's family in Norfolk. They're paying their respects to the Duke of Norfolk as he shares a distant ancestor with Randall's family. Father knew Lady Marsh was here, so he felt Margaret would be safe under her care. He worries too much, she is twelve years old and very advanced for her age.'

'And Randall?' asked Anne. 'Is this his first time at court? Do we know him?'

'It's his first time at court and no, we've never met him before.'

'How old is he?'

'He's sixteen and has been studying in Norfolk under a series of tutors but he'll be spending time with us in the New Year to improve his prospects. He's an orphan with a vast inheritance from a distant uncle in Yorkshire as well as properties and land in Norfolk from his late father. He's a ward of one of his Tyrwhitt cousins but Father feels his sharp mind could be honed and made useful at court.'

'Another young buck to add to the mix of wards buzzing around Father,' said Anne.

'Randall is quieter and more intelligent than the fools who surround the duke,' said Meg. 'He's a poet and is hoping to meet Thomas Wyatt. He has long admired his work.'

'A poet,' said Anne in surprise as she wound a skein of mistletoe around a bay branch. 'It will make a change to be able to discuss poetry rather than endure the bragging from the boys about their endless conquests.'

Meg grinned, then said in a voice of mock seriousness, 'But, Annie, the wards are always composing poetry. They like to show off their skills of courtly love.'

'True,' agreed Anne, 'it's a shame their attempts are terrible.'

The girls giggled as they continued with their task of

winding bay, ivy, holly and rosemary sprigs into the fragrant fir branches.

'Hello,' said a soft voice and Anne looked up. Margaret Giggs had arrived. Her narrow face with high cheekbones, was pinched with nerves at being in the heart of the noisy, bustling, glamorous court.

She bobbed a greeting to Anne and Meg before turning to Lady Marsh who smiled and said, 'Welcome, my dear, come and join us in the garlanding.'

'May I introduce my cousin, Randall Hanworth?' said Margaret.

A young man, tall for sixteen years old, stepped forward. He bowed first to Lady Marsh before turning to the young women, who had dropped into shallow curtsies.

As she stood up Anne felt strangely conscious of the newcomer. The air around her seemed to thicken as she breathed in his scent of cinnamon and sandalwood. Randall had fair hair with dark blue eyes and when he smiled a dimple appeared in his cheek. Anne felt an overwhelming urge to reach out and touch it, tracing her finger around the tiny indentation. Behind her Meg gave a small cough and Anne dropped her gaze, cursing the blush staining her cheeks.

'Randall, you're very welcome to join us,' said Lady Marsh. 'I am Lady Elizabeth Marsh and this is Anne Brandon, daughter of the Duke and Duchess of Suffolk.'

'My lady,' he said and gave another bow in her direction.

'Come, Randall,' said Lady Marsh handing him a pair of sharp scissors, 'we need all the help we can muster.'

'You appear to be doing very well,' he said, admiring their handiwork.

'My father's wards, Edward Grey and Thomas Stanley, were

supposed to have joined us but as usual they've let us down,' said Anne.

'No doubt they've been delayed in the lists,' said Lady Marsh, not bothering to conceal the irritation in her voice.

Anne knew her father had told the young men to make their presence felt during the garlanding. It was an activity the king enjoyed and he noticed if the up-and-coming courtiers displayed their artistic natures by helping the ladies. The king perpetuated the image that he and Queen Katherine had created a merry Camelot in their court; he as the gallant and romantic figure of King Arthur, she as his beautiful wife, Queen Guinevere. He required his courtiers to help enact this mythical world, and the gathering of the greenery to create traditional Christmas garlands was a subtle test of chivalry. The king, her father had told her, knew courtliness was not only about the joust and the hunt but the love of nature and the appreciation of her bounty.

'You will have to advise me, Miss Brandon,' Randall said, standing between Anne and Meg. 'I am clumsy when it comes to such delicate work.'

Margaret, who had moved to sit in a chair beside Lady Marsh, giggled when she heard her cousin's words.

'Don't believe him, Anne,' she said, holding up a ball of twine for the older woman to cut into lengths using a sharp silver knife. 'Randall is being modest. He's very artistic and has deft hands. His painting is superb and he carves intricate small wooden animals.'

'How interesting,' said Anne. 'We may have to put your artistry to the test but for now, we need your strength to move and lift the garland as Meg and I make it beautiful.'

'I'm yours to command, my lady,' he said and Anne cursed the deepening blush on her cheeks.

'Call me Annie, everyone does,' she said.

'Then you must call me Randall.'

Meg nudged Anne and said with mock pomposity, while making no attempt to conceal her gleeful smile, 'If we could return to the garlands, please. Randall, would you hold this end while Annie and I finish the weaving.'

'Of course,' he said and Anne was amused to see he was flustered, too.

'Evergreens are so mystical,' said Anne as she reached for a pile of thin bay twigs and began twisting them into place.

'As it's Christmas Eve these plants will bring us good fortune,' said Meg.

'Can we not bring them in sooner?' asked Margaret, who was laying out lengths of twine. Meg reached for one, tying it around a small bunch of red-berried holly.

'It's a tradition dating back to the Druids,' said Randall. 'They believed tree spirits dwelled in greenery and if they were indoors for too long during the dark days of midwinter they would cause mischief for the household.'

Finished with the bay, Anne moved further along the table and attached several branches of mistletoe, taking care not to damage the white berries. The lustre of the green leaves, the gloss of the holly and the white glints gave the garland a fairy-like shimmer.

'The Druids used mistletoe for healing during their midwinter ceremonies,' said Anne, adding a few more strands. 'According to legend, when enemies met under mistletoe they had to lay down their arms and observe a truce until the next day. It's where the custom of hanging a ball of mistletoe from the ceiling and exchanging kisses under it as a sign of goodwill and friendship began.'

'Really?' said Randall, and his cousin giggled again.

Anne had spoken without thinking and as Randall held up a branch of mistletoe, raising a curious eyebrow, their gazes locked. A disconcerted Anne was the first to look away.

'There are those who believe Christ's cross was formed from wood of the mythical mistletoe tree,' said Meg. 'The legend says that as a punishment after the crucifixion the plant shrivelled and was forever more bound to being a parasitic vine, while the holly represents Christ's crown of thorns. Although, there are many who claim his cross was made from holly wood. It's suggested this has imbued it with protective qualities and is why it's supposed to repel goblins.'

'Ivy guards against evil spirits too,' chipped in Margaret as she unwound the tangled tendrils, 'as do rosemary and bay.'

'Then we're safe,' said Randall, handing Anne another mistletoe branch to weave into the garland.

They worked in silence until Anne and Meg stepped back to inspect their creation.

'This is finished,' declared Anne. She reached across the table where a pile of silken ribbons waited, and tied blue and gold bows around each end to indicate it was from the Suffolks. She summoned two pages to carry the garland away to join the growing pile in the centre of the room.

'Shall we do a holly wreath next?' suggested Meg as Anne and Randall cleared away the detritus.

'Yes,' said Anne, 'the willow frames are over there.' She pointed to the back of the room. 'I'll fetch two.'

'I'll help you,' said Randall, following her.

Anne was conscious of people watching as she and Randall made their way to the table where the evergreens were piled high. Sir Henry Norris, a friend of her father's, was presiding.

'Hello, my dear,' he boomed, his cheeks pink from a surfeit of wine, 'what would you like next?'

'Willow frames for two wreaths, please, Uncle Henry,' she said, bobbing a curtsy.

'And will this strapping young man be carrying your greenery?'

'This is Mr Randall Hanworth, he's staying with Sir Thomas More and is a cousin of Margaret Giggs.'

'Welcome, young man,' said Sir Henry and Randall made the requisite bow.

Norris called to one of the servants who milled around the table and they gathered the items Anne requested and returned to their table.

* * *

As the servants placed the branches in a pile, several slipped onto the floor.

'Careful,' said Randall, bending to disentangle a sprig of holly from Anne's skirt.

Anne remained motionless as he unwound the thorned leaf from the delicate fabric with gentle care. She was intoxicated by his scent, by the long, elegant tapering shape of his fingers and, as he stood, towering over her, the overwhelming masculine nearness of him.

'Thank you,' she said, in a whisper.

'You're most welcome,' he replied and again their eyes locked.

The sound of the trumpet caused them both to jump. Anne's heart was pounding but before she could begin to understand her rush of confusing emotions, the minstrels had struck up a lively tune to indicate the arrival of the king and queen.

There was a rush of feet and a group of young men hurried into the hall via a side door. They skirted around the edge of the crowd, heading towards Anne, Meg, Margaret, Randall and Lady Marsh. Tall, confident and wealthy, these were the courtiers-in-waiting; the group who would soon be taking wives, learning the skills of diplomacy and courtliness. The men who would one day wield the power of life and death over vast swathes of people.

'We were in the lists,' whispered Edward Grey, 3rd Baron Grey of Powis, as he scooted to a halt at Anne's side. His cheeks were flushed scarlet and his dark hair stood up in a shock on top of his head, 'but your father caught us and said we had to join in with the garlanding as it's tradition.'

He nudged Anne out of the way with his hip, leaning towards the pile of holly.

'And, the king is about to arrive,' said Thomas Stanley, another of the Duke of Suffolk's wards who was catching his breath. 'It's always good to be seen to be involved with court frivolities. Meg, pass me one of the rings of willow, then you can weave the holly through it.'

'Who are you?' asked Edward, noticing Randall for the first time.

'This is Randall Hanworth,' said Anne, 'Margaret's cousin.'

'Do you joust?' asked Thomas.

'Of course,' replied Randall with an easy smile.

'Good man,' said Edward, 'now, let's make a start, we want to look industrious when the king arrives.'

They plunged their hands into the evergreens and with much laughter and shouts of 'Ow!' as the holly prickled them, Anne and Meg directed the wreath making.

'Here, Randall,' smiled Anne, passing him another willow ring, 'we'll work on this one.'

The first song ended and as it did a fanfare rang out. Everyone stopped, all eyes on the vast double doors where a herald announced, 'Their majesties, King Henry and Queen Katherine.'

As the king and queen entered, the courtiers sank into deep bows and obeisances, their lowered heads forming a sea of coloured velvet hats and hoods, their brilliant jewels glittering like painted frost in the glowing afternoon candlelight. Anne held her breath. She had curtsied awkwardly and her ankle was beginning to shake, she wobbled, terrified she would fall when a hand steadied her waist. The king's booming voice, full of laughter and excitement, called: 'Rise, rise, my friends, let us continue with the garlanding for there is much mischief to be made this festive season. Music, let us have joyous music to please the angels and the Lord himself.'

'As well as many prayers,' said the queen, but her tone was gentle. The king kissed her hand.

'Thank goodness we have you to care for our souls, my love,' he said leading her to an ornate chair where she sat as the musicians began to play again.

Randall helped Anne to stand.

'Thank you,' she said. 'It would have been awful if I had fallen.'

'I will never let you fall, my lady,' he replied before turning back to the garlanding table, leaving Anne flustered but amused by his attempt at a comment in the tradition of courtly love.

Pages hurried forward putting a low table in front of the queen, before the royal botanist placed a three-quarters finished wreath before her. The queen waved her hand and four of her senior ladies – including Anne's stepmother – hurried forward to help, the rest were dismissed to join their families and friends around the room.

Anne saw the king and her father laughing as they joined the table where several of the queen's ladies had gathered.

'There's no sign of Mistress Blount,' whispered Edward, and Thomas sniggered.

'Enough, boys,' snapped Lady Marsh. 'This is neither the time nor the place to make such comments. They are dangerous in the extreme.'

Edward blushed and Anne wondered if he might argue but instead he bowed his head and mumbled his apologies.

'If the rumours are correct, despite giving the king a son and a daughter, Bessie Blount is no longer in favour,' whispered Meg to Anne as she passed her a swirl of golden ribbon. 'My father has hinted the king is interested in Mary Carey.'

'Anne Boleyn's elder sister?' asked Anne in a low voice.

'Yes, look at her and her husband,' replied Meg.

At first, Anne could not understand what Meg meant. A surreptitious glance at the table where Mary and her husband, William Carey, a gentleman of the Privy Chamber and an Esquire to the Body of the king, as well as a distant cousin of the monarch, were standing either side of Henry. All three were laughing as they added red winter roses to the garland spread before them. Yet, as Anne watched more intently, she realised Mary's eyes were red-rimmed and when the king looked away, her smile drooped. William's demeanour mirrored that of his wife and when they caught each other's eye, a look of despair passed between them but the moment the king commented both Mary and William beamed, their smiles so wide Anne felt their faces must hurt.

Her eyes were drawn irresistibly to the queen on the opposite side of the room. Queen Katherine was laughing with Lady Elizabeth Boleyn, mother of Mary Carey, but neither woman could stop their eyes from flashing towards the king and Mary. The forced jollity was broken when an imposing young woman with dark hair, dark eyes and a confident walk traversed the room, halting beside Lady Elizabeth Boleyn.

'It's Anne Boleyn,' gasped Anne Brandon in delight.

'Do you know her?' asked Edward, his eyes alight with curiosity.

'Yes, we were girls together at the court of the Duchess of Savoy,' she said. 'Anne was already there and she helped me to feel at home.'

'She arrived at court a week ago,' said Edward. 'Your father said she's causing quite a stir with her French manners.'

Anne did not know how to reply, instead she returned to the wreath. When she and Meg exchanged secrets, it felt innocent but whenever Edward served up court gossip, there was a hard edge to his words, a sneer of contempt, especially when it concerned women. Beside her Randall was silent.

Laughter floated towards them, mingled with the music and chatter. Anne looked up, searching for her father and as she did, Anne Boleyn walked from the queen's group towards the king's table where the Duke of Suffolk was at the heart of the activity. The two women stared directly at each other and Anne Boleyn started in surprise.

'Annie?' she mouthed, and Anne Brandon nodded.

A moment later, Anne Boleyn was by her side.

'It's good to see you, my dear,' she said, sinking into a deep obeisance. 'The daughter of a duke and a dowager queen for a stepmother. How things have changed.'

'Please stand up,' laughed Anne Brandon, and in a moment of spontaneous joy, the two friends embraced.

As they parted, Anne realised her father, the Duke of Suffolk, was watching them, his eyes narrowed in displeasure. The king also followed his gaze and for a moment he stared at Anne Boleyn, then he turned away, a frown on his face.

5

DEXTER'S PLACE, ST ISHMAELS, MBROKESHIRE, APRIL, PRESENT DAY

Caroline's phone pinged.

EVE

Is it safe to come in?

CAROLINE

For you, yes, come around the side.

She then turned back to the letter in her hand, frowning as she reread its contents. With a shake of her head, she placed it on the kitchen table then hurried to the side entrance where a slight blonde woman was waiting at the locked gate.

'Eve,' Caroline exclaimed as she let her inside. 'It's so good to see you.'

'You too,' Eve Darnell replied as the two friends hugged. 'Wow, look at your hair. It's stunning.'

'I decided to go back to my real colour,' she said, running her hand through her copper tresses. She was delighted to have her red hair back but it continued to be a shock whenever she caught a glimpse of herself in the mirror.

The old Caroline, she thought whenever she saw her reflec-tion, *or is it the new?*

'How are you coping without Dexter?'

'Fine,' said Caroline. 'We knew it was coming.

'It doesn't make it any easier though.'

'True,' admitted Caroline, who was surprised at she was missing her irascible grandfather. 'Were th photographers or television crews outside?'

'No, the media has gone. There was one guy in a car bu didn't look like paparazzi. He had a dog with him and I think was lost because he was studying a map.'

'A map?'

'Yes, the signal for satnav up here is horrendous. He must know the area well enough to have an atlas with him.'

'Thank goodness the reporters have gone,' said Caroline. 'It was carnage here until last week.'

'It will be again when Dexter's final book is published,' said Eve, following Caroline through to the kitchen.

'Blanche has arranged a big launch in London so hopefully there won't be a repeat performance down here.'

'When is it out?'

'A few months, at the Summer Solstice, 21 June. Tea, coffee? Cold drink?'

'Coffee,' replied Eve and Caroline busied herself with the machine.

'It's strange to think this is the end of *Ether Heracles* and the crew,' admitted Caroline.

'Will you miss them?'

'Yes, they've been in my life for years and feel like real friends.'

'There are the films, so it isn't a complete goodbye.'

Caroline passed Eve her coffee, then picked up her own mug

and led the way to one of the prettiest spots in the house: a raised balcony overlooking the ancient woodland on the boundary of the garden of Dexter's Place.

Caroline settled herself in a cane chair with squashy cushions, grinning as Eve placed her coffee on the occasional table before throwing herself onto the chaise longue opposite Caroline. The two women stared out over the fresh green leaves beginning to cover the gnarled branches with springtime vigour.

Caroline and Eve were a similar age and had become friends several years earlier. Eve's family, the Mundys, ran a local hotel, The Orwell, and she was the youngest of five sisters. She had moved away to train as a chef and, after she had married her childhood sweetheart, Robbie Darnell, another chef, they had both established their reputations before returning to Pembrokeshire to open a bistro on the nearby Milford Haven Marina. One evening, when Caroline and her ex-fiancé, Travis, had been the last lingering customers, Caroline and Eve had begun talking and they had become firm friends.

Eve was one of the few people who had been to Dexter's Place. Usually Caroline held guests at bay, meeting friends away from the property, but Eve was different. She came from a huge family and understood the complexities of family politics. She did not find it unusual that Dexter would remain hidden throughout her visits.

'What do you plan to do next?' asked Eve, picking up her coffee.

'I have a few thoughts,' said Caroline. 'One is to research the history of this place,' she waved her hand around to encompass the house.

'It's Arts and Crafts, isn't it?'

'It edges into the Arts and Crafts movement, the core of the house is late Georgian,' said Caroline, 'but it's the woodland and the surrounding land I want to research. There are ruins in the wood and I'd like to discover what they were.'

'A long-lost Druidic temple used for human sacrifices, perhaps?' said Eve, laughter in her voice.

'I don't think they're quite that old,' said Caroline. 'They could be Tudor or a bit earlier.'

'What makes you think they're Tudor?'

'I was over at the Mary Fitzroy Heritage Centre a few days ago and there are some old maps of the area, one of which included the far corner of the woodland. There were some handwritten notes on the map, so I contacted the Centre and they sent me more detailed images. The writing says, "Hanworth House, private property".'

Eve sipped her coffee, wrinkling her nose as she thought.

'Hanworth is in west London near Heathrow Airport, isn't it?' she said.

'Yes, and there's a Hanworth in Norfolk too,' replied Caroline. 'It's intrigued me, so I've contacted a few of the second-hand booksellers Dexter and I used when we needed out-of-print books, and they're searching for old maps and books that might have any information.'

'You could try Marquess House,' said Eve. 'Their archive is enormous.'

'I've emailed them, too,' she said.

'Do you hope to turn this research into a book? A novel? Non-fiction?'

'Perhaps a novel but I'm not sure how viable it would be. People associate my name with Gramps and the *Ether Heracles* books.'

'Wouldn't that be a good thing?'

'Perhaps, but Gramps has left big shoes to fill. I might be accused of cashing in on his name.'

'Don't let other people's narrow-mindedness stop you following your dreams,' said Eve. 'You put a huge amount of effort into your grandfather's books. I saw how hard you worked editing them before they went to the publisher. Robbie and I have always thought you should have had joint authorship.'

Caroline felt a flutter of nervousness that she disguised with a laugh.

'Hardly; editing is one thing but staring at a blank page and creating a world as complex as Dexter did is a whole other level.'

'I suppose, but you were the one who kept track of the story.'

'What makes you say that?' asked Caroline bemused. She had never discussed the finer details of how she and her grandfather worked with anyone outside her family, Dexter's agent or his publisher.

'Travis mentioned it to Robbie one night when they were out.'

'Did he?' she said, her eyes narrowing with fury at her ex-fiancé.

'Robbie told him about the spreadsheet he'd been creating to help with our ordering and how he'd got confused. Travis suggested he ask you because he said he'd seen the vast spreadsheets you'd created for your granddad to help him keep track of the story over the ten books. He said it was a work of genius.'

'Right,' said Caroline, draining the final dregs of her cold coffee. 'Yes, the spreadsheet was enormous. Did Robbie manage to sort yours out?'

'No, but Tabs did,' said Eve, referring to one of her elder sisters, Tabitha. 'It's handy having so much expertise to call on.'

Eve's four older sisters fascinated Caroline. She and her sister, Flavia, had been close growing up and were best friends but the idea of there being five girls always made her think of the March sisters in *Little Women* or the Bennetts in *Pride and Prejudice*. Eve's eldest sister, Suzannah, was a solicitor who specialised in land disputes, next was Tamar who was a doctor, then Bathsheba, a scientist specialising in DNA and Tabitha, the closest in age to Eve, who was an historian and lecturer at Warwick University.

'Speaking of expertise, do you think Suzannah might be able to help me with something?' asked Caroline.

'I'm sure she would but doesn't Dexter have a fearsome bank of lawyers you can consult?'

'He does; he did,' she corrected herself, 'but this is a land inquiry which is more Suzannah's thing and I wanted some general advice to see whether I should call in the big guns.'

'What's happened?' asked Eve.

Caroline pulled a face, unable to disguise her concern.

'Wait here,' she said and hurried to the kitchen to collect the letter she had been reading when Eve arrived. She handed it to her friend. 'This arrived this morning. It's from a construction company called Salter Holdings who are trying to obtain planning permission to build a complex of exclusive holiday chalets with access to the private beach—'

'Your private beach,' interrupted Eve.

'Yes, the beach owned by this property, which they want to lease. The trouble is, for the visitors to reach it, they would need to access the oldest part of the woodland where the ruins are, and so the company wants to buy it. They've also hinted they have paperwork that might prove the woodland isn't actually part of the deeds of Dexter's Place.'

'That's nonsense though,' said Eve. 'You've always said

Dexter was fierce about his land and access across it. If there were any doubts, he would have sorted it out years ago.'

'I know,' said Caroline, 'but this letter feels like such an intrusion on my home. It's upset me and I wanted advice on the quickest way to shut it down.'

'Do you think they'll be given planning permission?'

'It would be tricky,' said Caroline. 'This is part of the National Park and as an organisation they hold a lot of power over planning permission. The Park Authority works closely with the council and are very particular about allowing people to build in remote areas. The development would border my land, which would give me grounds to object.'

'Let me ring Zannah,' said Eve, and pulled her phone out of her pocket.

Caroline, half-listening to the conversation, was relieved to have confided in Eve. She knew her agent, Blanche Fellowes, would be happy to call in the lawyers but there were other things she needed to discuss with Blanche first and she wanted to know her legal position on the land as quickly as possible.

Eve hung up and turned to Caroline. 'She said not to worry and to send her a copy of the letter. She'll look into it and if need be, send them a stern reply.'

'Thank you,' said Caroline unsure why the letter had caused her such unease.

Eve checked her watch.

'Sorry, Caro, I'm going to have to go, but before I do, there's news.'

'What?' asked Caroline, her fingers crossed in her lap.

Caroline knew that Eve and Robbie had been trying for a baby but instead Eve said, 'The large unit on the marina has been let.'

Caroline stared at her in surprise. This was the last thing she had expected. 'Another restaurant?' she asked.

There had been several ill-fated attempts to turn the two-tier unit into a variety of themed eateries but none had grabbed the local trade.

'No, it's going to be a Ten-to-Midnight bookshop,' said Eve.

'You're sure?'

'Yep, the sign was delivered under wraps a few days ago and Robbie bribed the workmen with coffee and bacon rolls to let him see it. The fitters will be done this weekend, then the books are being delivered and it'll open at the end of the month. You've been saying for ages you'd love there to be a bookshop on the marina.'

'I have,' agreed Caroline, but she was unsure how she felt about this particular chain infiltrating her adopted hometown.

* * *

Caroline watched as Eve roared away in her bright yellow Renault Clio before returning to the balcony and sitting down. She gazed towards the woodland but she did not see the ancient oaks. Instead, a rush of emotions assaulted her: delight, excitement, fear and another she refused to acknowledge. The thought of the bookshop had even pushed the niggling worry of the land request from her mind.

He will have a branch of his bookshops here, she thought with a shiver.

Was it coincidence or had he remembered her mentioning this part of Pembrokeshire? She pulled her phone from her pocket and flicked up his world-famous logo, feeling as she always did, a thrill of recognition. The image comprised a clock with its hands set at ten to midnight, hanging over it was a bunch of mistletoe, while on the left side was a small pair of DM boots with ribbons instead of laces and on the other a crash helmet.

'Gideon Morris,' she said in a low voice, and her mind flew to a night many years earlier when ten-to-midnight had held such significance.

It had been a long time ago, fleeting moments, lost to the past. When her second chance came, she had destroyed it with the lies. At the time, her choices, her decision to keep her secrets had seemed the most sensible path. But now, all this time later, what would he say if he discovered the truth? Could she tell him? Should she tell him?

She gave herself a mental shake and said aloud, 'He's married to Margot Bullington, you fool. Nothing has changed.'

She stood abruptly and marched inside, irritated with herself for allowing her imagination to slide in his direction. Gideon Morris was in her past. She doubted he would even visit the Milford Haven bookshop such was the size of his business empire. She stowed the mugs in the dishwasher and walked into her office, determined to spend the day doing something useful rather than brooding over lost teenage dreams.

6

WESTHORPE HALL, SUFFOLK, MAY 1522

Anne crept through the house towards the side door that led to Westhorpe Hall's extensive gardens. Her stealth was to avoid disturbing her father who was in his study further down the corridor. A satchel full of letters had arrived earlier and he had closeted himself away with instructions not to be interrupted while he dealt with the machinery of government and the royal court. Anne suspected this intense diligence was a panacea for his grief. They were a house in mourning and the darkness in their hearts was a sharp contrast to the golden summer's day outside.

Her six-year-old half-brother, Henry, had died a week earlier. His death had been unexpected and the more terrible for the swiftness of his end. Two weeks earlier, he had complained of a sore throat, then a fever had taken hold and a day later he had been struggling to breathe. To Anne's relief, her pregnant stepmother had been at home in Suffolk, excused from her duties with Queen Katherine and could oversee the nursing of her son.

'The queen struggles when her ladies are with child,' her stepmother had explained when she had gathered Anne and her sister, Mary, at the end of March and announced they would all be returning to Westhorpe Hall for the foreseeable future. 'She is older and unable to bear more children. This makes her sad.'

'Of course she hates seeing you while you're with child,' her father had scoffed. 'You're everything she isn't: young, beautiful, bountiful, and the king's favourite sister.'

'You fool, Charles,' Mary had giggled but she had not contradicted her husband's assessment.

None of them had expected that within a few weeks, tragedy would overwhelm their happy family. When it became clear the fever was serious her father had been summoned home from London. He had arrived an hour before Henry had died, his parents either side of his bed. Ever since, her stepmother, Mary, had been in her bedchamber and her father looked grey and old, his eyes filling with tears of sadness instead of their usual twinkle of happiness.

On silent feet she trod through the puddles of shadow created by the blinds at the windows. In their well of sadness, they were cold from shock, grief and loss, yet Anne longed to feel the warmth of the sun's rays. Along with the rest of the family, she was heartbroken at the death of her half-brother but a welcome distraction had arrived for her among her father's correspondence – a parcel from Meg More. When her father's steward had handed it to her, she had been overwhelmed with the desire to step away from her misery for a few moments; to return to the ease of her life before their loss. This package was her link to her friend, to the court where she had been happy, and she craved the simplicity of these emotions.

Anne skirted around the house and when she knew she was out of sight from most of the windows, she gathered her skirts and ran. The path led away from the lawn and under a walkway covered in wisteria to a tumble of ruins that she and her younger sister, Mary, called the temple.

Many years ago, the collection of fallen walls and piles of stone had been an old chapel. Lightning had struck it during a winter storm and the ensuing fire had left it burned beyond repair. When the Suffolk family had moved to Westhorpe Hall, Anne and Mary had found this secret corner where a hyssop bush grew in a sheltered spot. Beside it the two remaining walls formed a low curve making a perfect seat. Even better, it was hidden from prying eyes. For Anne and Mary it was the ideal place to talk, to daydream and to discuss their possible future husbands.

Anne sat on the warm stone seat and leaned into the arc of the wall, relaxing into the embrace of the ancient stone. With careful fingers, she opened the parcel, excited to read Meg's news. Inside was a note and a copy of *In Praise of Folly* by Desiderius Erasmus, a book she had wanted to read for a while.

'Meg, you're so kind,' she murmured, flicking through the pages.

As she shook out the wrapping another letter fell into her lap and her heart quickened as she saw the handwriting. It was from Randall Hanworth, the young man she had met at Christmas. They had been exchanging notes for several months but she noticed this was the first time he had addressed it to 'Annie' rather than 'Miss A. Brandon'. It felt intimate, as though he had taken her hand or stolen an unexpected kiss and for a moment her nerve failed. Flustered, she reached for the comfort of Meg's familiar hand instead.

The short message explained that Meg's father, Sir Thomas

More, had suggested Anne might find the Erasmus treatise interesting, even diverting during her time of grief. This was followed by the words:

> *Randall remains in our household as a senior page to my father. He is quick-witted and funny but also has a kindness of nature often lacking in the other young men with whom we associate. When Randall discovered this package was for you, he asked if he could enclose a letter. We often talk about you and the happiness of the Christmas we all shared. I hope the memories of our laughter will be a balm during these difficult days.*

A secret smile stole across Anne's face at the thought of Randall discussing her with Meg. Christmas felt an age away but its sprinkling of magic remained, as though the spells they had cast with their evergreen garlands had imprinted themselves on her heart. Whenever she looked back to those heady weeks, images of the lavish bathing, the masque and, vain though she knew it was, her hair in its riotous curls filled her mind.

When Bridget had released the tight plaits her often limp hair had been an explosion of waves. It had gleamed with life, shining chestnut and red in the candlelight as she had carried her stepmother's train during the elaborate Christmas masque. Most eyes had been upon her stepmother, but when Anne had looked up, Randall had been staring at her with curiosity and another expression that Anne could not name but which made her tingle.

Days of feasting, dancing and misrule had followed as the court celebrated the Twelve Days of Christmas. It had filled Anne's heart with glee, especially when her old friend, Anne

Boleyn, had sought her out. They had reminisced about their time together in Mechelen with the Duchess of Savoy. One afternoon, encouraged by Anne's mother, Lady Elizabeth Boleyn, the two girls had demonstrated one of the dances they had been taught to huge applause. This had been followed by the recitation of a poem about courtly love where they took alternate lines, a party piece they had often performed at the Mechelen court. Again, there had been shouts of delight and Anne Brandon had glowed with pleasure when her father had hugged her tightly and said: 'You're becoming a true lady of the court, my sweet. It's as though you've grown up overnight. I shall have to begin my search for a suitable husband.'

Her father's eyes had shone with pride as the king congratulated him on his daughter's vivacity, but they had all noticed his eyes flickering towards Anne Boleyn as though she were a curiosity he could not yet fathom. Even after the festivities were over, the Suffolks had remained at court, with Anne being part of a group of younger people, all of whom were learning the way of life that her father and stepmother promised would one day be hers.

What her parents had not known was that the real reason for her smile throughout this joyous time was the growing friendship between her and Randall Hanworth. She blushed; perhaps more than friends, she thought, after their stolen kisses under the mistletoe a few minutes before midnight on New Year's Eve. Her fingers brushed her lips as she thought of his mouth on hers. The gentleness which had nevertheless promised so much more.

With a shiver of remembrance, she placed Meg's letter inside the Erasmus book for safekeeping and reached for Randall's note. She tried to imagine his face as he had written her name. Had he smiled? Had he been thinking about their moments alone? There was a slight tremor in her hands as she broke the red seal embossed with his crest of an acorn on two chevrons.

My dearest Annie,

Meg has told me the sad news about your brother and I offer my condolences to you and your family. This must be a difficult time and you are in my thoughts and prayers. If it is not indelicate, when your family is once again ready to receive visitors, I might ask your father if there is room in his household for me. Would this idea have any appeal for you? Sir Thomas More has taught me well and it is his suggestion that I would learn even greater skills for advancement with the Duke of Suffolk. My potential future is a happy prospect but the thought of being near to you is my true desire. My heart has been captured and I count the days until I can see your smile again. My fondest thoughts to you, my beloved Annie.

Until we meet again.

Anne's cheeks burned at his words. She knew his extravagant comments were part of the tradition of courtly love encouraged by the king but beneath the overblown charm, his sentiments felt genuine. He wanted them to be together. A slew of emotions engulfed her: delight, a whisper of fear and then hope. Randall had a vast inheritance but no title and she knew her father was determined she and Mary should both become ladies of rank when they married.

She wondered if she would be able to persuade her father to take Randall into the household. She was certain that if the duke was able to witness the younger man's wit, cleverness and charm, he might prefer a potential suitor with a fortune rather than a member of the nobility. After all, her father was always struggling to repay the debt he owed the king.

'Hello, my lady,' said a gentle voice and Anne jumped, letting out a small shriek.

'My most humble apologies,' said Edward Grey, Baron Powis. 'I was returning from a walk and had intended to pause in the temple myself. It was beyond my wildest hopes to think a beautiful maiden was awaiting my arrival.'

Edward Grey bowed low. As he stood up, he ran a hand through his medium-length black hair so it fell in waves around his handsome face. With his clear skin, high cheekbones and twinkling brown eyes, there was no denying Edward's good looks but for Anne, he held little appeal. During their time at court, she had watched him and had been surprised to see how many girls had responded favourably to his charms, giggling over his dubious poems and blushing at his grandiose flirting. She had always felt his attempts at courting were false, insincere and lacking the light-hearted touch other boys had perfected. To her, his good looks were surface deep, spoiled by his arrogance and self-satisfied swagger.

'Were you asleep?' he asked.

'I was praying,' said Anne with hauteur, her fingers crossed in her lap to exonerate herself from her deliberate lie. 'You startled me.'

She took pleasure in Edward's discomforted look, surreptitiously slipping Randall's letter into the Erasmus book alongside Meg's.

'I'd been reading a letter from Meg More. She sent me a new prayer to help with my grief,' she elaborated. 'After this, I planned to study her comments on Erasmus's words. It was why I didn't hear you approach.'

Edward rolled his eyes as though such a way to spend one's

time was beyond tedious, then appeared to remember they were a house in mourning and rearranged his face into one of polite interest and concern.

'Is that why you came out here?' he asked.

'Yes,' she replied. 'The house feels too full of grief at present. I wanted to be able to breathe.'

'May I sit?'

Unable to think of a good enough reason to refuse, Anne shuffled over to make room. It was a small space and their legs brushed as he squeezed in beside her.

'You must be very sad,' Edward said. 'My half-siblings live with my mother in Lincolnshire. Mother writes of their antics and, although I rarely see them, her words make me feel as though I am there with them joining in their fun. It would be devastating if one of them were to die as suddenly as Henry.'

Anne glanced at Edward in surprise. He had been part of the Suffolk household since her father had bought his wardship in 1517 and whenever the other young men dared to show any sort of emotion, Edward was the first to jeer, to belittle their woes and tell them to be real men. This was the first time she had ever heard him speak with any sensitivity. He gave her a crooked half-smile.

'You did not think I was able to feel so deeply?' he asked.

'No, I didn't,' she said. 'You're not known for your thoughtful nature, it's your no-nonsense strength of character which is usually praised. It's gladdening to know there is a heart in your chest, after all.'

'You despair of me, don't you, Annie?' he said, but there was amusement in his words.

'I do,' she agreed. 'You're overwhelming with your spirited nature and I find it...'

She hesitated, not wishing to insult him. Edward was her

father's ward as well as a baron in his own right. His father had died when Edward was an infant and he had inherited the title while in his crib. A title of any sort was to be treated with respect.

'Rude?' he suggested. 'Arrogant? Annoying? Stop me when I reach the correct word.'

'Forceful,' suggested Anne, smothering her smile as Edward grimaced.

'It's difficult to understand how to behave,' Edward said and Anne realised he was being honest, there was no jest in his voice.

'What do you mean?'

'I'm a baron and have been since before I can remember,' he said, 'which means I have a certain status, but all my money is in the wardship, so I have no freedom until I come of age. Your father teaches me to be confident, to walk with pride and show I'm a man of substance, yet I can do nothing without his permission. Even worse, my ancestral home, Powis Castle, is shared with the Dudley family. I'm a baron-in-waiting with half a castle. It's frustrating.'

'Your home is jointly owned?' said Anne. 'How can that be?'

'In 1421 when Edward Charleton, 5th Baron Charleton and the then Lord Powis died there was no male heir and the castle and estates were divided between his daughters, Joan and Joyce. Joan married Sir John Grey and Joyce married Sir John Tiptoft. It became very awkward because both families lived in the castle.'

'How confusing,' said Anne who had no idea Edward's family history was so complicated. 'Did both heirs have a claim on the title?'

'The title went to the eldest daughter's husband upon her marriage. This was Joan Charleton who was my ancestor and she married John Grey making them Lord and Lady Powis. The Tiptoft heir is John Sutton, Baron Dudley, who is Joyce's great-grandson.'

'What a mess,' said Anne.

'This is what happens when there is no male heir, only daughters,' said Edward. 'Your father was in a similar position until young Henry was born—'

Edward stopped abruptly when Anne gave him a shocked look. Edward squeezed her hand in apology. He made no attempt to disentangle his hand and Anne felt it might be construed as insulting to free herself from his grip.

'Powis Castle is even more confusing,' he continued. 'The Outer Ward belongs to the Tiptofts and the inner ward to my family, the Greys. When I reach my majority, I intend to persuade Lord Dudley to sell me his half of the castle and restore it to its former glory.'

'You've never spoken of this before,' said Anne.

'It's a secret,' he said. 'Lord Dudley may not wish to sell in which case I shall use other means to reunite the two halves. Unless I have the castle and the barony, I won't consider myself a real man. It's important to me to reclaim my heritage. However, before then, I intend to marry and raise sons of my own so the title can continue through them.'

'Thank you for trusting me with your dreams,' said Anne.

Edward continued to hold her hand, his thumb making circling movements across her fingers.

'What are your dreams, Annie?' he asked.

An image of Randall flashed across her mind.

'To marry a kind man who has an edge of excitement, to have a beautiful home and to be able to have fun,' she said. 'These are not such worthy ambitions as your own but women have very little say in where the path of life might take them.'

'You didn't mention healthy sons,' he said, winking.

'Sons and daughters will come if God intends,' said Anne. 'These are other things over which we women have little control.'

'Your father is a good man,' said Edward.

'Indeed, but he will ride with the devil when needs must and I'd like such a courageous and dashing man by my side, too.'

Edward considered her, then gave a slow, gentle smile. She had never seen such a warm expression on his face before and it changed him. He looked more mature, his features were softened and for a moment she understood why others found him attractive.

'There are rumours that now we are at war with France again, your father will soon be leading the troops for the king,' said Edward. 'If he goes, I shall join him. It's time to prove myself on the battlefield so when I take my place at court the Powis title will stand for honour, valour and steadfastness, a worthy supporter of my liege – lord King Henry.'

'Edward, these are fine sentiments—' began Anne.

'There is another reason,' he interrupted. 'I wish to prove myself worthy of your hand in marriage, Annie. When your father bought my wardship five years ago from my grandfather, he admitted he was considering me as a future son-in-law. You are a vision of beauty. You have strength, intelligence and elegance. It would be my humble joy to imagine you as my ravishing Lady Powis. Would you find it an exciting quest to help me regain my castle? To rebuild it? To be mother to a castle full of sons?'

His face was eager, his eyes were shining; Anne stared at him aghast but before she could reply, she heard her name being called and felt a wave of relief.

'It's Lady Marsh,' she said.

'My lady, you should leave first to avoid suspicions of a tryst,' said Edward.

Anne gathered her book and the parcel wrappings, bobbed a curtsy of farewell and fled. As she hurried towards Lady Marsh, her mind whirred with all Edward had said and she wondered how she would be able to dissuade him from his plans of marriage.

7

SUFFOLK PLACE, SOUTHWARK, MARCH 1524

'The king has forgiven me,' said the duke as he raised his glass for it to be filled.

The duchess smiled, placing her hand on Charles's arm and squeezing it in a playful fashion.

'As I knew he would,' she said with a laugh.

Anne watched as Thomas Stanley hurried forward to pour the Gasçon wine into her father's glass. She wondered how the young man, who was due to inherit the ancient Monteagle titles, felt about being a sewer. This was the term for a servant of high rank, but nevertheless, a servant. It was a task many of the wards undertook as part of their education with the duke and for the evening Thomas was responsible for ensuring the correct courses and drinks were served.

It was one of the many strange things about the nobility, she thought. These young men from high-ranking homes are taught to serve their elders and betters but whether this built respect or resentment she was unsure.

Thomas Stanley stepped back and Anne saw her aunt, the Duke of Suffolk's elder sister, Anne, Lady Shilston, who was seated beside the duchess, give her brother a wry look after his hubristic comment.

'As if the king would have done anything else, Charles,' she said. 'Henry has always admired you. We all know that even if you had unseated him and deposited him in the mud he would have roared with laughter. However, a word of warning, my dear brother, he is the king. Mary knows better than anyone how he can change his mind in the beat of an angel's wing.'

Charles looked suitably abashed.

'You're quite right, dear sister,' he said.

'I warn him all the time,' said the duchess. 'Don't fret, sister, it's only when he's here he allows a shimmer of overconfidence to show.'

'It's with good reason the king trusts you, Charles,' said Sir John Shilston. 'You're a champion of the joust, a successful diplomat and you've led many successful military campaigns. Even with the disaster of our French adventure last year, the king knew its failure was not of your doing but down to the machinations of the Duke of Bourbon...'

A flurry of music began and a few seats away, Anne Brandon, who had been listening avidly to the conversation between her father, stepmother, aunt and uncle could no longer hear the discussion over the flowing notes. The war in France was a constant topic of conversation in Suffolk Place, the elegant and expansive palace on the Southbank of the River Thames where the Brandons lived when they were in London. In France, her father had once again triumphed despite the failings of the campaign overall and with him, Edward Grey and another rising star at court, Edward Seymour. Her father had been impressed with Seymour and had knighted him in the field – a high honour indeed.

Anne glanced around wondering if Seymour was at the gathering to celebrate her aunt's birthday but she could see no sign of his narrow face and cruel mouth. She was relieved. She had not liked the man when they had met at court the previous week. Despite Seymour's absence, Suffolk Place was bursting with guests, many of whom Anne knew, although there were enough new faces to keep things interesting. Her father had informed her that the king had been invited but other duties had kept him away.

Other duties, mused Anne. She wondered if this included Mary Carey who was said to be the king's mistress and possibly carrying his child.

Beside her, Edward Grey, Baron Powis, raised his glass for more wine, imitating the duke's confidence but, whereas Charles Brandon's subtle request had been carried out with a quiet air of sophistication, Edward's had a flourish of arrogance. Thomas Stanley glared at Edward and summoned a lower servant to his side, whispered an instruction in his ear and sent him to their group.

The young man, a newly arrived page, blushed a deep red as he filled first Anne's, then Mary's goblets before passing Edward and topping up the glass of the girl on his other side, Jane Orwell. With a final flourish, he attended to Edward's drink. Anne waited for the explosion of temper but instead Edward laughed and held his glass up in a salute to Thomas Stanley who was watching from his position behind the duke and gave a mock bow. The two young men had known each other for years and were involved in an endless game of friendly rivalry.

'Why is Thomas serving?' asked Anne. 'Mama said he would be sitting between Mary and me.'

'He cheeked your father when we were in the lists today,' said Edward. 'The Duke had no option but to issue a punishment.'

'Cheeked or teased?' asked Anne.

'He crossed a line and made the sort of comment he might have made to one of us,' Edward waved a hand to indicate the group of younger people, 'suggesting the duke might need to have his eyes checked. Unfortunately, the Duke of Norfolk was nearby and while you father might have let it pass if there had been no one around, he couldn't be seen to be insulted by his ward in front of another duke.'

'Why would he make such a comment?' asked Jane Orwell. 'Does the Duke of Suffolk have trouble with vision?'

Anne and Mary suppressed their snorts of laughter. Jane Orwell was new to the household and had a distant connection to the Brandon family through Anne's great-great-grandfather, Robert Brandon, and his links to the Guild of the Holy Trinity. Jane's father, Sir Lewis Orwell, was descended from a cohort of Robert Brandon's and the two families had often aided each other in times of trouble. When Jane had arrived with her younger brother, another Lewis, but known to all as Ludo, the Duchess of Suffolk had invited them to join the 'younger set' as she referred to Anne, Mary and the wards. Ludo had quickly made his mark among the young men as he was an expert hawker. However, Jane's vapid comments and tendency to over-dramatise situations had been trying Anne and Mary's nerves for the past few days.

'There was a minor accident,' explained Edward. 'The duke and the king were jousting but the king had forgotten to lower his visor. The duke didn't hear the shouts of the crowd to stop and because his vision was impaired by his own helmet, he rode straight at the king. He broke the lance on the helmet, narrowly missing his majesty's forehead and covering him in splinters of wood.'

Jane gasped, holding her linen napkin over her eyes and whispering a prayer.

'The poor king,' she murmured, as Anne and Mary rolled their eyes.

'There was no lasting damage,' Edward assured her, 'in fact, the king laughed.'

'But why didn't the duke stop when he saw the king wasn't correctly attired?'

'In order to protect the eyes, the slit in a knight's visor is very narrow,' said Edward. 'When you're travelling at speed it's hard to see anything except for what's directly in front of you.'

'It's important to protect your eyes though,' said Jane, gazing into Edward's. Mary giggled, hastily stifling it as Anne stepped on her foot under the table.

'It doesn't always work,' Edward said. 'Splinters can fly through even the smallest of gaps which is why most knights raise their chins at the point of contact. You lose sight of your opponent but your eyes are spared. If the duke was already raising his chin, he wouldn't have seen the king at all.'

'It sounds very dangerous,' said Jane. 'My mother believes tournaments are not suitable places for a young, unmarried lady so my experience is limited. Can men die during the joust, Baron Powis?'

'There are accidents, particularly if a knight falls from his horse, but the lances are tipped with coronals which blunts them so there is no real damage done,' replied Edward.

Anne watched the exaggerated manner with which Edward swigged his wine and knew he was flattered by Jane's attention. The Orwell siblings were among a number of new faces, others included the trainee lawyer, John Beaumont, who had come highly recommended from Sir Thomas More. He sat opposite Anne and beside him was Elizabeth Hastings, next to her were

Isabelle Dutton and Lady Lucy Somerset, a maternal cousin of Anne and Mary's.

Anne picked up her goblet and watched Edward over the rim with an amused expression.

If Randall were here, she thought, he would be laughing at Edward's pomposity.

'Do you understand how jousting is scored, Jane?' Edward asked, taking a slow sip of wine, holding her gaze.

'Not really,' she admitted, unaware she was being teased.

'Let me explain,' said Edward, 'then if you ever watch me, you'll know when to cheer.'

Jane blushed and John Beaumont murmured, 'Steady on, old man.'

Edward ignored him and continued.

'A match is three lances. One point is earned for breaking a lance on a man between the waist and the neck. You gain two points for breaking it on the helmet. The higher score is because this is a much smaller area and helmets are designed to sweep backwards over the head so the lance can slide off it. Finally, a knight earns three points for bearing a rider to the ground. If you're able to do this, you also win his horse.'

Jane stared at Edward in awe.

'You're so wise, Baron Grey,' she said.

Edward gave her a condescending smile before returning his attention to Anne.

'Has your father spoken to you yet?' he asked in an undertone.

'About what?'

'You'll find out soon enough,' he said and bestowed upon her the same expression he had given Jane before resuming his conversation from earlier with John about horses.

He's so arrogant, thought Anne. Not like Randall.

* * *

Anne's friendship with Randall Hanworth continued and he was the standard by whom she judged the other young men around her. For a number of happy months, Randall had been part of the Suffolk household but his responsibilities had forced him to return to Norfolk. He wrote regularly, confiding in Anne.

> *My aunt, Ethelreade, has requested my presence to help her with issues over the land my father left me. An uncle is trying to claim a portion of the inheritance in lieu of a debt he states my father left but it's nonsense. My father's accounts are scrupulous and any legal challenges will easily be dismissed. My friend, John Beaumont, is helping me to resolve the issue.*

Randall's words had proved true. The case had collapsed but he had felt it was prudent to remain at the family manor and help to run the property that would be his as soon as he reached his majority. Three weeks earlier he had written again and Anne's heart had leapt at his words.

> *Perhaps, when I inherit my lands, I can persuade your father that I will be able to keep you in the proper style befitting the daughter of a duke and the stepdaughter of a dowager queen.*

The words kept Anne warm at night as she prayed fervently for her dream of becoming Randall's wife to become a reality. The talk of marriage was a favourite topic among the glamorous, wealthy group of whom she counted herself a member. Too young for real court duties, they were nevertheless invited to the occasional event, as though they were being allowed to try on their impending adulthood to see whether it fitted. As the Duke of Suffolk's eldest daughter, Anne enjoyed a higher status than many of the other young women, viewed as an eligible maiden, her value diminished only by her small dowry. This was a result of her father's endless financial struggle as he tried to repay his debts to King Henry.

'My dear, would you care to dance with your father?'

Anne had been so lost in thought over Randall she had not heard the duke approach.

'Why, Papa, of course,' she said and, rising from her seat, curtsied.

The duke bowed and led her to the dance floor. His presence meant other couples could dance and within moments the space between the U-shaped arrangement of tables was filled. Out of the corner of her eye, Anne saw her stepmother giving instructions to the chief steward to push the tables back to give the dancers more room.

Over the past year, since the birth of her newest half-brother, also named Henry, after the son who had died, the Duchess of Suffolk had been instructing Anne and her sister, Mary, in the correct way to run an estate.

'Men fool themselves that they are the power in any household,' their stepmother had said with a tight smile, 'however, we women know the truth. We are the guiding hand that ensures everyone is fed, paid and clothed. Never expect your future husbands to show gratitude for this Herculean effort because they simply don't understand.'

Anne had bristled at these words, men always wanted praise for their achievements, no matter how small. Why should women be denied acknowledgement of their contribution to the family well-being? Not only did they bear the children, they ran the homes, accompanied their husbands about their business and ensured their husband's lives ran smoothly when they were in residence.

When Anne had asked why they could not expect praise, the dowager queen had shrugged and said: 'Because this is a woman's lot. Ever since Eve was blamed for Adam's fall from grace in the Garden of Eden we have had to carry the burden of blame. Any actions we take to improve the lives of those around us are considered penance.'

A slow, molten fury had flowed through Anne and she had written to Meg More about the situation. Meg had replied in equal anger:

It's insufferable...

she had written,

...but what choice do we have, Annie? It is either abide by these age-old laws or be left unwed with no household or income. Neither of us wish to become nuns, so we must follow this path. We must be subtle in our discussions when others are nearby or we may be accused of unnaturalness and witchcraft...

The music began and Anne was drawn from her thoughts as her father spun her around.

'You have grown so tall,' he said as he led her through the *gavotte*, their faces flushed and laughing as they trod steps they had danced since Anne was a child.

When she had been tiny, he had carried her in his arms as he spun around to the music, throwing her in the air until she screamed in excitement. Then, as she had grown older, she had danced with her feet on his as he had swept her through the moves. Her father was a tall man but Anne came to his shoulder and felt safe as he now guided her through the steps.

'I'm seventeen, Papa,' she said. 'A woman grown.'

'A beautiful woman,' he said, 'which is why it is time to announce your betrothal.'

'My betrothal?' she said, her feet faltering slightly. 'You promised I would have some say in my future husband but we haven't discussed any young men.'

'True,' the duke said, 'but I didn't think it was necessary as I believe you shall be satisfied with my choice. I have long watched you and this young man and believe there is an accord.'

Anne's hope rose as she twirled under her father's arm and danced around him, clapping her hands in time with the music.

'Is it Randall?' she said.

For a moment her father looked nonplussed.

'Randall?'

'The wealthy young man with whom you were so impressed in the summer...' she stopped as she saw a look of sadness pass over her father's face.

'But he has no title,' said the duke.

'Does it matter? He has a vast fortune,' she said, then in a less certain tone, 'and we are in love.'

'Oh, Annie, I had no idea,' the duke said, the laughter draining from his face. 'I thought I had always made it clear, it's essential you and Mary marry titles.'

'Why?'

'Your stepmother is a princess, the children I have with her all carry her royal blood and will always be protected by their status as the grandchildren of kings. You and Mary are but Brandons and we have a chequered past. The best way to keep you on an equal status with your siblings is for you and Mary to marry as high a rank as possible.'

'What do you mean? A chequered past?' asked Anne in surprise.

'The Brandons were not born to power,' he said. 'We've worked our way up from a start as lowly men. Our high status is new and because of the toughness we've had to employ in the past to gain our position we continue to be mistrusted by many of the noble families.'

'But, Papa, you're a duke.'

'I wasn't always,' he replied. 'My great-grandfather was an esquire which is a rank below a knight but he schemed and toiled, climbing his way up the social scale. His son, William Brandon, who was my grandfather, made enough money to own a ship. This gave him status and wealth, but William was a difficult man and not well liked.'

'How so?' asked Anne.

'There was a court case, long, long ago when he was accused of numerous violent and distasteful acts,' said the duke, his revulsion reverberating through his words. 'It wasn't until William was pardoned of all offences and made Marshal of the Marshalsea Prison in Southwark that our rise to real respectability began in earnest. It's why this house, our beautiful home, is in Southwark, it's where the Brandons made their fortune. Once my grandfather had established himself at the Marshalsea, he became an advisor to your stepmama's grandfather, King Edward IV.'

'And this was when the Brandons' fortunes grew?' asked Anne.

'For a while,' replied the duke, spinning her around, 'until my late father, William, was charged with High Treason.'

'What? Why have you never told me this before?' she said in horror, as she and her father crossed in front of each other. 'Was he executed?'

'Oh no,' said Brandon. 'The accusation was made by the usurper king, Richard III. He had declared your stepmama's mother and all her siblings illegitimate in order to claim the throne, and during an argument over some land that had once belonged to my mother, Elizabeth Bruyn, he threatened my father with a charge of High Treason. By then, my father was loyal to Henry VII and when the battle for the throne came, my father was Henry Tudor's standard bearer at Bosworth. God looked down from his heavens that day to ensure the true king triumphed and when his righteous reign began all thoughts of treason against my father were removed.'

He spun her around again.

'Your mother, Anne Browne, was a distant cousin on my mother's side,' he said. 'She was beautiful, Annie, like you. The land I own in Warwickshire was part of the dower your mother brought to our marriage, this is why I've bequeathed it to you in my will.'

'Why are you telling me this, Papa?' asked Anne. 'Are you ill?'

'No, my sweet child.' He laughed. 'I'm hale and hearty but I wanted you to know there is substantial provision for you when I'm no longer here to protect you. Annie, you're my first born and I am prouder of you than I can say but being the eldest brings responsibility. If you were a son, you could marry a wealthy heiress without a title because you would inherit mine but you're a girl. Therefore, to give us respectability and to further our family name you must marry a nobleman.'

Anne understood his words even if she did not like or agree with them. She also knew her father was implacable; there would be no chance of negotiation or persuasion.

'Who do you propose, Papa?' she asked as her father whirled her into his arms and hugged her tightly.

'Edward Grey, Baron Powis. You and he are friends, you spend time together, I thought you would be happy with this choice.'

Anne could not speak. Edward had suggested their marriage many times but she had ignored it, thinking he was teasing her. How could she have missed his intent? With her head so full of Randall she had never imagined her life with another. Her father's arms enclosed her and she knew he was doing what he thought was best. Edward Grey was a good match, a handsome young man with a title, money and a castle. She would be a baroness.

'Thank you, Papa,' Anne said at last. 'You are indeed a thoughtful and kind parent. I hope Edward and I shall be as happy as you and Mama.'

The duke gave her one final squeeze then released her.

'He's a good man with great prospects,' he said, his tone was gentle.

'I know,' she said, but her voice was tiny, choked by the tears of disappointment.

She forced a smile and as she did, she saw Edward Grey watching them as he danced with Jane Orwell, a smile of smug satisfaction marring his handsome face.

8

MILFORD HAVEN MARINA, PEMBROKESHIRE, APRIL, PRESENT DAY

Caroline parked her car and pulled the zip of her puffa jacket up to her chin. It might be April but the wind whistling through the marina held more hints of winter than spring. The forest of masts on the row upon row of moored boats chimed and clanged with the age-old song of the sea as Caroline buried her hands in her pockets. She turned into the breeze and headed towards the shops, cafés and restaurants that made up the bustling waterside community.

As she rounded the corner, she saw it: the shop she had been pretending to herself held no interest whatsoever. The double-storeyed corner plot glowed with light on the gloomy day, the purple Ten-to-Midnight logo offering a warm point in the grey backdrop.

Even if she had not been collecting a package, she knew she would not have been able to resist the pull of the bookshop. She had squared it with herself by saying it was far easier to pick up the items they had sourced for her in person instead of having them delivered but she knew this was a lie. She wanted to see his shop.

The marina was quiet with a few hardy souls battling through the cold. Caroline smiled at a woman she recognised who was carrying a tray of cups from her coffee run to Eve and Robbie's bistro, then paused to gaze at the boats again before turning her eyes to the vast estuary.

Oil refineries had once brought wealth to the town of Milford Haven but as they had closed one by one, leaving only a few to offer employment, the fortunes of the area had shifted and turned as often as the tides. Caroline thought there was a majesty to the remaining oil industry that brooded on the banks of the estuary. Vast metal containers stood sentinel in front of huge chimneys which burned away the excess gas and fuel. Around these was a myriad of mysterious hangars and pipelines, all served by tankers so huge they seemed to defy the laws of physics.

She breathed in the salty air and felt her head clear. Should she return home? she wondered, looking at the shop again. It would be simple to send a message and ask for the books to be delivered or she could ask Eve to collect them on her behalf.

Am I a behaving like a fool? she thought. Was entering the bookshop the equivalent of cutting the thread on a seam and watching as her life unravelled, falling into tatters on the ground.

Her conversation with Blanche Fellowes earlier in the day had unsettled her and she knew this was why she was jittery. Blanche had sent Caroline a Zoom link and the moment she had appeared on the screen Caroline had known it was going to be a difficult conversation.

'I've read your email,' Blanche said. 'Caro, what were you thinking?'

'What do you mean?'

'Why is Travis still living rent-free in your riverside London apartment?' Blanche exclaimed.

'You knew I'd let him move in when he took the job with the Metropolitan Police. He wasn't earning much when he first moved back to London,' Caroline said. 'I didn't want him to be homeless—'

'It was supposed to be a temporary arrangement while he settled in,' Blanche interrupted. 'He left you nearly a year ago because he was seeing Bella. Did you think the two of you would be reunited?'

Caroline, who unimpressed at being treated like a child, felt her own temper flare.

'Yes, back then I'd hoped when the situation had calmed, we might make a go of it again. When he left, we agreed we'd discuss things in six months' time.'

'But that didn't happen,' said Blanche, 'and now the woman he left you for has moved in.'

The discovery three days earlier that Travis Hibbert had ensconced his girlfriend, Bella Arnold, into Caroline's apartment had been a shock. Travis had sent a terse text informing her of this development before demanding Caroline speak to the security company who managed the building and officially add Bella's name to the apartment. Travis was furious that not only had security tried to deny Bella access; they had also clamped her car when she parked in one of the two residents' bays that went with the flat.

'He's played you, Caro,' Blanche said. 'He's taken advantage of your good nature.'

Caroline had not replied. When thrown at her with such blunt ferocity she realised the stupidity of her actions but at the time they had seemed reasonable. She and Travis had been together a long time, he had known things with Dexter would change eventually. It was because of this she had been confident their separation was nothing more than a small bump in the road.

'Have you any idea of the danger of this situation?' Blanche asked, and Caroline admitted defeat with a single nod of her head. 'Do you want the legal team to serve notice on them?'

'Yes, please,' she replied. 'It's time I moved on. Travis and I are over.'

Blanche's face had softened at Caroline's woebegone voice. She had run a perfectly manicured hand with its chunky silver rings through her streaked blonde and grey hair. Caroline was never sure whether the blonde or the grey was natural but it suited Blanche's ice-blue eyes and high cheek-boned face. Thin to the point where it was bordering on dangerous, Blanche's uniform of impeccably tailored suits in a wild array of colours worn with a man's white shirt were her trademark. Yet Caroline knew underneath Blanche's apparently cold exterior, there was a kind heart and a determination to protect and champion her many clients.

'Leave it with me,' she said. 'I'll ask the legal team to give him three months' notice. Does that sound fair?'

Caroline agreed then – insisting she had an appointment – leaned forward to disconnect but as she did, Blanche said, 'I like your hair. It's good to have you back.'

Caroline had smiled her acknowledgement through gritted teeth, then spent twenty minutes pacing her office until fuelled by her anger with Blanche, Travis and herself, she had jumped into her car and driven to the marina. As she relived the conversation in her head, her fury flared again and with a determined step, she marched towards the new shop.

From the angle she approached, Caroline caught a glimpse through one of the side windows. The interior of the Ten-to-

Midnight bookshop looked welcoming, with piles of books and a collection of armchairs grouped around a roaring log-burning stove. But, when she saw the picture window at the front, she wondered if she should flee.

'No,' she exclaimed.

A huge cardboard publicity image of her grandfather's, as yet unpublished, new book *Ether Heracles and Ishtar's Legacy* dominated the display. It was suspended on transparent fishing wire to make it look as if it were flying through the star-strewn backdrop. A toy version of the spaceship, *The Oisin*, flew towards it, and hung at different heights were copies of the rest of the series. There were editions ranging from the original, well-thumbed paperbacks to glossier special collector's items. In among these were a variety of pictures of the actors who played the crew of *The Oisin.*

Caroline squinted at a few of the smaller items and realised they were props from the earlier films. One was a cap badge from the costume worn by Connie Wells who played the female lead: Chief Engineer, Allegra Cadwallader, the second-in-command on the rebel spaceship.

'Connie,' Caroline murmured to herself, although she could not help but smile.

The stars of the *Ether Heracles* films were all huge fans of the books and the stealing of tiny artefacts was a badly kept secret on set. Everyone on the production team was aware of the pilfering and towards the end of each shoot would circulate a list of items that would not be needed in future episodes so crew members, stars and extras alike would be invited to keep a memento.

'Very cheeky,' murmured Caroline.

The tinkling of the bell over the door announced her arrival and she was not sure whether to laugh or weep when she saw the life-size cardboard cut outs of *The Oisin* crew arranged around the shop.

Caroline gazed from one to the other, these people were as familiar to her as family. There was Joe Newman who played Ether, she was godmother to his youngest son, Ether, which made her wince. A cut-out of Simon Keystone, the man who had been cast in the part of Beau Ferris in the fourth film, *Ether Heracles and The Race of Jupiter* glared menacingly from another corner. When the book had been released eleven years earlier it had been a turning point for Dexter as this was the first time fans had queued around the block on publication day, desperate to find out what happened next. When it was revealed that Allegra, who all the fans eagerly wanted to marry Ether, married a new character, Beau Ferris, there had been uproar. Beau Ferris had become the most hated man in the world.

The cardboard figures were from one of the premieres, given away free once the red carpet event was finished, and she wondered whether it was Gideon who had requested them or whether the manager of the new shop was the super-fan. The thought Gideon might have read the books tingled through her like an electric shock.

Caroline wandered away from the *Ether Heracles* display, down the winding corridors created by the shelves, breathing in the scent of the books. There was nothing so wonderful to her as a bookshop. Around another corner, the counter came into view and she realised she had been led in a circle. It was a clever design because here was the hub of the place: the log burner was to the left of the counter and to the right were the stairs that led up to the performance space and café. She glanced towards the counter but it was empty.

Typical, she thought with a wry smile. *Everyone is so trusting here, unless they have incredible security cameras and even now I'm being biometrically scanned and my details stored in a secret database...*

She forced herself to break off the path her overactive imagination was taking. *This is what has brought disaster to my life,* she thought. The need to exaggerate, to embellish, to lie. There would be no more, it had already cost her too much.

Caroline moved to an octagonal table that was laden with books, a selection of new and classic. Then, she heard familiar music and the opening scenes of the second film in the series: *Ether Heracles and The Lake of Tawaret* coming from the rear of the shop.

ETHER
We have to use the Blast Drive, Allegra. It's our only hope of escaping The Wicked.

ALLEGRA
But, Lucifer said the mechanism was loose and it would have to be operated manually. (A BEAT AS SHE TURNS TO HER COMPUTER SCREEN) He lied. Lucifer must have switched the blasters off. I'll reboot them.

ETHER
(OPENING COMMS) Crew to bridge. This is Code Gold. This is NOT a drill.

The film stopped and a man's voice said: 'Look, there, when all the extras who are crew come in, the woman with the blonde hair, it's definitely her. Not only that, she crops up in all the films.'

Caroline froze, she recognised the voice. A cold shiver ran down her spine.

'Maybe. She has red hair though,' another man replied.

'It's a wig.'

'Look closer, that woman has brown eyes. Hers were bright blue.'

'Could be contact lenses.'

'Perhaps...'

'Do you think she's forgiven us yet?'

'I hope so.'

Despite the fact she had a package to collect, Caroline turned to leave. The second voice had caused her as much angst as the first. *Why were they both here?* This was a nightmare. She could not stay.

But you knew it was a possibility, her conscience whispered, and Caroline could not deny the truth. It had seemed unlikely though; especially for them both to be on the premises. His final question, had she forgiven them? She had, many years ago but, she wondered as she turned on silent feet and moved towards the door, *will they forgive me if they ever discover what I've done; the lies I've told for so many years?*

Her hand was on the door handle when she heard Gideon say, 'I'm so sorry, I heard the bell but was distracted by...' he let the sentence drift. 'Is there something I can help you with?'

Her hand trembled but she could not ignore him, she had never been able to resist his voice – soft, melodic, a hint of London in his vowels. She took a deep breath.

'I've come to collect two items you've sourced for me,' she said and turned to face him for the first time in twelve years, but as she did, he ducked down behind the counter.

'Of course. Ms Harvey?' he questioned. '*The Brandon Letters* and *Maps of Tudor Pembrokeshire*. The Brandon book is rare, there are very few copies available but we were able to source this through our Canadian connections.'

There was a thunk as he placed the heavy package on the counter and straightened up. Caroline waited, then he looked at her properly. His dark green eyes narrowed and his face registered confusion. Caroline smiled; he had not changed much. His thick dark hair was greying at the temples and he had laughter lines around his green eyes. His clothes were more expensive versions of his preferred jeans and shirt combination from his college days, but he remained the Gideon Morris she remembered.

'Caro?' he said in astonishment.

'Hello, Gideon,' she replied and the broken heart she had tried so hard to tell herself had healed, cracked a little bit more.

9

'Caro Drover! Oh my goodness, it is you! Ben, get out here. You'll never guess...'

A moment later, she was enveloped in a hug.

'This is astonishing, but why was your package addressed to Harvey?'

The delight in his eyes seemed to fade.

'You're married?'

'No...' she replied, although she was not sure why she felt the need to explain, especially with his own high-profile marriage to actor, Margot Bullington, but before she could say any more another man emerged followed by a golden retriever.

Time had not been as kind to Ben Hastings as it had to Gideon Morris, his once unruly mop of curls had thinned and he looked careworn.

'Caro?' he gasped, then looked shamefaced. 'I'm so sorry—'

'Ben, we split up sixteen years ago. I'm over you and you're forgiven,' she said with a laugh.

The dog sniffed her hand, then sat beside Gideon.

'This can't be Ewan,' she said, 'but it looks like him.'

'It's Ewan's grandson; this is Ken.'

Ben grinned and for a moment as the three old friends stared at each other, it was impossible to believe so much time had passed.

'Why are you two here?' she asked. 'You own the company. Don't you have a manager?'

The Ten-to-Midnight Books chain had begun online, selling new and second-hand books, often rare titles. When the first shop had opened in west London, Caroline had watched its progress with interest. In a small outlet with a downstairs, the shop was one part of the business. The basement had been converted into a performance space that held weekly book readings, as well as the occasional poetry slam, hosted authors and opened its doors to local book groups. It had been a huge success and more branches had sprung up all around the UK, then the world.

As the popularity of the bookshops increased, the owners, two old friends, had done a great deal of publicity. The fact one partner was Gideon Morris, a high-profile TV and film producer, had helped. Ben Hastings had often completed interviews looking shell-shocked at his own success. It was their natural on-screen banter that had helped to create a buzz around their business.

'Stacey Jones is the manager, but she doesn't start until later this month. We thought we'd rent a place down here for a while, have a bit of a holiday and set it up ourselves,' said Gideon. 'It's been ages since we've done one and I miss the challenge. We always do a soft opening first. It gives us a couple of weeks grace in case of any problems before the advertising kicks in and the launch events begin.'

'And, super-fan here, wanted to find Dexter Blake's house so he could worship at his gates,' added Ben, nodding toward Gideon.

His words were said with affection.

'You're a heathen, you've never fully appreciated the Arthurian beauty of the *Ether Heracles* books,' Gideon said.

'Unfair, I've read them all.'

'You're a fan?' asked Caroline, touched that both these men had read her grandfather's books.

'Huge—' began Gideon.

'Obsessed is more accurate,' said Ben. 'He claims he can empathise with Ether, as though his beloved hero can read his mind. It's why he bought this unit, to be near the home of Dexter Blake.'

Gideon took the teasing with good humour.

'It wasn't the only reason,' he said. 'We wanted to expand into Wales and when we discovered this space, it was perfect.' He hesitated, then continued in a more uncertain tone. 'Actually, Caro, perhaps you could answer something for us? If you don't mind.'

'If I can,' she replied with trepidation.

Despite his fan status, it appeared Gideon had not yet made the link between her new name and Dexter Blake.

'Were you ever an extra in the *Ether Heracles* films?'

'Er—'

'Leave her alone,' said Ben.

'There's a woman who's been in all of them and she looks like you, except blonde. Were you wearing a wig?'

'Gid, you nutter, leave her alone.'

Gideon held up his hands in mock surrender.

'Sorry, he's right, I do get carried away. My sister-in-law is in the films and I feel there's a family connection. I was hoping I'd spotted you there.'

'As I've said many times, why would she be?' said Ben.

Caroline listened to the exchange with growing discomfort. How much should she tell them? It was on the tip of her tongue to deny everything, to lie again, but a rush of rebelliousness filled her. She did not want to lie any more.

'Yes,' she said, 'it is me. I'm in all of them.'

'I told you!' crowed Gideon, punching the air as Ben groaned.

'Are you a fan too—?' began Ben, then Gideon stared at her and she could see he had finally understood. He looked at the package on the counter.

'Caroline Harvey?' he said and there was awe in his eyes. 'You're Dexter Blake's granddaughter.'

'Yes.'

'But I met your granddad at your eighteenth birthday party, we did karaoke together.'

'That was Dad's dad, Granddad Brian,' she said, anxiety rising. 'Dexter was Mum's dad.'

'Oh yeah, my mistake,' said Gideon. 'Why did you wear a wig?'

She had forgotten about his forthright manner, the inability to stop asking questions, but she had always found it endearing, almost childlike as he felt his way into conversations. She would draw a question mark in the air if his interrogations became overwhelming and he would apologise, backing off.

'It wasn't a wig. I was blonde for a long time.'

'Why?'

She drew a question mark in the air and Ben hooted with laughter as Gideon apologised with good grace.

'And you're straight back under the thumb,' Ben said.

Caroline blushed.

'Hardly,' she said. '*You* were my boyfriend, remember?'

'I know, but you worshipped Gid from afar,' said Ben.

'What? I didn't—'

'Caro, it was years ago. I knew you fancied the arse off my best friend but he only had eyes for Nadine Keating.'

'Who turned out to be bisexual and is now happily married to a lovely woman called Daniella with two sons,' said Gideon.

'No way,' said Caroline her eyes wide with surprise. 'How wonderful!'

The bell over the door rang and Gideon went into professional mode, greeting the new customer and hurrying behind the counter to check the database to see whether they stocked her requested book. Ken followed Gideon and was fussed by the customer.

'Here you are,' said Ben handing Caroline the heavy package. 'Are you researching something?'

'The history of Dexter's house,' she said. 'I think these might have some useful information.'

'Sounds interesting. I did a history degree, perhaps I could help?'

Caroline stared up into his familiar face and grinned. 'Perhaps you can,' she said.

'Come upstairs and I'll make us a coffee,' he said. 'Then we'll give you a proper tour.'

'Are you sure?'

'Yes, it's wonderful to see you.'

Caroline followed Ben up the wide staircase. The ease with which they had fallen back into their old bantering manner made her feel more like herself than she had for years. They saw her as fellow student and old friend, Caro Drover, not Caroline Harvey, granddaughter and public face of Dexter Blake. She realised how much she had missed being herself, talking to old friends, sharing a history, but she had chosen to step away, to close those doors to the past. In a moment of panic, she wondered if she deserved this rush of affection from the two men, particularly Gideon.

He's married, she reminded herself. He's forgotten about our entanglements, but as Ben, at the top of the stairs, spread his arms wide in the manner of a magician's assistant and said, 'Ta da, the newest branch of Ten-to-Midnight books.' Caroline realised she was continuing to delude herself because she could not deny the name of his shops and its connection to the significant moment they had shared all those years ago.

It must be a coincidence, she told herself for the umpteenth time. A quirky name, nothing more, but she knew this was a lie too. The tiny DM boots on the logo were based on the pair she had worn, adorned with ribbons instead of laces, the crash helmet was Gideon's from the days he had owned a battered purple moped they had both loved. She shifted the heavy package from one arm to the other and allowed Ben's enthusiasm to envelope her, pushing away her thoughts from the past.

'It's wonderful,' she said staring around.

They were standing in a large room but with the use of clever spacing between the furniture and different flooring it had been divided into clear sections. Where Ben stood was the café and bar area with tables grouped to give maximum advantage of the views of the marina and the estuary beyond. In the far corner, there was a large section of tiled floor with a low stage in the centre creating the performance space. Around this were sofas and armchairs with lower tables and there was room to add extra chairs for an audience. Bookcases were tucked into unexpected places and a sign on the wall announced:

Please read as many books as you like!

A line of green tiles drew the eye towards the double doors leading out onto a small terrace where there was more seating. All around the walls were framed prints of giant book covers intermingled with famous quotations and signed photographs of authors.

'Grab a seat,' said Ben. 'Do you want coffee or tea?'

'Coffee, please,' she replied, placing her package on one of the tables that looked out to sea.

Instead of sitting, Caroline wandered around, studying the books on the shelves, smiling in remembrance. The bare brick walls, the sprawling sofas and even the rug with the yin and yang image were as familiar as her own skin. She had known what to expect because she had visited other branches of Ten-to-Midnight and each performance space was identical: a sophisticated recreation of Gideon's teenage bedroom. It was the place where The Seven had spent many hours, talking, laughing, discussing their plans for the future and rehearsing their drama practical.

She walked back as Ben placed three mugs on the table before disappearing into the kitchen again. Caroline was impressed by the attention to detail; the mug was from a local pottery and the signs above the counter advertised the coffee as a variety made a few miles away. It was this level of care that had made the Ten-to-Midnight brand so successful.

'Here,' said Ben, placing a plate of pastries in front of her. 'When Gid's wife saw the first shop and performance space she said, "Do you think it's a bit too book-y?". But then, she's never been the sharpest knife in the drawer.'

'Do you mean Margot Bullington?' asked Caroline unable to resist discussing Gideon's marriage.

'Yes,' said Ben, his eyes flashing with anger. 'I've never

understood what Gid saw in her. She's one of the most spiteful women I've ever met.'

Caroline did not reply. In his teens, Ben had been very easy-going, although always protective of his friends, and the hurt in his eyes on Gideon's behalf told her more than his words.

'Between us,' Ben continued, 'another reason we came down here is to give Gid a break. He and Margot are divorcing and the decree absolute will be through later this week.'

'You're joking,' whispered Caroline. 'I thought they were supposed to have one of the most trouble-free marriages in the celeb world.'

'Nope,' he said, taking a glug of his coffee, 'she's been leaving him, having affairs, then returning to Gid for years and he forgives her every time.'

'It doesn't sound like the Gideon I knew,' she said. 'He was adamant he'd never forgive anyone's infidelity, not after the way his parents' marriage ended.'

'I suppose we change. As teenagers, you think you know exactly how to behave in relationships but as adults we often do things we never imagined we would,' said Ben. 'The reason Margot kept running back to Gid was because he was the one with the BAFTA for his documentaries and not her. Why he kept taking her back, I have no idea.'

'But Margot's family is famous,' said Caroline. 'Wasn't her dad in that film we kept watching when we were at college, *Mongoose Summer*?'

'"*A poignant and daring cross-cultural love story*" that was actually so terrible it was funny and that's why it became a cult classic.'

'True,' agreed Caroline, 'but the Bullington family is old acting royalty in this country. Isn't her uncle Bullington Bullington famous for a TV detective series in the eighties?'

'Yes, *Jet Spencer, P.I.* and her cousin, Tallulah, presents *Psychic Pets* on an American cable channel. His father thought the Bullington name was iconic and decided to use it as his eldest son's forename too.'

'There's her sister, Connie Wells, too,' said Caroline. 'She's the most talented. She plays Allegra Cadwallader in granddad's film adaptations.'

'Yet, the rest of the family refuse to acknowledge her talent which is why Connie decided to use her married name. And, of course, there's Margot the haemorrhoid cream queen,' said Ben, and Caroline tried not to laugh. 'Her advert for: "Haemorrhoid Healer, the gentler way to ease your pain" has been her most prolonged TV appearance ever. What concerns me though is Gid's tipped to win another BAFTA for his latest documentary series. Did you see it? The one that followed the group of friends through drug rehabilitation and helped them as they all signed up to various local research projects.'

'Didn't they help save an old manor house by proving it was of historical importance?' said Caroline, who had watched it avidly.

'Yes and they all learned skills to help with its restoration.' Ben said.

'It was wonderful watching them overcome such huge difficulties and succeed.'

'I'm worried Margot might try to stage another reunion if he wins.' Ben confided.

'But you said they're getting divorced,' said Caroline.

'Yes, she had another affair and he told her it was the last time. He filed for divorce but it doesn't mean she won't try to persuade him to marry her again. In every other way, Gideon is one of the strongest people I've ever met, but when it comes to her, he crumbles.'

From below they heard the shop bell ring and voices as the customer left.

'Anyway, I've told you so you understand Gid's mindset. He's pretending to be fine but he's angry and heartbroken at Margot's betrayal.'

'Does he want her back?' asked Caroline.

'No, but on the other hand who wants to be divorced? I've got two under my belt and it's horrible.'

'What?' gasped Caroline.

'I'll tell you another time,' he said and Caroline saw the sorrow in his eyes. 'Try one of these, they're from the amazing bistro a few doors down called, Morforwyn. Do you know it?'

Caroline smiled.

'Yes, it's run by my friend, Eve, and her husband, Robbie,' she replied.

'I'm a fool,' laughed Ben. 'You're the local, we're the incomers but it feels so strange. Whenever I think about you, it's in west London when we were teenagers.'

'"*We're a long way from home...*",' she replied, a famous quote from her grandfather's books.

'"*But the view is beautiful...*",' came Gideon's voice as he emerged at the top of the staircase, followed by Ken.

'Get a room, you two.' Ben said with an exaggerated groan.

'I've put the "Closed" sign on,' said Gideon, sitting beside Caroline, while Ken climbed onto a large armchair and observed them for a few moments before settling down and resting his head on his paws. 'It's such a miserable day, apart from you and the lady who's just left, we haven't seen a soul.'

'Eve and Robbie, at the bistro,' added Caroline when Gideon raised his eyebrows questioningly, 'are lucky, they usually have a steady trade in the mornings but at this time of year it slows down after lunch. Even they have quiet days when they only see one or two people.'

'So, tell us why you wanted the maps?' said Gideon, picking up a fruit tart and biting it in half.

Caroline sipped her coffee. 'My plan had always been to research the ancient woodland around Dexter's Place because there are ruins among the trees and I'd like to know more about them. It feels even more urgent now because I had an unexpected letter.'

She explained about the request from Salter Holdings to gain access over her land, to lease her beach and the veiled threat that she might not own the woods.

'Luckily, Eve's elder sister, Suzannah, is a solicitor who specialises in land disputes. She's looked into the deeds and there's no doubt whatsoever about ownership, the land is mine. Well, it was Dexter's but he left me everything,' she said, and under the table she crossed her fingers. 'Suzannah said this company, Salter Holdings, is renowned for being ruthless. She's agreed to take over any correspondence and liaise with Gramps's legal team if necessary.'

'Do you think the old maps will help?' asked Gideon. 'It seems as though you've got everything in hand.'

'If the site is one of historical interest or value, it'll protect me even further from Salter Holdings should they try to gain the land illegally. Even if they don't, I've always been interested in the history but this is the first opportunity I've had to look into it in more depth.'

'Do you know anything about the ruins?' asked Ben.

'I've discovered a few things. When I visited an exhibition at the Mary Fitzroy Heritage Centre there was a map that showed the corner of my woodland with the words "Hanworth House". I contacted the heritage centre who put me in touch with both the Pembrokeshire Archives and another research centre nearby, Marquess House. It transpires, in the mediaeval period, the land was owned by the Marquess House estate and in their archive there was a deed of sale, complete with the plans of a mediaeval manor. These show the house was renovated – rebuilt by the looks of things – in 1535 when the estate was bought by a Randall Hanworth. They also found a handwritten journal from the early nineteenth century containing local folklore about the oak trees in my wood.'

The two men made suitably impressed noises.

'And you think this manor could be your ruins?' asked Gideon.

'I hope so,' replied Caroline. 'So far, all I've discovered about Randall Hanworth is his connection to Anne Brandon, who was the daughter of Charles Brandon, Duke of Suffolk. Brandon was the best friend of Henry VIII.'

'Why would a man connected to the Suffolks have a house this far from court?' said Ben.

'A question I can't answer yet,' said Caroline.

'My degree covered the politics of Henry VIII's reign,' said Ben. 'As far as I'm aware, the Brandons had no link to this part of the world, but for the Tudors it was a very special place. Henry VII was born at Pembroke Castle and he landed at Mill Bay in Dale, which is near here, before the Battle of Bosworth when he defeated Richard III. By the time Henry VIII became king, Haverfordwest was a very busy port – it's what? Seven or eight miles from here? – and being near Ireland, who were forever squabbling with the monarch, this part of Wales was of real political importance. Although, I'm not sure if Henry VIII himself ever came this far west.'

'Ben's degree comes in useful,' said Gideon, with affection

and pride in his voice. 'It's why I use him as a consultant on my projects.'

'It could turn out to be very handy,' agreed Caroline. 'Do you know much about henges?'

'No, not especially,' said Ben. 'Why?'

'The ruins are one thing but the wood has a separate history,' she explained. 'The handwritten journal contains a legend about an oak henge. The tales claim the ring of oak trees was once the entrance to a sacred land and centuries later, druids worshipped there.'

'Do you know the story?' asked Ben. 'The historian in me is desperate to hear it.'

'And the producer in me is already considering camera angles,' said Gideon.

He stood up and went behind the bar where be picked up a bottle of red wine.

'Let's sprawl on the sofas and you can tell us all you know so far,' he said. 'It'll be like old times.'

10

'What do you mean – like old times?' asked Caroline, following him across the room.

'When you used to tell us the tales of King Arthur during our drama practical lessons and we listened, spellbound.'

Caroline stared at him in surprise.

'I always got the impression you were all bored and humouring the nerd.'

'Well, perhaps Nadine,' said Ben with a grin, 'the rest of us, me in particular, gazed at you in awe.'

'Oh, shut up,' she said, throwing a cushion at him.

Caroline had a glimpse of them as their younger selves – laughing, teasing, tumbling over each other with a complete lack of self-consciousness as they rehearsed. She wished things were as simple as they seemed in this moment but in her heart, she knew these high spirits were superficial. The friendships could splinter again and when they discovered what she had done, she suspected neither man would forgive her this time.

They flopped onto the sofas and Caroline pushed her thoughts aside. Gideon and Ben would be here for the first few weeks of the shop's opening, then they would return to their normal lives.

Enjoy this, she told herself, you love both these men and they're part of your soul. Kick back, stop worrying and have fun. When was the last time you laughed like this? But she could not remember.

Ken climbed up onto the sofa and placed his head on Caroline's leg, nudging her until she began stroking his silky ears. Gideon poured the wine and Ben disappeared to the kitchen, returning with bowls of crisps, olives and feta cheese cubes.

'This is civilised,' said Caroline, raising her glass to Gideon and Ben, 'but I'm driving. One glass for me.'

Gideon twirled an imaginary moustache.

'My evil plan to tempt you with drink has failed before it began,' he said.

'Fool,' she said.

Ben sat in the armchair nearest Caroline while Gideon took the other end of the sofa much to Ken's irritation.

'No wine for you,' said Gideon to the dog. 'You were a right misery the last time you had a hangover.'

Ken wagged his tail in response before covering his nose with his paw.

'Come on, then, tell us about the mythical henge in your ancient woodland,' said Ben, his face alive with interest.

Caroline placed her glass on the table before twisting in her seat and striking a dramatic pose with one hand raised.

'Legend tells us,' she began and the two men cheered, making Ken bark.

It was the way she had always started her stories about King Arthur back in Gideon's bedroom. Caroline beamed at their reaction, took another sip of wine, settled back against the cushions and continued. 'There was once a ring of oak trees laid out like the henges of old. Oval in shape, with a protective internal ditch. This sacred space was said to have been the entrance to the hidden kingdom of Mabe, the fairy queen of misrule—'

'I've never heard of Mabe,' interrupted Ben, 'and mythology was one of my specialisms. There's Mab, the queen of the fairies, but she was first named by Shakespeare. There's Maeve, which is the English translation of *Medb*, the Queen of Connacht from the Ulster Cycle in Irish mythology.'

'Could Mabe be either of those but with a local dialect?' asked Gideon. 'Although, isn't there a standing stone in St Ishmaels called Mabe's Gate? It's what's known as a Bronze Age Longstone and is supposed to be the tallest in the county.'

'How do you know?' asked Ben.

'You're not the only one who does research, History Boy—'

'Hello? The legend?' said Caroline interrupting them.

'Sorry, Caro,' said Gideon and Ben in unison, and she giggled.

'You're right, Gid,' she said. 'The standing stone is on the edge of the wood in Dexter's Place. It's strange, haunting because it stands alone, staring out across the sea to Ramsey Island, Carn Llidi and Pen Berry as though it's keeping watch.'

Gideon held the bottle above her glass, his eyebrows raised for permission to top up her drink. Caroline was about to refuse but then she changed her mind. Her grandfather and his books had ruled the majority of her adult life, forcing her to kow-tow to his whims, but Dexter was no longer awaiting her return with a list of demands. She was free. If she chose to stay here on this miserable afternoon to drink wine and laugh with old friends, it was her decision. She could leave her car, collect it in the morning and order a cab to take her home.

She smiled and pretending to flutter her eyelashes like a

heroine from a black-and-white film, she declared in a Southern belle accent, 'Why, Mr Morris, are you trying to get me drunk?'

'Why, yes, Miss Drover, I mean, Harvey, I believe I am,' he replied in kind.

'In that case you'd better fill my glass to the brim.'

'What about your car?' asked Ben but he clinked his glass against hers in delight.

'I'll collect it in the morning.'

'One of us can fetch you,' said Gideon. 'No more interruptions, let's hear your legend.'

The two men looked at Caroline in anticipation and she began her tale.

'In the dark, cold days, on the edge of time when this land was newly made, there was a wild goddess of misrule called Queen Mabe. She had dominion over the chaos of the oceans with their broiling storms of yore, the whirling sea mists and the terrible monsters of the deep. On land, she was an undefeated warrior armed with lightning forks created from the black waves of the high seas. She would smite all who challenged her to dust and of her beauty, there was no equal. If she were to smile with the glint of allure in her eyes, no living creature could resist.

'Mabe was served by her tribe of loyal warrior women in a land hidden in the soul of the earth. Each of her followers knew the price they would pay if their loyalty to Mabe wavered: a death of great brutality. But the life they lived with Mabe offered freedoms and adventures and all swore happily to remain in the beauty of their home.

'The entrance to this opulent realm was guarded by a lone watcher, appointed to protect all within. For this was a place of feasting and song, of power and destruction and no human who witnessed the hall was ever the same again. Many were lured by the songs of the earth. They danced and ate, taking pleasure with the women but when they awoke, far from home, on storm-tossed islands in raging seas they would wander alone forever until they were claimed by the water.

'Whenever she departed her realm, flying high over seas and oceans, conversing with the stars and dancing with the winds as they tore across the cosmos, Mabe would appoint a regent to stand at the entrance of the hidden land to await her return. One day, she appointed her daughter, Heri. As tall as Mabe but with a softer, gentler heart, Heri waited, watching the horizon for her mother's homecoming. Each day was the same, the broiling seas, the eerie mists and the spikes of rain as winter roved mercilessly across the land. Heri kept her vigil.

'As the earth turned and Mother Gaia awoke from her frosty sleep, spring crept across the fields and oceans and, one morning, Heri saw a young man, a shepherd tending his flocks. He was tall and handsome but what intrigued her was his kindness to his charges. She watched as a skittish ewe fled into a bush, catching herself in the thorns, but rather than laugh and leave the creature to struggle, the young man spoke to her in soft tones, soothing her while he unwound her fleece from the brambles. Heri had never been shown such care and was curious to know how it felt.

'Whenever the shepherd passed, he smiled but they did not speak, until one morning, when Heri said, "Hello." They exchanged greetings. He told her his name was Drustan and she said she was Heri. As the days turned into weeks, they spoke more and more. He was careful of her feelings, giving her small gifts of flowers and unusual stones. When the weather was hot, he offered to share the fresh spring water from his flask and when it rained, he sheltered her under his cloak. With the passing of time, they fell in love. Every evening, as he returned with his flocks, Drustan would ask Heri to leave with him, but the princess was loyal to her mother, Mabe, and she refused.

'The changing of the weather indicated Mabe would soon return and, with a breaking heart, Heri told Drustan they must part. She knew if her mother were to discover her feelings for the man, he would be punished; lured below into Mabe's kingdom, to suffer the fate of losing his mind and his life. It was a punishment she could not bear for her beloved shepherd. She explained why he must leave, assuring him it was the way to save them both and with a kiss, they parted.

'Unbeknown to Heri, Queen Mabe, was watching from on high and as Mabe saw her daughter and the man weeping together, she mistook their actions, believing Heri was planning to abandon her and the other women.

'Mabe flew into a jealous fury and materialised in front of the sobbing lovers in an explosion of lightning. She screamed in fury as she smote the young man, leaving nothing but a patch of blood on the ground. This seeped into the rocks, giving them the red hue which they still carry today, thousands of years later. Then, she turned to Heri and before her daughter could explain, Mabe raised her hands and, invoking her terrible wrath, she turned Heri to stone.

'Her sister warriors were saddened. They tried to persuade Mabe to free Heri but the queen refused. At the entrance to the hidden land, Heri stood, a lone watcher to the passing of time, gazing out to sea, pining for her lost love.

'As happens with the ancient ones, Mabe and her warriors felt the pull of time and, summoned by new adventures in the star-strewn sky, they vanished. The marker to the hidden land was all that remained. Tales of Mabe became fireside whispers and the stone was forever called Mabe's Gate to pay tribute to the truculent queen. But, as Heri's family left, a group of human women arrived, the sisters of Drustan. These women knew the story of the lost lovers but they feared building a monument of stone or wood in case Mabe became enraged. Instead they planted a henge of trees to honour the love of the fallen princess, Heri, and her shepherd, Drustan.

'The trees stood for centuries and as time passed, they became a sacred grove to the Druids. For hundreds of years, they worshipped in the henge of oaks, healing the sick, guiding kings and passing on the wisdom of the Ancients. Until the Romans came, cutting a swathe across the country and destroying all they did not understand. The Druids fled, taking refuge with their brothers and sisters in the stronghold of Anglesey. The Romans were scared of the power of the Druids and as punishment they destroyed the oak trees, leaving only one standing beside the lonely stone.

'The tree was imbued with the kindness and magic of the Druids. It refused to let its family die and as it wept for its lost loved ones, it continued to nourish the stumps through its roots, keeping them alive. As word spread of the magical tree, people came to worship and the oak would grant wisdom and wishes. Then one day, Merlin visited. In great reverence, he listened to the tree's wish to be reunited with his slain fellows. Merlin raised his arms aloft and in an instant the trees were restored. The oak henge was left in peace until age and time took back the trees and they died together, their branches and roots entwined.

'New trees grew to protect the sacred site and when a young man arrived to build a home in the centre of the henge, he knew to make an offering. He sang to the trees of the love he felt for a maiden who was not his, a maiden whose father had forced her to marry another. He promised the henge he would save her from this rascal's clutches and bring her to a place of safety if they would offer their wisdom and their shelter.

'The woodland decided this man was pure of heart and before his eyes the tangle of branches and bushes, oaks and leaves cleared and a house emerged from the stones of the ground, the timbers grew from the trees of the forest and the moat from the waters of the river running through the woodland. The man cried in relief and in due course, he rescued his maiden and together they lived in harmony in their home.

'When she died, he buried her on the edge of the ancient henge, then he lay down beside her and died with his arms around her, so they could spend all eternity together. The ancient grove reclaimed the house and, legend tell us it lies, waiting for a man of honest love who will once again call the magical house from the ground and live happily with the maiden of his soul.'

When she had finished, there was silence, until she realised both Gideon and Ben had tears in their eyes. She smiled, wiping away her own as her two old friends reached forward and pulled her into a many armed hug.

11

SUFFOLK PLACE, SOUTHWARK, MARCH 1525

I am married. The words ran through her mind but they were difficult to comprehend. She was Baroness Powis and Edward Grey was her husband. Was it real or a dream from which she would awaken? The noise and revelry, the excess of food and drink, the many congratulations raining down upon her forced her to accept that after months of planning, her married status was true. The service had been attended by the important nobles of the land, including the king, who had given them a generous gift of a silver dish with a lid.

In a few days, she and Edward would depart for his family home hundreds of miles away in Wales, the vast Powis Castle in Welshpool, where she would be the lady of the house. The power of her new status appealed to her; she would be able to make decisions, to help Edward reclaim the entirety of his legacy from his cousins, and to build a strong family of her own. She glanced around the room and saw a number of familiar faces, relieved that when she undertook her journey, she would not be alone.

Over the past few months, her stepmother had worked hard to ensure Anne would be accompanied by a group of loyal women who would help her transition from daughter to wife. Elizabeth Oxenbridge née Puttenham and Ellen Guyban née Audley were both distant cousins on her father's side, while Beatrice Ogle née Cooke was the step-granddaughter of Margaret Penning, an old friend of the Duchess of Suffolk.

The two women had been close since their time together as ladies-in-waiting to Katherine of Aragon. Beatrice's husband, Richard, was considerably older and she was his second wife. His duties kept him at court and when the request came from the Duke of Suffolk for Beatrice to join Anne to help her settle at Powis Castle, he had agreed. Charles Brandon knew Richard Ogle was hoping to buy some land adjoining his estate in Pinchbeck, Lincolnshire, and had suggested he might be able to help smooth the deal if Beatrice could be spared.

'She and Anne are friends from childhood,' Charles had reminded Richard. 'Beatrice would be an asset.'

Richard agreed with a hearty smile.

Emma Meverell was a distant cousin on her mother's side of the family and, to Anne's dismay, Jane Orwell, with her Brandon connections, was the last of her ladies. Jane's brother, Ludo, was part of Edward's entourage, as were Emma's betrothed, Thomas Cradock, and Elizabeth's husband, Tom Oxenbridge. Ellen Guyban and her husband, another Thomas, were a few years older than Anne and Edward and would be the senior members of the household to advise the young couple during their first years. The Guybans would be accompanied by their young children, Ursula and John.

Across the room, a shout of laughter attracted Anne's attention and she watched as Edward Grey, encouraged by his friends, drank a huge goblet of Gasçon wine. She smiled. Despite their differences and her disappointment at not being able to marry Randall, she and Edward had reached an understanding.

'We're friends, Annie,' he had said after the betrothal had been announced. 'We respect each other, love will come.'

Anne had agreed. She knew her duty was to help strengthen the dynasties of both the Greys and Brandons. Her battered heart was her own to deal with in private.

My husband, she thought, as she watched the young men carousing, an ebullient Edward at their centre. *He is my husband.* The words, although strange, felt less startling with each repetition. She knew her situation could have been worse. Her lady-in-waiting, Beatrice, was married to a man twenty-seven years her senior. At least she and Edward were similar in age and there was no denying his good looks. Her father had been thoughtful in his choice of spouse, even if he had overruled her own feelings.

A wave of laughter rippled through the room as Thomas Stanley, Baron Monteagle, hooted and said: 'You'll need to keep your strength up tonight, Edward. You're a married man now!'

There was a ribald cheer and Anne felt a wave of appreciation towards her stepmother who had forbidden the ritual of the young couple being carried to bed by the other members of the wedding party.

'It's archaic and appalling,' she had stated when her husband had suggested it a few weeks earlier. 'You might think it's a merry entertainment, Charles, but for the bride it's humiliating and terrifying. Do you wish Anne to begin her marriage in such a manner? Isn't it enough we will shortly lose her to the wilds of Wales without sending her off in distress?'

The Duke of Suffolk had considered her tirade before replying, 'Do you know, my dear, I've never thought about it from the woman's perspective. Yes, I can see why the boisterous behaviour of a group of drunk young men might be disturbing.'

Anne had listened in relief. The idea of being placed in a bed and enduring the bawdy revelry of all the men with whom she had grown up as they deposited Edward beside her, had been an appalling thought.

'I shall insist Edward comport himself in the manner befitting the status Anne enjoys. He might be a baron but he is marrying the daughter of a duke and queen,' the duke said.

'Quite right, dear,' Mary replied. 'Edward has never known a true father, his own died while he was a baby. It's important you step into this role and advise him on the courteous and respectful ways a husband should behave.'

'Are you well, my dear?' her stepmother's voice was near and Anne started, pulled from her thoughts and back to the present.

'Yes, thank you, Mama, I am just a little overwhelmed,' she said.

'Weddings are emotional,' agreed the dowager queen. 'Come to my solar for a short break to recover your equilibrium.'

Anne fell into step beside her stepmother. Lady Marsh followed as did Anne's younger sister, Mary, and Meg More. Meg reached over and squeezed her hand, their friendship about to change irrevocably as they were soon to be parted. Meg was to marry the scholar, William Roper, and, at first, they would continue to live at her father, Thomas More's, house until William took possession of his family's home in Hertfordshire. It was many miles from Anne's destination of Welshpool.

As Anne made her way through the throng, she wondered if her father had spoken to Edward or, whether as was often the case with the duke when he found a job uncomfortable, he had 'forgotten' to educate his future son-in-law in the correct etiquette for a wedding night. Edward was swaggering around the room accepting the congratulations of his contemporaries but as she reached the door, she noticed he looked over in concern and the arrogance fell from his face as he mouthed: 'Are you well?' She nodded. He gave a shy smile and turned back to his friends.

The door swung shut and the silence enveloped her. After the raucous excitement of the wedding banquet, the peace of her stepmother's private solar was a welcome respite.

'Sit,' said the duchess to Anne, ringing a bell for the page, 'you look very pale and it wouldn't do for you to faint on your wedding day. Have you eaten?'

'Not much,' admitted Anne. 'This dress is tighter than I am used to and it makes eating difficult.'

The duchess and Lady Marsh exchanged an understanding glance.

'Alas, sweet child, you're a married woman and a member of the nobility, thus you are expected to follow the court fashions and tight bodices are no one's friend.'

'Come, Anne, let me loosen it for you while you rest,' said Meg. 'Mary, can you help?'

Mary Brandon hurried forward and Anne sighed deeply as her friend and her sister worked their fingers through the laces of her bodices, loosening the constricting cords. The square neckline gaped forward, allowing Anne to take several deep breaths.

'Thank you,' she gasped. 'I thought we wore our outfits tightly laced already but I was wrong.'

'Your maids will take care of everything,' said her stepmother. 'Miriam and Alice have been well trained and you will have your ladies with you to help too.'

'It feels strange to think I shall be in your position, Mama. The household will be mine to run as I choose.'

'My dear, we have enjoyed many long talks about the duties of a wife,' she said. 'I hope I have trained you to run a property as well as your mother would have done.'

'You have, Mama, and I am most grateful,' said Anne. 'It will take time to be as proficient as you though.'

'Imagine how I felt,' laughed Mary, 'the first household I had to run was a palace as Queen of France. It was an ordeal, especially when Louis sent half of my ladies away.'

The pages arrived with a tray of refreshments: small cakes with swirls of candied orange on top, rose petal marchpane and trays of comfits. When they had left, Anne ate two cakes in quick succession and drank deeply of the sweet wine. During the banquet her plate of food had grown cold before she could eat much as she had been inundated with well-wishers offering congratulations.

'Elizabeth, could you tell Charles we shall be remaining here for a few moments?' said her stepmother. 'You go, too, Mary, Meg, I wish to speak to Anne alone. We shall return shortly, then Anne and Edward will lead a pavane.'

Lady Marsh, Mary and Meg left. The duchess turned to Anne who hoped her stepmother was not about to explain again the wonders of the marriage bed. Each conversation they had shared being more awkward than the last.

The duchess hesitated, then sitting beside Anne, she took her hand and said, 'Last night, your father told me about Randall.'

Anne felt as though all the air had been sucked from her lungs. This unexpected mention of his name proved she was not over her former love. When her father had announced her betrothal to Edward she had written to

Randall and he had replied, his heart as shattered as her own.

We were foolish. In the joy of our love we forgot we both have duties to those around us. Annie, my love, I blame myself for this disaster but please know, whatever happens, my heart is yours. The only comfort I can take is that Edward Grey is a good man and I pray he will make you a gentle husband. We must make the best of this terrible tragedy.

Anne had replied with equal sadness though they knew there was no choice but to end their tentative relationship. She had written with tears in her eyes:

Perhaps one day we will meet again...

After sending the letter she had packed away the small gifts Randall had given her – a silver chain with an amber pendant, a series of poems he had written and a small disc bearing his family's coat of arms – and turned her attention to Edward Grey.

Over the next months, as the young couple were trained assiduously in the art of creating a successful partnership, Anne had discovered attributes within Edward she could admire. He was fierce in his devotion to his friends, a loyal soldier to her father whom he had joined on the French campaign. He could be funny and kind but he also had a quick temper and could hold a grudge with bitterness and malice.

Edward, too, seemed to make an effort and as they approached their wedding day, Anne had begun to feel hopeful that they could make a successful union. Despite the enormity of being mistress of a castle, Anne was looking forward to the freedom her marriage would afford her.

'You'll be living in an ancient stronghold, you have history on your shoulders,' the duchess had said during one of their many discussions. 'You'll no longer simply be Anne Brandon, you will be Lady Powis and you will carry the power of every woman who has ever held the title, each woman who has ever lived in Powis Castle.'

The duke had likewise insisted that Edward Grey shadow him, taking him to court, introducing him to important men, making it clear Edward was a rising star. The Duke of Suffolk had also approached the Dudley claimants to try and secure full ownership of Powis Castle on Edward's behalf. He was confident that an arrangement would be reached.

Anne had been caught up in the whirl of preparations, her days so busy she could not brood, but at night, in the darkness, in the bed she shared with her sister, Mary, her thoughts would turn to Randall and what might have been.

'Last night, your father gave you a book,' said her stepmother, bringing Anne back to the room.

'Yes, a copy of *Tristan and Iseult*.'

The leather-bound copy of the Arthurian legend was a work of art. She had run her fingers over the engraved cover, aware of the love story within; a tale where three people who cared for each other were caught in an impossible tangle of emotions. When Anne had opened it, she had been surprised to see blank pages among the illuminations and the neat rows of text.

'We decided upon it together and thought it would be useful for you to make notes about your household,' said Mary. 'However, it's important that what I'm about to share with you remains a secret between us.'

'Of course,' said Anne.

'When I was young, I was betrothed to the Prince of Castille. I didn't love him, in fact, we never met. There was another who had already caught my heart. A man who I believed would never be mine. A charmer who continues to hold my love.'

'Papa?' asked Anne in surprise.

'Yes, your father.' She sighed, her eyes bright with reminiscence. 'He was always the best looking, most dashing of all the young men at court. Every night I prayed that one day, Charles and I would be together. Even while I had to endure my marriage to Louis, I prayed for Charles. Then Louis died and my brother sent Charles to fetch me. It was the sign I'd been waiting for and I grasped it with both hands.'

'You were very brave,' said Anne.

'Perhaps; foolish was the word my brother used,' she replied. 'But it taught me that if your love is pure, eventually, it will find a way. True love is a powerful force and it can never be destroyed, and if you truly love Randall, then trust in your feelings for each other, Annie. With all my heart I hope Edward and you will find love but if you and Randall are meant to be together, then love will prevail.'

Mary placed her hand on Anne's cheek.

'Even as a princess I had no choice in the affairs of the heart so remember this always. If an opportunity presents itself, don't lose love a second time.'

A knock on the door interrupted them as the Duke of Suffolk requested their return to the celebrations.

'Let me tighten your bodice,' said Mary as her husband withdrew from the room.

'Do you know how?' asked Anne in surprise.

'I might have been born a princess but I'm a woman first and this is a skill we all acquired in the court. I grew up surrounded by female friends and they're still important to me today. Why do you think I put such care into helping you choose your women for Powis Castle? I wanted to ensure they're loyal to you rather than your husband. You'll need their friendship.'

With a final tug, the Duchess of Suffolk tied the strings on Anne's bodice.

'And now, my dearest girl, I shall pass you to your husband's care. Remember my words though. True love will always prevail.'

12

POWIS CASTLE, WELSHPOOL, JUNE 1526

'How can you ask if I'm with child?' Anne said as Edward glowered down at her. 'The moment I have such an inkling, I shall tell you.'

'It's important to me,' he said but the hardness of his expression marred his handsome face, making him look older than his years. 'A family of my own, a son to pass on my title is my heart's desire.'

'You're not the only one who is sad at the loss of our baby,' she said. 'My job is to provide your heir and yet the babes slip away after a few weeks.'

Anne turned away, stifling her sob. Her delight at discovering herself with child not long after their wedding had turned to sadness when she had miscarried. Despite following advice from every woman she knew, the next two pregnancies had ended the same way, with the most recent just a month earlier.

'No wonder the king dallies with other women,' said Edward, his words edged with scorn. 'When we were at court I didn't understand, but after this mess,' he gestured towards

Anne, 'his wisdom at welcoming other women to his bed rings clear.'

His words cut through her like a blade.

'You wouldn't?' she said, turning to face him. 'We've barely been married a year and you would consider bedding another?'

Anne was shocked at how much this comment hurt her. Despite the lack of an heir, they were young and, as those around them continued to say in comforting tones, there was time to have a family. Anne had thought she and Edward were building a happy, successful life but his barbed words undermined her confidence. Edward's threat hung in the air between them and to Anne's horror, tears welled in her eyes. She raised her hand to brush them away but felt his touch on her arm.

'Forgive me, Annie,' he said. 'I shouldn't be so base. It was my disappointment speaking but you're right, this is your pain too. How do you feel? Are you well? Shall I call Beatrice with a tincture to soothe your nerves?'

'It's considerate of you,' said Anne, 'but I have no wish for yet another mug of warm camomile while everyone fusses around me as though I were made of glass.'

Edward chuckled, a boyish grin replacing the sneer of earlier. Despite being relieved at his return to a more reasonable frame of mind, Anne found his quicksilver changes of mood unsettling.

'We know the history of Queen Katherine,' Anne continued, 'she struggled but eventually she and the king were blessed with the Princess Mary. We shall have a family, I know it.'

She shook back her long dark hair and gazed up at her husband. His eyes were gentle and his brow creased as he frowned.

'You're right, my love, we must pray for healthy sons and they will arrive.'

She smiled, hoping he would not insist on trying again this afternoon. He claimed his desire for her was such that he could not always control himself but Anne found his swift, almost brutal couplings difficult to bear, especially when she felt unwell, as she did today.

The air had been thick with summer showers and after the midday meal she had retired to her room, her limbs heavy with fatigue. The same symptoms of exhaustion and despair had haunted her for weeks after each pregnancy ended. Even her closest friend in the household, Beatrice Ogle, was pushed away as Anne grieved alone. Today, after issuing instructions for food to be brought to her room, she had asked Jane Orwell to oversee the evening meal, a task she knew the younger woman enjoyed.

Upon entering her bedchamber she had stripped off her restrictive clothing and pulled on the soft lawn nightdress Meg More had sent her as a gift to cheer her up. Her maid, Miriam, had helped her to release her hair and brush it out in tumbling waves, then she had slumped on the bed. For an hour, she had lost herself in *Utopia*, remembering the day she had first read it and revelling in the innocence of her youth. Then her eyelids had grown heavy and she had slipped into a dreamless sleep. Edward's knock had awoken her.

She gazed up at her husband and considered sending him away but with his kind mood restored, she changed her mind. The loneliness of loss was the hardest thing to bear and, unexpectedly, she craved the company of the one other person who truly understood her sorrow.

'Why don't you stay awhile,' she said, smiling, 'and tell me the news from court?'

Edward had received letters earlier that day, many of which were from friends who attended the king. Although they were far away from London in the ancient stronghold of Powis Castle, they were well connected for social life and for news from court. Ludlow Castle where Princess Mary ruled over Wales was forty miles away and there were other great houses in between.

One of Edward's favourite pastimes was discussing the other nobles at court. He felt he was superior to them all and could resolve their issues with ease. During the first few months of their marriage, Anne had tried to argue with many of his illogical suggestions but this had sent him spinning into a violent temper. On one occasion he had lashed her hard across the back of her legs with his belt and ever since, she had allowed him to ramble, smiling at the nonsense he spouted while missing the reasoned discussions she had once enjoyed with Meg More and Randall.

'Where would you like me to start?' asked Edward, leading Anne towards the bed. He kicked off his boots and climbed on, arranging the pillows in a comfortable V-shape before opening his arms to her. Relieved he was calm again, Anne slipped off her soft embroidered slippers and clambered up beside him, settling back into the crook of his arm. 'There is gossip aplenty.'

'Do you mean the king and Mary Boleyn?' she asked.

'Oh, my darling, you're very behind the times,' Edward said with a cruel laugh. 'No, the king moved on from Mary Boleyn long ago.'

'But she had his son at the beginning of the year,' said Anne.

She knew her miscarriages and the illness she had suffered after her second loss had kept her thoughts centred on her home rather than court but she was startled by this news. She wondered why none of her own friends had mentioned this betrayal.

'The king has decided he doesn't need another illegitimate son,' said Edward.

Poor Mary, she thought, to be thrown aside like rubbish.

'Anyway, it's not the king who's causing problems, it's the poet, Thomas Wyatt.'

'Lizzie Brooke's husband?' asked Anne.

Elizabeth Brooke was the daughter of Thomas Brooke, 8th Baron Cobham and Dorothy Heydon. Baroness Brooke was a first cousin of Thomas Boleyn and Anne remembered her friend, Anne Boleyn, discussing the links between the Wyatts, the Boleyns, the Brookes and the Heydons when they had been together in Mechelen as girls.

'Yes, there is unhappiness in the house of Wyatt,' Edward said with a sneer.

'What's Tommy done?'

'First, he began a dalliance with your old friend, Anne Boleyn, but for some reason he backed off...'

'The Boleyns and the Wyatts lived near each other, they've been friends for years, so have the Brookes. I can't imagine Anne flirting with Tommy Wyatt. It's more likely she was taking him to task about treating Lizzie so badly—' Anne said.

'Did you want me to tell you or not?' asked Edward, his voice cool.

'Yes, my love, sorry,' Anne said, and gave him a shy smile.

Mollified, Edward continued. 'Once Anne Boleyn was out of the game, it seemed Tommy took up with another of Queen Katherine's women, Lady Elizabeth Darrell.'

'But what about Lizzie? She and Tommy married when they were teenagers and their son was born when Lizzie was only seventeen.'

'The word at court is that they've grown apart but while we all know Tommy is on the lookout for someone new, he's managed to pass the blame off on Lizzie. He accused her of having an affair instead,' said Edward with a roar of cruel laughter.

'How dare he?' exclaimed Anne.

She did not know Lizzie Brooke well but on the occasions they had met she had been charmed by her sunny temperament and loyal nature. To think Lizzie's husband would try to besmirch her name rather than take responsibility for his own adultery appalled Anne.

'With whom is Lizzie supposed to be sleeping?' asked Anne, her voice low with anger.

'No one knows, no one cares, it's taken the heat off Tommy and she's run home to her parents at Cobham Hall in Kent. They're officially estranged.'

Anne did not know how to respond. She lay in silence, staring up at the Arthurian figures embroidered on the canopy above her bed.

'There's more though,' said Edward, relish in his voice as he pushed himself further back into the pillows, pulling Anne tightly into him, his thumb grazing the underside of her breast. Anne forced herself not to flinch.

'Is that not scandal enough?' she said, trying to keep her voice light.

'The whisper is, the reason Wyatt backed off from Anne Boleyn is because the king is said to be infatuated.'

'With Anne?'

'Yes, this is why he abandoned Mary Boleyn.'

'Edward, this is awful. What about the queen?'

'Serves her right for not giving the king a son,' he said with a shrug. 'I'm surprised the king hasn't offered to marry Bessie Blount, after all, she's the mother of his eldest illegitimate son, Henry Fitzroy. The king has elevated Fitzroy to the double dukedom of Richmond and Somerset; after the monarch, Fitzroy is the most powerful man in the land. Most people think the king might make Fitzroy his heir. Imagine that, an illegitimate son inheriting the throne? I wonder what it would mean for other families where the only potential heirs are bastard born?'

Anne did not reply. Edward's callous descriptions of people she knew, women she cared about, people whose lives were being torn apart, upset her deeply. His tone suggested it was a game and their feelings were not worthy of proper consideration. She had thought Edward – who considered himself one of the more progressive men at court – would have eschewed the uncaring ways of her father's generation. It appeared he was treading the same path as many men before him.

Randall would never have found this situation humorous, she thought.

'Anyway, my love, I understand you will be remaining here for the rest of the evening,' said Edward.

'Yes, if you don't mind,' she replied, bringing her thoughts away from Randall. 'I've asked Jane to oversee the meal.'

'Have you? Not Ellen? She's the most senior woman in your household.'

'No, Jane needs the practice. She'll be betrothed soon, I'm sure of it, and I thought she'd enjoy presiding in my place.'

'What do you mean?' asked Edward, his voice sharp.

'My place at the table, beside you,' she said. 'You know she adores you.'

Edward grinned like a naughty schoolboy.

'Then I shall leave you in peace,' he said, 'and give Jane a thrill by flirting with her. She'll never replace you though, my beautiful Annie.'

He rolled off the bed, pulled on his boots, then with a deep, theatrical bow, he left. As Anne heard him pounding down the corridor she could not shift a deep sense of unease.

13

POWIS CASTLE, WELSHPOOL, SEPTEMBER 1526

The fire crackled and Anne glanced around the table ensuring her guests had all they required. In the flickering candlelight, she watched Edward who was deep in conversation with the lawyer, John Beaumont. The two men had met several years earlier at her father's house in Southwark and when Edward was in need of a man who specialised in property and land, it was to his old friend he had turned.

It was becoming more fashionable to dine in smaller numbers rather than the entire household from the master and mistress to the lower staff, all eating together in the great hall. This room was part of their wing of the castle but this was the problem; the property continued to be shared with Edward's cousins. He was seeking John's advice to resolve the matter and was hoping he would be able to force his relatives to sell him their share.

The outer ward of the castle belonged to the family incorporating the Tiptofts and Dudleys, while the inner ward where they lived was the Grey legacy. Other properties within Edward's inheritance were Charlton Castle and the manor of Pontysbury.

He had also recently acquired more estates and now owned the manors of Plas Y Dnas and Trewern in nearby Montgomeryshire. However, the close proximity of another family within the walls of Powis Castle irritated him on a daily basis.

Around the table were Anne's closest friends in her household: Beatrice, Elizabeth and Emma. Ellen and her husband, Thomas, were away visiting his estates in Lincolnshire and Jane Orwell and her brother, Ludo, were in London having been summoned to court by her father, Sir Lewis Orwell. Her mother, Mary, was ailing and Jane had gone to nurse her, while Sir Lewis wished to discuss his son's future. Anne was relieved to be spared Jane's company for a few weeks.

She tried her hardest but she found the young woman difficult to like or trust. Jane appeared perfect – quiet, demure – but she knew from the others in the household she could be manipulative and spiteful, as well as being adept at pushing the blame of her own misdemeanours onto others. Her endless longing glances towards Edward which Anne had at first found amusing, were now unnerving. At first, her husband was a touch embarrassed but he no longer laughed at Jane's devotion. Anne often saw the two together, walking, laughing, their closeness more intimate.

'And yet,' Anne heard her husband exclaim, 'my own home, my ancestral birth right is shared with the Dudleys, all because there was no male heir. It makes a mockery of my title and my position.'

'Quite right, Edward, but there are always ways to circumnavigate the law,' said John Beaumont.

'Women, again, you see, John,' exclaimed Edward, 'failing in the one task for which they were placed on the earth: to provide healthy sons. I have all sympathy with the king, no wonder he has decided to throw the queen aside.'

Anne felt sick at Edward's words but before she could comment the woman to Anne's right leaned over and squeezed her hand, distracting her from the conversation. Isabelle Beaumont, formerly Dutton, was now John's wife and when they had arrived they brought news that the king continued to pursue Anne Boleyn with an even greater fervour.

The king's open wooing of Anne Boleyn had begun six months earlier when at the Shrovetide joust he had used the motto: *Declare, I dare not.* It was a signal of his feelings for Anne, suggesting the depth of his emotions and his desire to share them. At first, Anne's parents had whisked her home to Hever Castle in order to protect her from gossip and, Annie wondered, from witnessing a second daughter coerced into the king's bed. Henry, however, would not be dissuaded from his pursuit and the rumours were the king had sent her endless letters full of declarations of love and passion. It was said Anne Boleyn was beginning to soften towards Henry's overtures. The queen retained a dignified silence but Anne felt sympathy for Katherine.

'Don't fret, Annie,' said Isabelle. 'John often makes ridiculous claims when he's had too much wine, no doubt Edward is the same.'

'You're very understanding,' said Anne. 'Although, it isn't his wild talk about the king and queen that's upsetting me, it's his comments about reclaiming his property. My father is already speaking to other members of the Privy Council to persuade Lord Dudley to sell his portion to Edward but these things take time.'

'Then you shouldn't worry—' began Isabelle, but Anne shook her head.

Anne leaned closer and said, 'I'm more concerned about other land deals Edward wishes to embark upon. I feel not all of them are fair. After our marriage, my father told Edward that he has put a vast tract of land in Warwickshire aside for us in his will. Edward believes this land is his already and is trying to borrow against its value. Father was unimpressed when Edward wrote to him asking for his support in this matter and explained it would be unwise. The land came to father through my mother, Anne Browne, and represents our connection to her family. He has refused Edward access to it.'

'John's a member of the Inner Temple, he'll ensure your husband remains within the letter of the law,' said Isabelle but the women exchanged a concerned look.

'What other news is there from court?' asked Anne, not wishing to dwell on Edward's behaviour.

'Apart from the rumours about Anne Boleyn? There are further suggestions that the king will soon name Bessie Blount's boy, Henry Fitzroy, as his heir. Fitzroy has moved to Sheriff Hutton where he is being given the education of a prince.'

'But Princess Mary is at Ludlow Castle, which is where the heirs of the monarch are sent to learn how to rule,' replied Anne in surprise.

'The king is ensuring the future of the Tudor crown by training both his children to have the skills to take the role of monarch.'

'What of Mary Boleyn's children?'

'If the king is intent on pursuing a relationship with her sister, he can't be seen to have slept with her. It would bring the legality of any relationship and possible offspring into doubt,' said Isabelle. 'Mary Boleyn has been cast aside.'

'The king is cruel,' said Anne.

'He's a man,' replied Isabelle coolly, 'and he's determined to secure the Tudor line.'

'Is there any word of Lizzie Brooke?' asked Anne.

'Her family is trying to broker a reunion but I don't think either Tommy or Lizzie is interested,' said Isabelle. 'John told me that Baron Brooke has approached Chancery to force Tommy to take care of Lizzie financially but it's messy and unpleasant. She doesn't deserve all the spite that is being aimed at her.'

'Women never do,' said Anne, 'yet we are blamed for men's woes.'

'We should blame Eve,' said Beatrice, who had been listening.

'No,' said Anne, 'we should blame Adam for allowing Eve to be tempted.'

Isabelle and Beatrice exchanged curious looks.

'What do you mean, Annie?' asked Isabelle.

'It's something Meg and I discussed when we were younger,' said Anne. 'Men claim they are superior to women; they are cleverer, stronger, wiser, yet when Eve was tempted by the serpent in the Garden of Eden, Adam didn't challenge her or try to protect her, he simply took the fruit without question. Surely, if he was the superior of the two, he should have reasoned with her and resisted. In so doing, he could have persuaded Eve to reject the forbidden fruit, thus protecting them both from the evils of Satan.'

'But this was the allure of the serpent and of Eve's womanly wiles,' said Beatrice. 'They fooled Adam.'

'Then Adam was not as wise or holy as we are led to believe,' replied Anne. 'If Adam were superior, he could have saved Eve from temptation and we would all be living in paradise. Instead, men use this story to punish women, blaming them if things don't go as they believe they should.'

Anne sipped from her goblet, enjoying the stunned looks on

the faces of her friends. She missed Meg and their intellectual debates.

'Your sentiments are interesting,' said Beatrice. 'Perhaps there are others who agree. There's no doubt the moral lines at court continue to be blurred. There are rumours of new liaisons every week, all claimed to be within the tradition of courtly love which the king admires.'

* * *

The food was cleared and Anne lost track of the conversation as she issued directions to her staff. By the time the trays of sweets and marchpane fancies had been served, the conversation had moved on and the women were discussing the latest fashions while the men were talking about the possibility of hunting the next morning. Anne listened, nodding, occasionally making a comment.

Then Isabelle said, 'I came across an old friend of yours while I was at court: Randall Hanworth.'

'Randall?' said Anne, shocked.

'Yes, he was visiting his cousin Margaret Gibbs and asked after you. He said he'll be travelling to see family and friends not far from here soon.'

'Really?' said Anne, her heart pounding. 'I shall tell Edward and we must extend an invitation. They were friends when they were at my father's house.'

At the other end of the table, Edward caught her eye and Anne smiled.

'Come, ladies,' she said, 'let us retire to my solar.'

Anne rose, indicating the end of the meal. The men stood as Anne led the women through the double doors of the dining chamber and along the corridor towards her solar. Around her the women chatted but her mind was elsewhere. Randall would soon be nearby, the thought made her heart pound. Despite her best intentions to put him from her mind, Randall was never far from her thoughts. She knew seeing him again would be both wonderful and unbearable in equal measures, yet how could she resist?

'Anne, there is one more thing I must warn you about,' whispered Isabelle, slipping her arm through Anne's as they walked, bringing her from her thoughts of Randall.

'Warn me? What about?'

'Jane Orwell,' said Isabelle.

'Jane? She's harmless.'

'I overheard her telling her sister-in-law, Margery de Ponte, that she believed Edward to be in love with her,' said Isabelle.

'Foolish girl—' began Anne, but she paused at the stricken expression on Isabelle's face.

'No, she must be taken seriously,' whispered Isabelle. 'With all the upheaval at court, things have become less rigid in the matter of marriage vows being kept. With the hints that Fitzroy might be made heir, men with no sons are wondering if they can look elsewhere to sire a son. This is a bad time for women like us, Anne, women who are unable to bear a child. Jane believes she will soon be a permanent addition to this household as Edward's lover.'

Anne listened but the words made no sense. This was like a tale from the legends of King Arthur: of Tristan and Iseult and their forbidden love; of Arthur, Guinevere and Lancelot. Was this how the king saw his relationship with her old friend, Anne Boleyn? A love triangle of beauty, recreating the chivalry of old, while the reality was painful beyond belief.

'Thank you for passing on your suspicions, Isabelle,' said Anne. 'I shall think hard on your words.'

As they entered the solar, the fire blazed and the other women settled in chairs, picking up embroidery or prayer books. Anne took her seat beside the hearth but she felt chilled. Would Edward do such a thing? Could he be so cruel? It would be the greatest of humiliations if he were to parade his mistress in front of her, but Edward was a determined man.

Her mind flickered to her father, Charles Brandon; had he not cut a swathe through the women at court? He had abandoned her own mother, Anne Browne, for several months, leaving doubts over Anne's legitimacy when he had married the elderly Margaret Neville and taken her money and lands, as was a husband's right. The duke had then annulled the marriage to marry Anne Browne, leaving Margaret to fight to have her wealth returned.

After the death of her mother, Charles Brandon had been betrothed to Elizabeth Grey, 5th Baroness Lisle and on the strength of her title, been created 1st Viscount Lisle. It was without a qualm he had ended this agreement to marry her stepmother, Princess Mary. His past was chequered and full of deceit and Anne realised he treated women as nothing more than interchangeable commodities in order to further his ambitions and gain power. Was this what Edward had learned from her father? He had been his ward for many years, travelled to war with the duke and been tutored in the skills of the courtly life by him. Her father was a ruthless man and it seemed his influence had created her husband in the same mould.

14

PEMBROKESHIRE, MAY, PRESENT DAY

Caroline slipped off her jacket as she walked across the car park towards the Mary Fitzroy Heritage Centre. The weather was playing its usual games and after the deluges and icy winds of the previous week, when it felt as though winter had returned, the day was soft and golden with all the promise of early summer. Excitement bubbled inside her as she hurried to her meeting with Mark Llewellyn, head of The Dairy, the research centre at Marquess House.

She had spoken to Mark the previous day and his voice had been full of enthusiasm about their discoveries.

'The information you pointed out to us about Hanworth House has solved a mystery we've been pondering for a while,' he had explained. 'We all thought it might refer to Hanworth Manor in west London which was once the home of Queen Katheryn Parr but the dates and information didn't tally. However, a Hanworth House in Pembrokeshire would make far more sense. Especially when you factor the names Randall Hanworth and Anne Brandon into the search. The hits were popping up all over the place. Even more interesting, we knew Anne Brandon had been with Anne Boleyn in Mechelen at the court of Margaret, Duchess of Savoy, but we hadn't realised they had remained friends. This estate once belonged to Anne Boleyn as part of her Welsh holdings when she was created Marquess of Pembroke on 1 September 1532 and there are deeds showing a parcel of land was sold to Randall Hanworth in 1535.'

Mark had asked her if she was available to view the documents and she had jumped at the chance.

'I'll book one of the seminar rooms at the Heritage Centre,' he had said. 'We should be able to compile a sizeable digital archive for you to keep. There are a few items we think would be of interest. They're beautiful but too fragile to lend.'

The glass doors of the centre swished open and Caroline felt the change in air temperature. The entire museum was climate controlled to protect the more delicate exhibits. In the atrium was a portrait of a woman in her mid-forties below which was a plaque:

Mary Fitzroy, painted in 1975.

It went on to explain that her granddaughters, Perdita and Piper Rivers, had inherited her estate and this museum was their tribute to her.

The building had once been an old farmhouse with a series of barns and outbuildings but the entire complex had been converted into a heritage centre. Alongside the restorations of the original buildings, there were new galleries and chambers. These were made from glass and steel, built in curves like the hull of the ship, *The Arbella Stuart*, which was the focal point of the museum. The wreck had been found in nearby Dale and had been raised several years earlier thanks to funding from Marquess House.

Work continued on the restoration of the shattered hull, decks and mast but the vast ship's figurehead in the shape of a mermaid, which had been rescued first, dominated the central gallery. It rested on a Perspex wave, supported by a cat's cradle of cables from above. Caroline had been astonished the first time she had seen it and paused again to gaze up at the serene beauty of the ancient carving.

A café-bar stretched along one side with an art gallery and gift shop, while in the main chambers were exhibits from the local area. To one side was a Victorian wing, complete with small theatre which housed a vast collection telling the story of a local woman, Esme Blood, who had been a music hall star. Mark had told Caroline to follow the signs for this exhibit, which would lead her to the corridor where the seminar rooms and a small lecture theatre were situated.

As she rounded the corner a man came hurrying towards her. Tall and thin, wearing jeans, a checked shirt and Timberland boots, a pair of tortoiseshell glasses perched on his nose, he beamed when he saw her and extended his hand to shake hers.

'Caroline?' he asked. 'I'm Mark Llewellyn.'

He was not what Caroline had imagined from their conversations. She had imagined a small, besuited professor with a pince-nez not this outdoorsy looking man.

'Hello,' she replied. 'It's so kind of you to spare the time.'

'We're a research centre, we all love a new puzzle but especially me, and your request has been fascinating,' he said, then he cleared his throat nervously. 'Do you mind my asking, your name, Caroline Harvey, are you connected to Dexter Blake?'

'Yes,' she said, 'he was my grandfather.'

Mark blushed scarlet and stared at her in wonder.

'I'm a huge fan,' he said, overwhelmed, and Caroline grinned.

Her grandfather might have shied away from fans but she found their enthusiasm both humbling – that they should adore the books with such intensity – and their love for Ether and the crew, endearing.

'It isn't long until the final book,' said Mark. 'Has filming begun on Book Six, *Ether Heracles and The Elegua Crossroads*? It's probably my favourite so far.'

'Really?' said Caroline, surprised. 'It's not as popular as some of the others, readers found the names of Luna the Alien's 1,200 cousins and siblings confusing. Dexter was annoyed when they complained about it in the reviews.'

'People are foolish,' said Mark. 'Luna's one of my favourite characters. The recurring theme of her resurrection at the end of each book really underscores the high stakes and dangers the crew face with every journey. It frustrates me that few other fans have picked up on the way Ether revives her each time. It's a huge clue to the part Ether must be destined to play in the defeat of the Boucicauly.'

Caroline stared at Mark in bewilderment.

'I don't suppose you have family trees with the names of all Luna's cousins in your research, do you? It would be fascinating to study it,' he continued.

'Actually, I do,' she replied. 'It was a labour of love that Dexter and I worked on for about two months. Would you like me to email them to you?'

Mark gasped. 'Would you?'

'Of course, I'll send them over later.'

He gazed at her for another few seconds then seemed to remember her purpose for visiting and pulled himself together.

'My apologies,' he said, leading the way into a large square room, 'my wife, Stephanie, teases me about my Ether obsession. Anyway, you're here for the Tudors not to listen to me expound on your grandfather's books.'

'It's fine,' she said. 'It's always great fun to hear people's thoughts on the story.'

'You're very kind,' he said. 'Now, the mystery of Hanworth House. As we've already explained, your grandfather's land once belonged to the Marquess House estate. Do you know much about our background?'

'No,' admitted Caroline, 'until I began researching the woodland, I hadn't given it much thought.'

'Brief history lesson then,' said Mark. 'A few years ago, Perdita – she and her twin sister, Piper, own Marquess House – discovered a deed of ownership from King Henry V for the land, then known as Llanismael, which is the old name for the villages of St Ishmaels. The bulk of it was given to the church but a large portion, which was centred around an existing sixth century tower, was given by royal charter to Sir Stephen Perrot to build a house. This was in 1457 when he married the Lady Ann Tudor, half-sister of King Henry VI. We've subsequently discovered this was the origins of Marquess House and the tower which is still at its centre.'

'How amazing,' said Caroline. She had no idea how this was connected to her enquiries but it was fascinating.

'Perdita had to do a great deal more research to discover whether it was a genuine document because there were a number of concerns about the dates and the suggestions of Henry VI even having a half-sister. The entire story would take far too long to explain but the document has since been authenticated. Further research revealed the house fell under the auspices of the Marquess of Pembroke, which is where our connection to Anne Boleyn appeared. Have you had a chance to read the transcript of the journal from the early nineteenth century?'

'Yes, there's a great deal about local issues as well as a myth about the oak henge and the ruins.'

'Exactly,' said Mark. 'Did you notice the final section of the legend, concerning a man who needed to rescue his lady-love from a cruel husband?'

'Yes,' said Caroline, remembering the afternoon she had told the tale to Gideon and Ben.

'After a great deal of discussion, Perdita, her husband, Kit, and I think this might refer to Randall Hanworth and his love affair with Anne Brandon, or as she was by then, Lady Powis, wife of Edward Grey, Baron Powis.'

'Isn't that quite a leap?' said Caroline.

'Yes, and if we hadn't found these,' Mark indicated a cotton cloth covering several bulky items on the table beside him, 'we wouldn't have made the suggestion. They were in an archive Perdita and Piper inherited more recently. It's been a treasure trove of history and it was wonderful to discover these items were connected, albeit loosely, to the Marquess House estate.'

'Ready?' he asked and Caroline could tell he was enjoying the theatricality of the moment.

He pulled back the cloth to reveal an ancient leather-bound book resting on a foam wedge. Beside this in a Perspex box was a pile of yellowing letters. Caroline stared in awe.

'Here,' he said, handing her cotton gloves, 'you'll need these. This is a copy of *Tristan and Iseult*. Do you know the story?'

'Yes, it's one of my favourite Arthurian tales,' said Caroline.

'One of mine too,' he said. 'There's Arthurian influence

throughout the *Ether Heracles* books, isn't there? Sorry, sorry... This copy is from the earlier part of the sixteenth century and as well as the beautiful illustrations, there are sections that were used as a journal. Even better, the name at the front is "Anne Brandon, Lady Powis".'

'This belonged to Anne Brandon?' gasped Caroline. 'Are you sure?'

'Yes, we've done multiple tests including the use of our scanner which captures colour nuances of non-photographic materials such as papyri, parchment, vellum and fabric. The level of light it uses can highlight hidden messages. Steganography is Stephanie's area of expertise.'

'What?'

'It's the practice of concealing a message within another message or physical object, and focuses on ensuring this information is undetectable. Cryptography is the art of protecting the contents of the data alone, while steganography concentrates on the process of concealing the entire content rather than simply the message.'

Caroline stared at him in bemusement.

'Do you mean invisible ink?' asked Caroline.

'Yes, or even ink that's faded with time,' he said. 'It's quite a puzzle though because the Brandon family had its roots in Suffolk and Norfolk. One of the earlier Brandons I've been able to trace was Robert Brandon of Lynn, Norfolk. He was mentioned in the *Little Domesday Book*...'

'Is that different from the *Domesday Book*?'

'It was a first draft,' explained Mark. 'It covered Essex, Suffolk and Norfolk. It was never included in the final *Domesday Book*, so is known as the *Little Domesday Book*. There's an *Exon Domesday* at Exeter Cathedral which is similar and covers the south west of the country.'

'Robert Brandon was listed as receiving securities from the Exchequer for the keeping of…' she reached into her bag and pulled out a slim folder containing items she had thought might be useful for this meeting. 'Here we go, the keeping of "La Lovecon" in Lynn. I presume it's a house. In the early 1420s he became a member of the Guild of the Holy Trinity and by 1433, he was the guild's treasurer. Robert Brandon was the great-great grandfather of Anne Brandon,' said Caroline. 'I sourced two quite rare books from Ten-to-Midnight.'

'They're a great bookshop, it's very exciting to have a branch on the marina,' said Mark. 'Have you seen the window? Did you help with it?'

'No, my friend Gideon who runs the shops is a huge fan,' she said. 'The display was all his own work.'

'You know Gideon Morris?'

'Yes, we were at college together when we were teenagers,' she replied and had to suppress a smile at Mark's further admiration. 'I'll introduce you if you like but first, these were the books he found for me.'

She pulled out the copy of the Tudor maps and the slim volume of letters.

'*The Brandon Letters* edited by Jericho Fleming,' said Mark examining the book. 'This is very interesting and will be a real help to fill in the gaps from the cache of correspondence we discovered.'

'The letters are nearly all written by men,' said Caroline. 'I was hoping it would be similar to the *Paston Letters* where a number of women wrote too but these cover the older Brandons. One of the few women featured is Margaret Brandon who married Sir Walter Guybon before 1421. This is dated 1421 and she's enquiring about a reliable wet nurse from her friend Lady Alice Tay. Sadly, the historical records show she died giving birth to her son Lawrence Guybon. Margaret was Anne Brandon's great-aunt.'

'How interesting,' said Mark. 'Was there anything in the maps?'

'Perhaps, but there are so many, it's taking me time to wade through them. I was hoping you might have found more details about Randall Hanworth,' she said.

'He's proving even more elusive than Anne Brandon,' said Mark but he looked delighted about this situation. 'From what I've discovered, Randall Hanworth was a courtier descended from the brother of Hugo de Hanworth who was Archdeacon of Stow and Lindsey in Lincoln. He had links to the Doughty family who were the main landowners in Norfolk and they have a blood tie to the Browne family, which is Anne Brandon's maternal line.

'There's also a possibility he had a distant connection to the Howards. The name Hanworth is quite unusual but there was Haworth and Howarth both of which could have been forerunners of the Howards, who by the time Randall and Anne were alive, were the Dukes of Norfolk. There was no standardisation of names in Tudor times, so Hanworth could have been a variation on either. The question is, how did they end up in Pembrokeshire?'

Caroline shrugged. Mark pointed to the Perspex box.

'Luckily,' he said, 'we've found an astonishing array of letters between Anne Brandon, Margaret Roper, who was the daughter of Thomas More, Lady Eleanor Brandon, who was Anne's half-sister and Anne Boleyn, which is where we discover our Pembrokeshire link.'

'Honestly?' said Caroline.

'Yes,' he said, 'and even better, such is the brilliance of our team, they finished transcribing them last night along with the entries in the copy of *Tristan and Iseult*.'

He handed her a memory stick.

'We've put it all on here for you,' he beamed. 'Happy reading.'

It was Caroline's turn to gaze in awe.

15

DEXTER'S PLACE, ST ISHMAELS, PEMBROKESHIRE, MAY, PRESENT DAY

Caroline was engrossed in the transcript of Anne Brandon's diary from the ancient copy of *Tristan and Iseult* which had been written in faded and invisible ink. This was the first transcript she had decided to read in the vast number of documents Mark and the Marquess House team had digitised for her. Each was numbered and itemised with notes giving summaries and cross-references. When she had approached the heritage centre for help, she had never imagined they would discover so many references to Anne Brandon and Randall Hanworth in connection with their own property or in their wider archive.

'It's great to have someone researching a new area of the Tudor court,' Mark had said when she had emailed him to express her gratitude. 'The problem we have is finding the time to explore the documents we protect. There are thousands, so this has been a huge help.'

As she lost herself in words written centuries earlier, Caroline's heart broke for the long-dead woman who had tried so hard to do her duty by her father and her husband. Her sense of outrage grew as Anne was blamed for her string of devastating miscarriages and she was reading Anne's feelings about Jane Orwell when her phone buzzed, making her jump.

Her phone was hidden under the pile of overlapping print-outs that were strewn across the kitchen table. As she rescued it, she saw Blanche Fellowes's name flashing like a demon. Even before Caroline could say hello, Blanche barked, 'Caro, why didn't you tell me about Salter Holdings and their land request to gain access to your private beach?'

'Good morning to you, too, Blanche,' said Caroline.

'Sorry,' said Blanche, her tone softening, 'but we've had an email from them this morning and its contents are concerning.'

Caroline explained Salter Holdings had contacted her but Suzannah had dealt with it and as far as she was aware the matter was over. There was such a long pause, Caroline wondered if Blanche had been cut off.

'Blanche, are you there?'

'Caro, this matter is not over,' said Blanche and the seriousness of her tone caused a shiver to run down Caroline's spine. 'I received an email this morning demanding you reconsider your position. They've widened the request and have stated they're interested in buying part of the woodland too. There is a very clear threat within their terms that suggests they're prepared to use forceful tactics.'

'What do you mean?'

'At the end of the new proposal they have asked why a Caroline Drover from Twickenham is listed as buying the house named Beach View in May 2013 when all Dexter Blake's publicity states the same property, known as Dexter's Place, has been in his family for over three generations?'

'No,' gasped Caroline. 'How could they know?'

'Land Registry,' said Blanche. 'We're good at covering our tracks but we can't actually make documents disappear from public record. Well, not easily. Caro, this could be a big problem, especially with Dexter's final book due out in a few weeks and the global publicity building. You should have sent it straight to me not used some local person.'

'Suzannah works for one of the biggest law firms in London,' retorted Caro, 'and she did it as a favour because she's a friend. I had no idea they were going to cause such problems.'

'Were you aware that Salter Holdings is part of Arnold Constructions?'

'No,' said Caroline, horrified, 'but Travis is going out with Bella Arnold, the daughter of Lee Arnold who owns Arnold Constructions.'

'Exactly,' replied Blanche, 'which explains how they discovered the private beach at Dexter's Place. When did the first letter arrive?'

'A few weeks ago,' she said.

'Around the time Bella moved into the apartment?'

'Yes,' agreed Caroline. 'Oh, Blanche, I'm such a fool for not realising.'

'You weren't to know but I wonder if this more aggressive stance is because of the notice to quit we've since sent Travis,' said Blanche.

'It's possible.'

'Probable,' said Blanche, then her tone became businesslike. 'Leave it with us, Caro. We'll dig out Travis's Non-Disclosure Agreement and remind him. He's not going to want his bosses at the Metropolitan Police discovering he's involved with dubious land deals.'

'Are you sure?'

'Trust me, I have contacts everywhere and there's a very pleasant Detective Chief Inspector who owes me a favour.'

'Blanche, thank you,' said Caro.

'No problem,' said Blanche. 'There's one more thing, too. Flavia's been in touch, the social media trolls are making a noise again.'

'What about this time?' asked Caroline.

'Dexter's death,' said Blanche, and again her tone was serious. 'An online fan group, although they're not real fans, they're troublemakers, has begun a whisper campaign suggesting Dexter was murdered.'

'Murdered? By whom?'

'You.'

'Blanche, no, that's awful,' said Caroline, genuinely shocked.

'Flavia's going to ring you later, she's trying to have the posts removed. Don't worry, Caro, we'll do all we can to protect Dexter and Ether.'

Caroline hung up, wondering why Flavia had gone to Blanche with the problem rather than contacting her direct. For her sister to have taken such serious action meant it was more than the usual nastiness. Although she was relieved Blanche and Flavia were helping, she felt resentment rising at Blanche's final comment.

'Always Dexter and Ether,' she muttered as she tossed her phone onto the kitchen table. 'Never me, always bloody Dexter. Dexter Blake who has caused me so much misery. Never, *"You must be upset, Caro, discovering your former fiancé has betrayed you..."* No, let's consider the impact it might have on BLOODY DEXTER.'

She shouted the last two words, unsure if she was angry or hurt or even whether her emotions were being caused by Travis's perfidy, Blanche's inability to see beyond Dexter or the insidious rumour about her murdering Dexter.

Would Travis really stoop so low as to pass on information to Bella and her father? Caroline wondered.

The word, *yes,* floated into her mind. The flat in question had been the most expensive thing Caroline had ever bought. When the first film was made, in gratitude, Dexter had insisted on giving her a vast bonus. With several million pounds in the bank, her accountant had advised her to spend a chunk of it on property. Caroline loved the Southbank in London and decided to purchase one of the apartments on the banks of the Thames near the Tate Modern. Travis had adored the flat and they had spent many happy times there.

Breathing deeply in an effort to calm her fury, Caroline felt tears of frustration prick her eyes. Of course this had come from Travis. Why else would a subsidiary of the company owned by his girlfriend's father make an unexpected bid to buy the land beside her house and request access to a beach very few people knew existed. The question was, how much had he said?

A chill ran through her. Could he have revealed enough to ruin everything? She was so near the end. The final book was mere weeks away and then it would be over. If the films were made, then they were made but that was never what this had been about. It was about the story: the epic tale of friendship, romance and true love conquering all. It was what she had given everything up for and if it was ruined at the last moment, she did not think her heart would cope.

She picked up her phone and scrolled through her numbers until she came to Travis Hibbert. Should she call? Ask if he had accidentally let information slip? A mistake, it could not have been deliberate. He was aware there were others, innocent bystanders who would be damaged by a revelation about Dexter. Would he be this cruel?

Her thoughts were chaotic as she fast-forwarded through all the potential damage Travis or Bella, if he had told her, could do to all she, Dexter and Blanche had worked so hard to create.

Leave it to Blanche, she told herself. *We have the law on our side, even if Travis might think as a police officer he's above it, he isn't.* As for the rumour about Dexter being murdered, they had weathered such storms before.

These rationalisations offered no comfort and she pushed herself back from the table, letting herself out of the French doors into the garden. Fear was making it impossible to remain still, she wanted to walk but the anxiety caused by the phone call conversely made her crave the safety of home. She marched to the centre of the lawn, which felt like a good compromise, before criss-crossing backwards and forwards as she tried to control her thoughts. Images of her and Travis flitted through her mind. In the past, there had been several occasions when he had hinted he might one day reveal her secret.

'Lies, all lies,' he had once jeered during a row about them returning to their lives in London rather than remaining in Pembrokeshire. 'Your entire life is a lie and I could tear it down with one phone call.'

'You wouldn't,' she had gasped. 'Do you want to destroy Dexter too?'

Travis had always been jealous of Dexter, frustrated that the old man's career had consumed their lives. It was part of the reason their relationship had faltered and then ended. And now, with Dexter dead, unable to defend himself, would Travis have his revenge? Punish the man whom he believed had been the cause of Travis's lack of promotion at work.

Her phone buzzed again and Caroline answered it without looking at the caller ID, assuming it would be Blanche.

'Hi, Caro, it's Gid.'

'Hello,' she said in surprise, her emotions notching up another level at the sound of his voice.

They had all exchanged numbers when she had finally left

the bookshop a week earlier. Her promise of one drink had become many more as a second bottle had been opened but a call to Eve and Robbie had solved the problem of her finding her way home.

'We came in together this morning,' Eve had said, grinning. 'I can drive you and your car home. You can introduce us to the mysterious Gideon, we've only met Ben so far.'

The introductions had been made with promises of working together and the swapping of numbers before Eve and Robbie led a smiling, hiccupping Caro away. As soon as they were in the car, Eve had said, 'Do you remember the day I visited and said there was a man in a car with a map?'

'Yes,' Caroline had said, shutting her eyes to stop the world spinning.

'I'm pretty certain it was Gideon.'

'Really?' said Caroline. 'It's probably because he's a huge Dexter Blake fan, he was trying to find the house.'

Eve had questioned her about Ben and Gideon all the way back to Dexter's Place.

'We're friends, nothing else,' Caroline had said as they arrived.

'Yep, you keep telling yourself that,' Eve had laughed as she climbed into Robbie's jeep.

* * *

'Is everything all right? You sound stressed?' Gideon asked now.

'My— well, she's mine and Dexter's agent, has been on the phone. There are a few problems to do with the launch,' she said, then inwardly cursed herself for lying but at this stage the entire situation felt too fraught to discuss with anyone other than those involved. 'She'll sort it out. How about you? How's the bookshop?'

'Going well. The new manager, Stacey, is settling in and I think she'll be a real asset,' he hesitated. 'In fact, she's doing so well, she doesn't need both me and Ben. He offered to stay so I wondered if I could come over to yours? Although, if it's a bad time...'

He let the sentence hang and Caroline bit her lip. Her initial reaction to Gideon had been a rush of excitement, followed by apprehension. Very few people visited Dexter's Place because her grandfather did not like it, then she remembered: Dexter was dead. The house was hers, she could invite as many people as she liked. *But what if Blanche or Flavia were to call?*

She dithered wondering whether to turn Gideon away, to make herself available for any calls as she had always done in the past. No matter her plans, she had always changed them if Dexter or his wider world had needed assistance. She was about to suggest he visit another day, then she realised she *wanted* to see him, she did not want to face another crisis about her grandfather alone and a wave of recklessness washed over her.

'Where are you?' she asked.

'I'm parked by the St Ishmaels Sports Club,' he said and Caroline laughed.

'You just happen to be in the area?'

'It was Ken, he insisted. He wants to see the standing stone from your story.'

'And we wouldn't want to disappoint Ken,' she said. 'I'll give you directions.'

Caroline heard Gideon start the car and as she guided him to her house on the edges of the village, she ran upstairs to brush her hair and apply lip gloss.

'I'm at the gate,' Gideon said, and she could hear the excitement in his voice.

As she hurried down to let him in, she wondered whether the allure of visiting was down to her or the possibility of seeing Blake's inner sanctum. He parked beside her silver Land Rover and she felt a thrill of anticipation as he and Ken climbed out of the car and walked towards her.

'Hey, you,' he said, bending to kiss her cheek. Ken licked her hand. 'Wow, so this is Dexter's Place.'

Caroline's heart sank.

'Sorry for having a fan-boy moment but I can't believe I'm at Dexter Blake's house,' he said, his eyes sparkling.

Caroline's smile became more rigid, 'It's nothing extraordinary.'

'It's the place where *Ether Heracles* was created,' he said in disbelief, throwing his arms wide. 'This is the place where a new world was built—'

'Stop it right now,' said Caroline but even through her whirling emotions after her phone call with Blanche she had recognised the signs: the exaggerated tone, the glint in his eye. He was teasing her, as he had done throughout their friendship and particularly during their brief but perfect relationship one summer. 'If you carry on like this, I won't let you inside.'

Gideon grinned. 'Too much?'

'Way too much.'

'Sorry,' he said. 'I wouldn't want you thinking the house was the reason I visited.'

'Well, that's a relief,' she said coolly but her smile relaxed. 'Come in and if you promise not to be too weird, I'll show you Dexter's writing shed.'

'I promise,' he said, pulling a serious face.

Ken gave a woof of disgust at Gideon's behaviour and with dignified grace, marched inside the house.

16

'The tour then,' said Caroline as she shut the front door behind Gideon. 'Living room,' she pointed to the bright sunny room to her left, 'then through there – the kitchen and dining area. There's another living room beyond and a smaller snug which was Dexter's favourite. Through there,' she pointed to the right, 'is my office and beside it is the room we've always called the library, although it's a rather grandiose description for a medium-sized room with lots of bookcases. Upstairs are a variety of bedrooms and bathrooms.'

'And Dexter worked in the garden?' asked Gideon gazing around.

'Yes, he always claimed it made him feel as though he was properly going to work if he had to leave the house. He could also lock Ether and the gang outside so they wouldn't bother him at night.'

'I imagine they could be troublesome,' said Gideon.

'You have no idea,' replied Caroline. 'Come through, I'll put the kettle on.'

Ken's nails tapped on the polished wooden floor, the tune

changing as he entered the kitchen and encountered the stone tiles.

'I don't have a cushion large enough for Ken, will he make do with the sofa?' asked Caroline pointing to the two large settees positioned at right angles to each other to maximise the views across the garden and over the bay.

Gideon looked at Ken and said, 'Sofa?'

With a sigh of 'If I must', Ken trotted to the seat on the left and made himself comfortable. Caroline filled a ceramic bowl with water and placed it near the dog.

'What's his full name?' she asked as she flicked on the kettle and reached into the cupboard for a packet of Earl Grey tea.

'It's Kenneth Aloysius Morris and his dad was Percival Gawain.'

'Very Arthurian,' she said. 'Wasn't Ewan – your dog when we were at college – Ewan Bartholomew?'

'Good memory,' he said as he wandered over to admire the view.

'It's beautiful,' he said. As he walked back towards Caroline he was distracted by her photographs. 'Hey, it's us!'

Caroline's hand shook as she poured the water into the teapot and cursed herself, how could she have forgotten her picture gallery? There was an alcove in the living room, a small nook that was lined with personal photographs. *Calm,* she told herself. *It's Gideon, he's your friend.*

Wiping her sweating palms on her jeans, she took deep breaths as she joined him.

'It's great to see this picture again,' he said studying the image Caroline had recently found of The Seven in their costumes. She had framed it and added the image to her wall of happy memories. 'Is that your sister, Flavia?'

'Yes, with her husband, Steve, and their sons, Logan and

Finn,' she said, pointing to the boys in order of their names on the photograph below.

'Who's the other little boy?'

'Jonah, their cousin,' she said and nudged Gideon towards an image of herself in a wheelchair with a plaster cast.

'Is that you and Dexter?' he asked.

'Despite the broken leg, I love that picture of Gramps,' she said. 'It was taken a month after Flavia knocked me over reversing out of the drive.'

'Yes, she was a terrible driver,' said Gideon. 'Do you remember when she collected us from the station one night? How we managed to avoid that bus...'

Caroline grimaced.

'Running me over on the driveway was the moment Flavia realised she should organise more driving lessons. We were always astonished she passed her test at all, she was so erratic behind the wheel.'

'Remind me exactly how it happened,' he said, gazing at the image of the teenage Caroline balancing on crutches beside her grandfather.

'Flavia asked me to guide her out of the driveway,' said Caroline. 'I was standing in what I considered to be a safe place, beckoning her into the road. We lived in the quietest cul-de-sac but she was so nervous about reversing. She was edging backwards and then her accelerator foot slipped and in her moment of panic, she forgot the brake was next to it, pushed her foot down hard on the accelerator pedal and shot out of the drive. She screamed and took her hands off the wheel so the car swerved and came straight at me. I dived out of the way but it clipped my leg and broke it in two places.'

Gideon winced. 'It must have been agony.'

'It wasn't great,' she agreed. 'Flavia was in a state, Mum came flying out of the house to comfort her and didn't realise I was on the ground behind the car. I rang the ambulance myself, then passed out. I woke up on a stretcher with Flavia sobbing over me and begging for forgiveness.'

Gideon stared at her and she could tell he was working hard not to laugh.

'It's funny now,' she said.

'The accident changed everything for you,' said Gideon.

'Yes, I deferred my place at Hull University and helped Gramps with his first *Ether Heracles* book,' she said. 'By the time my leg was healed, we'd developed a real working partnership. He asked me to stay and help. Neither of us ever dreamed *Ether* would become such a huge success.'

'A worldwide phenomenon,' he said, then his voice tailed away as his eyes flicked back to the image of the three boys.

'When was that taken?'

'Last summer when Steve's sister was staying,' she said. 'She took the picture.'

'So, he's a nephew through her husband's side,' Gideon murmured but Caroline did not comment. Gideon did not seem to be able to stop staring at Jonah. 'He looks familiar.'

'He's an actor,' said Caroline, quickly. 'When he was young he loved performing so much his mother decided to send him to stage school and he's thrived. You probably recognise him from the adaptation of *Oliver Twist* last year. He was the Artful Dodger.'

Relief flooded Gideon's face.

'Yes, we loved that series.'

'You and Margot?'

'No, she never watched anything other than *Mongoose Summer* or reality television,' he said bitterly. 'Me and Ben.'

'Tea?' reminded Caroline, and led the way back to the kitchen.

'Earl Grey, you remembered,' he said taking the mug.

'It's because the first time I drank it was at your dad's place and I thought it was disgusting.'

'But you drank gallons.'

'I was too polite to say I didn't like it,' she said.

The statement held a hint of truth. Her shyness back then had stopped her asking for a different drink but she had been desperate to appear sophisticated in front of him. When Nadine had complained about it, Caroline had taken great pleasure in drinking mug after mug of Earl Grey even though she found its floral bouquet too perfumed for her palette.

'Why do you have it in your cupboard if you don't like it?' he asked.

'Dexter drank it,' she replied.

'A man of taste,' said Gideon.

Caroline picked up her own breakfast tea.

'Are you in the middle of something?' asked Gideon, pausing by the kitchen table.

'The beginnings of research,' said Caroline. 'I'd usually be in my office but at the moment it's full of boxes of books for me to sign.'

'For *you* to sign?' asked Gideon.

'Yes,' she replied. 'I'm letting you into a huge secret here but Dexter never signed the books, he said it was frivolous and pointless. I created the cipher he used as a signature and when I showed it to him, he loved it. We agreed it would be used in the books because I was able to do it for him. As he refused to do live events, Dexter never signed a book in his life, it was always me.'

Gideon stared at her in astonishment.

'Have I disappointed you?' she asked.

'No, not all,' he said. 'I'm amazed at how deeply you were involved. Ben and I were discussing it last night and we wondered how it worked, whether you were a researcher or a PA.'

'I was both of those, as well as a carer and an integral part of the *Ether Heracles* world,' she hesitated, wondering whether to explain further, then decided she could trust Gideon. 'About ten years ago, Dexter was diagnosed with macular degeneration and his sight deteriorated. By the end, he was dictating everything and I was transcribing it. Then we'd work on the edits together.'

'You were practically the co-author then?'

'We were a team.'

'How are you going to explain the signed books to his fans?' asked Gideon.

'A social media message will state that when he knew it was possible the final book might be published posthumously, Dexter signed one hundred loose bookplates which have been stuck into the first books off the press.'

'They'll become collector's items.' Gideon sipped his tea, then he said, his voice more gentle, 'You must miss him.'

'Yes, but it's also a relief to be free,' she said. 'He could be a difficult man.'

They stared at each other. She did not want to shatter the dream of his hero but she could no longer lie about the negative impact Dexter had had upon her life. Over the years he had come between her friends and family as his demands grew more intense, but she realised this was not the time to elaborate. Gideon had been allowed the knowledge of two of Dexter's secrets, it was enough.

'I'm also slightly overexcited to think the final *Ether Heracles* book is in the next room,' said Gideon, defusing the sudden seriousness. 'We won't have them at the shops until the day before the launch.'

'With all my heart I wish I could give you one but there are trained snipers surrounding the house who'll be triggered if anyone other than my biometrically scanned fingers touch them,' she replied, paraphrasing a famous scene from *Ether Heracles and The Tropic of Pisces*.

'Who are the signed books destined for?'

'They're going to random bookshops around the world including the online shops. One hundred lucky readers will receive a copy,' she paused. 'Actually, ninety-nine will.'

'Ninety-nine? What about the other one?'

'You can have it.'

Gideon's eyes lit up, then he shook his head.

'No, that's unfair, I'd be depriving a fan somewhere.'

'You're a fan, you're very welcome to have one of the limited edition signed copies, it'll complete the collection you used in the window of the shop in the marina,' she said. 'Unfortunately, I can't give it to you until publication day but then I'll drop it off.'

'Caro, are you sure?'

'Of course. Dexter would have liked you and your enthusiasm for books.'

Gideon reached over and squeezed her hand in gratitude. Caroline felt as though her skin had been scorched but he seemed unmoved as he released her and pulled the ancient atlas towards him. 'Are these maps of your woodland?'

He pointed to the cotton markers she had used and Caroline felt a wave of relief. She had expected him to ask to see Dexter's summer house next but he must have sensed her need to change the subject. Even when they were teenagers they had been in tune with each other's sensitivities. It was one of the things she had missed most when he vanished from her life.

'Yes, that's the book Ten-to-Midnight sourced for me. I was going through it earlier before I was distracted by Anne Brandon's diary.'

As she said the name of the shop, she saw the side of his mouth quirk into the half-smile she had once found so irresistible.

'Her diary?'

'Marquess House, the research centre I mentioned to you and Ben has found an astonishing amount of information which they've shared.'

'Was the book helpful?' he asked.

'Yes, I ordered it to try and find the map used in the exhibit at the Mary Fitzroy Heritage Centre and I was lucky.'

'You've found it?' asked Gideon.

'Yes,' she said. 'There are three maps showing the land around the house. This one is the oldest and gives the outline of ecclesiastical buildings, which makes me wonder if it was once a monastery, especially as the cove further up is called Monk Haven.'

'Interesting,' said Gideon. 'When did Henry VIII close the monasteries?'

'In England and Wales the closures began in 1529 after the king was refused an annulment for his marriage to Katherine of Aragon. From then on monasteries were sold and converted all over the country. The second map that's been useful is from 1535 and refers to a building named Powis House which, if it was the monastery conversion, would make it one of the earlier properties to be commandeered – Lamphey Palace, which is near Pembroke, didn't become a secular dwelling until 1546. But, the third map, which is dated 1552 and was in the image used at the

Mary Fitzroy Heritage Centre names the property as Hanworth House.'

'Could it have changed hands between 1535 and 1552?' asked Gideon.

'It's possible but the two names, Powis and Hanworth are linked.'

Gideon sipped his tea, asking the occasional question as Caroline explained all that Mark and the Marquess House team had discovered.

'I'm halfway through the transcript from Anne Brandon's *Tristan and Iseult* and it's heartbreaking,' she finished.

'Poor woman,' said Gideon. 'Her husband sounds like a very traditional Tudor male.'

'I'm trying to see his actions relative to the times but his mood swings are challenging,' she said. 'It'll be interesting to read the letters, too. They might cast light on other people and events.'

'You love history, don't you?'

'Yes, I hadn't realised how much until I began researching the historical side of the *Ether* stories for Gramps. Until then, I'd always thought my writing skills lay in literary fiction. Perhaps my next project will be an historical novel.'

'No wonder you and Ben were so close when we were younger,' he said and she could not decide whether his tone was sad or bitter. 'He's always loved history too. What did you research for your grandfather?'

'Genghis Khan, Alexander the Great, the Romans, the Vikings, as well as mythology, particularly of the British Isles. There are so many local tales we were able to incorporate. In Book Three, *Ether Heracles and Lugh's Hands*, I drew on Celtic mythology. Lugh was a warrior who was also a master craftsman; he wielded an unstoppable spear, a sling stone and had a hound named Failinis. This was the basis for the battle scene for the new Lugh or leader in the opening chapters.'

Caroline drained her almost-cold tea.

'*Lugh's Hands* is one of my favourites in the series,' said Gideon. 'There's a lot about Allegra and the crew. She's the one who I like best.'

'Not Ether?' asked Caroline.

'He's great but Allegra's my girl. It's odd, especially now I know how closely you're involved with the books because she always reminded me of you.'

Caroline felt a chill run down her spine.

'Of me? Why?'

Gideon shrugged.

'In the same way Lucifer Transmere, before his escape pod exploded, made me think of Ben.'

'What did you make of Beau Ferris when he married Allegra in the fourth book, *The Race of Jupiter*?'

'I wanted to punch him.'

'You and all Ether's fans,' Caroline said. She stood up, gathering their mugs, placing them in the dishwasher as Gideon pulled the vast atlas of ancient woodlands back towards him.

'And all that's left of the original manor is a few stones?' asked Gideon.

'Yes, would you like to take Ken for a walk in the woods and see the ruins?'

'Of course,' he said. 'Then maybe I can see Dexter's writing shed on the way back.'

'Let me fetch the keys and we'll head off.'

17

The speedwell-blue sky was patterned with wisps of swan-white clouds that drifted like ballet dancers through the endless light. Caroline breathed in the salty air and allowed contentment to envelope her. Gideon's arrival had been the perfect distraction from her worrying call from Blanche. Ken, like all Gideon's dogs, was a canine with good manners whom it was a pleasure to walk, although Caroline laughed when he gave Gideon a you-may-have-called-me-but-I'm-a-dog-on-a-mission look before bounding off towards the wood.

'He's safe,' Caroline assured Gideon, 'the cove is fenced off. He can't get onto the beach until we let him through the gate.'

'Ken's far too sensible to do anything reckless like visit an unknown beach alone,' said Gideon, then gazed around and added. 'This place is huge.'

'Yes, Gramps loved the fact he could be isolated but that the village was a short walk for me. He knew his reclusiveness was difficult for the family but he couldn't bring himself to leave the safety of Dexter's Place.'

'Was it agoraphobia?'

'No, he claimed he'd seen enough of the world and no longer wanted to worry about it on a day-to-day basis. He had his books, his cricket and until his sight made it impossible to tinker with them: his cars.'

'Do you still have them?'

'No, Gramps sold them years ago,' replied Caroline.

'There was a rumour that the reason he'd retreated was because he'd been a spy during the Cold War and he was in hiding,' said Gideon.

'Yes, we saw that in one of the tabloids. It was suggested there were high-placed people within governments across the world who would be happy to silence Dexter Blake. Complete nonsense, of course, but we never managed to discover the source of the rumour,' said Caroline.

'There were people who thought his name was a secret code,' said Gideon. 'Did you see it on the fan sites?'

'Yes, they said Dexter Blake was not his name but an anagram and if it was cracked, it would reveal Cold War secrets,' Caroline said.

'There was an entire website dedicated to that theory for a while.'

'There was,' said Caroline, 'but Flavia managed to have it taken down.'

They had reached the edge of the garden where the cultivated section gave way to the wilder areas.

'This path,' said Caroline, pointing to the woods, 'leads down to the ruins. The other one,' she pointed to her right, 'goes to the cove. Salter Holdings want to buy this section.'

She pointed to back half of the garden.

'Do they want the wood, too?'

'Yes,' she replied, 'it's a ridiculous suggestion because it would deny me access across my own land. Blanche and Dexter's legal team are dealing with it.'

'But this is hidden from view,' said Gideon staring around. 'How could they have known about the beach?'

'My ex-fiancé, Travis, is going out with the daughter of the man who owns Salter Holdings,' she said.

'Caro, that's dreadful,' said Gideon. 'Why are people so vindictive?'

His voice was harsh and she was surprised when he pulled her into a tight hug.

'Ben and I will do all we can to help,' he said. 'Dexter's fans would definitely give you their support, too. Bullies should never be allowed to win.'

'Thanks, Gid,' she said, as he released her.

'Are the ruins through here?'

'Yes, you'd better call Ken.'

Gideon whistled and Ken crashed through the bushes to join them, padding along at his master's side.

'Won't you ruin your boots?' said Gideon as Caroline led them along the muddy path.

She looked down at her battered Dr Martens boots.

'These are old now,' she said. 'They've been demoted to casual and garden wear.'

'But they're embroidered with roses,' he said.

'Hence the reason they're garden wear,' she said, and for a moment their eyes locked.

'Do you remember the DMs you had at college with the purple swirls and ribbons for laces?' asked Gideon.

Caroline felt her heart quicken.

'I loved them,' she replied. 'Do you still have your moped?'

'Sadly, no, it died a long time ago,' he said. 'I have the crash helmet though.'

'The crash helmet...?'

'The one you customised for my birthday. You lined it with the embroidered version of my favourite poem. *He Wishes for the Cloths of Heaven* by Yeats. "Tread softly because you tread on my dreams",' said Gideon. 'My mother has it in LA for safe keeping.'

'You kept it,' she said, stunned.

'Of course,' he replied. 'It mattered.'

Around them, the air seemed to thicken with the intensity of their gaze. Was he remembering too she wondered? The illicit kisses one New Year's Eve, the beginning...

Ken nudged her hand and Caroline jumped.

'It's this way,' she said, pushing back a low branch.

Her hands were sweating and she felt breathless. *He walked away from you,* she reminded herself as they rounded a bend and Gideon exclaimed over the tiny waterfall in the stream. *He married another woman and ignored your emails. He left you when you needed him most. Be careful.*

They walked past a patch of vast gunnera swaying like giant prehistoric rhubarb, skirting around bright patches where hydrangea bushes bloomed. Caroline tried to ignore her confusion by chatting about the wood, the plants, anything to avoid more personal discussions. As they reached a bush studded with huge white flowers, she paused.

'Around this corner, there's an extraordinary clearing,' she said. 'I think it might be the inspiration for the oak henge in the legend.'

She stepped aside and allowed Gideon to walk into the green-gold light in all its beauty.

'This is astonishing,' he exclaimed as he and Ken wandered through the dappled shade.

Caroline followed, breathing in the wild smell of leaves and earth. This was her favourite place on the estate: another realm, a place of magic; the ancient Welsh fairy land of Tylwyth Teg. A place to sit, to think, to dream, to listen, her heart ever hopeful she would hear a message from these ancient giants on the breeze.

The largest oak had spreading branches opened wide, like arms welcoming all-comers into the space. Around the circle were gaps where trees had died or been felled. The loss of each one, even though they had been before she lived at Dexter's Place, had made Caroline weep. Of those that remained, the branches created a cathedral to nature, a sacred space.

'This place is magical, Caro,' said Gideon.

She watched as he moved around the clearing, staring up at the trees, pausing to run his hands over the roughness of their bark, drinking in the other-worldly atmosphere.

'Let me show you something,' she said and led him to an enormous tree stump, Ken walking between them.

The middle of the stump had long-since rotted away, reduced to mulch, but with her thumbnail, Caroline gently scraped away a tiny piece of bark.

'Can you see?' she said. 'It's green.'

'Doesn't that mean it's still alive?' said Gideon.

'Yes,' she replied.

'But that's impossible,' he said. 'For the tree to have rotted away in the centre, it must have been cut down hundreds of years ago.'

'This is the wonder of the clearing,' she said. 'I was so intrigued, I did some research and it seems that on very rare occasions trees pump natural sugar nutrients into tree stumps to keep them alive.'

'How?'

'Scientists think the food is delivered from neighbouring trees through the roots.'

Gideon stared at her in astonishment. 'But why?'

'There's no definitive answer but it's been suggested trees are often family groups and if one dies, the others will nurture it for hundreds of years, even though the rest of the tree is dead. They're showing their love for a lost family member,' she said, tracing her fingers along the blackened wood. 'It's one of the reasons this space is so special.'

'It reminds me of the Arthurian legend, *Tristan and Iseult*,' Gideon said. 'Do you remember telling it to us one rainy afternoon?'

* * *

The memory held a bright clarity. Ben had been trying to persuade her to tell a story because he did not want to do any work. She had refused because their exams were edging ever nearer and they were struggling to find a workable idea for a play. In the end, Gideon had suggested they might be inspired if she told them an Arthurian tale. Never able to refuse him, she had recited the story of the two lovers, Tristan and Iseult, caught in an eternal triangle with Iseult's husband, King Mark of Cornwall. A tale of love and difficult choices where all three participants cared for each other but the wrong two people had fallen in love.

At the time, with her crush on Gideon causing her sleepless nights, she had hoped he might pick up the message and respond to her feelings. Instead, when she had finished speaking, Nadine had snorted with derisive laughter and said they needed something edgier than a love story first written in the twelfth century. Caroline had been crushed when Ben had laughed, too, but Gideon had held her gaze.

'I think it has a deeper meaning and we should use it as a basis for a modern-day version.' Gideon had said.

The discussion had begun and they had decided to set it in 1940s Chicago.

'The version you told us said a rose tree grew over Iseult's grave and a vine over Tristan's, which wove itself around the tree. Whenever either of them was cut down, they grew back again. The lovers wouldn't be parted, even in death,' said Gideon. 'After that, it became my hobby to find versions of the tale because it reminded me of you.'

'I'd no idea you'd even remember,' she whispered, a lump in her throat.

'You were very hard to forget,' he said.

As she looked into Gideon's familiar green eyes, Caroline realised they were both single. They were adults. They might have a chequered past but the feeling between them remained.

Time stretched around them, cocooning them until Ken barked and they stepped back. Gideon gave her his lopsided smile and ran his fingers through his hair, a gesture of nervousness from his teens and said, 'Are the ruins far?'

'No,' she said, hoping her voice sounded normal. 'They're beyond the new trees over there. I've often wondered if this grove was planted around the original church to protect it or whether they were planted when the church buildings became a home. If we follow the path, we'll go past them and reach the standing stone Mabe's Gate on the other side.'

Gideon held out his hand.

'Come on, Caro, let's have an adventure.'

It was a phrase he had used in their past. Back then, life had been an endless journey of excitement and opportunity for

Gideon. In his enthusiasm and confidence, he had dragged her from her shyness into a world of possibility.

They wandered past the ruins, examining them with care while Ken circled, excited by the new smells, then they turned the corner.

'There she is,' murmured Caroline as the red-hued standing stone rose in magnificence.

The monolith stood alone, staring out to the choppy Celtic sea, bleak yet beautiful in its isolation.

'Incredible—' began Gideon, then his phone buzzed.

He looked at the screen and all the happiness leached from his face.

'I'm sorry, Caro,' he said, his voice tight. 'I have to take this, it's Margot.'

He turned away and Caroline felt as though she had travelled back in time, as once again, another woman claimed his attention, leaving her to watch from afar.

18

HAMPTON COURT PALACE, SEPTEMBER 1531

Anne, Lady Powis, smoothed down the front of her heavily embroidered kirtle, ensured her elegant overskirts were straight, then linked arms with her friend, Beatrice, Lady Ogle. They left Anne's elegant rooms and made their way to the vast main hall of Hampton Court Palace, their excitement growing as they speculated who might be in attendance. The noise of the gathering reached them first and when they entered, Anne gazed around in awe. The room was packed with people dressed in their finest. There was a glitter of gold and jewels, with flashes of iridescent colour whisking through the air like sprites. The buzz of conversation was intense, a nest of wasps murmuring as they aligned with their chosen faction: the Queen or the Lady? Who would succeed and what price would the losers pay?

It was the first time Anne had stayed at the vast and ornate residence commissioned by Cardinal Thomas Wolsey and as she searched the ever-swirling mass of courtiers for her husband, she observed the delicate panelling peeping out between the heavy tapestries. The images were enormous, depicting the biblical story of Solomon. Anne knew the story well, Solomon was promised wisdom, riches and a long life if he were to continue in righteousness before the Lord. However, as the morality tales of the scriptures are wont to do, rather than showing a man of humility and compassion, it told the darker tale. Around the room, delicately embroidered thread displayed Solomon's inability to use his wisdom, instead he was punished by a disappointed God. Solomon's kingdom was taken from him with the declaration from the Lord that one of his servants would rule instead.

The extravagance of the room was like nothing Anne had ever experienced. *If I am dazzled,* she thought, *a girl who has been brought up as the stepdaughter of a princess and well used to opulence, it was no wonder this palace is the talk of Europe.* It was every bit as grand as her friend, Meg Roper formerly More, had described.

> *Ever since Cardinal Wolsey died last year, His Majesty has been taking great delight in the beauty of his newly acquired palace. The Lady Anne Boleyn is always by his side and they boast about their conquests on the hunt...*

Anne might spend a large portion of each year at Powis Castle but every member of the nobility was aware of the scandal rocking the court. Anne felt closely connected because the power games involved her father, stepmother and her old childhood friend, Anne Boleyn. The rumours had begun in May 1527 when the king had led Anne out as his dance partner. Her stepmother had told her this had caused a stunned silence before, with various degrees of curiosity and surprise, the courtiers had followed the gimlet-eyed king and the flustered Anne in the galliard.

Since this auspicious event, the king had taken advice from

his wise councillors and declared his marriage to Queen Katherine illegal. He stated it was his duty as monarch to insist upon a divorce in order to marry Anne Boleyn, whom he knew would give him healthy male heirs. It had become known as the King's Great Matter and was the topic of conversation throughout the land. Her stepmother, Mary, was saddened by events and in their regular exchange of letters, Anne had become her stepmother's confidante.

Katherine has been my sister-in-law for most of my life. I was five years old when she married my older brother, Arthur, and thirteen when she wed Henry and became queen. It's awful to watch as she struggles to understand her loss of status. When I was in France, Anne Boleyn was one of my ladies-in-waiting and her skill with languages was an asset. Who would have guessed these two women who have offered me kindnesses in different ways would both be the object of my brother's desire? Mark well, Annie, the heart is a capricious mistress and will do as she chooses, even if propriety forbids her desires, the yearning for true love will aways find a way…

To Anne's surprise, Anne Boleyn had become a regular correspondent too. Anne wondered if her former youthful companion wrote because of their time together or because she needed someone outside her family whom she could trust.

The world is a strange place, Annie. I returned home to marry an earl but now there are plans afoot to make me a marquess to give me a high enough status to be elevated to queen. Will love survive this strange, dark path on which we find ourselves or will the brutalities of life wear us down?

Whenever she replied, Anne tried to offer solace as it was clear her friend was struggling with the pressure of her unexpected betrothal to King Henry.

How would it feel to have the king love you, Anne wondered. Would it be thrilling or frightening to carry such a weight of expectation upon one's shoulders?

Queen Katherine had failed to deliver a male heir and because of this the king was doing his utmost to replace her. She, too, had not yet given her husband a longed-for child. The cradle at Powis Castle remained empty. She could not help but speculate as to how Anne Boleyn would fare. It had never entered her own mind that she would not be able to do the very thing for which she had married, to have a living child. Would Anne Boleyn suffer the same fate?

* * *

'Anne,' her husband's voice called across the crowd, cutting through her reverie. She glanced over, assessing his mood. It was a relief when she saw his smile and responded in kind. Behind him was George Boleyn talking spiritedly to the courtier, Henry Norris, another close friend of the king.

'This is where I shall leave you, Annie,' said Beatrice, her excitement muted by disappointment. 'I must join my husband and see you on the morrow.'

'Are you not staying?'

'My stepmother, Lady Margaret Pennington, would be most displeased if she knew I was fraternising with what she calls the "Boleyn Faction",' she nodded towards George Boleyn who was moving through the crowd, his voice slightly too loud, drawing attention to himself. 'She's been a lady-in-waiting to the queen for many years and is loyal to her. I must show my support for her. My husband, Sir Richard, and our sons and daughters are waiting for me to join them in our rooms.'

'Very well, Beatrice, please send them my regards,' said Anne. 'It's a dilemma my stepmother faces too. She feels loyalty to Queen Katherine, while my father understands the necessity of supporting the king.'

Beatrice dropped a curtsy and Anne watched as her friend made a discreet exit. There were many who felt as Beatrice, her husband, Sir Richard Ogle, and Beatrice's stepmother, Lady Pennington, but she was not going to allow their feelings to spoil the excitement of being at court again. She and Edward were very much part of the new young set supporting Anne Boleyn, even if it did cause her stepmother some woe. Her father was in a similar position, he owed loyalty to his wife but he was the king's closest confidant, his best friend and was therefore complicit in helping the monarch to achieve his much-longed for divorce.

As Anne pushed her way through the crowd to her husband, she watched as he laughed at a comment made by one of his companions. A woman she did not know shot him a covetous glance but Edward did not notice. Anne knew why women often watched her with envious eyes. Edward had always been a good-looking youth and as he had matured his looks had become more dramatic. His dark hair and eyes, high cheekbones and ready smile with straight white teeth were impressive. When coupled with his love of good clothes which hung well on his athletic figure and his ancient title, he was not a man to be ignored, even in a glamorous crowd.

Oh, if only you knew, Anne thought, raising her eyebrows at the woman as she arrived at Edward's side and gave a small curtsy.

'Annie,' he murmured, taking her hand before returning to

his conversation with Henry Courtenay, Marquess of Exeter, and the lawyer, John Beaumont.

They both murmured a greeting of 'Lady Powis' but returned their attention to Edward.

'The judge claimed the charge could be construed as champerty,' said Beaumont.

'Which is what?' asked Courtenay.

'A slippery but ultimately illegal action where the plaintiff and the judge have an agreement before a lawsuit is brought. These cases usually involve land. The plaintiff brings the charge when he believes someone else has taken his land. He will sue the perpetrator for the return of the property he believes is his by right.'

'It sounds reasonable,' said Courtenay.

'Perhaps,' said John, 'but in the case of champerty, the plaintiff will have made a deal beforehand with the judge agreeing to sell him the land at a lower price than it's true value once it has been granted to him.'

'In other words,' said Courtenay, 'the judge finds for the plaintiff, he buys the land at a reasonable price and everyone benefits.'

'Except the person who really owns the land and is being fraudulently sued,' said Beaumont.

'Land deals are never simple,' said Edward, and began to explain his own precarious situation with the dual ownership of Powis Castle.

Anne had heard the tale so many times, she allowed her attention to drift as her husband listed his grievances. Another man joined them and nudged Anne. She looked around in surprise but her face relaxed into a smile when she saw her brother-in-law, Thomas Stanley, 2nd Baron Monteagle. He too had been a ward of her father and in 1527 had married Anne's younger sister, Mary. Thomas gave her a theatrical formal bow making Anne giggle and in return, she went into a deep obeisance.

'Lady Powis,' he said.

'Lord Monteagle,' she replied. They laughed again as he drew her to her feet.

'Look at us all grown up,' said Thomas. 'Do you remember when we used to skulk around watching our elders, desperate for the day when we were the ones with the power?'

'It seems a long time ago,' agreed Anne. 'Is Mary with you or is she at Suffolk Place with William?'

Mary and Thomas already had one son and Mary was pregnant again. Anne was pleased for them but there was a hint of sadness in her smiles whenever she hugged her nephew.

'Yes, she's here somewhere,' he replied gazing good-naturedly around the crowd. 'I think she was looking for your father.'

'He's probably with the king,' she replied.

Edward squeezed her hand and she turned towards him.

'The Marquess has invited us to join The Lady Anne in her quarters later,' he said turning to look at Henry Courtenay. 'She has a number of entertainments planned including a recital by Tommy Wyatt.'

'Thank you, Marquess—' began Anne.

'Henry, please,' he interrupted.

As first cousin to the king, there was no denying the family resemblance. Both men were tall and handsome with red hair and fair skin which had a tendency to flush but while the monarch had followed the broad-shouldered build of their shared grandfather, Edward IV, Courtenay was of a more slender build, following the elegance of the Woodville line through their shared grandmother, Elizabeth Woodville.

Henry Courtenay was the son of Catherine of York, who had been the sister of Henry VIII's mother, Elizabeth of York. Courtiers often commented on the similarity between the men and while Courtenay was a favourite of the king, there was always an edge of uncertainty surrounding him. He had a strong blood claim to the throne, which made the king nervous.

'Henry, you're most kind to include us,' she replied.

It would not do to steal her husband's moment of pride in having secured them such a privileged invitation. She had not seen him since the morning when he had joined her father and many other men to hunt with the king. He was unaware that earlier in the afternoon a note had arrived from Anne Boleyn inviting them to her evening entertainments. Anne knew Edward resented the fact she was the one at court with the more exclusive connections. He pretended it was his name that cut their swathe to the top of the nobility and to suggest otherwise could lead to an explosion of anger.

The crowd ebbed and flowed as friends and family greeted them, laughing and talking, the room a shimmering whirl of excitement and glamour. Anne hugged her sister when she arrived and, stepping away from the men, they caught up on each other's news.

'Mama is furious about the King's Great Matter,' she whispered. 'Papa is, too, but he has no choice. Everyone is saying Anne Boleyn has used the dark arts to capture the king. You know her, Annie, is she a witch?'

'You know very well that's nonsense,' Anne said. 'Anne is being pushed forward by her ambitious uncle, the Duke of Norfolk. He practically forced her sister, Mary, into the king's bed and when that didn't capture the king, he tried another tactic. The king wants a legitimate son. He'll do whatever it takes and Norfolk will do whatever he can to have a Howard heir to the throne.'

Mary looked doubtful but before she could reply, a trumpet fanfare sounded and the atmosphere in the room tautened. As though they had been given a signal, all eyes turned to the giant double doors, the tension increasing with every breath. Two of the king's personal guards in their Tudor green uniforms threw them open and the king entered. At his side, her hand resting on his arm, was Anne Boleyn dripping in pearls. A few steps behind looking uneasy were the Duke and Duchess of Suffolk.

Anne dropped into a deep obeisance, her head bowed, waiting for the command to stand, which came within seconds. The king's laughter filled the room and Henry Courtenay hurried forward to greet his cousin. As Anne took her place beside her husband with her sister on her other side, she saw her father scanning the crowd and when it reached her and Mary, a wide smile creased his face. He gave a nod of acknowledgement and Anne beamed back.

Since her arrival in London a few days earlier, she was yet to see her father, although she had briefly seen her stepmother. He had sent her a note promising they would spend time together at this gathering. Anne well understood the whimsies of the court; the king often called upon her father's services at the last moment, making it difficult for him to be definite about his plans. Amidst the noise surrounding the arrival of the royal party, the banquet was announced and Anne was surprised to find Edward take her hand.

'We're seated near the king,' he whispered. 'People will see us and understand my importance.'

'Of course,' she replied, wondering if this was a taunt.

They both knew the reason for their prestigious position was due to her father and his friendship with the king. Without this, they would be relegated to the middle of the table with the other lower-ranking nobles. Anne decided it was unwise to challenge Edward. Her marriage was a constant balancing act and she was often exhausted pandering to her husband's moods.

Edward waited for Anne to sit, before taking his place to her right, opposite were Mary and Thomas. As Mary greeted Edward, Anne heard a gentle cough to her left and a shiver of anticipation filled her heart. When he slipped into the seat on her vacant side, his leg brushing hers, she swallowed her gasp of pleasure.

She had known Randall was in attendance even though she had not seen him yet this evening. As soon as she had written to say they were travelling to London to join the court, he had assured her he would be among the crowd.

* * *

Seven months earlier, shocking news had arrived. Meg Roper had written to tell Anne that there had been an attempt on her father Thomas More's life. His chef, Robert Roose, had tried to poison not only More but John Fisher, Bishop of Rochester. Anne and Edward had been horrified, so when a letter had arrived from Randall a few days later stating he was nearby at Ludlow, wondering if he might visit, Edward had been delighted by the distraction.

'It's been years since we've seen him and whenever we encountered him at your father's house he was always a solid and trustworthy fellow,' he'd said. 'We must invite him to stay.'

'Are you sure, Edward?' Anne had replied, her heart pounding at the thought of seeing Randall again.

'It would be good to catch up with the old crowd,' Edward

had said, 'and it's not as if you're busy doing anything else, is it? The last time I checked the nursery was empty. You have plenty of time to entertain my guests.'

The subject of children was a constant emotional battle between them. Three more miscarriages had led Edward to cruelly shout 'I should never have married you. I understand why the king wishes to get rid of the queen.'

An hour after Edward's outburst, Beatrice had entered Anne's rooms, her face full of concern, to inform Anne that Edward had taken Jane Orwell hawking.

'He claims they will be away for several hours,' she'd said, and Anne had felt a confusing mixture of despair, anger and relief.

Despite her best efforts, Anne could not warm to Jane, nor was she comfortable with the way the younger woman would arrive unannounced before leaving on a whim, usually stating she had been called away on family business. When she had challenged Edward on this peculiar behaviour, he had said in a tone which Anne knew was not to be argued with, 'Jane asks me and I give her permission.'

When Randall arrived a week after they received Meg's letter, he was taller and broader than when she had last seen him and with an air of maturity that enhanced his looks.

'My lady,' he'd said, his eyes twinkling when he'd greeted her in the great hall of Powis Castle, 'this is an unexpected pleasure.'

'My husband was most eager to see you,' she'd said with a curtsy.

'And you?'

'I am always ready to please my husband,' she'd replied with a wide smile.

He'd held her gaze a heartbeat longer than necessary and

she'd felt her old feelings for Randall clawing their way through the walls she had placed around them many years earlier.

'Randall,' Edward had exclaimed, hurrying into the room. 'What a pleasure. The next few weeks will be a delight.'

Anne had watched as Edward had borne Randall away on a tour of the castle and wondered.

* * *

'Are you well, Lady Powis?' Randall asked now, drawing Anne back to the present. As he made himself comfortable beside her, he nodded greetings to the extended Suffolk family.

'Extremely,' she replied. 'It's stimulating to return to court, to be among the finest thinkers, the fashionable elite and the most daring in the land.'

'Not to mention the chivalrous men of Camelot?'

'The king encourages courtly love, who are we to question his rules?' she replied, and under the table Randall squeezed Anne's hand.

19

Thomas Wyatt bowed to the select group of courtiers. The candlelight flickered on the tapestries, picking out the glints of gold and silver in the thread. Yet none looked finer than Wyatt; resplendent in a jewelled doublet and hose, a huge pearl, a present from his lover, Lady Elizabeth Darrell, pinned to his hat. As it caught the light, glimmering with ethereal colours Anne remembered the story she had heard so many years ago about another pearl. One that had been attached to the huge diamond: the Mirror of Naples.

Around the room more gems reflected the flickering light and Anne could not help feel a surge of pride that she was among the favoured of the court. This was the inner circle, the powerful, the elite and the glamorous. Every eye was upon Wyatt and he preened under their gaze as they awaited his recital. Anne was unsure whether to be amused by his strutting, cockerel-like demeanour or shocked by his lack of regard for those in power who beheld him.

Beside her, Edward drank in the atmosphere, his eyes roving across the lounging courtiers. It was a relief for Anne to have returned to the world where she had grown up, surrounded by friends and family rather than arguing with Edward at Powis Castle. At least here, there was plenty to occupy them both and since their arrival they had hardly spent any time together. Whenever they did meet at meals or in crowds such as these, it was easy to show a superficial front of happiness and unity, even if the truth was a different story.

There were many familiar faces but a few were unexpected. In one corner, Sir Edward Seymour laughed at a comment made by Sir Francis Bryan, another of the king's close friends. A girl with a wide strip of blonde hair showing under her French hood stood with them, her eyes merry as Sir Francis slipped an arm around her waist.

'Who's the girl with Sir Edward Seymour and Sir Francis Bryan?' Anne whispered to Edward.

'I think that's Edward's sister, Jane. Francis Bryan is a distant cousin. He champions the younger Seymours at court.'

Anne watched the trio with interest. Sir Edward Seymour hailed her husband, who acknowledged the other man with a lordly wave. Jane Seymour looked over and, when she smiled, her ordinary features lit up making her beautiful in the candlelight.

'It's a surprise to see Seymour here,' muttered Edward. 'He might be brave but he's the dullest man you could ever meet.'

'He looks very pleased with himself,' she murmured.

'Arrogant is the word, my dear,' said Edward. 'Look at him eyeing up the women. He thinks he's irresistible. The trouble is, his wife, Catherine Filliol, wasn't convinced and rumour has it she had an affair with her father-in-law, John Seymour, while Edward was in France.'

'But it was a rumour, nothing more,' said Anne.

'Was it? Why are they separated? Why has she been forced

into a convent? Stay away from him, Annie, he's not to be trusted.'

Anne watched as Seymour's eyes skittered from one woman to the next, an unnatural lust sparkling on his pale face. Even without Edward's warning she would have kept away from Seymour. There was an air of desperation about him, a desire to succeed, no matter the cost. No wonder his wife had looked for a kinder man, thought Anne.

Wyatt flourished his hat and the crowd stilled. The king took Anne Boleyn's hand.

'Your Majesty, my Lady, ladies and gentlemen,' Wyatt began, 'It's an honour to be here this evening. My Lady Boleyn has asked me to recite a tale of excitement, love, difficult choices and friendship, ending in the most tragic demise of two lovers.'

He paused while his audience gasped appreciatively.

'Legend tells us,' he said spreading his arms wide when the room was quiet again and the king roared with laughter at what was obviously an old joke. Wyatt winked at him, 'of the tale of Tristan and Iseult and their forbidden love. The gentle pair who, when faced with true love, could not deny their passion. A love of such magnitude that even death was unable to part them. My gentle audience, make yourselves comfortable, sip your wine and together we shall follow the path of these star-crossed lovers, Tristan and Iseult.'

There was a ripple of applause but Wyatt held up his hand to quell the noise. He circled the performance space, then after a cheeky wink at Anne Boleyn, he declaimed, 'Sir Tristan of Lyonnes was the son of King Meliodas and his queen, Elizabeth. She was a beautiful princess through her own blood and was the sister of King Mark of Cornwall. Yet, young Tristan's life, which should have been full of happiness and joy, began with sadness. His mother died at his birth, her final act was to give life to a strong healthy son. His father, the king, raised the boy well and in due course, Tristan entered into the service of his uncle, King Mark.

'Over the years, Tristan and Mark grew to love each other. Many said they were as loyal as father and son rather than uncle and nephew. But, as so often happens, envious minds were at work and there was a king in Ireland who was jealous of Mark and wished to bring him low. In order to humiliate him, the King of Ireland demanded a tribute but King Mark was a proud man, and he refused. In revenge the King of Ireland said Mark must select a champion to fight his fiercest warrior, Marhaus. In a heartbeat, his nephew, Tristan, volunteered.

'When Marhaus arrived at the court of King Mark, he strode the length of the hall in anger. He was the brother of the Irish queen and he had promised her he would win. Tristan was an honest man, a true knight who fought with valour and purity. As the men began their battle, Tristan beat Marhaus back with every blow, until at last, he was victorious but as he swung his final deadly blow, Marhaus threw a poisoned knife and it glanced Tristan's skin.

'King Mark's physicians and wise healers examined Tristan and declared there was but one place where it would be possible to heal the poisoned wound, in the land whence it came. Mark was told the only person who could save his nephew was Iseult, the daughter of the Irish lord, King Anguish. Tristan had no choice but to travel to Ireland where he was led to the beautiful Iseult. Her gentle hands stroked the wound and using her knowledge of herbs, she cured Tristan.

'Upon his return from Ireland, Tristan told King Mark of the wondrous lady and, so taken was the king, he negotiated with King Anguish to marry his daughter.

'Tristan volunteered to fetch Iseult but on the return journey to Cornwall, a dreadful fate befell them. On board the ship was an apothecary and in his many bottles was a love potion. It was intended for the betrothed couple, King Mark and Iseult, to ensure their union was happy and fruitful.

'But, one night, whether through malice and mischief or a genuine mistake by the apothecary, Tristan and Iseult drank this potion. As they stared into each other's eyes the pair felt their hearts cleave in a life-long bond. It was a love as deep as the ocean, a fiery unstoppable passion. They knew this love was wrong and they fought hard to resist but they could not deny their feelings.

'When they arrived in Cornwall, Iseult saw that Mark was a good man. She understood how the king and Tristan loved each other. Iseult prayed to be a good wife, to love Mark with the purity and desire she felt for Tristan, but no matter how hard she tried, her heart yearned for Tristan. The soul-felt love caused them to meet in secret even though neither wished to hurt Mark.

'Tristan was in despair. He loved his uncle and could bear to betray him no longer. In tearful tones he explained to Iseult that their love was doomed and with a breaking heart he departed King Mark's court to settle in Brittany. Here he married Iseult of the White Hands, the daughter of King Havelin. But such was his love for another, the marriage was never consummated.

'His wife grew jealous of the woman who held her husband's heart. Yet despite this Tristan became firm friends with his brother-in-law, Kahedrin. Together they embarked on many quests until eventually they were welcomed into the merry band of brothers at Camelot where Sir Tristan of Lyonnes sat at the fabled round table.

'One day when he was out hunting with Kahedrin, he fell from his horse and scratched himself on the dread belladonna bush. He believed the only way he could be saved was with the help of his true love, Iseult. He sent a ship to Cornwall to fetch her but before he did, he made the captain promise to fly white sails if Iseult were aboard and black if she had refused his request. His wife, seething with envy and hatred, lied to Tristan. When she saw the fluttering white sails and knew the woman who had stolen her husband's heart was aboard, she ran to Tristan and with a voice full of malevolence she told him the sails were black as night.

'A wave of grief so intense washed through Tristan. He could think of no reason Iseult would refuse his request unless she was dead. In despair, Tristan allowed the poison he had been trying to resist to do its evil work and died with a shiver of sadness. When Iseult, his true love, arrived and found his lifeless body, the pain was more than she could bear and she, too, died.

'King Mark, who knew the forbidden love between his wife and nephew had been the cause of his beloved Tristan leaving his side, wailed with remorse when he heard of their deaths. He buried them side by side and on their graves he planted two oak trees, which wrapped themselves around each other, together for eternity. True love will always find a way and it will last forever.'

The final line was said to Anne and Henry, as though Wyatt were giving them the secret to their marriage. There was a pause, then a roar of approval from the king, followed by ringing applause.

Anne had listened to the tale and wondered, was it a justification for the king and Anne? Were their feelings of the same intensity as if they had swallowed a magical love potion? Perhaps they were trying to show they had not set out to hurt people but had fallen in love despite themselves. If so, these were emotions with which she could sympathise.

She glanced over at Edward who looked uncomfortable. He gave a muttered excuse and wandered towards a page who held a tray of goblets, his eyes searching the crowd.

'Music,' shouted Henry, and minstrels struck up a lively tune.

The king led Anne Boleyn out to dance and as other couples joined them, laughter and noise filled the room. Wyatt and Lady Elizabeth Darrell spun past, followed by Sir Edward Seymour and a woman Anne did not know. To her surprise, she saw Thomas Howard, Duke of Norfolk, dancing with Lady Elizabeth Holland and wondered where the Duchess of Norfolk was that night. Rumours abounded that the Norfolk marriage was an unhappy and violent relationship and that the duke and Lady Holland had long had an agreement. As Anne watched she realised none of the couples were husband and wife.

Across the room, she saw Randall, who had moved after Wyatt had finished his tale, but she did not dare approach him. A few feet away, Jane Orwell emerged from behind a pillar and Anne felt a wave of irritation. She had invited Randall with Anne Boleyn's approval but had Edward invited Jane? She was not of a high enough rank to have warranted inclusion otherwise.

Anne's gaze moved to her father who was watching the king through narrowed eyes but there was no sign of her stepmother. Was Mary's absence her way of showing her disapproval?

Edward appeared by her side, his hand snaking around her waist as he pulled her close and whispered, 'Annie, will you be satisfied with Randall's company?'

Anne looked at him in surprise.

'Of course, my dear, is there something amiss?'

'No, but I have to speak to John Beaumont. We wish to continue our conversation about land deals and he has a wealth of legal expertise. Henry Courtenay has invited us to play cards while we discuss matters and I know cards bore you.'

Edward waved Randall over to their side, 'Would you take care of Annie for a few hours?' he asked. 'I believe there's some sort of poetry contest taking place after the dancing. It might appeal to both of you, but not to me. I shall see you later, my dear.'

As he departed, with Courtenay and Beaumont, Anne saw Jane Orwell drifting like a shadow in their wake and as they were ushered into an adjoining room, Edward reached for her hand. Jane's presence confirmed Anne's suspicions about their affair. She waited to feel the pain of Edward's betrayal but there was none, only relief. Randall took the seat beside her, accepting a quill and parchment from the king's niece, Lady Margaret Douglas.

Yet, she thought, *I cannot criticise Edward for I too have broken my marriage vows.*

'We can teach those bards a thing or two,' Randall said and she smiled.

'Our version of the courtly tales of King Arthur will be a sensation.'

When he reached over to kiss her, no one gave them a second glance.

20

LONDON, JUNE, PRESENT DAY

Caroline's eyes widened in surprise. She was reading the transcripts of the letters given to her by Mark at Marquess House. During the previous weeks, she had cross-referenced them with the book of Brandon letters she had bought from Ten-to-Midnight and the tale of Anne Brandon was slowly revealing itself. The night at Wyatt's retelling of the Tristan and Iseult legend was a revelation. This confirmed that not only were Anne and Randall together, they were not troubling themselves to hide their affair. And, she thought, Edward seemed to have an agreement with Jane Orwell. She was intrigued, having always imagined the past to be staid, limited by strict rules of etiquette but from the letters sent between Anne and her friends, the Tudor court was a hotbed of extra-marital affairs.

She was in bed in her sister Flavia's spare room. Shades of pale green and white, with floor-length white curtains and pale wooden furniture created a tranquil air. Caroline loved staying there, even when her nephews invaded with war cries at the crack of dawn. This morning, they had been and gone, shouting their farewells as their dad, Steve, ferried them to a swimming gala. She punched her pillows into a more comfortable position and pushed her laptop onto her bended knees.

The affair was an unexpected development in Anne's story. Over the years, the research Caroline had done for Dexter had given her knowledge of Henry's 'Great Matter' as he referred to his divorce. In his quest to end his marriage to Queen Katherine, the king had turned to the wisest minds of his time and used as his defence the biblical quotation:

> If a man takes his brother's wife, it is impurity... they shall be childless.
>
> — LEVITICUS, 20:21

His argument suggested the word 'childless' meant to have no sons within the union, ignoring the fact he and Queen Katherine had a healthy daughter, Mary. However, the argument was thin and was countered by the queen's advisors quoting the *Book of Deuteronomy*, which stated:

> The widow of the dead man shall not be married outside the family, her husband's brother shall take her as his wife.
>
> — BOOK OF DEUTERONOMY, 25:5

Before being married to Henry VIII, Queen Katherine had been the wife of Henry's older brother, Prince Arthur. Alas, he had died in April 1502, aged fifteen, leaving her a widow. Whenever Caroline had read about the issue of the divorce, she had never before considered the effect it had on those around the monarch.

In the history books, the focus was always on the three main players – Henry, Katherine and Anne – but having read Anne Brandon's diaries and letters as she witnessed events, Caroline could now sympathise more acutely with the families and friends of the royal trio. Henry's determination to marry Anne Boleyn had been a period of intense destructiveness, forcing the members of his court to choose a side. Caroline had never before considered the difficulty of Princess Mary, Duchess of Suffolk's predicament, torn between her brother, her husband and her sister-in-law. The atmosphere must have been tense, frightening, as Henry bullied his way to his ultimate aim.

'Their whole world was ripped apart,' she murmured, then jumped as the bedroom door eased open.

'I could see the light beneath the door,' said Flavia, handing Caroline two mugs of tea before climbing in beside her and taking one drink back. 'It's been ages since we've sat in bed and chatted.'

Caroline had arrived the previous day and a hectic evening at the nearby bowling alley with Flavia and her family had followed. Steve, Logan and Finn had been excited to have Caroline staying and the fun had been infectious. Caroline had tumbled exhausted into bed far later than usual.

'When was the last time?' asked Caroline.

'Years,' said Flavia, 'when you were with Travis, you always stayed at your flat. I hate him for messing you about with it but in a funny way, I'm glad because it means we have the chance to spend time together.'

'True, we should make a point to do this more often,' she said and they clinked mugs.

'What were you reading?'

Caroline explained her research and the transcripts she had been sent.

'How interesting,' said Flavia, 'and Anne Brandon was right

at the heart of things as Henry VIII divorced Katherine of Aragon?'

'Yes, she was torn over who to support because her stepmother had been close to Katherine most of her life but her father was very much enthral to the king. Anne herself was old friends with Anne Boleyn.'

'It sounds as though the court was a den of wife-swapping. Imagine if they'd had reality TV back then.'

'I think they preferred to use the term "chivalric code",' she said, 'but from what Anne Brandon has written there appears to be a great deal of bedroom hopping and not a great deal of chivalry.'

'Will you be able to use the research or is this a personal project?'

'Do you mean in a book?'

'Yes, why not? You've always wanted to write literary novels, perhaps an historical tome would be a good place to start; give Anne Brandon her voice at last.'

'Perhaps,' said Caroline, 'let's allow Dexter's last book to have its moment, then I'll consider what to do next.'

'Have you heard any more from Travis about the flat?'

'One snotty letter from his solicitor which stated they were checking the legal validity of his Non-Disclosure Agreement.'

Flavia looked startled.

'He couldn't...'

'No, it's legally binding and would enable us to gag any newspaper or publication with a super-injunction if he tried to sell his story.'

'It would be more difficult if he decided to write an anonymous online dump?' said Flavia. 'We can usually have them taken down but in extreme cases when the perpetrator hops IP addresses to hide their trail it can take a few weeks. He could do extensive damage before we could stop him.'

'Would anyone believe him once we publish a counter-piece saying he's my ex and is being vindictive? There have always been rumours circulating about Dexter. This would just be another one.'

'But, Caro, he knows everything,' said Flavia. 'He could damage so many people. I know Dexter's public biography is full of untruths – remember Gramps always claimed he never spoke to the rest of the family and that Mum died in a freak accident – but it was all done to protect him and you.'

'Exactly, which is why Blanche is attacking this with such ferocity.'

Caroline watched as Flavia sipped her tea. She could almost hear her sister's brain whirring as she considered the carnage Travis could wreak through all their lives.

'Are you going to tell Gideon?'

'What?' asked Caroline. 'Why would I tell him?'

Flavia gave her an arch look.

'Be careful, Caro,' she said. 'From what I've been told, when his and Margot Bullington's divorce is finalised, she won't be going quietly.'

'Tell me,' said Caroline.

Flavia's social media and publicity contacts were extensive, which often meant she was privy to embargoed information.

'My friend Louise sent me this late last night. I wasn't sure when to show you,' Flavia said. 'It'll be out in a couple of days.'

She pulled her phone from her dressing gown pocket and opened an email.

Caroline stared at the screen in dismay. It was from one of the more respectable gossip magazines and showed a black-and-white photograph of a pensive looking Margot Bullington gazing into the middle distance under the headline:

I'll save my marriage, no matter what...

'Ben said she wouldn't go without a fight,' said Caroline.

'Caro, if you're seeing Gideon again, this could be disastrous.'

'I'm not "seeing" Gideon,' she replied and her heart contracted with disappointment. 'He's rented a cottage near St Ishmaels because he wants to avoid Margot until the divorce is finished. I imagine he guessed or knew she'd sell her story far and wide. Ben's staying too. They're planning their next shop, overseeing the new one and Gideon is working on ideas for a possible documentary series about standing stones and burial mounds. I've seen them both. Ben's helping with my historical research and Gideon's—'

'The love of your life,' finished Flavia.

'Flav, stop it,' said Caroline banging her mug down on the bedside table. 'There's nothing between me and Gideon any more. I have to remain focused on the launch of Dexter's final book and stay in touch with the film crew in LA to ensure the secret sections aren't leaked before this evening when we make the announcement. The rest of the filming will begin in the UK in the next few weeks. The historical research is my distraction from work. I don't have time to become involved with Gideon again. Even if he wanted to.'

Caroline continued to feel waves of humiliation whenever she thought about the day in the ancient woodland. One call from Margot had sent Gideon scurrying away and it was a week before she had heard from him again. When he did call he was quiet and withdrawn, claiming stress and a migraine. She had expressed sympathy but when she had bumped into Ben at the supermarket a few days later, he had begged her to have a coffee and had unloaded twenty minutes of anger about Margot onto her shoulders.

'By the way,' said Caroline, in a falsely bright voice as she returned her sister's phone, 'are Dexter's fans continuing to accuse me of murder?'

'Caro, it isn't funny,' said Flavia. 'The ground swell against you is growing.'

'Have any of them thought to find Dexter's death certificate?' she asked.

'Not yet and let's hope they don't,' replied Flavia. 'It would be a total invasion of privacy.'

'Flav, try not to take this so seriously,' said Caroline. 'We know the truth.'

'You're right but the level of curiosity and the number of people who are beginning to question Dexter's death is alarming.'

'In what way?'

'Two reputable newsreaders who are big fans have chimed in with a few comments which has sent the Internet into a frenzy.'

'The official launch is tomorrow,' said Caroline. 'At midnight tonight, the covers will be whipped off the tables of books and the reading will begin. In a few months' time, everything will have calmed down. We might have a few more rumbles when the film of *Ether Heracles and the Elegua Crossroads* is released but I think once everyone knows how the story ends, the intensity levels will minimise and the scarier fans will find another craze to follow obsessively.'

'Perhaps,' said Flavia, but she sounded unsure.

Caroline kissed her sister's cheek, then threw back the covers.

'We've weathered worse than this before,' said Caroline, getting up and opening the curtains on a perfect summer morning.

'Does Travis know about the secret section?' asked Flavia, her voice quiet. 'And the names of the actors?'

Caroline spun around to look at her sister.

'Yes,' she replied, and for the first time she fully understood the damage her ex-fiancé could cause if he revealed her secrets.

21

Caroline felt a small clench of sadness. This was the final book, Dexter would never write again. It was the last launch and at midnight, people would know the end of Ether's story. The message that had been hidden all around Ether's fictional universe would be revealed and his quest would be over. The function room at the Dorchester Hotel on London's exclusive Park Lane had been decorated to look like a cross between the interior of Ether's spaceship, *The Oisin,* and the elaborate ballroom which featured in the new book, *Ether Heracles and Ishtar's Legacy*. It was magnificent.

The legend which had inspired the final story had its hero walking through seven doors which led to the Underworld. At each level, Ether was forced to explain his feelings on love. One of these included a dream sequence where he danced in a ballroom with his heart's desire, Allegra. Caroline could not believe how accurately the set designers had followed the descriptions on the page.

'What do you think?' asked Tanya Ross, the head of marketing at Antrobus Publishing.

'It's incredible,' said Caroline. 'Exactly as I imagined it.'

'You imagined it?' asked Tanya.

'When I read the first draft,' Caroline added. 'This looks as though it's going to be quite a party.'

Bar staff were lining up tray after tray of champagne, canapés were waiting to be circulated and an army of helpers were ready for the second it struck midnight when they would distribute goodie bags to the guests. Each contained copies of *Ether Heracles and Ishtar's Legacy,* replica crew badges, a bar of chocolate bearing an image of *The Oisin* and a watch identical to those worn by the Ether and Allegra in the films.

'The TV crews are setting up,' Tanya said, pointing to one corner before leading Caroline to the bridge of *The Oisin,* 'and this is where you'll be standing when the clock begins the countdown to midnight. You'll push the red button and all around the world the purple cloths will be whipped off the displays and *Ether Heracles and Ishtar's Legacy* will be live.'

'Thank you,' said Caroline. 'You've all worked so hard, although, had he been here, Dexter would have been suitably grumpy about the idea and gone to bed early.'

'He's lucky to have had you by his side all this time,' said Tanya, her phone began playing the *Ether Heracles* theme tune from the film series. 'Sorry, have to answer this...'

The click-clack of heels announced Blanche's arrival and she pushed a glass of champagne into Caroline's hand.

'You look divine,' Blanche said.

'Back at ya,' Caroline replied.

Blanche was wearing a fitted black dress with a plunging neckline and impossibly high red shoes. A pendant with a single diamond hung around her neck and gold bangles circled her arms. Caroline was in a shimmering purple gown, laced up the back like a corset and split up one leg to reveal a pair of tights decorated with the covers of all the Ether Heracles books. She had worn a pair to every launch and they had become her trademark. The thickness covered the scars on her leg from when it had been broken. She felt these marks were intrinsically linked to the *Ether Heracles* stories, Dexter Blake and the changes both had wrought in her life.

'Glad to see you've come as Caroline Harvey,' said Blanche with a wink.

'For the final time,' she replied as she swished the blonde hair extensions the hairdresser had spent the afternoon clipping over her red hair.

A car had collected Caroline from Flavia's house at midday to deliver her at the Dorchester where hair and make-up were ready for her transformation. When she had arrived, she had disappeared into the Ladies to put in brown-tinted contact lenses to cover her blue eyes and then submitted to have her newly returned natural hair colour hidden for the evening.

'Flavia's upstairs with Steve,' Caroline informed Blanche. 'They'll be down in a minute.'

'And your parents?'

'They decided not to come. Dad's arthritis has flared up and they thought it was safer.'

'Probably wise,' agreed Blanche. 'Any word from LA?'

'Yes, I spoke to the chaperone, Wendy Philips, and all is well,' she said. 'The flashback scenes in *The Elegua Crossroads* book have always been popular so it was great to include them in the film. I've seen the preview clip we'll be showing this evening and it's extraordinary.'

'Fifteen minutes until showtime. Incidentally, I've discovered what Travis is planning,' said Blanche, glancing at her watch.

'Which is?'

Blanche showed Caroline her phone, swiping through a series of images of Travis with his girlfriend, Bella Arnold, every inch the glamorous London couple.

'Bella's bought Travis a brand-new BMW iX M60 which cost nearly £125,000. This is them leaving Nobu two nights ago.'

'Where did you get these?' asked Caroline.

'The agency has often had private investigators following him. It's our way of ensuring you and Dexter remain safe,' she replied.

Caroline was about to complain but this had always been part of their agreement, even if the subterfuge made her uncomfortable.

'From what the detective gleaned, Travis is hoping to blackmail you into signing the flat over to him.'

'He'd never sink so low.'

'Look at the pictures, Caro. The man's a player.'

Caro stared at the images, flicking backwards and forwards. She could not deny Blanche's words. Travis had never lived within his police salary, he had insisted on a joint account with Caroline. Disconcerted by this, Caroline had placed a sizeable sum in there each month but never disclosed the true amount Dexter paid her. The money she contributed to her relationship with Travis was substantial but her ex-fiancé would spend up to the overdraft limit each month. It seemed when he had left her, he had found another wealthy woman to allow him to continue his expensive, pampered lifestyle.

'Bella Arnold might claim to be a PA but she works for her father who is a multi-millionaire tycoon. I would suspect even if her salary is that of a PA, her allowance is larger than her wage.'

'But when we last had the flat valued the price had rocketed, it's worth nearly ten million pounds.'

'That's what he's after,' said Blanche.

'Why would I hand over my apartment?'

'To be rid of him,' suggested Blanche. 'To ensure they both sign an even tougher legally binding document to stop them revealing the truth.'

'The NDA already does that—'

'But what if they separate? If Travis has told Bella anything, she could cause havoc. We need leverage to make her sign an NDA too.'

Caroline could feel her fury building but she was not sure whether it was directed at Blanche, herself or Travis and Bella.

'He's motivated by money,' continued Blanche. 'If you'd rather, we could make an offer to sell him the flat. His salary won't cover it but Bella's might and if not, her father would probably snap it up.'

'But, Blanche, the flat's worth ten million pounds,' she reiterated.

'And how much is Dexter worth? How much are you worth? I know you hate talking about it but you're a very rich woman, Caro, and quite rightly after all the hard work you've put in over the years. It isn't ideal but think how much more it could cost you. How would you feel if Travis revealed everything before you'd had a chance to try and mend the past? It might be irreparable.'

Caroline stared ahead, her mind whirring. She gulped her ice-cold champagne and pushed the phone back at Blanche.

'Would it matter if he sold his story?' she asked. 'Would it really put all we've built at risk?'

'Are you mad?' asked Blanche, shocked.

'Is it because of the money? Or is it because even though Dexter's dead you'll do everything you can to protect your investment?'

'It has nothing to do with Dexter,' said Blanche, her voice

low, hurt. 'Everything we've done has been to protect you and the secret you've been keeping.'

'A secret you've colluded with,' snapped Caroline, but she was shaking.

'This is the final book in the series,' said Blanche, forcing calm into her voice. 'By the end of the year, it'll be over and you can disappear from the public eye. All we need is another six months and then you're free. You can date whomever you choose, you can travel anywhere in the world, live wherever takes your fancy and, at last, should you choose to, you'll be able to reveal your secret. Although, I find it hard to believe you'd throw away all the hard work so easily.'

'Easily? How can you even begin to think any of this has been easy?' said Caroline. 'You know the reason we made these decisions, you've been there beside me every step of the way. You encouraged me, you've never once said, "Just bite the bullet, Caro, let's face it and see what happens. We'll do it together." Every time I wavered, said he should know, you dissuaded me. You kept saying it would be a disaster to reveal the truth—'

'I said those things because at the time we both thought they were right,' interjected Blanche, she gazed at Caro with her shrewd blue eyes. 'What's changed, Caro? Why are you so ready to risk the truth being revealed now?' There was a pause, then Blanche asked, 'Have you met somebody?'

Caroline had often wondered if Blanche could read her mind.

'Nobody new, no,' she said, and Blanche's eyes widened in surprise.

'Is he back?' she asked and with great reluctance Caroline nodded.

'Doesn't that make things more complicated?'

'Things have changed,' said Caroline. 'Tomorrow there's

going to be an announcement in the press. He and Margot are divorced.'

'Divorced? I thought they had one of the most untroubled marriages in showbusiness.'

'No, she's been leaving him and coming back for years but he's had enough,' said Caroline.

'Where did you find him?' asked Blanche.

'He's opened a bookshop near me.'

'He owns bookshops all over the world but that doesn't mean he visits them.'

'He's a huge Dexter Blake fan. It was part of the reason he decided to open a bookshop in Milford Haven. He knew Dexter lived nearby but he didn't know I was Dexter's granddaughter. He'd never made the connection.'

'Are you going to tell him?'

'About my connection to Dexter? He knows and he spotted me in the films...'

'No, Caro, that's not what I mean. Are you going to tell him?'

Tears welled in her eyes and the lump in her throat made her gasp.

'I have no idea. How would I even begin the conversation?'

'Oh, Caro,' said Blanche and hugged her. 'I'm sorry to have mentioned Travis tonight but I wanted you to be on your guard. If I'd known what was happening, I'd have waited until next week.'

Caroline gave her a watery smile, then wiped away a tear.

'It's always better to be prepared,' she said, 'even if the knowledge is uncomfortable.'

Blanche glanced at the large clock over the bridge of *The Oisin.*

'Two minutes until the party starts,' she said. 'Let's try and enjoy tonight. We'll deal with problematic men next week.'

22

There were familiar faces and strangers, old friends and new acquaintances. Caroline accepted condolences and sympathy at every turn. She knew Dexter would have been unimpressed by the rush of emotions sent in his direction. On paper he had been able to transport people with his emotive words, but in reality he had never chosen to be effusive with his own feelings. As the line of arriving guests dwindled, Caroline saw Flavia in a figure-hugging shocking pink dress bearing down upon her with a glass of red wine.

'Thanks, sis,' said Caroline, handing her half-drunk glass of champagne to a passing waiter.

'Bubbles make you sneeze and I thought you might prefer this,' she replied. 'Any surprises in the line-up?'

'You mean Travis?'

'No, I was wondering if your nemesis might tag along with her sister.'

'Margot Bullington? Would she dare?'

'The woman has no shame.'

'Connie isn't here yet,' said Caroline, glancing around. At

nearly six foot tall with waist-length inky dark hair, bright blue eyes and porcelain skin, Connie Wells, who played Allegra Cadwallader, was hard to miss.

'Are you sure?' replied Flavia and Caroline felt two arms snake around her waist from behind.

'Sorry we're late, darling, the traffic was awful,' said Connie. 'Give us a glug of that wine.'

'I'll ask a waiter for one,' laughed Caroline as she fought her way out of Connie's grip. 'It's wonderful you're here.'

'It's the final book, I need to know how it ends between Ether and Allegra. Does she finally get her man?'

'Let's hope so,' said a familiar voice and Caroline turned to stare into Gideon's beaming face.

'Gideon,' she exclaimed.

'Surprise,' he said, but he looked nervous, unsure of her reaction. 'Bart was held up at work, I was staying with Connie while I had a few things to do in London and she invited me.'

'My darling husband, Bart, is never very comfortable with "arty types" as he refers to my friends, whereas Gideon is one of us,' she said, but neither Caroline nor Gideon heard as they continued to stare at each other.

'Why are your eyes brown?' he asked, breaking the growing tension between them with his usual directness.

'Tonight, she's Caroline Harvey,' said Flavia stepping forward. 'Hello, Gideon, it's been a long time.'

'Oh my goodness, Flavia, still my blonde goddess,' said Gideon hugging her.

'You're looking well, Gid,' she said. 'I'm sorry to hear about you and Margot.'

Caroline noticed Gideon's face close but with what seemed a huge effort on his part, the shadow passed and he said, 'Thanks,

Flav,' as he turned to the waiter Connie had summoned, taking a large glass of red.

'You have unusual mix of names,' said Connie savouring a deep gulp of wine and sighing as though she had been given the kiss of life. 'Flavia and Caroline. Where did they come from?'

'Flavia means golden or yellow-haired and as Flavia has always had her white-blonde hair, which was evident almost from the moment she was born, Dad suggested it and Mum agreed,' said Caroline.

'Yours is unusual these days too, Caro,' continued Connie.

'Old-fashioned, you mean,' she said. 'Mum chose it because it means strong, free, independent woman.'

'Well, she got that right,' said Gideon.

'And you, former brother-in-law?'

'"Great warrior",' he said. 'Ben and I looked them up once. His means "son of the right hand" or "son of the south", which he thought was a bit disappointing.'

'Mine is utterly boring,' said Connie, 'it means "steadfast" which is why I love playing Allegra because her name derives from the Italian for joyful.'

'Do you know why and where Dexter collected his characters' names?' asked Gideon.

'Ether is obvious,' said Caroline, 'it's because he's everywhere, he's in the ether. Heracles was the Greek hero who had to complete numerous tasks, again, like the many difficulties Ether must overcome as he searches for the answers to the clues to the prophecy. The others, Gramps gathered over the years.'

'Including Ken,' said Gideon.

'The Egyptian Goddess of love,' replied Caroline. 'Gramps liked eclectic names.'

Connie stopped a passing waiter and took a canapé.

'Are we all set for the announcement later?' she said, eating the spaceship themed choux pastry in one bite.

Flavia widened her eyes in warning but Connie shrugged.

'Gid and Mad Margot might be divorced but as far as Bart and I are concerned he's family, he'll keep our secret,' she turned to Gideon and continued. 'Tonight, Caro's announcing the names of the two youngsters chosen to play young Ether and young Bylgja. There's been Internet chatter for weeks about whether or not the flashback scenes will be included and this evening we're showing a clip, aren't we, Caro?'

'We are,' Caroline said. 'You probably already know, Gid, because Connie is terrible at keeping secrets but young Bylgja is being played by Maddie.'

'Your *daughter* Maddie?' he asked Connie, and she beamed.

'Margot's going to be furious, two of you in the franchise and she never even made the audition.'

Caroline swallowed. Gideon's divorce was final, so he was a free man but he did not seem to be able to resist mentioning his ex-wife.

'Actually, way back at the beginning, Blanche and I considered Margot for Luna the Alien,' Caroline said.

Both Connie and Gideon stared at her agog. Flavia giggled at their stunned expressions.

'But she's never said,' said Connie.

'She doesn't know,' said Caroline. 'The director of the first film, Jesse Kapell, had worked with her before—'

'He directed her advert for Haemorrhoid Healer,' interrupted Connie.

'Yes, he said it took 436 takes to record thirty-seconds of useable footage and he was unsure his patience or stamina could cope if she was involved in a full-length feature. He recommended Geraldine Leaf and as soon as she read the first scene with Joe Newman we knew she was perfect. The chemistry was electric between them: friendship and respect but with no sexual tension.'

Gideon snorted as he tried to suppress his laughter.

'Wait until I tell Ben,' he exclaimed.

A moment later, they were engulfed in a crowd of excited guests and Caroline was monopolised by Peter Conrad, the head of Antrobus Publishing. He led her around the room, introducing her to many of his foreign counterparts but wherever she moved, she was aware of Gideon's eyes upon her. When she flicked her long hair extensions over her shoulder, she saw Blanche and Flavia in deep discussion. Caroline turned her back guessing their conversation included Travis, Gideon and the current situation.

It's none of their business how I live my life, she thought. A defiance roaring through her as she accepted another large glass of wine from a passing waiter.

Canapés were circulating, along with an endless flow of drinks. Caroline watched as the guests explored the ballroom, all wondering how and where it might fit into the final story.

'Do you think Ether and Allegra are married in the ballroom?' one woman suggested.

'How can they be?' her friend replied. 'Ether's been wed to Bylgja since childhood and Allegra foolishly committed to Beau when they were on Jupiter in book four.'

'Perhaps their union isn't legally binding...'

Caroline smothered a smile and turned away, searching the crowd for Blanche. The time was approaching for the preview clip to be shown. Instead of her agent, it was Gideon who caught her eye and wandered over.

'More wine, m'lady?' he asked.

'No, thank you, kind sir. A few of those mini-cheeseburgers

would be good though,' she said, and Gideon beckoned over a waiter. They both loaded up a napkin with multiple burgers, giggling when they could not hold any more. 'Are you enjoying yourself?'

'It's been a great night and exactly what I needed after today,' he said. 'The divorce is complete. I'm a single man again and the relief is enormous.'

'If you were unhappy, why did you stay so long?' asked Caroline, then shuddered. 'Sorry, the wine has loosened my tongue. Look, filling my mouth so I can't speak.'

She shoved two burgers in, chewing with ferocity. Gideon laughed.

'Your eating habits have always been disgusting,' he said. 'Do you still eat instant mash with grated cheese?'

'It's a delicacy,' she said through the canapés. 'You've never appreciated the finer things in life. Wasn't your favourite food potato waffles with spaghetti hoops?'

'Perhaps...'

'But why did you?'

'Why did I what?'

'Stay.'

Gideon stared down at her and she wondered whether she should back away, find Blanche, have her make-up repaired before she introduced the preview.

'My marriage to Margot is not a relationship I can easily explain—'

'No, I understand. The heart wants what the heart wants,' interrupted Caroline.

'Caro, no,' he said, and there was an urgency to his voice. 'No, you're wrong. I never loved Margot.'

'Why did you marry her then?'

'Next week, when we're home, back in Pembrokeshire, I'll

explain everything but there is one thing I must say to you tonight.'

Caroline swallowed the canapés, waiting, wondering whether the butterflies in her stomach indicated good news or bad.

'What, Gid?' she prompted.

'I should have said this years ago,' he murmured, then he took her hand and with an air of determination, as though his nerve might fail him, said, 'I love you. I've loved you since we were teenagers and during our summer together. I have never stopped loving you and if the things that happened hadn't ruined my life, I wouldn't have left you.'

'But...' Caroline stared at him, unable to take in this rush of emotions, of hearing the words she had always dreamed to hear. 'You love me?'

'Yes...'

'You ignored my messages, you married Margot two months after our perfect summer together in 2012. You didn't love me then.'

'Will you let me explain?' he asked and the urgency returned to his voice. 'Please, when we're home. I tried to make it clear you were in my thoughts by naming my bookshop after you.'

'Ten-to-Midnight,' she murmured. 'I wondered but couldn't believe you meant it.'

'You remember?' he asked.

'Yes, we were at Julian's house for a New Year's Eve party. Nadine had disappeared and Ben had passed out on the sofa. It was ten to midnight and we kissed...'

'It was more than a kiss,' he said.

'But the next day, we decided to put it behind us because of Ben and Nadine,' said Caroline.

'Until the summer I saw you again and realised I loved you,

that I'd always loved you and the kiss had been the beginning—'

'I'm sorry to interrupt,' said a female voice, and Caroline jumped as Blanche gripped her arm. 'We need you to visit make-up and prepare for the announcement.'

'One second,' she said, shaking Blanche off and reaching for Gideon's arm.

'I have things to tell you too,' she began but Tanya Ross appeared at her other side and she knew there was no time.

'When we're home,' he said, squeezing her hand. 'We'll tell each other everything.'

Caroline turned to Blanche, who looked steely. As Caroline was marched away, she looked behind her and saw Flavia and Steve standing on either side of Gideon, with her sister throwing concerned glances in their wake.

* * *

The next half an hour passed in a blur. People fussed around her and she was forced to tear her teeming mind away from Gideon's revelation. She took deep, calming breaths as Blanche recapped on the running order, watching her with eagle-eyes as she ran through Caroline's cues.

'It's the last one, Caro,' Blanche hissed as they took their places on the stage between Tanya Ross and Peter Conrad. 'Hold it together for tonight, then tomorrow, we'll talk.'

Caroline squeezed her agent's hand, for all Blanche's abrasiveness, she knew she was always on her side.

'We'll do it for Dexter,' said Caroline. 'One last time.'

The lights dimmed and the crowd fell quiet as Joe Newman, who played Ether Heracles, bounded onto the stage. A huge cheer filled the room as he welcomed the audience before one by one introducing his fellow crew mates: Connie Wells, Sky Baxter, Geraldine Leaf, Simon Keystone, Tegan Marriott, Justin Stein and Soozie Restwell. A cheer greeted each actor and while the others formed a semi-circle behind them, Connie remained by his side. Joe waited for the audience to calm, then he held up a hardback book that was wrapped in plain purple paper.

'The final instalment,' he said to more applause, punctuated by whoops of excitement and whistles. 'All the secrets are revealed. At last, we'll discover the answer to the clues and the consequences this will have on Ether's world when he fulfils the prophecy and speaks it aloud.'

The audience oohed and ahhed in appreciation.

'But first, we have a surprise. As you're all aware, the sixth *Ether Heracles* film *Ether Heracles and The Elegua Crossroads* is being filmed. The rumours online have been astonishing, even for *Ether* fans, but one question keeps appearing: will there be a young Ether and a young Bylgja?'

Caroline stared around, the loyalty of her grandfather's fans always left her awed. She had never imagined *Ether Heracles* would ever become such a phenomenon.

'Tonight,' shouted Joe, 'we can exclusively reveal the names of our two newest crew members. Ladies and gentlemen, please give a huge round of applause for Jonah Stoppard who plays Young Ether.'

A spotlight fell on a boy of twelve, his thick brown hair brushed back, his green eyes alight with excitement. Caroline felt her heart lurch as he bounded onto the stage and stood beside Joe.

'And Maddie Wells as the Young Bylgja.'

A girl the same age as Jonah appeared, wearing a bright blue dress, her dark hair swinging in a high ponytail. Tegan Marriott, who played Bylgja Opus, stepped forward and took the girl's hand. However, there was no mistaking she was Connie's daughter.

'Ladies and gentlemen, we have an exclusive preview of these two youngsters in action and then I'll be handing over to Caroline Harvey, Dexter's granddaughter and spokesperson, for the countdown to the launch of the final Dexter Blake book.'

Above Joe a screen unfurled and Caroline watched, her heart bursting with pride as Jonah and Maddie raced across the screen escaping from their evil overlords the Boucicauly. Caroline felt into the side pocket of her dress to check her speech was there. It was short and she knew it by heart but she had insisted it was printed in case the emotion of the moment overwhelmed her. A roar of applause went up and Blanche beckoned her forward.

Caroline walked to the microphone, the crew of *The Oisin* shuffled backwards to make room. She stared out over the crowd and felt an unexpected sadness that this would be the last time the *Ether Heracles* books would draw people together in such a manner. Tonight, everyone would know the end of the story. There were no more mysteries, the secrets were set free and she would say a final farewell to her grandfather.

'Hello,' she said to the hushed crowd, 'for those of you who don't know me, I'm Caroline Harvey, Dexter Blake's granddaughter,' the excitable audience cheered. 'Thank you all for coming. The last book will soon be with you, the culmination of years of work. The *Ether Heracles* series has been Dexter's lifelong passion and it's strange to know, like him, it has reached its conclusion. There have been many things written about my grandfather since his death earlier this year and I hope you'll indulge me while I pay my own tribute.

'Gramps – Dexter – was an extraordinary man. He was irascible, awkward, frustrating but also funny, kind and loyal. As many of you know he long held an interest in the Human Potential Movement. The belief that once a human's basic survival needs have been met, their desire to grow in mental and emotional dimensions increases. He studied the works and lectures of Abraham Maslow, the American psychologist who championed the organisation.

'Through interviews with psychiatrists, psychologists and other mental health experts Maslow learned that the most we use of our brain is ten per cent. He believed if we were able to tap into the rest, we would release untold potential.

'This idea inspired the early drafts of *Ether* and the crew. In every story, Dexter enjoyed pushing his creations to the limits of what was thought humanly possible in each of their missions and the crew always excelled. After several drafts of the first manuscript, this theory of understanding our potential gave Dexter the idea for the character of Luna the Alien. She might die at the end of every book but through her understanding of her immense potential and with Ether's help, she was able to restart her body and live again.

'Alas, Gramps hasn't been able to regenerate himself but through his stories he will live on. He has changed my life. We worked closely on the books and tried to include references from his favourite legends and poems. *The Space Sirens* was a book we both adored because of its references to Arthurian literature, particularly the tale of *Tristan and Iseult*, the lovers who tried to resist their attraction. In *The Lake of Tawaret* we were inspired by the tale of *Gawain and the Green Knight* and in the final book, *Ishtar's Legacy*, we wove in a few hidden strands of poetry from Gramp's favourite poem, *He Wishes for the Cloths of Heaven* by W.B. Yeats.'

Caroline could not resist looking at Gideon but he was staring at Jonah Stoppard, a perplexed expression on his face.

'So, as the clock ticks down to midnight and Ether's final adventure, I'd like to thank you all on behalf of Dexter Blake for staying with us on this epic journey. It's been astonishing. As you read my grandfather's last words, remember each day is a new beginning, one where you can stretch your human potential to greater levels. Whenever things become difficult, think of Ether and his loyalty to his crew, their friendship and their determination to succeed. Dexter and I always said, if we could create this extraordinary world in our heads, then so can anyone. Live to your fullest potential and remember, love is always the answer.'

'And now,' she said, 'will you join me in counting down to the release of the last-ever book in the *Ether Heracles* series.'

The audience took up the chorus and as the clock reached midnight a huge cheer erupted as live feeds from across the world showed the surge of people grabbing copies of the book. At the Dorchester, the waiting staff, now dressed in crew uniforms, circulated, handing out goodie bags with the books inside.

Caroline stepped back, overwhelmed with emotion. This was it. It was the end. It was over.

She stumbled off the stage away from the clamouring cheers and found a quiet corner, wiping her eyes, composing herself before returning to the hordes of people. She let out a long breath and shook back her hair, then she felt a hand in hers and arms circled her waist.

She looked down and eyes wide with delight she hugged Jonah Stoppard back, tears welling again as he said, 'Don't cry, Mum. Your speech was brilliant.'

'Oh, my darling, I've missed you,' she said.

'I've missed you too,' he said, then he whispered, 'Is my dad here?'

'Yes, he arrived with Connie.'

'I thought so.' Jonah grinned. 'He was in the crowd, watching me.'

A shadow fell across them and Caroline looked up. Gideon was staring down at them, colour rising in his cheeks.

'Your nephew's cousin, from the photograph in your office,' said Gideon, but his voice was harsh. 'I thought he must be a cousin on Flavia's husband's side but it was spooky because he looked like me when I was young.'

Caroline did not respond. She and Jonah stared at Gideon.

'He's your son, isn't he?' said Gideon.

'Yes, but—'

'How old are you, Jonah?' Gideon cut across her.

'Twelve,' he replied, looking from Caroline to Gideon.

'Is he my son too?'

Caroline considered lying but to start the whole terrible cycle again was more than she could bear. She had endured enough pain. She stared at Gideon, tears spilling down her cheeks.

'Is he my son?' demanded Gideon.

'Yes,' she whispered.

23

THE STRAND, LONDON, MAY 1536

'It is done then?' said Anne, and Randall wiped his hand across his beard in distress. 'There was no last-minute reprieve to send her to a convent?'

'No,' he replied, his voice tense as Anne stifled a sob. 'The queen is dead. She was dignified to the end but the king didn't spare her. He sent his son, Henry Fitzroy, to watch, the poor boy was shocked when the swordsman swung—'

'Enough, Randall,' Anne gasped, her stomach churning with revulsion. 'The king is free to marry Jane Seymour.'

'Poor woman,' said Randall pouring himself a pewter tankard of ale from the jug on the table.

'Do you mean Jane or Anne?'

'Both,' said Randall, collapsing into the chair beside the table where piles of paper fluttered in the breeze of his movement.

Anne slid the piece of parchment she had been writing on under a legal document concerning her father's Warwickshire holdings. She did not want Randall to see she had been practising her husband's signature.

The past five years had been turbulent. The king's obsession with Anne Boleyn had not abated and in his desperation to take a new wife, he had turned the religion of the country upside down, breaking with Rome and the Catholic faith, declaring himself head of the Church of England. Once empowered he claimed his marriage to Queen Katherine was illegal and encouraged Thomas Cranmer, the new Protestant Archbishop of Canterbury, to grant him a divorce, enabling him to marry Anne Boleyn.

Yet, the story of their love had not been smooth and when Anne failed to deliver the longed-for male heir, instead giving birth to the Princess Elizabeth, Henry had fallen out of love with his new wife. His roving eye had turned to others including Anne Boleyn's cousin, Madge Shelton, followed by the mysterious Imperial Lady; Jane, Lady Stukley; Mary Berkeley, Joanna Dingley and Jane Ashely. However, it was during the Summer Progress of 1535, the king had noticed Jane Seymour, the daughter of John and Margery Seymour, when they entertained the royal party at their country manor, Wulf Hall.

A few months later, Anne had announced another pregnancy but the king was torn between his wife and his compliant new love, Jane Seymour. When Queen Katherine died in January 1536, followed by Anne's miscarriage shortly after, the court felt the waves of change. Under instructions from the king, Thomas Cromwell had moved with deadly speed. Anne was arrested and charged with adultery with Sir Henry Norris, Mark Smeaton, Sir Francis Weston, Sir William Brereton, Sir Richard Page and her own brother, George Boleyn. The poet, Sir Thomas Wyatt was arrested but released without charge, as eventually was Page.

A trial was held where the queen was allowed to plead her case but the result was a foregone conclusion. The men chosen to hear her evidence were all enthral to the king, including Anne Brandon's father, her husband, Edward Grey, Baron Powis and her brother-in-law Thomas Stanley, Lord Monteagle. Anne Boleyn was found guilty and sentenced to death by her own uncle, Thomas Howard, the Duke of Norfolk. In what he considered to be an act of kindness, Henry declared his wife could be executed using a sword, which would be quicker than being hacked to death with an axe. The king had sent for a man from France to despatch her with all haste. Henry even helped with the design of the scaffold himself, his final gift to the woman he had once loved enough to recreate the country's religion in order to marry her.

'Anne Boleyn didn't deserve to die,' Randall continued, draining his tankard, 'and Jane, well, she doesn't deserve whatever is coming to her.'

They were in the private solar of the house Lord Powis rented in London. It was a vast property on The Strand with gardens overlooking the River Thames. This room was space shared by both Edward and Anne, although husband and wife had suites of their own at opposite ends of the grand manor. Randall was a regular visitor and Anne wondered if her husband realised the friendship her lover showed to him was superficial. Randall's reason for being in the property was her and the loving relationship they had built over the years. Today though, there would be no question as to why he was in the house. Anne Boleyn, the erstwhile queen, had been executed on Tower Green on charges of adultery and nobles from across the land had come to act as witnesses to the historic event.

'Do you think the accusations against her were true?' asked Anne.

'It's unlikely,' said Randall. 'You know yourself, the queen was rarely alone, there were always ladies-in-waiting and servants around. When would she have been able to have assignations with so many men? There are whispers that Cromwell used Anne's fall as a way to clear out men he viewed as troublesome. The truth is the queen's life was in danger from the moment she miscarried the baby in January.'

Anne forced herself not to flinch at Randall's words but it was difficult. All around her women continued to bear children for their husbands while the Powis cradle remained stubbornly empty. Her younger sister Mary, Lady Monteagle, had four children and was pregnant again, even her younger half-sister, Lady Frances Brandon, now the Marchioness of Dorset was hinting she might be pregnant with her first child. Would the king's actions against a wife unable to bear an heir have far-reaching consequences for women such as her? Would he pass a new law allowing frustrated husbands to dispose of wives they felt had outlived their usefulness as Henry had done with Anne Boleyn and Queen Katherine? The thought sent a cold trickle of fear down her spine.

'The king wants a son,' she said.

'Exactly,' said Randall. 'What has your father said about the trial?'

'Nothing,' said Anne. 'To comment could be construed as treason and my father is a cautious man.'

'What do you mean?'

'None of us imagined the king would ever turn on his trusted advisor Sir Thomas More but when he refused to take the Oath of Supremacy or acknowledge the king as supreme head of the Church of England, Uncle Henry was brutal. Prior to this he had adored Thomas More above all others. My father is another whom he admires but the king is quicksilver. Papa doesn't dare challenge him. Although we haven't discussed the matter directly, Papa has hinted he would have preferred Anne to be sent abroad instead of executed.'

Randall poured himself another drink and sipped it, considering her words. His next comment took her by surprise.

'How did the king react when your new half-brother was born?'

Anne scowled. Her beloved stepmother, Mary, had died in July 1533 and, in her view, her father had behaved appallingly in the aftermath. Within two months of his wife's death, the Duke of Suffolk had married his fourteen-year-old ward, Lady Katherine Willoughby, and gained access to her vast fortune. All the Brandon girls had been shocked by their father's actions. As far as the family had known, Lady Katherine was supposed to have been a potential wife for their youngest brother, Henry, Earl of Lincoln, the son of Princess Mary who was born the same year – 1522 – the older Henry had died. For the forty-nine-year-old duke to have taken a fourteen-year-old bride, while not frowned upon by society, caused shockwaves among his children.

When in March 1534, nine months after the death of Mary, Duchess of Suffolk, the young Earl of Lincoln had died, the duke called his daughters and their husbands to a dinner explaining his wisdom in marrying Katherine and ensuring her fortune stayed in the Suffolk coffers.

'I knew my son ailed,' he said, blustering as he struggled to justify his actions, 'and if Katherine had been betrothed to Henry, it would have been impossible for she and I to be wed.'

The new young duchess kept her eyes on her plate and said nothing. Later, Anne sought her father out.

'She's young enough to be your granddaughter,' she hissed at her father in fury.

Anne knew, as his daughter, it was not her place to challenge him and expected an angry retort. It was a shock, therefore, when he collapsed into a chair and hid his face in his hands.

'You're right, Annie,' he groaned, 'and I promise I'll be kind to her but without her money, I'd be bankrupt. The debts Mary and I owed the king for our illegal marriage continue to drain my coffers and without Mary's dower payments from France, my income has halved. Try not to think badly of me, Annie. This was for the family, not just me.'

When her father had written the previous autumn to rejoice that Katherine, Duchess of Suffolk, had been delivered of a healthy boy, Anne was unsure of her emotions. They were a complicated mixture of disgust at the thought of the now sixteen-year-old Katherine with her father, relief both were well and the deep bitterness in her soul as she struggled with the fact that once again another woman had done something which continued to elude her.

'The king was intrigued that my father, who is older than him by seven years, could have a son at his stage in life,' Anne said to Randall, 'and I believe this is another reason he was interested in finding a younger queen.'

'Let us all pray that Jane Seymour is able to provide a son or the king might start cutting a swathe through the ladies of the court as he tries to begat a legitimate Tudor heir,' said Randall and Anne shuddered.

They fell into a brooding silence, each lost in their own thoughts at the horror of the violence that had taken place among the people they classed as friends. A clatter of hooves outside and the call of voices alerted them to the arrival of Lord Powis. A few moments later, he strode into the solar.

'Randall,' he exclaimed in delight, 'this is indeed a pleasure. Did you witness the execution? The king was a wise man to empty his bed of the she-devil; she was always a troublesome whore. Her best effort was to produce a daughter, although,' he shot Anne a contemptuous glance, 'a daughter is better than nothing.'

Anne felt her temper rise at both her husband's words and his ebullient manner caused by Anne Boleyn's death. His tone suggested the entire saga was little more than an entertainment, a masque or jousting competition which would soon be forgotten, rather than the death of a woman, a queen; her friend.

'Thomas Cromwell did a good job clearing out the dead wood in the court, too,' he continued, ringing the bell for a servant. 'Wine,' he demanded when Dodman, the chief steward arrived, 'strong as we have, and food. Death makes me ravenous.'

He roared with laughter and a beat later, Randall forced a smile.

'Will you be staying, Randall?' asked Edward. 'There are more friends visiting soon, you'd be most welcome.'

'In that case, yes,' said Randall, and Anne felt a thrill of pleasure.

'Anne will have Dodman prepare your usual chambers,' he said. 'How's your building project taking shape in the wilds of Pembrokeshire? Honestly, man, I admire you. How did you discover it?'

'The building and conversions are going well,' replied Randall. 'The land came to my notice thanks to John Beaumont. He knew I wished to have a property that gave me access to the Irish coast for the import and export of minerals from my estates across the country.'

Anne turned away. No one but herself, Randall and John Beaumont knew that the vast holdings in Pembrokeshire had been sold to Randall by the now deceased Queen Anne Boleyn.

When the young Lady Frances Brandon had married Henry Grey, Marquess of Dorset, the king and Anne Boleyn had attended the wedding. Pregnant with the future princess, Anne had been made comfortable from the summer heat on a vast chaise under silken banners draped between trees in the beautiful gardens of Suffolk Place.

'Please don't curtsy,' the queen had hissed when Anne edged into view. 'I'm so bored with people bobbing up and down in front of me. It's worse than being on a barge on a choppy day on the Thames.'

Anne had laughed as she slid into the seat beside the queen. Around them, a sea of nobility ebbed and flowed around the king, towards the newly married couple and then back to the king.

'You're queen,' Anne had said.

'It's hard to believe,' Anne Boleyn had replied.

'And how is it? After all these years, was it worth the wait?'

'I hope so but the politics of court are an endless game of chance,' the queen had replied.

'How so?'

'When I became queen, I thought this would allow me control over my own destiny at last. My court of women would be my place of joy and sanctuary but this couldn't have been further from the truth. Thomas Cromwell controls the court and is keen to advance himself at every opportunity. My father, my brother, my uncles all think I'm there to grant them personal favours while the king expects me to be at his side whenever he desires it. When we were courting, he listened to my thoughts, my views but as his wife my opinions are no longer required. Instead my presence is demanded to bolster his own hubris.'

Anne had looked at the queen in surprise, then said, 'There are few people destined to be happy in these marriage games.'

The two women had glanced towards the young married couple who were being feted by all around.

'It's true then?' the queen had said. 'All is not happy in the House of Powis?'

'Edward is disgusted by my inability to bear a child,' she'd said. 'He has taken a lover: Jane Orwell.'

'And what of the delicious Randall Hanworth?' the queen had asked with a knowing raise of her eyebrows.

'Annie-Bee, stop it.' Anne had giggled, lapsing into the old nickname from their younger years. 'Anyone might hear.'

'There's nobody near enough,' the queen had replied. 'Is it true?'

'Yes,' Anne had admitted. 'We became reacquainted several years ago. For a long time, our relationship was friendship.'

'But since you've discovered your husband is bedding Jane...?' the queen had let the question hang but Anne's flaming cheeks had given the answer. 'Then let me help at least one person I love,' the queen had continued. 'Do you remember, before I married the king, I was created the Marquess of Pembrokeshire?'

'Yes, of course...'

'A house came with the title, an old manor belonging to the crown and at its heart is an island with a convent. Further away are a series of newer monastic buildings but these will soon be the property of the crown. As they come under my dower, it's my choice where to bestow them. If Randall were to apply, I could ensure he was granted them. They are in a remote part of the country but it would mean the two of you have a place of safety should it ever be required.'

'Anne, this is very generous—' Anne Brandon had begun, but the queen shook her head.

'We must be quick, the king and your father are coming this way,' she'd whispered. 'There is one small condition.'

'Of course, anything.'

'Should I ever need a place to hide, then you will open these properties to me without hesitation.'

Anne had stared at her in confusion.

'But, why would you—?'

'Please, Annie,' she'd implored, and with a nod of Anne Brandon's head, the deal was agreed.

The request had bemused her but in the excitement of her and Randall securing such powerful support for their relationship, she had not questioned her friend's fears any further. It was when the queen had been arrested Anne wondered if her friend had long suspected her end would be swift and brutal.

* * *

'John Beaumont helped smooth out any difficulties when it came to taking over the land. He's quite ruthless, isn't he?' Randall said, the clatter of his tankard on the table bringing Anne back to the conversation.

'A very able man to have on your side if you find yourself in a difficult situation concerning the law. Did you hear? His wife, Elizabeth, is pregnant. He's a wise man. Another one who has moved on from a woman who was useless in the area of childbed. I told him so myself when he remarried. Ah, here's the wine.'

Anne's friend, Isabelle, John Beaumont's first wife, had died in childbirth the previous year. A few months later John had married Elizabeth Hastings but Anne did not think Edward was correct in his assumption that Beaumont had moved on in such a callous manner. She wrote to him after Isabelle's death and the words of his reply revealed his heartbreak at the loss of the woman he loved and the child he had never been given the chance to meet.

The correspondence between them continued and Anne was the first to hear about his new marriage, although, she had not shared this with Edward. Anne stood. She had no desire to hear her husband decry another woman's failures in the marriage bed. Another loveless coupling with him at Christmas had resulted in a pregnancy but the child slipped away in the third month.

'I shall organise the rooms for Randall,' Anne said. 'How many other guests will be joining us?'

'I don't know how many of your ladies will be here but I've invited John and Elizabeth Beaumont, Jane Orwell, her brother Ludo, who will soon be off to France, Edward Seymour with his wife, Anne, and young Gregory Cromwell, son of the Lord Privy Seal, Sir Thomas Cromwell. There's a rumour he's been suggested as a possible match for Elizabeth, Lady Ughtred.'

'Jane Seymour's sister?' said Anne.

'She's the widow of Sir Anthony Ughtred who was Governor of Jersey and everyone has learned from watching the Boleyns that this is the time to manoeuvre for positions of favour. It's a shame we don't have any daughters we could parade before the king...'

'I shall speak to Dodman,' said Anne and strode towards the door, furious at Edward's snide comments but as she brushed close to Randall, she felt his fingers briefly entwine with hers and the barbs from her husband no longer mattered.

Edward might strut and preen, a cockerel crowing his dominance over his household, but she was not the meek, cowed creature he imagined. She and Randall had been in love for years and with him under their roof, she felt safe, protected by the secret of their union. There was no doubt Edward would summon Jane Orwell to his chambers later and, when she was certain all were asleep, she would take as much pleasure inviting Randall to her own bed.

It took all her self-control not to laugh in Edward's arrogant face as she swept from the room.

24

The evening passed with painful slowness. Anne and Edward fell back into their familiar roles as host and hostess. The veneer they had established – the small smiles, the jokes, the harmony with which they oversaw the meal – belied the true state of their marriage with its constant bitter battles. Seated on either side of Lord and Lady Powis were Sir Edward Seymour and his second wife, Anne Stanhope, a couple Anne found venal and smug.

As the brother of the queen-in-waiting, Seymour had become an important man at court. Edward Powis was excited to be able to claim him as a friend from their shared youths and to entertain the Seymours in his home. As the wine flowed, Anne watched as her husband became more obstreperous, leaning across her to speak to Seymour, revelling in the downfall of the Boleyns and the executions of both the queen and her brother, George.

A few seats away, Randall chatted to Beatrice and her husband Richard Ogle, Jane Orwell on his other side sending flirtatious glances towards Edward, while her brother Ludo scowled at her behaviour. John Beaumont and his wife, Elizabeth, were beside him, opposite was Beatrice Ogle, one of Anne's senior ladies, with her husband, Sir Richard, who were entertaining Gregory Cromwell. Despite herself, Anne liked Gregory. He was shy with none of the arrogance of his father, Sir Thomas Cromwell, and was bemused to find himself in such august company.

Although, thought Anne, as she watched him, if he is to marry Elizabeth Seymour he will have to grow up. The marriage will raise his status even higher and he will be related to royalty with all the excitement and terror such connections bring.

Since the death of her stepmother, the number of invitations to parties and masques had lessened. She was no longer the stepdaughter of a princess and the subtle laws of the court had shifted. For a while her friendship with Anne Boleyn had kept them in the inner circle but as the Boleyns' star had waned, so had their inclusions to the glamorous events at court.

Edward had berated her, blaming Anne's connections to the disgraced queen as the reason they were being sidelined. It never occurred to Anne to tell her husband that she and Randall were often invited to small, exclusive parties and it was Edward's arrogance and cruelty, which offended so many of the nobility, that left him excluded. She knew Edward hoped his old friendship with Seymour would see him drawn into the exclusive upper echelons again.

However, she thought, my links with the queen's court continue, even though Edward is, as yet, unaware.

Earlier in the afternoon, a note had arrived from her father. He had explained that he had arranged for a place among Jane Seymour's new ladies-in-waiting for her younger sister Mary, Lady Monteagle.

'As soon as there is a suitable opening, I shall try to place you in her household,' he wrote, 'but I suspect with the rumours at court concerning the difficulties in your marriage, the new queen might wish to distance herself from potential scandals. The king claims Jane's intentions are to have a quiet and demure court.'

Anne had crumpled the letter and thrown it in the fire. From what she had heard of Jane Seymour, Jane's behaviour had once been more outrageous than Anne Boleyn's. Ever since she had come to the attention of the king, these rumours were quashed and her past reinvented as pure and wholesome.

Events were moving with a frightening speed and Anne found it difficult to comprehend or forgive. Her friend was barely cold in her grave and the new queen's court was assembling. She wondered how Jane Seymour felt but could not begin to imagine – was she excited about her new position or terrified, having witnessed what happened to wives who displeased the king? Anne was grateful she had been passed over for a place at court. Her feelings towards Jane were ambiguous but she would struggle to be civil to the king, the man who continued to insist she call him Uncle Henry.

Edward roared with laughter, bringing her from her thoughts. She signalled to the page to top up Seymour's goblet, then murmured to her husband, 'The ladies and I shall retire to my solar,' she said.

He waved his hand in acknowledgement but did not respond, instead returning to his conversation with Seymour. Anne rose and led the women away. As she had requested there were tisanes and cordials, sweet wine and brandy, with delicate pies and cakes awaiting their arrival. Outside, she heard a clock strike ten and wondered how much longer she would have to endure the night. To her relief, Beatrice intercepted Jane Orwell on her trajectory towards Anne, distracting her by asking if she would recite a poem. Anne smothered a sardonic smile, Jane was fond of reciting, Beatrice had known this would divert her. For Anne, it meant she would not have to listen to the other woman's sly comments about the state of the Powis marriage.

It was less than ten minutes later when Sir Edward Seymour tapped on the door, thanking Anne for her hospitality and requesting his wife as he, Lady Anne and Gregory Cromwell were due back at the Palace of Whitehall. The rest of the party faded away too. In her room, Anne bade her women goodnight as they dispersed to their chambers leaving Anne with her senior maid, Alice Ramkin, who always slept in the room with her.

Once prepared for bed, Anne walked to the window, staring out at the river with its eerie covering of silver mist. The distant cries of the water boatmen carried towards her like the call of magical birds and she shivered in anticipation of the secret tap on the door. There was always a risk when Edward was in the house but she knew Randall would not be able to resist.

'Is that all, Lady Powis?' asked Ramkin, as she folded away the last of Anne's clothes, closing the cedar trunk where they were stored with a gentle thunk.

'Yes, thank you,' Anne replied. 'I crave solitude this evening. You shall sleep in the dressing room.'

'Of course, my lady,' she replied, and the two women exchanged an understanding look.

There were no secrets between a lady and her maids, which was why Anne was convinced Anne Boleyn had been innocent of the charges laid against her. Perhaps her women might have been able to smuggle one lover into the queen's bedchamber but to suggest they had accommodated Mark Smeaton, Sir Francis Weston, Sir Henry Norris and Sir William Brereton was ludicrous. The one man who would have had access to the queen would have been her brother, George Boleyn, but the idea of incest was repugnant and Anne knew this was the ultimate insult Henry and the queen's other accusers had been able to concoct.

'Leave the door unlocked between the rooms,' she said. 'In case I need you.'

The woman gave a curtsy, gathered Anne's discarded undergarments and scurried through the door to the adjoining room. As Anne climbed into her wide, warm bed, she wondered whether Edward had continued to drink. If so, she thought, he will likely pass out at the table.

She propped herself against a mound of pillows, the candlelight flickering, and smoothed her hands over the copy of *Tristan and Iseult* which was open on her lap, wondering at the path her life had followed. Despite her love for Randall, when she married Edward she had intended to be true to him. With her marriage vows, she had felt confident of building a partnership, a marriage, creating a Powis dynasty. However, her endless tragic miscarriages combined with Edward's callousness had worn her down.

She remembered the first evening Randall had slipped into her rooms at Powis Castle, a shadow in the night. The conversation that followed had contained promises of love and discretion on both sides but for weeks afterwards she had struggled with her conscience. She knew her husband had long since invited Jane Orwell into his bed; this behaviour was his own business and she did not feel it justified her finding solace in another man's arms.

Yet, as she observed the behaviour of those around her –

other courtiers, even her own father – she realised their actions and their words were a contradiction. To hear them speak, each would agree that marriage was sacrosanct, children must be born in wedlock in order to inherit, to bed another while you are married was a sin. But, while they paid lip service to the ancient laws of marriage, she had seen with her own eyes many felt these rules did not apply to them.

She remembered the night at Anne Boleyn's court, when Thomas Wyatt had recited the tale of *Tristan and Iseult*. Afterwards, when the merriment had begun, none of the people present had danced with their spouses. It had been a revelation, especially when Randall had kissed her in full view and no one had noticed. Was this the reason her stepmother had given her a copy of the story so many years ago? Was it some sort of code? A message hinting that if you were to follow your heart away from your marriage vows, be subtle?

* * *

Anne knew her father had strayed during his marriage to Princess Mary but the discovery had shocked her. It had been at her sister Lady Frances Brandon's wedding when he had revealed his misdemeanour. Frances had married Henry Grey, the Marquess of Dorset in 1533, and as Anne and her father traversed the sunlit lawn during the celebrations afterwards, they had discussed married life.

'How is your marriage, Annie?' he had asked as they made their slow way across the garden, skirting around the wedding guests. 'You have no children to show for near eight years of marriage.'

'The babes do not wish to stay,' she had said, her voice unexpectedly thick with tears. 'Edward and I have suffered many tragic losses and now he has another to take my place in his bed.'

Charles Brandon had given a sad nod.

'I wondered if this was the case. Your mama hinted as much. However, you are Lady Powis and only children of your body will be able to inherit. His mistress will never be able to replace you.'

'Oh, Papa, you're so old-fashioned,' she'd said. 'Have you not seen the example the king is setting?'

'What do you mean?'

'His illegitimate son, Henry Fitzroy, Duke of Richmond and Somerset, is being educated as a prince. There are many who believe – and my husband is among them – that if the new queen is unsuccessful in providing a male heir, the king will elevate his eldest son – legitimate or not – to inherit the crown. If he does, other men who have had children out of wedlock but none from the marital bed may also be able to bestow their titles and wealth on these bastard children.'

'Annie, this is nonsense,' Charles had said. 'To allow such heresy would cause chaos in ancient families. The Privy Council would never allow it.'

'Yet, each day, Fitzroy draws closer to the king and possibly the crown.'

It was something she and Randall had discussed, a path she thought would have been ruminated upon at court, however, the distress on her father's face suggested otherwise.

'Then pray your friend gives the king a son,' her father had said, 'or, if what you allude to comes to pass, the realm could again be plunged into civil war.'

'Would it?' she had asked, this time it had been her turn to register alarm.

'There are many young men who talk of birthrights, who

suggest they can claim dukedoms, earldoms, because their mothers have told them their fathers are noble and wealthy men. In fact, there is a rumour that the king has an illegitimate daughter with a member of the yeomanry class, a girl named Ethelreade Malte. Imagine if she had been a boy?'

'Papa, women generally know the identity of their child's father and very few would lie. The consequences for them would be severe if they were caught to be spreading salacious falsehoods.'

'Perhaps,' the duke had admitted, 'but if these children felt they were able to claim titles and lands, it would change the natural order of the nobility. It could lead to brothers and half-brothers fighting for their supposed rights. The disgrace it could cause to men who have made mistakes...'

He had shaken his head, a faraway look in his eyes.

'Do you have other children?' Anne had asked, expecting a denial but the duke had flushed. 'A son?'

Charles had nodded, his face a mask of shame.

'And a daughter,' he'd confessed. 'They're well cared for and your mama is understanding but my other son is older than your brother Henry, who is styled Earl of Lincoln. Would it be fair to Henry if another were to try and take my title?'

'How could you?' Anne had hissed. 'How could you betray Mama in such a heartless manner?'

'It is the way of things, Anne,' Charles had snapped. 'You're a married woman, you know men have needs which can't always be satisfied by their spouse.'

'So, you lay with another woman, then make excuses,' she'd said. 'Do any of you men consider how hurtful this is to the wife you have left behind.'

'I do,' he'd replied, 'and I was never more ashamed. Believe me, Annie, when your marriage was arranged I thought Edward to be a good man; that this would be a fruitful match. It seems I was mistaken and for this, my dearest daughter, I am sorry but, like so many women before you, it is imperative you understand that a man will always look for comfort elsewhere.'

'You don't need to tell me,' Anne had said.

'However, if he is cruel, Annie, remember you are the daughter of a duke and the stepdaughter of a princess. You are at the heart of a powerful family while Powis, despite what he might think, will always be on the periphery. Suffolk House will always be your home and I will protect you.'

'Thank you, Papa,' she had said as he hugged her.

* * *

What would he think of my liaison with Randall? she wondered, as she let the memories of the conversation float away, making herself more comfortable in her bed.

She had loved Randall since she was a girl. It was he and he alone she adored, not the thrill of the chase.

'I love him,' she murmured, dipping her quill into the tiny inkwell on her bedside table.

She turned the pages until she came to one bearing an image of the ship heading towards the dying Tristan, the white sails clear for all to see, despite the lies told to the ailing man by his jealous wife. She wrote in tiny letters between the elaborate scrolls that formed the sea:

I will always come to you, my love

When the ink was dry, she closed the book with care and placed it on her bedside table. If he visited her tonight, she would hand him the book. If he did not, she would leave it somewhere for him to collect in the morning, so he could read her message of devotion. Throughout their time together the leather-bound copy of *Tristan and Iseult* had been used as a method of private communication. They would write messages and mark the pages for the other to find. It gave them both a tantalising thrill as they shared their loving notes under Edward's nose.

Anne stretched, enjoying the coolness of the sheets, and stared at the canopy above thinking about Randall. Over the years, their meetings in the Powis home had been memorable, often chaste due to their fear of discovery. Yet, there were many occasions where their passion had overflowed, their desire too intense to contain. She groaned thinking of Randall's touch; the gentleness of his hand smoothing her flesh, the whispers of his words of devotion and the reverence with which they made love. Beatrice Ogle had proved a surprising ally and had often allowed them to use a secluded house in St Giles Cripplegate that was part of her dower.

'He will be here soon,' she whispered into the darkness and shivered in excitement.

Half an hour later, there were two short knocks, then a pause followed by three more. Anne sprang from the bed. This was the secret code Randall had created to prove his identity. Anne opened the door on the dimly lit corridor where Randall waited. She moved aside and he entered on silent feet.

'My love,' he whispered, pulling her into his arms. For a moment, Anne was lost to his kiss, then self-preservation and sense forced her to murmur.

'Where's Edward?'

'In his cups,' he replied. 'I was reading in my chamber when I heard Jane giving orders for him to be helped to his rooms and for his men to prepare him for bed.'

Anne felt a wave of relief. If Jane was with Edward, then they would not be disturbed. She kissed Randall, her hands exploring the familiar muscles and strength of his body. Whether it was the wine or the deep sense of injustice she felt concerning the treatment of her old friend, she was in a wild, reckless mood. She wanted to feel alive, to allow passion to race through her until she could not breathe, to feel Randall tremble under her touch.

She broke from him and locked the door, before stripping away her finely embroidered lawn nightgown. She beckoned him towards the bed, her face glowing with impish delight. Randall threw his heavy satin gown to the floor and wrenched his nightshirt over his head. His eyes ablaze with passion as she pulled him to her, kissing him with her heart and soul.

It was several hours later when the noise awoke Anne. Disorientated she sat up, taking the covers with her. Randall groaned as the draught wrenched him from his slumber. The noise came again and her hand flew to her mouth in fear as she realised its source: there was someone outside twisting the door-knob. As she struggled into her nightgown, she mimed to Randall to put on his clothes, then they both froze as the handle rattled with increased violence.

'Anne,' Edward's voice was deep, slurred, a feral growl, 'unlock this door.'

Anne and Randall stared at each other in horror. Randall pulled his nightshirt over his head, gathered his robe and secreted himself behind the arras.

'Anne, let me in, I'm your husband...' Edward banged on the door.

She lit the candle and holding it high to ensure Randall was hidden, walked to the door on cautious feet. With trembling hands, she turned the key but before she could retreat Edward stormed inside, his face livid with rage as he grabbed her by the hair, jerking her to an abrupt halt. She screamed but Edward tightened his grip.

He wore the clothes from dinner, although his feet and legs were bare and his doublet had been loosened.

'You useless whore,' he hissed, pushing his face close to hers.

His breath was sour with alcohol, red veins pulsed in his wild eyes, globules of spit and dried wine gathered in the corners of his mouth. He was beyond reason and as he bared his teeth, his face alight with malice, Anne felt true fear.

'I should have done this years ago,' he hissed. 'Thank goodness the king is a man of wisdom. On your knees, woman.'

'Edward, no,' said Anne, struggling to push him away but his hands tightened as he tried to force her to the ground.

Terror pulsed through her. She pushed back, straightening her legs, forcing him away; she would not give in without a fight. Taken by surprise, Edward stumbled, loosening his grip on her hair as he fought to regain his balance. Anne took her chance to stagger away but it was then she saw it, glimmering in the candlelight: the wicked glint of metal on an unsheathed sword.

'Alice—!' Anne screamed. 'Ramkin, help—' but her entreaties were cut short as Edward caught her hair again and dragged her towards him, pushing his lips against hers, silencing her as he forced his tongue into her mouth with such violence it caused her to gag.

'All these years, I've waited patiently for an heir but, nothing,' he hissed, twisting his hand in her hair so she screamed with pain. 'It was prudent to keep you as wife while you had royal connections. Even after your stepmother died, your friendship with the Goggle-Eyed Witch kept us in the highest circles of the court. But she's dead too and your usefulness is at an end.'

Anne screamed in pain as Edward hooked one foot behind her knee, forcing her to the ground.

'Help—' she shrieked as her maid appeared in the doorway, her face white with horror. Alice Ramkin gave a sob but the only exit was the door behind Edward.

'Kneel before me, wife,' hissed Edward.

'Lord Powis, no...' implored Ramkin. 'Please, sir, stop...' but Edward turned to the woman and spat in her face.

'Shut your noise,' he screamed, flailing his sword, 'or you'll be next.'

He turned back to Anne, his face twisted with such loathing he looked bestial.

'You are my chattel, wife, and I am at liberty to do with you as I wish and I wish to slice off your head. Is it not amusing that like the king, I am ridding myself of a useless whore called Anne in order to replace her with a simple woman called Jane who will never challenge me?'

He let out a hysterical roar of laughter. Anne screamed, a crumpled heap on the floor, powerless to move. Edward raised his sword.

'No!' shrieked her maid as Anne threw her arms over her head, tears filling her eyes, bracing herself for the slicing death blow of the sword.

'Die, whore,' screamed Edward and Anne began to pray through her sobs.

There was a shriek followed by a crash and a groan, then silence. Anne tensed but there was no whipping sound of metal through the air, no fierce sting of death against her slender throat. Instead, two strong hands pulled her to her feet and embraced her. Randall glowered down at the swearing heap on the ground that was Edward. Blood seeped from a cut across the back of his head, matting his hair, his eyes out of focus. Beside him was a heavy metal candlestick, the cause of the injury.

'You bastard,' groaned Edward. 'You bed my wife in my house, then you try to murder me. I'll see you hang for this, Hanworth.'

'Try your hardest,' said Randall, his eyes narrowed in incandescent rage. 'You're the worst example of a man I've ever met. Anne, call your women, we leave now.'

Anne was shaking, her eyes flicking between the two men, unable to move. The noise had woken the household and faces were appearing in her doorway including Beatrice and Richard, followed by her other maid, Richardson. In the distance, the heavy footsteps of the steward, Dodman, were coming towards them with Mrs Loose, the housekeeper, scurrying along in his wake.

'Dodman,' said Randall taking command of the situation, 'Lord Powis has drunk something which has disagreed with him and has had a fall. Take him to his quarters and ensure his men dress the wound. It would be wise to keep him there until morning, when I shall send one of my representatives to discuss events. After that, please send word to the stables and the staff at the Duke's house to expect us within the hour. Lady Powis and I shall be leaving immediately for Suffolk Place. Mrs Loose, pack a travelling chest for Lady Powis.'

Anne watched as the household followed Randall's commands, her legs shook and she wondered how long they would continue to hold her up. Beatrice entered the room and led Anne to the bed. Randall knelt before her, taking her hands.

'My love,' he whispered but his words seemed to come from far away, 'I shall return to my rooms and dress, then we shall depart. Until then, stay with Beatrice.'

'He was going to kill me,' she whispered, forming the words even though they made no sense.

'Yes, my love, I believe he intended you great harm.'

'My father, we must tell my father.'

'We shall be with him soon and after that, I will never leave you again.'

Anne stared into Randall's eyes and despite the horror of the past hour, a small shoot of hope burst into her heart.

25

SUFFOLK PLACE, LONDON, JULY 1537

'I have written to Sir Thomas Cromwell on your behalf. There's no reason why your husband should not continue to support you with your payments of £100 a year,' said the Duke of Suffolk as Anne fidgeted about the room.

'Edward sent me a note refusing,' she replied. 'He claimed his finances were stretched.'

'It's utter rubbish,' said the duke. 'I've spoken to Cromwell and he's assured me that Edward has a strong room bulging with money. In the past months he has benefitted from a number of properties that belonged to the Catholic church: Harnage Grange, Hatton Grange, Gofford Grange as well as properties all over Salop and Wales. He's a very wealthy man.'

'Why is he being so parsimonious then?'

'To upset you,' her father said. 'By the look of it, he's succeeding.'

'He's never forgiven me for taking legal action against him when he tried to have Randall and me accused of his murder,' she said.

'Well, my dear, it's his own fault. Randall was defending you, the first blows came from your husband. Edward shouldn't have tried to kill you, no matter the provocation and to attempt to do so in front of witnesses was a far greater mistake. How is Alice Ramkin?'

'Her nerves continue to worry her. She lives in the country with her sister and brother-in-law. I believe there's a suggestion she should wed but she's resistant. Edward and I were not a good example for the married state.'

'Are any of us?' He sighed. 'Annie, for goodness' sake, sit down. You're exhausting me with your wanderings.'

Anne slumped into the chair opposite him. In the year since her marriage had ended there had many acrimonious discussions between her father, Sir Thomas Cromwell, who was the Lord Privy Seal, and her husband concerning finances. What surprised Anne was her continuing welcome at court and the inclusion of herself and Randall in the social whirl. Edward, Lord Powis, was less evident in the higher echelons of society but two months earlier, at a gathering given by John Dudley, her husband had been present and on his arm was a pregnant Jane Orwell. When Anne overheard Jane requesting another guest refer to her as Lady Powis, Anne had laughed in her face, as had all those connected with the Brandons.

'Have you heard word about the child the Orwell girl is carrying?' asked the duke as Anne fanned herself in the summer heat.

'Why would I care?' she asked.

'Do you and Randall plan to have issue?'

'You know it's unlikely,' Anne snapped. 'Any babe has always slipped away from me before its time. It's what drove Edward and me apart.'

There was a pause as they both stared out over the ornate gardens of Suffolk Place. In the distance, Katherine, Duchess of Suffolk was walking with her mother, Maria, Baroness Willoughby de Eresby. The Baroness was in her late forties but was fit and healthy with a passion for plants.

'We move to Grimesthorpe Castle next week,' said the duke. 'It'll be our new base.'

'Has the king banished you from court?' asked Anne, but her tone was teasing.

'No, he's given me Tattershall Castle in Lincolnshire to use as a headquarters to improve the protection of the county. The king has asked me to make it a permanent position in order to ensure his presence is known in that part of the world. I will continue to visit court on a regular basis.'

'Is this anything to do with the Pilgrimage of Grace?'

The duke shuddered. The Pilgrimage of Grace had been a frightening time for the king when in October 1536, thousands of people in the north of England, led by Robert Aske, had marched in protest against Henry's reforms of the church. The pilgrims were unhappy that he had changed the country's religion from Catholicism, creating the Church of England, over which the monarch ruled supreme rather than following the Papal law of Rome.

The protestors believed if they were able to speak to the king, he would understand their grievances and be merciful. An uprising in Lincolnshire at the same time had seen ten thousand people march to and occupy Lincoln Cathedral. The king had sent Charles Brandon to disperse the hordes. By the time the duke arrived, most had gone but Henry punished the ringleaders of the rebellion cruelly.

Anne knew the subsequent slew of executions had caused

her father to have nightmares. The brutality with which the king insisted the men be punished was terrifying. In total 216 people had been executed including abbots, lords, knights, Lady Margaret Bulmer was burned at the stake and men from every village that had taken part in the uprising were hanged. Even Thomas Moigne, the MP for Lincoln, was hanged, drawn and quartered. Although the duke made no public comment against the king, Anne knew her father had been revolted by the carnage and she wondered whether his move away from Henry's increasing violence was perhaps being encouraged by the duke himself.

'The king feels it is prudent to flex his authority and now my son, young Henry, has recovered from smallpox and Katherine is over her ague, we intend to make our family home in the property left to her by her father. Her child will be born in September and she'd like to be settled by then.'

'Another child for you, Father, you're prolific,' Anne's voice was light but there was disapproval in her tone.

'I have another heir,' he agreed, 'but as I have already buried two sons, I understand the importance of fathering as many children as possible. My girls grow strong, my boys are weaker. Another son will ensure the continuation of the Brandon and Suffolk names.'

'It appears there will be a rush of children born in the early autumn – your child, Edward and Jane's child and, if the rumours are true – the king and queen are also anticipating a happy event.'

'Indeed, the child the queen is carrying has quickened which means all is well. The king is delighted. Queen Jane has a craving for quails and Henry has sent messengers far and wide to ensure a steady supply.'

Anne focused on the swaying branches of the oak tree on

the edge of the lawn, its bright green leaves ruffling in the soft summer breeze. Children everywhere, she thought. No matter where I go, the conversation is always about the birthing of heirs. Men are obsessed with the desire to pass on their names.

'Let's hope it's a boy this time because there can be no doubt the king and queen are legally married, his first two wives are both dead.'

The duke shot Anne a warning glance. Even in the privacy of Suffolk Place it was unwise to speak of either Anne Boleyn or Queen Katherine. Both their daughters, the princesses Mary and Elizabeth, had been declared illegitimate.

'Since the death of Henry Fitzroy a year ago, the king is even more desperate to have a son,' said Brandon, then he shifted in his seat, leaning forward, his fingers splayed wide on his desk. He stared at them as he spoke, avoiding Anne's gaze. 'This brings me to another development concerning the king and you.'

'The king and me?'

'Henry has requested that tomorrow evening I take you to Bishop Gardiner's house on the other side of the river to dine with him. Randall is not invited.'

'Why?' said Anne, but a sense of unease enveloped her. Bishop Gardiner's house was notorious for the group of prostitutes he maintained there, known as his geese. It was rumoured the king met his mistresses there when he wished to discreet.

'During her confinement, the queen will be unavailable for certain duties,' the duke said. 'It's imperative the king is entertained through this period and he has been asking about you. He's hinted that you've grown into a fine-looking woman and he enjoys watching you dance...'

The duke's voice ground to a strangled halt.

'Papa, no,' said Anne in horror.

'The king is my best friend; how do I deny him?'

'And I am you daughter,' she replied. 'You remind him I'm his niece by marriage.'

'There is no blood connection,' said the duke. 'The king has pointed this out to me on numerous occasions.'

Anne stared at her father. The words 'numerous occasions' struck her like a slap. For how long had the king and her father been planning to ensnare her?

'You must be mistaken, Papa,' she said.

'No,' he replied. 'There is no mistake. Henry is most insistent he would like to spend time with you, learn what makes you happy.'

Anne felt acid bile rise in her stomach. 'You would offer me up like a common whore to the king's bed while the queen is with child?' she said.

'He won't listen to reason, Annie.'

There were tears in Charles Brandon's eyes and he seemed to have aged a hundred years since the beginning of their conversation.

Shock brought Anne to her feet. Her father remained seated and she glared down at him, her hands balled into fists to stop them shaking.

'The king has known me since birth,' she said, her voice thick with disgust. 'When we dance, he insists I call him Uncle Henry. Will he want me to call him Uncle while he undresses me, pushes me onto to my back and forces my legs apart—'

'Anne, please, no,' her father cried, covering his eyes as though they were scorched by the image.

'You must refuse,' she said.

'He's the king...'

There was an angry silence, then Anne said, her words dripping with scorn, 'What has he offered you in return for my presence in his bed? What price will you receive for selling me like a prize mare? You're already a duke, how much grander a title do you wish to bear? Are you hoping "Uncle Henry" will make you king of your own kingdom? Perhaps crown you King of Ireland as he considered with his son, Fitzroy? Or are you reaching even higher? Are you placing me in this position in case the queen dies in childbed? Who would be better placed than you to suggest he marry me instead, make me queen, then you would be father-in-law to the king?'

'This is not of my doing,' said the duke, guilt and fury bringing him to his feet too so he towered over Anne. 'The king's been watching you for months. Why else do you think your and Randall's relationship has been tolerated? From the moment the queen believed she might be carrying the future king, Henry has been asking about you. Have you not noticed him singling you out? Dancing with you? Ensuring you and Randall are included in all the court activities? You are the one who has flaunted herself in his presence with a man who is not your husband. You have brought this upon yourself with your whorish ways.'

Anne felt the air leave her lungs as she struggled to catch her breath at his words. It had never occurred to her there might have been an ulterior motive to her inclusion in the lavishness of the court. In her naïvety she had assumed it was due to the king's love for her as a niece and in remembrance of her stepmother, the king's beloved sister. She had been wrong and worse, her father, the man she loved and admired most in the world, had colluded with the king and betrayed her in the worst possible way.

Father and daughter stared at each other, neither spoke but the tension between them deepened. They were courtiers to their fingertips and understood the strange dark underside of the glamorous world they inhabited. Was this how Mary and Anne Boleyn felt? thought Anne as she turned away, unable to look at her father any longer. The shocking realisation that as women we are no more worthy of consideration than a prize bitch who can improve the purity of the bloodline.

'Are there other women who have caught his eye?' Anne asked.

'Yes, there is always more than one,' replied the duke. 'There is a wench, not high-born, with whom the king has more than a passing fancy. She lives near Hampton Court. However, he wishes to have a lady in London, too. He will be generous and has offered you a suite of rooms near his, they are sumptuous.'

'And Randall?'

'He will be given an earldom but will be asked to leave court for the duration.'

Anne felt disgust as she glimpsed the look of relief on her father's face. It was clear that by asking these questions, discussing the terms of the king's twisted arrangement, he thought she was giving her consent.

'And if I refuse?'

'You would put us all in danger.'

Anne did not reply to this threat.

'Think of all we could gain,' her father continued.

'And what about how much I would lose?' she said. 'My self-respect, my status and possibly Randall, the man I love. I have already lost him once, when I married Edward at your command. Would you ask me to risk my heart again?'

'But, Annie, it's the king...'

'Then you must choose, Papa,' she said. 'Me or him.'

'You dare to question me?' asked the duke and his eyes narrowed, a shadow marring his handsome face.

'No, Papa, I ask you to protect me as you once promised you always would.'

'And if I choose the king.'

'You will never see me again.'

They stared at each other in shocked silence.

'Annie, at least discuss it with Randall,' the duke said.

And with his words, Anne knew she had lost. Her father had chosen the king and he would try to intimidate Randall into coercing her into the royal bedchamber. She shuddered; her husband, Edward, would have agreed to this plan in a heartbeat, leading her to the king himself but Randall loved her. He would be disgusted and as he had no desire to attain titles or land, his loyalties were to their relationship, their love, not the king and the court.

'Very well, Papa,' she said, a plan forming in her mind. 'I shall consult Randall.'

Charles Brandon smiled and the tension in his shoulders loosened. Anne stared at her father and for the first time she saw him not as her charming, smiling papa but the venal man who would do all he could to protect himself and his position. Anything and everyone was dispensable, she realised, including herself.

Anne hugged her father and gazed at his face, memorising it, knowing she would never see him again.

'Goodbye, Papa,' she said.

As Anne left Suffolk Place, her palfrey frisking with excitement, she gazed around bidding a silent goodbye to the bustling city that held her heart, then she dug her heels into horse's side, urging her forward. Anne's face was set and her eyes were clear with determination as she planned her next move. Her father's actions had destroyed her love for him, turning her emotions to ice and anger. The duke had once told her the tale of the Brandon's troubled rise to power, their violence, larceny and misconduct. Despite his fine clothes and his titles, her father was no different from his forebears, he was as ruthless and cruel.

'And so am I,' murmured Anne as she urged her horse onwards. 'The Brandon blood is dark with hidden crimes, with lies and treachery and as it flows through my heart, my vow is this: they will all pay.'

26

DEXTER'S PLACE, ST ISHMAELS, PEMBROKESHIRE, JULY, PRESENT DAY

Caroline swirled the vibrant Aperol spritz in its plastic wine glass, fishing out the slice of orange and sucking it as Flavia talked.

'We have to take this seriously,' her sister reiterated. 'The call for an investigation into Dexter's death is growing.'

'Why though?' said Caroline. 'We issued a statement saying he died at home after a short illness.'

'But one of his fans tried to find Dexter's death and birth certificates and drew a blank.'

'That doesn't prove anything,' said Caroline but her stomach clenched. 'Anyway, we both know why: Dexter wasn't his real name.'

'*We* know that and so does Blanche but this is being driven by someone in the shadows,' said Flavia. 'For some reason, they want to publicly humiliate you and they think suggesting you were responsible for your grandfather's death—'

'Our grandfather.'

'Whatever,' exclaimed Flavia and Caroline was surprised to hear real anger in her sister's voice. '*Our* grandfather, happy now? The rumours about you being a killer might have begun as a joke but both Blanche and I believe there is a more sinister motive behind the campaign.'

'Do you think it's Travis?' asked Caroline. 'Blanche is sure he's trying to scare me into handing over the flat. We're receiving daily letters from Salter Holdings each more threatening than the last.'

'He knows everything, Caro, he could cause a great deal of damage. But, in answer to your question: it's possible Travis is involved but he wouldn't be able to do this alone.'

'Tell me,' said Caroline and she gave Flavia her full attention.

If her sister was this concerned then Caroline realised there were true grounds for her fears. They had spent so long ignoring the trolls and the Internet nasties that the insults no longer bothered her. In the past, she and Flavia had made a game of it often reposting the more ludicrous insults online themselves to ridicule the crazed keyboard tappers but there was a seriousness on Flavia's face she had never seen before.

'Does Gideon know?'

'About what?'

'Dexter?'

'No,' said Caroline. 'Do you think it's him?'

'Of course not,' replied Flavia, 'but it could be Margot, possibly in conjunction with Travis.'

Caroline considered this suggestion before replying.

'A few questions,' she said and Flavia nodded. 'First, would Margot have the capability? Second, why would she care? And, finally, how would she and Travis have met and hatched their campaign?'

'Margot Bullington's nowhere near as helpless as her woe-is-me image suggests. If she doesn't have the technical skills, she has the wealth to pay for the necessary expertise.'

'But why?'

'Perhaps because of the picture of you and Gideon outside his shop which was posted online a few weeks ago,' said Flavia. 'It might be enough to give Margot motive.'

Caroline remembered her shock at seeing the image. It had been accompanied by a ghoulish feature speculating on the identity of the mystery red-haired woman cosying up to BAFTA award-winning producer and bookshop entrepreneur, Gideon Morris, days before his divorce to Margot Bullington had been announced. Gideon had told her to ignore it but for some reason the vitriolic piece had unnerved her. At least with the return to her natural hair and eye colour no one had recognised her as Caroline Harvey or linked her to Dexter Blake.

'The trolls have been suggesting Dexter's death was suspicious for a few months so why would a blurred online picture of Gideon Morris with a "mystery red-head" give her motive for a prolonged online attack on me via Dexter.'

'True,' said Flavia, 'but you pay me to be suspicious and to look for all possibilities in order to protect Dexter's image.'

'What can we do to find the perpetrators?'

'Blanche has asked the management company's legal team to look into it but they haven't come back to me yet,' said Flavia. 'I'm sorry to discuss it while we're supposed to be relaxing but I thought you should be aware the situation was becoming more serious.'

Caroline sipped her drink as her sister's warning hung in the air between them like a grey cloud marring the beautiful summer's day. They were lying on two loungers that Flavia's husband Steve had brought down to the private beach, helped by Jonah and Flavia's twin sons, Logan and Finn, earlier in the day. A large umbrella offered a sizeable patch of shade and to one side were several portable barbecues for later. A cool box full of drinks was behind them and her parents had insisted on visiting the nearby supermarket for supplies for the barbecue.

She gazed over to where the three cousins, separated in age by a year, were crabbing in one of the larger pools in the red-tinged rocks. The bright fishing nets waved like banners and the cove echoed with their shrieks of excitement, their joy was simple and infectious. Steve, as eager as the children, was grinning, his deep laugh rumbling, merging with the music of the waves and the calling of the gulls.

'Flav, I appreciate your warning and I shall be more aware in future but as we both know these are ridiculous claims. I'm confident they'll die down soon.'

Flavia rolled her eyes at Caroline's use of words. It had been deliberate. There was no case to answer although, she had to admit the idea fans were trawling the records for Dexter's birth certificate was disconcerting.

They'll never find it, she thought.

Comforted by this, she told herself to relax, to enjoy the sunshine and being with her son and her family. A shout came from the pathway to the beach and her mother, Linda, arrived with more towels, then to her surprise, she saw Ben Hastings carrying two large cool boxes, chatting with her father, Alan.

'Look who we met in the supermarket,' Alan called. '"A lost soul, a long way from home".' A quote from *Ether Heracles and the Tropic of Pisces.*

'Hope you don't mind me gate-crashing,' Ben said, dumping the cool boxes in the shade of the umbrella.

'Of course not,' said Caroline. 'You're practically family, Ben.'

In the flurry of her parents and Ben arriving, Caroline was able to move away from Flavia and her dire warnings. She knew her sister meant well but she did not understand why she was so stressed about this particular online bombardment. *We've survived worse rumours than this*, she thought as she wandered down to where the boys were clambering over the rocks, searching for more unsuspecting crabs.

'Mum, come and see how many we've caught,' shouted Jonah, beckoning her over.

'Poor things,' said Caroline, looking in the large bucket where the creatures swam and crawled around and over each other. 'Put them back soon, please, we don't want to hurt them.'

'Uncle Steve said we could have a few more minutes, then we have to release them.'

'Good boy,' she said but Jonah had scampered away, summoned by his cousins.

Caroline loved having him home, carefree and cheeky, having fun. It had been a busy school year for her son and she wanted his summer to be as relaxing as possible. He would be back on set for the *Ether Heracles* film in September but to her relief the remainder of the shoot would be in the UK.

* * *

'So, that's Jonah,' said a voice, and she started. Ben had approached on silent feet. He handed her a bottle of water.

'Gideon told you?' she asked.

'Yes, he needed to tell someone and—'

'You're his best friend,' she finished. 'Do you hate me for keeping Jonah a secret?'

'No,' said Ben. 'You must have had your reasons.'

'I did,' she replied, 'and much as I'd like to tell you, Gideon must be the first to hear them.'

'He'll be back next week,' said Ben.

'I know. We've spoken a few times.'

The night of the party had been an impossible place to talk about Jonah, especially as the whirl of publicity around the boy had been enormous. All Caroline had been able to explain to Gideon was the reason he used the stage name of Stoppard which had been his great-grandmother's surname.

'To protect his link to me and Dexter,' she had explained. 'It was all to keep Jonah safe.'

His chaperone, Wendy Philips, had sat with Jonah during the brief press conference rather than Caroline and since then Blanche's extensive management company had dealt with all interview requests. It had been decided not to reveal he was Dexter Blake's great-grandson yet. As soon as the press conference had finished, Gideon had been whisked away by Connie who was eager to take Maddie home once her professional commitments had been fulfilled, leaving no chance to discuss things further. Caroline had taken Jonah upstairs to the suite they were sharing.

Gideon had promised to call and true to his word, the next morning he had contacted her.

'Caro, I'm not angry,' had been his opening words. 'I know you well enough to understand there were reasons. From working out when he was conceived, I suspect my engagement to Margot might have been a problem.'

Caroline had been overwhelmed by his honesty.

'Yes, it didn't help,' she admitted.

'I wish you'd told me though,' he said with sadness. 'Things could have been so different. Please, Caro, give me a chance to explain. I owe you a huge apology leaving you in this position.'

Caroline had been stunned. She had expected fury, denial and many other emotions but not an apology.

'You know Gid,' said Ben drawing her back to the present. 'He always rings.'

'Yes,' she said, 'he does.'

The morning after their kiss at ten-to-midnight that fateful night Gideon had called and after a few awkward moments, they had realised to reveal their moment of passion would be hurtful to both Ben and Nadine. They had decided to keep it a secret. *The first*, thought Caroline, *of so many secrets, each making the next easier until I'm trapped into the silence of my lies.* Unable to speak the truth because to tug on one deceit and reveal it would cause the entire structure to collapse and then there would be hell to pay.

'How's the history research going?' asked Ben.

'It's very interesting,' she replied, relieved at the change of subject. 'The Marquess House archive has given me a huge amount to work with: household documents, letters, legal records. There's also a collection of letters, some of which are replies to reproductions published in the book Ten-to-Midnight sourced. The maps have been useful, too, they pointed me towards papers in the National Archive showing ownership of monasteries after the Dissolution. Lord Powis, Anne's husband, made a huge amount of money from the redistribution of property around then.'

Flavia had joined the boys and Caroline felt she could wander away to talk to Ben.

'The new information is quite widely spread but as I've been piecing it together, it's given me an incredibly different view of the Tudor court,' she said as they made their way back to the encampment of chairs, blankets, beach umbrellas and loungers. 'In one entry in her diary, Anne describes being present at a reading by the poet Thomas Wyatt. It's so vivid, if felt as though I was there beside her.'

'Wow,' said Ben, 'could I read it?'

'Of course,' said Caroline. 'Even more extraordinary was the audience, she name-checked Jane Seymour, the Duke of Norfolk and Sir Francis Bryan among others. Even more surprising, the married members of the audience, Anne included, were there with people other than their spouses.'

'Thomas Wyatt and his wife, Elizabeth Brooke, had a very troubled marriage,' said Ben. 'From what I can remember, Wyatt lived openly with his lover, Lady Elizabeth Darrell, and they had three sons. For a while he continued to support his estranged wife, too. His involvement in the scandal of Anne Boleyn's arrest brought things to a head between Elizabeth Brooke and Wyatt.'

'What happened?'

'He was arrested and the Brooke family was shocked. Wyatt was questioned, then released thanks to his close friendship with Thomas Cromwell. Historians have suggested he might have been a spy for Cromwell. After his release, Wyatt refused to support his wife and son, Thomas Wyatt the Younger. He insisted Elizabeth return to live with her brother, George Brooke, Baron Cobham. The Brooke family was appalled but when Wyatt was arrested for treason again in 1541, it was Elizabeth's connections that helped to clear his name. The family tried to effect a reconciliation but the couple refused.'

'You know a great deal,' said Caroline, impressed.

'It was part of my dissertation,' said Ben. 'In the end, Elizabeth Brooke lived with her lover, Edward Warner, of Polsteadhall in Norfolk. When Wyatt died in October 1542, they were married and went on to have three sons who all died in infancy. Although, for a while, it was rumoured the king was interested in making her wife number six after the death of Catherine Howard in February 1542.'

'It sounds as though Elizabeth Brooke had a lucky escape by

marrying Edward Warner. Henry married Katheryn Parr instead.'

'Warner did well at court, especially under the Protestant Edward VI but when he died and after Lady Jane Grey was deposed, he ended up on the wrong side. When the country rose to support Mary Tudor as the true queen, the country returned to Catholicism and Protestants like Warner were in danger.'

'Was this around the time of Wyatt's Rebellion?' said Caroline. 'I've never really connected it before but was that led by Elizabeth Brooke and Thomas Wyatt's son?'

'Yes, in early 1554, four men led a rebellion expressing concerns about Queen Mary's plans to marry the Catholic foreigner, King Philip II of Spain. They were Wyatt, Sir James Croft, Sir Peter Carew and Henry Grey, who by then was Duke of Suffolk, having inherited the title via his wife, Lady Frances Brandon.'

'She was Anne Brandon's half-sister,' said Caroline as her understanding of the family ties fell into place. 'Lady Frances and Sir Henry were the parents of Lady Jane Grey.'

'Yes,' confirmed Ben. 'Is that important?'

'I'm not sure,' said Caroline. 'Anne Brandon was Lady Jane Grey's aunt, so it must have been awful to watch her niece being sent to the block.'

'Part of the reason Lady Jane was executed was so she would no longer be a figurehead for rebellions such as Wyatt's.'

'What happened to the ringleaders?'

'Wyatt was hanged, Carew and Croft were eventually pardoned, Suffolk was beheaded,' said Ben. 'One of the other men involved was Edward Courtenay who had a claim to the throne through his grandfather, Edward IV. Mary's advisors thought he and the Princess Elizabeth intended to marry and challenge Mary for the crown, it was the reason Elizabeth was sent to the Tower of London. There was no evidence against them and both were eventually released. At first Elizabeth was kept under house arrest with Sir Henry Bedingfield but she had returned to court by the end of 1554. Courtenay was released from the Tower in 1555 but was exiled to Europe.'

'It must have been frightening,' said Caroline. 'To think Anne Brandon lived through all this and was related to a number of the key players. It's strange, there are lots of similarities between Anne Brandon and Elizabeth Brooke's stories.'

'In what way?' asked Ben.

'Anne and Elizabeth both struggled to have children, were in unhappy marriages and lived openly with their lovers and, it seems, their choices to do this were accepted by the rest of the nobility,' she said. 'There are the other echoes, too. Mary Tudor and Lady Jane Grey were second cousins, one queen executing another. An event which repeated itself in February 1587 when Mary Queen of Scots was executed on the orders of her second cousin, Queen Elizabeth I.'

'True, although some historians dispute Lady Jane was ever queen,' said Ben. 'What else has cropped up about Anne Brandon?'

As Caroline explained all she had read, her eyes continued to flicker to Jonah, checking he was safe and enjoying himself. A loud and enthusiastic game of beach cricket was being played as she finished telling Ben about Mary, Duchess of Suffolk's funeral and Edward's perfidy.

'I think she was better off without him,' said Caroline. 'He was a typical Tudor man, only interested in his wife until he has an heir, then when she has or he realises she can't provide an offspring, he's off elsewhere.'

'It's not only Tudor men,' Ben said sadly.

'What do you mean?'

'I'm not proud of it but that was the reason my marriage failed. We didn't have children,' he clarified, 'but I was so impressed with myself for actually finding someone who wanted to marry me, it went to my head and I had a string of affairs.'

'You said you'd been divorced twice,' said Caroline.

'Yes, from the same woman,' he said.

'Oh, Ben, no.'

'Remember when we split up...?'

'When you dumped me by text, you mean?' she said, but there was humour in her voice. Ben hung his head.

'I was such a coward,' he said.

'You were young, inexperienced and very bad at discussing your feelings.'

'That's kind of you to say,' he said, squeezing her hand, 'but it was a cowardly way to end our relationship.'

'It was years ago,' she said. 'We were kids, even if our raging hormones made every emotion seem desperately intense.' He gazed out to sea and she nudged him. 'You were saying, remember when we split up...'

'Paige and I had met the previous week,' he said. 'She was a friend of a friend and it was like being hit by a thunderbolt. Our relationship was extreme, fiery, passionate and we married three weeks after graduation. We divorced a year later.'

'Ouch.'

'It was my own fault for sleeping with one of her friends,' he said. 'We didn't see each other for five years, then bumped into each other at a mutual friend's wedding. The fireworks began again and we decided to give it another try. This time, rather than an impetuous register office marriage with two mates as witnesses, we did it properly. Gideon was best man, it was in a hotel by the river in Windsor and we were convinced it was forever.'

'What happened?'

'We survived for four years then we realised it was over,' he said. 'There was no particular reason, it was a hundred little things. We discussed it, even had counselling but in the end, we separated and were divorced for a second time.'

'Ben, that's so sad,' she said. 'Has there been anyone since?'

'A few dates from Internet sites but that feels soul destroying. For the past few years I've thrown myself into work and the bookshops,' he said. 'How about you?'

'I met Travis at a Comicon I was attending on behalf of Gramps in the early days of the *Ether* books,' she said. 'We began talking and it evolved from there. It was devastating when he left because he'd been there for me during the tough times when Jonah was a baby. Jonah always knew Travis wasn't his biological father but he was a huge part of our lives.'

'Were they close?'

'Not especially,' said Caroline. 'From a very young age, Jonah loved performing which Travis couldn't understand. He thought it was a bit effeminate and would try to "toughen" him up by taking Jonah to football and rugby matches. Jonah loves those too but ever since he was in a Nativity play in Year Two being on stage had stolen his heart. He was Joseph and he excelled. He asked to go to drama classes and there was a scheme running at The Torch, the local theatre in Milford Haven. During one of their shows he was talent spotted for an advert for a breakfast cereal. After that, he asked if he could go to stage school.'

'What did you say?'

'Travis and I discussed it. Gramps's fame was increasing and it was impacting on our lives, so we thought it might be better for Jonah to be elsewhere. You see the school he most wanted to attend – Baddeley Manor – was a boarding school.'

'I've heard of that, it's supposed to be very prestigious and difficult to win a place,' said Ben.

'Jonah was offered an audition on the strength of his advert and after they saw him perform he was given an unconditional place. He's been having a whale of a time ever since. When the part of Young Ether came up, the school put him forward for it under his stage name, Jonah Stoppard. No one in the production team had any idea of his connection to me or Dexter. Jonah won the part fair and square.'

'You must be very proud.'

'Words can't describe it,' she said. 'He acts because he loves it and if that ever stops, he can too. The decision will always remain with Jonah.'

'Were you pregnant with him when you met Travis?' asked Ben.

'Yes and Gid had announced his engagement to Margot,' she said. 'It's odd because I emailed Gideon telling him I had to speak to him urgently and, as we both know, he always replies but he ignored my messages.'

'Are you sure he received them?'

'They didn't bounce back, so they must have arrived.'

'It doesn't mean he read them, they could have been deleted.'

'By whom?'

'Margot.'

'I know you don't like her, Ben, but would she be so manipulative.'

Ben turned his kind, familiar face towards her and she was surprised to see the fury in his eyes.

'You have no idea what Margot Bullington is capable of,' he

said. 'It's Gid's story to tell but if he'd seen your message, he would have contacted you. He's been in love with you since we were teenagers, there's no way he would have abandoned you or your child.'

There was a call of 'Hello' from the path and Caroline turned to see Eve, Robbie, Mark Llewellyn and his wife, Stephanie, walking across the sand.

'Let him explain,' said Ben. 'He deserves a chance to put this right.'

Then they were surrounded by newcomers and Caroline had no choice but to smile and welcome them even though her heart was screaming for answers and her hands were shaking in shock.

27

'Hi, Caro, we bumped into Mark and Steph by the house. We didn't think you'd mind them joining us,' said Eve as she hugged Caroline.

'Everyone's welcome,' she replied. 'Mum and Dad have brought enough food and drink for at least thirty people.'

'We didn't intend to intrude on a family party,' said Mark, looking over at the game of cricket.

'Mark, you and Stephanie are very welcome. It's lovely to be able to share Dexter's Place with everyone at last. Gramps was unbelievably shy, which led to a great deal of his reclusiveness. It's a shame he missed out on so much love and fun.'

'This beach is extraordinary,' said Mark. 'I had no idea it was here.'

'It's my hidden piece of heaven,' Caroline replied.

'Well, thank you,' said Mark, then he grinned. 'And, we've found another interesting document concerning Anne Brandon, which will fascinate you.'

'He also wanted to visit because he's finished the final *Ether Heracles* book and wanted to discuss it with you, in depth,' said

Stephanie, amusement in her Canadian drawl apparent as she hugged Caroline.

'The ending was perfect, wasn't it?' said Ben as he introduced himself.

'Have you read it?' Caroline asked Ben in surprise. 'You didn't say.'

'Of course, I've read it, I told you, I've read them all. I had to know how it ended,' said Ben. 'The difference between Gid and me is that I'm not obsessed. He practically knows them off by heart. My favourite is *Ether Heracles and The Lake of Tawaret*. I love the scene when Despard the Pig-Lizard eats the scout from Soutus Major—'

'When they're in the Drylands,' interrupted Mark in excitement. 'Despard grabs the scout and—'

'—Eats him alive, from his feet first; like a Jelly Baby,' they finished together, laughing in mutual fandom.

'The stories are sensational,' said Mark, 'and *Ishtar's Legacy* is the best in the series.'

'It's a relief to know you enjoyed it,' said Caroline. 'We were concerned about whether the fans would like the ending.'

'The final chapters were everything I'd hoped for and more,' continued Mark. 'Dexter was true to each of the characters, all the loose ends were resolved and the secrets were revealed. I plan to read the entire series again from the beginning in order to enjoy the flawless storytelling.'

'You'll have to meet Gideon,' said Ben. 'He, Caro and I were at college together and Gideon has always felt he knows the characters, as though they're old friends.'

A huge cheer erupted from the game of beach cricket and the three youngsters ran across the sand their arms outstretched like aeroplanes.

'I think they've won,' said Caroline, relieved to turn away from Mark and Ben's enthusiasm.

She had not expected to struggle with the concept that the series was over, the secrets were told and she would never again discuss Ether and his antics with Dexter. Yet, whenever she was confronted with an eager comment the reality of the ending bit at her heart a little harder.

As Flavia and Steve linked hands, rounded up the boys and waited while Alan gathered the jumpers they had used as stumps, Caroline watched her family wandering towards her. Under the large umbrella, Linda was pulling iced drinks from one of the cool boxes, while Robbie was checking the food in the other.

'Caro, would you like me to start the barbecue?' he called.

'Yes please, if you don't mind.'

'You know Robbie,' laughed Eve, as she accepted the drink Ben offered, 'he can't bear to watch anyone else cooking. He's such a control freak.'

The words were said with love and Robbie waved back in agreement.

'Jonah, come here and put on dry clothes,' Caroline called, holding up a towel for him to change behind.

With minimal grumbling, Jonah changed out of his wet swimming trunks and T-shirt. It felt good to have her son home, to be able to look after him and be a mum. They spent months apart and they both enjoyed these interludes together. It was another reason why Caro had shifted her base to Los Angeles, to be nearby while Jonah filmed the secret sections for the new film. The break-up with Travis had cemented her decision to follow her son but she had always known it would be for a limited period because of Dexter.

'Mum, can I go and play Top Trumps with Logan and Finn?' he asked as he wriggled his head through a dry T-shirt.

'Yes, of course,' she replied. 'Do you mind if I stay here and talk to my friends?'

Jonah grinned. 'As long as you don't get overexcited and have a funny turn. You can't be too careful at your age.'

'Cheeky little—' she began as he ran off hooting with laughter.

'Are you sure we're not intruding?' said Stephanie, as Caroline handed her a glass of wine.

'You're definitely not,' Caroline replied.

'Your grandfather's reclusiveness must have had an impact on you,' said Stephanie.

'We found a way to make it work,' she replied.

'I didn't know you had a son. He's never been mentioned in any of Dexter's publicity.'

'No, he hasn't and I'm trusting you and Mark will be discreet enough to keep his identity secret. He was born about the time the books became famous and neither Dexter nor I wanted his life to be overpowered by them.'

'What about Jonah's father?'

Caroline sipped her drink, allowing herself time, but before she replied. Stephanie placed her hand on Caroline's arm in apology.

'I'm sorry, it's none of my business,' Stephanie said. 'It was a surprise, that's all, but yours and Jonah's secret is safe with Mark and me.'

'Thank you,' she said and was relieved when Eve arrived and began chatting to Stephanie.

* * *

The hustle and bustle of family life hummed around her. Ben joined Eve and Stephanie and began to chat to Stephanie about Canada, Linda hovered around Robbie beside the barbecue, Alan fell asleep with a book over his face, Flavia and Steve circulated, keeping an eye on the boys who had set up their own encampment a few metres away in the arms of two extending rocks which formed a miniature cove. Caroline was checking everyone had all they needed when Mark appeared at her side.

'Would this be a good time to show you the new document we discovered at Marquess House?' he asked.

'Yes, I'd love to see it,' Caroline said, as they settled on two deck chairs in the shade.

Mark opened an image on his phone and passed it to Caroline.

'We found a land document signed by the Duke of Suffolk and countersigned by Anne, Lady Powis, dated 1536. It was drawn up by a lawyer called John Beaumont.'

'Where did you find it?' asked Caroline widening the document so she could read it.

'It had been mis-filed with paperwork concerning another plot of land on the Marquess House estate that was sold in the 1840s,' he said, waving his arm in an arc to include the beach. 'Jenny Procter, our chief librarian, found it by chance when she was searching for details for another piece of research.'

'What a great find,' said Caroline.

'You'd be surprised how often this happens, documents appearing in unexpected places,' said Mark. 'There are so many papers in archives around the world, it's impossible to know all the secrets of the past.'

'What's so special about this one?' asked Caroline.

'At the bottom, there's a seal stating this deed was cancelled, which is suspicious enough, but what's so interesting is on the reverse.'

Mark leaned over and flicked to the next image on his phone. Caroline stared at the list of signatures, each with a slight difference, before handing the device back.

'Why has the Duke of Suffolk signed his name on the reverse twelve times?' she said.

'We don't think it was the Duke of Suffolk,' said Mark. 'The Marquess House team is convinced these are forgeries; somebody was practising the duke's signature.'

'Do you think it was John Beaumont?'

'It's possible and we wonder if this is the reason the document was cancelled,' continued Mark. 'The signatures on it are fake.'

'Anne Brandon's too?'

'Perhaps.'

'John Beaumont and Anne Brandon were friends,' said Caroline.

'Were they?'

'Yes, his name appears in her journals. She was close to John's wife, Isabelle and Anne Brandon's husband, Lord Powis, often worked with John on legal issues, particularly those connected to land.'

'Interesting,' said Mark. 'From the research we've done, Beaumont was a protégé of Thomas Cromwell who was the mastermind behind the dissolution.'

'Anne's husband was at the front of the queue for land,' said Caroline. 'I found a document online listing at least thirty properties which were granted to him.'

'We're going to keep searching to see what else might be hiding in plain sight,' said Mark. 'Anne Brandon has intrigued us all, especially since we've discovered her local connection.'

'Do you have any evidence she lived in the old manor house that was here?'

'Not yet, but we'll keep looking.'

28

HANWORTH MANOR, PEMBROKESHIRE, AUGUST 1545

Anne stared at the letter bearing the neat, childish handwriting of her younger half-sister, Lady Frances Grey, Marchioness of Dorset. It carried news she had been dreading. Her father was dead. Her ten-year-old half-brother, Henry Brandon, had inherited their father's title and was the second Duke of Suffolk.

I am the only one left, she thought. *My mother, my sister and now, Papa. All gone. Dead.*

She knew members of her extended family were alive but her core family, her parents, her full sister, the Brandon family as they had been, albeit briefly, was no more. Even her second family was depleted. Her two half-brothers, the sons of Mary Tudor, who could have claimed the throne of England, were dead. The only people who remained were her half-sisters, Frances and Eleanor, daughters of Princess Mary, and her two young half-brothers, the product of her father's marriage to Katherine Willoughby.

The hot sun beat through the diamond-paned windows but Anne did not see the perfect periwinkle blue sky, her eyes were full of tears. It was many years since she and her father had spoken, the rift between them had never healed but as time passed and her anger abated, she realised she had still loved him. He was her father, he was weak but he was her one remaining parent. Now, he was gone.

She crumpled the parchment in her fist, wiping away her tears with her free hand. A shout of laughter from her family, who were enjoying the hot weather made her smile. She was not yet ready to share her sad news, instead, she slipped the crinkled letter into her pocket and made her way along the corridor to a passage leading to the servants' exit into the courtyard.

Hanworth Manor was magnificent in the sunshine. Anne Boleyn had been true to her word and had arranged for a vast tract from her holdings in Pembrokeshire to be sold to Randall all those years ago. The property that was at first named Powis House in Anne Brandon's honour was hastily renamed Hanworth Manor when they had fled to the safety of its thick walls. Its roots as an ecclesiastic dwelling were evident in the elegance of the buildings but today Anne took no pleasure in its beauty.

Randall had mixed old and new to create a stunning home. The cloisters and part of the church had been incorporated within the house while the remainder had been remodelled and extended to spread over three grand floors. The local grey stones, dressed with slate, shimmered on rainy days but when the sunlight played across them as today, they took on an ethereal hue. The sun's rays brushed the whispers of quartz within the walls creating bursts of natural sparkle.

Built in a U-shape, two wings enclosed a bustling courtyard housing the stables and the kitchens, while to the front, Hanworth House boasted magnificent carvings of mythical beasts and the Brandon coat of arms. The glittering diamond-paned windows overlooked a vast formal garden which flowed as far as the eye could see, with the woods away to the west, where a path led to a sheltered cove. It was towards here Anne headed, swift feet carrying her to her favourite part of the grounds: the oak grove in the woods with the comfort of its magical gold and green light.

The trees, young and virile, towered above her, the leaves snapping in the breeze from the ocean. Two oaks stood near each other, Anne thought of them as the lovers, kissing. The taller of the two grew with branches open wide and in the space between nestled a smaller, slender companion. Whenever Anne saw them, she was reminded of the tale of *Tristan and Iseult* and wondered whether there were graves below the trees.

Death again, she thought. *Perhaps Randall and I should request to be buried here below the loving trees. Our love has survived, despite the vagaries of life.*

To one side of the grove there was a stump, newly cut after a storm had split the tree, making it dangerous. Anne sat, allowing the tranquil light and rustling breeze to soothe her heart even as a single tear tracked its way down her cheek. It was not her way to be melancholic but this was a milestone in her life and for the first time in years she mourned the fracture that had severed the relationship with her father.

The day he had suggested she replace the queen in King Henry's bed had changed everything. For the first time, Anne had realised the full strength of his ambition, understanding at last that no one was exempt from his plotting and scheming. Why she had ever thought she was different she had not known; the duke had always put himself first no matter the situation.

Upon her return home, she had informed Randall of the conversation and such was his consternation he had issued instructions for small trunks to be packed in haste. Later the same evening, the tide had changed in their favour allowing herself, Randall and a small group of loyal retainers to board a ship and head inland on the River Thames. They had sailed on one of the well-worn trade routes, traversing the waterways of England until they had arrived in Bristol a week later.

From here, Randall had chartered a boat, carrying them along the Welsh coast to the ancient walled town of Tenby in West Wales where a carriage had awaited to take them to St Ishmaels.

It was not long before a letter arrived from her sister, Mary, describing the duke's rage when he realised Anne had outwitted him and fled.

> *...Papa is angrier than I have ever seen him. He shouts of your perfidy and ungratefulness. He has threatened to send the Yeoman guards to bring you back by force. Our step-mama tries to calm him but he claims he shall disinherit you and give the Warwickshire lands intended for you to Frances instead...*

When Anne had shown the letter to Randall, he had pulled her into the safety of his arms and murmured into her hair, 'We don't need your father's money or his land. We're together and we're very far away. If the guards come, I shall protect you.'

The threat had been empty. No mounted force had arrived to drag Anne into the king's bed. Instead, three months later she heard her stepmother had delivered the second son her father had craved, Charles Brandon, named for his father. A few weeks later, Queen Jane gave birth to Prince Edward but this was followed by the sad news announcing her death, twelve days afterwards. The news which upset her most, however, was sent again by her sister. It was to warn Anne that her husband, Lord

Powis, was a father; Jane Orwell had delivered a healthy son. Mary stated that Edward was seeking legal counsel as he battled to ensure his son could inherit the Powis title despite being illegitimate.

Anne had not realised how much this would upset her but she had taken to her bed for a week after the news, devastated that Jane Orwell had succeeded where she had failed by providing an heir to the Powis estate. Over and over again she relived her multiple miscarriages, wondering why she had been punished so cruelly. Eventually, Randall had crept into bed beside her and told her about a distant cousin who had recently had a baby girl. The mother had died in childbirth and the child's father, Randall's cousin, Hugh, a month later from smallpox.

'She needs a home,' he had whispered. 'She needs a mother and you need a child.'

The little girl had arrived two weeks later and with the help of John Beaumont, Anne and Randall had legally adopted her, calling her Elinor, after Anne's great-great grandmother, Alianore Mautby.

'We'll use the modern spelling of the name,' Anne had declared.

As the years passed, they adopted two more children, a boy, John, and another girl, Ursula, from different distant branches of their families. Each morning as Anne awoke, she revelled in her new-found happiness.

Far away in London, events took a darker turn and whenever Randall returned from a visit, he assured Anne their decision to move to their remote home in St Ishmaels had been wise. In 1540, King Henry had married again, the foreign princess, Anne of Cleves, but this match was short-lived and when the next news arrived from London, Henry had divorced Anne to marry the youthful Catherine Howard. Anne could not help but wonder if the king's choice of bride was inspired by her father and his marriage to Katherine Willoughby when she had been just fourteen years old.

Two years later, Catherine was beheaded and Anne was reminded horribly of the events of 1536 when Anne Boleyn, a cousin to Catherine Howard, had also been executed. Two women from the same family, both married then destroyed by the king. Once again Anne gave thanks for her lucky escape. The king did not stay a widower for long and in 1543 he married Katheryn Parr, Lady Latimer. Anne heard from her stepmother that the court hoped she would be the king's final bride.

* * *

Anne looked down at the scrunched parchment in her hand and smoothed it out. In the house, she had read the first lines announcing the death of the duke but no more. In the ethereal grove, her heart aching, she returned to Frances's words. Details of the lavish funeral the king planned for his best friend spilled across the page: a grave in St George's Chapel at Windsor Castle, a vast procession of the nobility and a funeral service delivered by Stephen Gardiner, Bishop of Winchester and Henry Holbeach, Bishop of Rochester. Anne gave a sad smile, all this pomp despite the fact her father had long ago requested a quiet service followed by a burial in the chapel at Tattershall Castle.

'Oh, Papa,' she sighed into the green air of the grove, 'did you think as the king's former brother-in-law and his life-long friend and ally you would be allowed to languish in Lincolnshire?'

Anne returned to the letter but as she read further, her mood shifted. The words became bunched up and difficult to read as though they had been written in a rush, she could almost hear Frances's sanctimonious tone.

> *...Stepmama often spoke to Father, asking him to change his will but he was stubborn. We had hoped that he might have made alterations without our knowledge but, alas, Annie, his lawyers have assured us your name does not appear. We are sorry to inform you that the land in Warwickshire has instead been bequeathed to me and my husband. Henry is in negotiations with Lord Powis who would like to buy it...*

The letter ended with Frances giving Anne news of her nieces, the Grey sisters, who, according to their mother, were perfect in every way, even the new baby, Lady Mary Grey, rarely cried: Frances had always been competitive. However, her final line was a shock.

> *We have often wondered if the reason Papa never forgave you was because of the family you have had with Randall. You have always claimed your children are adopted but I suggested to Father they were naturally yours and the reason you never had any offspring with Lord Powis was because you wished to punish Father for making you marry Edward rather than Randall...*

Anne stared at this strange comment in bemusement. What was Frances suggesting? Was she hinting that Anne was capable of deliberately losing all the children during her marriage? Bile burned in her throat at having such an accusation thrown at her. Although she and Frances had never been close, Anne had believed their relationship to have been that of natural sisters but this comment made her unsure.

'You dare accuse me,' Anne said aloud, 'when you've just informed me that you and your husband have stolen my land.'

She and Randall did not need the wealth from the Warwickshire holdings but she remembered her father telling her they had once been Browne lands, given to her mother as part of her dower. Why had he left them to Frances and not Mary's husband? she wondered. Would this not have at least kept them in the Browne family line for Mary's children to inherit?

The answer floated into her mind: Mary's husband was not to be trusted with money matters. The duke had spent years bailing out Lord Monteagle due to the mismanagement of his finances. Yet to pass them to her younger sister who had no emotional link to the property was cruel, especially as Frances planned to sell them to Anne's estranged husband. It was a deliberate snub, a clear message Frances believed Edward's lies and posturing rather than Anne's account of the violence of the Powis marriage.

This cannot be allowed to happen, Anne thought, and as she closed her eyes, the gentle light of the grove flickered around her. Gossamer strands floated in the ether, silver whispers, wicked ideas all leading to a delicious revenge on both the father who had cut her from his life and the half-sister who challenged her version of the truth.

'The land is Warwickshire was promised to me,' she murmured, a slow smile spreading across her face, 'and I shall take what is rightfully mine.'

29

HANWORTH MANOR, PEMBROKESHIRE, DECEMBER 1545

'This is the paperwork bearing my late father's signature,' said Anne, passing the heavy scroll to John Beaumont. 'It's a document claiming a prior arrangement to transfer the ownership of the Warwickshire land to me. He promised me this settlement on the day he informed me of my betrothal to Lord Powis. If what you say is correct, this document predates his current will.'

John pulled the document towards him and studied it with care. His legal career was booming, he was now a double reader – duplex lector – at the Inner Temple and was soon to be appointed recorder of Leicester. He was also tipped to succeed Sir Robert Southwell as Master of the Rolls, a highly prestigious and powerful position.

Anne glanced over at Randall who was sitting opposite her at the wide desk. He shifted uncomfortably and refused to meet her eye.

'Signed?' Randall asked.

'Yes, if you'd like to see...'

Beaumont pushed the parchment towards Randall who studied the signature.

'Which of you forged the duke's signature?' Randall asked after a long silence. Anne tried to look affronted but a naughty grin ruined her attempt.

'As far as the world is concerned, neither of us,' she said, plucking the scroll away from Randall and returning it to John. 'The plan is simple. John presents this to the Duchess of Suffolk stating Papa left it in his charge shortly before his death. John will explain it's a legally binding document and, despite Papa being unable to change his will in time, this declaration is enough to ensure the land is signed over to me. Once we have ownership, I shall sell the land to John, therefore putting it beyond the reach of my half-siblings and, if he were foolish enough to challenge me for it, my husband, Lord Powis. When the furore has abated, John will sell or lease the land back to us, whichever is the safest way to ensure it remains in our ownership.'

As she spoke, Randall turned to look out of the window. He was watching their two eldest children playing in the sunshine with their nurses nearby. Other people might think this gesture was dismissive but Anne knew him as well as she knew herself and understood he was thinking hard; considering her comments, understanding her passion. His concerns would be for her and their family and the impact becoming involved in a shady business deal might have on the day-to-day life of Hanworth Manor.

She wondered: if he forbade her to continue, would she do as he asked? It was a question she had not yet been forced to confront but perhaps this was about to change. It was possible he did not understand her desire to own the Warwickshire lands was not simply born from the need for revenge on her father or to redress the balance of the spite of her half-sister.

Randall returned his gaze to her and said in a placatory

tone, 'Anne, there is no financial reason to claim this land or the money from the sale. We have wealth beyond anything we could spend in several generations. As for you, John, I'm surprised you'd be willing to risk everything you've achieved in your career to become involved in a case of champerty with Annie.'

'It isn't about the money,' said Anne, her tone matching his: low, calm, reasonable. 'It's to stop either my brother-in-law, Henry Grey, or my husband, Edward, receiving lands that were brought to my father's estate when he married my mother. These are Browne holdings and should belong to either myself or my sister Mary's family.'

'But your father changed his mind when you and he fell out —' began Randall.

'Have you forgotten what Edward did?' Anne interrupted, her voice rising. 'He tried to behead me in my own bedroom.'

'I remember,' replied Randall. 'It was me who saved you and the horror of his actions remain with me. Edward is a terrible person but you're free from him, Annie. We're happy, we have our family and a wonderful life. Don't ruin it all because of a misplaced desire for revenge.'

'Misplaced?' said Anne, her eyes shadowed with hurt. 'The scars of such attacks never fully heal, no matter how great the passage of time. Ask any woman who has been brutalised, humiliated or who lives in fear of her life. While we might continue with our everyday lives, we may laugh again, the haunting shadow of the violence never leaves us and it will resurface when we least expect it.

'This claim is for every woman who has been passed over in a will, whose dower has been halted by avaricious relatives or a bride whose inheritance has been stolen by a cruel husband. For any woman who has been forced to beg for money and lands that should have been hers by right of birth. The only time a woman has autonomy is if they are widowed but even then, male relatives try to force them into loveless marriages for money. The Warwickshire lands were my mother's dowry and for her sake, I want to protect them.'

Anne waited, watching as Randall resumed his staring out of the window. They were in the large wood-panelled room he used as an office. Shelves held leather-bound books of law, astronomy and a myriad other subjects. Anne felt it was the appropriate place for this discussion rather than her own more feminine solar with its intricately carved walls and delicate furniture. Randall knew she was not motivated by money, he understood this was a point of principle. The silence grew until eventually Randall turned to face her. His expression was benign and his eyes were full of love. Anne felt her heart leap as it had the first time she had seen him all those years ago.

'Very well, Annie,' he said taking her hands in his, 'if this is what you must do, then you have my full support. You're correct, these men who were supposed to love and protect you and all the other women you speak for, have failed in their basic task as gentlemen or caring husbands and parents. I understand why this is important but please heed my words of caution: you will be taking on two powerful nobles – your brother-in-law is a marquess and your estranged husband is a baron. I implore you to keep yourself safe and step away from this scheme if necessary. Do you promise you will drop this case if there is potential for harm to you or our children?'

Anne stared into his beloved face.

'Yes,' she said, hugging him. 'I promise to halt proceedings if danger arises. Thank you, my love, for trusting me.'

'I shall leave you and John to your discussions.'

Anne released him. Randall ran his finger down her cheek, then with a nod towards John Beaumont, he left the room. As the door clicked shut behind him, Anne sat beside John and smoothed out the stack of parchment he handed her.

'Sign your father's name at the bottom of each one,' John said, 'and I'll write the required legal documents as they are necessary.'

Anne dipped her quill in the inkwell and having blotted away any excess on a scrap of cloth, she focused on the faint line John had marked at the foot of each page. She took a deep breath and signed with a flourish. For years she had practised writing her father's signature. It had begun as a game when she and Mary were younger. He was newly created the Duke of Suffolk and he would sit between them, encouraging, laughing, correcting their attempts as they signed his name.

'Why, Papa?' Mary had once giggled as he challenged her to copy Thomas Cromwell's signature which she did with ease.

'The king has people who use a dry seal to sign his official documents when he's absent or too busy to be bothered with the tedium of running the court. I enjoy the idea of my daughters being able to sign my name in case I am ever otherwise engaged.'

The three of them had found it hilarious and it had been a tiny piece of life which was simply theirs, the Browne daughters, nothing to do with the extended line of royal Brandons. When Anne had married Edward, his rather childish signature had been easy to replicate and she had often signed it to pay bills or order goods when her husband was absent from Powis Castle. He had never questioned her running of the household and she had never told him her secret.

'Why are you doing this, John?' Anne asked as she signed the final page. 'You and Edward were such good friends; why would you help me to humiliate him and Henry Grey?'

John inspected her work and gave a satisfied nod.

'I also believed Edward was my friend,' he said, 'but when Isabelle died in childbirth, I turned to him for comfort and he dismissed me. He laughed at my grief and insisted I was better off without her. It hurt, Annie. Isabelle was my heart, my soul and to lose her and our child almost broke me.'

'Oh, John,' she murmured and squeezed his arm in a sympathetic gesture.

'When I married Elizabeth, Edward insisted she would prove to be a better wife, a woman who would provide heirs. He confided that he felt his life would be improved if he could marry Jane Orwell. He made many disturbing comments and I was concerned for your safety. When I heard what he attempted after the death of Queen Anne, my friendship with Edward became superficial.'

'But you helped him to acquire all the monastery lands,' said Anne in surprise. 'Randall showed me the list, there were dozens of properties.'

'The decision to pass those to Lord Powis were not mine but Lord Cromwell's,' said John. 'As Cromwell's student, I was encouraged to learn how to supervise the land transfers. My involvement was to ensure the correct paperwork and legal documents had been completed. It's interesting what one discovers as one advances. Not all the lands and properties are his in their entirety, many are leased and will eventually return to the crown but Powis is too arrogant to read the small print and realise his fortune is not as secure as he hopes. Ever since he was able to purchase the missing half of his castle from John Dudley, Powis has behaved as though he is king of his own realm. His comeuppance is due and our plan will help him on his way.'

Anne stared at Beaumont. His face was serious and there was bitterness in his eyes. Edward had made many enemies over the years and she wondered who else might try to avenge themselves.

'This world is one of illusions and lies,' she said. 'All these years I believed you and Edward were best friends yet it was nothing but fairy fire on the water, a flash of light, nothing substantial. Is there anything at court that is real?'

'There are a few things,' replied John. 'Your love for Randall and his for you has always been extraordinary. It was the reason your father didn't object to your friendship, even before your marriage to Edward broke down. The duke had seen other couples fall apart and the women treated with great cruelty when they did not deserve it—'

'Lizzie Brooke or Wyatt to use her married name,' interrupted Anne.

'Yes, there was Elizabeth Stafford, the Duchess of Norfolk, too. Thomas Howard, the Duke of Norfolk, flaunted his mistress, Lady Elizabeth Holland, whenever the opportunity arose. There were dozens of others but your father always thought you behaved with subtlety and honour. It was why he insisted Cromwell help you after Edward's attempt on your life and this is the reason I have agreed to help you too. You and your father may have been estranged but I'm confident the Duke always loved and respected you; I believe he would enjoy this scheme of yours. In fact, I wonder if it's what he intended all along.'

'Do you have knowledge I do not?' Anne asked, curious at his comment.

'Nothing in writing but the Duke loved to bend the rules and I think this would have amused him.'

'What would you think if I suggested another scheme?' said Anne, and John raised his eyebrows questioningly.

'Another land conspiracy?'

'Small ones designed to cause niggling problems rather than huge issues. Irritating snags with unexplained paperwork that nevertheless yield high financial rewards for us.'

'What did you have in mind?'

Excitement bubbled up in Anne. This was an idea she had long been considering. It was petty, she knew, but it was subtle enough for them to become the thorn in the side of men she believed should be punished.

'This is a list of the men who tried Anne Boleyn,' she said. 'They were chosen by the king and had been ordered to pronounce her guilty. Each of them was culpable in her death, an event which led to Edward thinking it was in his authority to do the same to me. How many other women have suffered behind closed doors since the king set a precedent on the removal of wives? My suggestion is to study their estates, then present them with documents stating they don't actually own certain sections, thus forcing them to buy them back from the anonymous plaintiff.'

'You want us to create documents to force people to buy land they already own?' clarified John. Anne nodded and John burst out laughing. 'It's a brilliant idea, Annie. Let me give it some thought as to how we can carry it out.'

His eyes travelled down the list again, this time with a professional interest.

'Your husband and your brother-in-law, Thomas Stanley, are on here,' said John.

'We'll leave Tommy for now,' she said. 'He has enough money troubles since my father died and is no longer able to bail him out. As for Edward, he can wait until we deny him the Warwickshire lands.'

A week later, John Beaumont left Hanworth Manor.

'The journey from here to my home Grace Dieu in Leicestershire is a long one,' he said to Anne and Randall as his belongings were loaded onto a wagon and his staff prepared the horses. 'It will be several months before I arrive in London but this is probably for the best because your half-sister and her husband will believe there are no challenges to the land. When I produce this document, claiming it has been in my possession for many years and can prove you already legally own the land, we shall be in a strong position to halt any claim they might attempt.'

'And if they are suspicious?'

'I'm a chancery judge, Annie. I can wield my power to ensure we are above suspicion.'

He shook Randall's hand, then gave a bow to Anne.

'Goodbye, Lady Powis. I shall write as soon as there is news but it could be many months before we are able to move this challenge to the court. Even if silence lies between us, don't fret, we shall succeed.'

30

DEXTER'S PLACE, ST ISHMAELS, PEMBROKESHIRE, AUGUST, PRESENT DAY

Caroline flicked on the kettle, her mind on Anne Brandon's scheme. The words written centuries ago had sent a rush of conflicting emotions through her. A small part of her was impressed at Anne's bravado in becoming involved in what was essentially a Tudor land heist but another part of her was concerned at the potential danger and damage such a risky venture could create for Randall and their growing family.

She had searched online and discovered information about John Beaumont but there was nothing further about Anne or what really happened.

The women of the Tudor period are shadows in the biographies of men, thought Caroline, the few whose names were known were infamous or powerful.

Anne Brandon it seemed had not garnered enough of either attribute to warrant a place in the traditional history books. However, through reading her diaries, letters and the numerous snippets of information from other people's biographies that she had gathered during her research, Caroline had formed an image of the long-dead woman which she greatly admired. There was a rebelliousness about Anne, a fearlessness. She had survived one of the most turbulent periods of British history and the fact the ruins of her manor house were on Caroline's land meant there was an even stronger link between them.

A shiver of recognition had fluttered through Caroline when she had read Anne's description of the oak henge. She wondered whether Anne had known the story of Mabe's Gate or whether this was created years later. The Victorians had been fond of moulding Tudor history and ancient folklore to their own image and there was a certain Gothic feel to the tale.

'Oh, Anne,' she said into the silence as she filled her mug with boiling water and prodded her camomile teabag with a spoon, 'what I wouldn't give to be able to sit in the grove and discuss your life?'

Anne had been brought up in a world of illusion and deceit. Every person of influence in her life was working to their own agenda, even if their actions were illegal. Caroline was unsurprised that as a result of these influences Anne had been prepared to take matters into her own hands, even if it meant breaking the law.

She flipped the teabag into the recycling bin and wrapped her hands around the mug, her bare feet enjoying the cool of the kitchen tiles on the stifling August day.

Was she the same as Anne she wondered. Bending the rules, lying in order to protect herself. *Although, where is my excuse for such behaviour? No one in my family has ever sunk to the level of lies which have shaped my life.*

Caroline turned, intent on continuing to piece together Anne's story, but the grandfather clock in the sitting room chimed midday and her breath caught in her throat. Gideon would be here in half an hour. He had returned to Milford

Haven the previous evening and messaged, suggesting they talk. He had written:

> I have so much to explain. I hope you can forgive me.

Caroline was unsure why Gideon felt he was the one who should atone when she was the person who had hidden the truth. Ben's words on the beach came back to her: *'He's been in love with you since we were teenagers, there's no way he would have abandoned you or your child... Let him explain. He deserves a chance to put this right.'*

She placed her mug on the kitchen counter and ran upstairs to her bedroom to brush her hair and reapply her lipstick. Jonah was out at a birthday party and sleepover with his best friend, Hywel. The two boys had been friends since their first day at school and kept in touch during term time by gaming together online whenever they were allowed. She had dropped her son at Heatherton, a nearby amusement park, earlier in the morning and he had raced off with a shouted, 'Bye, Mum,' over his shoulder as he headed for the zip wire. A carefree twelve-year-old out with his friends and no one giving him a second glance.

She inspected her reflection in the mirror, critical of her appearance, then she scolded herself.

'You're lucky he's even talking to you after all you've done,' she said, and pulled a face at herself before hurrying downstairs to wait.

The tea had cooled enough for her to drink it in three large gulps. Years of stressful deadlines and being on set as her grandfather's representative had taught Caroline that camomile tea was better to sip all day than coffee. Yet as she waited for Gideon its soothing properties were less effective than usual. When the gate buzzer sounded, her hands shook as she pressed the button to admit his car.

'Hello,' she said, opening the large front door as he and Ken, the golden retriever, climbed out.

Ken trotted towards her, wagging his tail and licked her cheek when she bent down, then he walked inside and she heard him sigh as he took up his position on the sofa. His bowl of water with ice cubes floating in it was waiting nearby in the shade.

'Hi,' said Gideon. 'How have you been?'

'Nervous,' she replied.

'Yes, me too.'

He edged past her and she saw the shadows under his eyes, the crease in his forehead where he was frowning. There was a tension in his gait as he walked through the house to the large living room and Caroline's hopes of their reaching a truce plummeted. He exuded a low-level of anger and she knew it was no less than she deserved.

In the living room, the enormous bifold doors were open and the summer breeze ruffled the long white cotton curtains. From outside came the sweet scent of honeysuckle and roses, mingled with the sharp tang of the sea. Ken was sprawled on the shady end of the sofa and Gideon was staring at Dexter's writing shed.

'Would you like a drink?' Caroline asked.

'Water would be great,' he said, and his voice sounded gruff, unlike himself.

Caroline filled a jug, adding ice and a slice of lemon before returning to the living room and placing it on the table between the sofas. Gideon was sitting beside Ken. Caroline poured water into two glasses before taking her position on the opposite chair.

'Have you heard from Jonah? Is he having fun?' Gideon asked.

Caroline had explained their son would be at a birthday party when Gideon had suggested they meet.

'He sent me a photo of himself on the zip wire,' said Caroline, and pinged the image to Gideon.

'It looks as though he's having a wonderful time.'

Gideon stared at the image, then to Caroline's surprise, tears welled in his eyes.

'You must hate me,' he said.

'Hate you?' she said. 'No, I could never hate you but you must be furious with me for hiding your son.'

'How can I be when you've brought Jonah up alone while I was married to...' he stopped abruptly.

Caroline swallowed hard. Her mouth was dry, she sipped her water. How much should she tell him?

'Who else knew about Jonah?' Gideon asked.

'My family and Blanche.'

'Did they know I was his father?'

'Yes,' she said, and Gideon looked as though he had been struck by physical pain.

'They must hate me too,' he said. 'I was so weak, such a fool.'

Caroline stared at him in surprise, he looked wretched.

'What are you talking about?' she said.

'Me, Margot, the entire mess that was our marriage. Caro, you've no idea...'

'Tell me then,' she said, a spark of irritation hardening her voice.

For years she had carried the guilt of hiding Jonah from his father. The decisions she had made had been to protect Jonah, Dexter and herself, especially when Dexter's books became a worldwide publishing phenomenon. The choices she had felt forced to make were heartbreaking but every time she suggested contacting Gideon to tell him the truth, Blanche had reminded her of the litigious nature of the Bullington family, and Caroline would back down. Her humiliation and pain at having lost Gideon to Margot Bullington outweighing her sense of outrage at his betrayal.

She placed her glass on the table and looked at Gideon. He was white-faced and his distress was growing. It was clear she was not the only one to have suffered but she did not understand why. It had been his choice to marry Margot Bullington, to live his life in the spotlight. Finally, she asked a question that had been as corrosive to her soul as water dripping on metal.

'Were you seeing Margot during our fling?' she asked, her cheeks hot with mortification.

When she had seen the announcement of Gideon and Margot's engagement so soon after his return to the States, a prior relationship was the explanation Caroline had settled upon. Her heart in tatters, she knew he had played her. Yet, this assumption did not tally with Gideon's usually considerate and honourable behaviour.

'No,' he replied, and his eyes clouded with fury. 'I knew her but there was nothing between us. The summer you and I spent together was idyllic. When I went back to America my plan was to rearrange things to enable me to move home to the UK.'

'What stopped you?' she asked. 'A better offer from another woman?'

'No, Caro, it was nothing like that,' he said.

Caroline raised her eyebrows in disbelief and he had the grace to look chagrined.

'This is difficult,' he began, running his hands through his hair in agitation. Caroline did not speak, she waited. 'In 2012, I was working for my stepdad's production company and he asked if I'd like to work in London for the summer – this was before I had my own company. There were two reasons I accepted the job, the first was to be in my home city, London, for the Olympics, which I love and the second was to find you, who I knew I also loved, and beg you to try again.'

'But you stopped writing to me in 2008,' she said, bewildered. 'You ended it.'

It was a few months after their A-levels that she had broken her leg, Gideon had been in LA with his actress mother, Suzi Ross, and stepfather, Sean West, but tipped off by Ben about the accident, he had begun writing to Caroline, proper letters on expensive notepaper. In delight, Caroline had replied and, after Ben ended their relationship, she and Gideon had both felt they could gradually start revealing their feelings for each other, tentatively finding their way to a potential relationship themselves. Caroline was ecstatic until one day, the letters from Gideon stopped.

'No, *you* ended it,' he said.

'I did no such thing,' she replied.

'You wrote saying you were unsure about taking things further because Dexter had asked you to help with his unexpected writing career.'

'You were supposed to tell me we could work it out and that this didn't need to be the end,' she exclaimed.

'I was supposed to do what?' he said. 'How was I supposed to realise? You told me it was over.'

'No, I didn't…' she repeated.

'"*Things are difficult here at the moment, Gid, I need my space*",' he interrupted and Caroline stared at him in amazement.

'You can quote the letter.'

'It's seared on my heart. To me, it felt as though you were ending it.'

'I was heartbroken when you didn't reply.'

'In my teenage mind, it felt the simplest way even though I knew by then I was in love with you.'

'It took you four years to find me again,' she said.

'My feelings for you didn't change.'

'Nor mine,' she murmured.

Caroline had been in a bar in Soho with her friends and her phone had buzzed. She had never deleted Gideon's number and when his name and the message:

Behind you!

had flashed across the screen her hand had trembled so much she had been forced to place her glass on the high table she was standing beside. Her heart pounding, she had turned with slow deliberation and peered through the noisy crowd and there he was, smiling.

'Hello,' he had said, and they had flung themselves into each other's arms.

For the next fortnight, in between their other commitments, they had spent as much time together as possible. He promised he would return and at first, his replies to her messages were prompt, they spoke every day. But, after a few weeks, her emails remained unanswered, his phone went to voicemail whenever she called, then the announcement of Gideon and Margot's engagement had shattered her hopes and her heart.

'You said you knew Margot,' said Caroline. 'How?'

'My mum knew her parents. Margot and I had met a few times when we were children, then she came to my mum's birthday party with her father, Tubshaw Bullington, up in LA.'

'You were friends?' clarified Caroline, and Gideon wrinkled his nose in distaste.

'We knew each other,' he said. 'Her family was famous and when I met her again as adults she seemed on the cusp of superstardom.'

'Did you fancy her?'

'I was young, she was pretty and yes, at first, I was flattered by her attention,' he said, 'but every time we met, which was always at functions or when other people were around, she listed her auditions, the jobs she was lining up, but it was always someone else's fault that she hadn't been given the part or been recalled for a screen test. When she asked to swap numbers, I resisted, explaining there was someone in the UK and I wasn't interested in a relationship with her.'

'How did she react?' asked Caroline.

'She cried,' he said. 'It was the night before I flew to London and she had turned up, uninvited, at the restaurant where I was eating with my mum and stepdad. It was awkward.'

'Did she contact you while you were here?' asked Caroline and Gideon shook his head.

'No and it was a relief,' he admitted. 'I thought she must have finally understood I wasn't interested in her.'

'Did you contact her?'

'No,' he said. 'which was why I was so surprised when she met me at the airport in LA. Before I knew it, a host of photographers appeared from nowhere. She claimed to be scared and insisted we leap into a cab, which screeched away in a blaze of publicity. I was furious because it was obvious she'd planned the whole debacle, either by tipping off the photographers or even paying them. She wasn't famous enough to warrant such attention from the usual paparazzi.'

'What did you do?'

'I told her I was seeing someone else,' he said. 'She took it calmly and dropped me home. However, the next day my picture was all over the tabloids being named as Margot's new boyfriend.'

'You announced your engagement a week later,' said Caroline.

'No, we didn't,' he said, and there was a hardness to his voice she had never heard before. 'Margot had landed a small part in a film and a magazine requested an interview. Her family connections made her newsworthy. Halfway through, she flashed a huge diamond ring on her left hand, then pretended she shouldn't have worn it and took it off, therefore making "a secret engagement" the story. The photographs of us at the airport made the journalist assume I was the mystery fiancé. Margot neither confirmed nor denied the suggestion.'

'Had you given it to her?'

'Nope. When the magazine contacted me asking for a comment, I was furious. I rang Margot insisting she call the journalist and explain there had been a mistake. She refused. She claimed she'd done it to help my career.'

'How?'

'My documentary series was about to come out,' he said. 'It was the first series I'd shot independently and if it was a success, I'd be able to give up my job for my stepdad's production company and work for myself full time. It would mean I could come home and work in London, near you. Margot was right, her interview had boosted my profile and suddenly, my name was everywhere. It was great publicity.'

'Why did she do it?'

'After the piece came out, the press camped on my doorstep and whenever I denied we were involved, it convinced them even more. Then one day, Margot rang and suggested she come over. I wanted to have it out with her so I agreed. She arrived with her father and they told me Margot had a rare form of cancer that meant she had less than four years to live. She declared undying love to me and Tubshaw asked if I could be generous enough to give Margot a few years of happiness. They hinted it was the least I could do after all the publicity they'd generated around me and my documentary series.'

Caroline stared at Gideon aghast.

'Why did you agree?'

'Margot is a better actor than people give her credit for.' He sighed. 'I believed her, and Tubshaw was the perfect picture of despair.'

'I asked for time to consider things because, obviously, I was in love with you and this was too bizarre for words but the next morning Margot released a statement to the press about our engagement. She hinted at being pregnant and how brave she would have to be considering her other "undisclosed" medical issues.'

'Was she pregnant?'

'No, I didn't sleep with her until about a week after our wedding and only then because I was drunk.'

'But why did you go through with it?'

'Because you emailed to say it was over between us and you never wanted to see me again, so I decided to do as Margot and her father had asked.'

'No, I didn't,' Caroline exclaimed.

'Margot showed me the email,' he said.

'I emailed to say we needed to talk because I had news and I hoped you'd think it was good but you never replied. I sent about ten messages.'

'But I never received them.'

They stared at each other.

'Did Margot have access to your emails?' asked Caroline.

'Yes, I suppose…'

'She must have deleted my messages.'

'What about the one ending things?'

'Perhaps she created a similar email address and banked on you not noticing through your distress.'

Gideon stared at her in stunned silence.

'Was this why you stayed with her? Her illness?'

'Margot isn't ill,' he said, and the words felt dark, unlike Gideon.

'Her treatment was successful?'

'My ex-wife was never ill,' said Gideon. 'She wanted a husband with dual nationality enabling her to work wherever she chose. I have both a British and an American passport.'

'It's a bit extreme.'

'Margot doesn't live in the real world, nor do her parents and brother. The only sane one is her sister, Connie, and they don't talk to her,' he said. 'For years, Margot ran rings around me. I've lost count of the number of affairs she's had but each time she held the threat of her illness over my head. She would be charming and sweet and I'd give her one more chance. Then, last year, I overheard Margot talking to her father and she laughed about my gullibility and how I continued to believe she was dying.'

'Gid, no,' said Caroline horrified.

'Margot had no idea I was in the house. I put my phone on record and when she hung up, I played her side of the conversation back to her, there was enough to be damaging. She tried her usual repertoire of guilt-inducing tricks – crying, shouting, threatening to ruin my career but none of it touched me because I knew the truth at last. Despite her early hope for stardom, it had never materialised. Instead she used my career, my hard work, my success to open doors for her, while she coerced and bullied me. It was Connie who confirmed Margot's ill health was totally fictitious.'

'And Tubshaw?'

'He thought it was funny.'

'Gideon, it's awful. She's abused you throughout the relationship.'

'Yes and when she rang the other day in the wood, I had to take the call because she was trying to halt the divorce, again. It wasn't a risk I could take.'

'She can't though,' said Caroline with a faint hint of panic.

'No, of course not,' he replied. 'But in her world, she believes she's a mistress of manipulation and can do whatever she chooses.'

'What do you think she'll do next?'

'I hope, nothing, but this is another reason why I've been careful about being seen with you. It isn't because I don't want to be with you. I don't trust Margot not to hurt you in order to have revenge on me. When I realised Jonah was my son, I was terrified about what Margot might do—'

'Margot Bullington has no power over me or Jonah,' said Caroline, pushing away her shiver of unease. 'You can't let her dictate your life any more.'

'Margot is dangerous when thwarted. If you have any secrets, she'll find and expose them.'

'Gideon,' said Caroline, reaching out to squeeze his hand, 'she doesn't have as much influence as you think.'

In the distance, the doorbell rang.

'One minute,' said Caroline, 'it's probably a parcel.'

Caroline hurried through the house, her mind racing at the horror of Gideon and Margot's relationship.

'Hello,' she said as she opened the door to a man and a

woman. Behind them, was a police car and two uniformed officers.

The man and woman held up police badges.

'Miss Harvey?' asked the woman. 'I'm DS Penn and this is DI King.'

'What's happened?' said Caroline. 'Jonah! Has there been an accident?'

'No,' said DS Penn. 'Can we come in?'

'Yes,' Caroline said, and to her relief saw Gideon and Ken hurrying towards her.

The police officers exchanged stern glances.

'Are you the granddaughter of the late Dexter Blake?' asked DI King.

'Yes.'

'And you are?'

'Gideon Morris,' he replied. 'What's this about?'

DS Penn did not reply, instead she moved in sight of the open door and beckoned to the two uniformed officers.

'Mr Morris, we're here to take you to a place of safety. You have nothing to fear.'

'What are you talking about?' asked Gideon as the uniformed officers entered and tried to guide him through the front door while Ken gave a low growl.

'We understand Miss Harvey has been keeping you here against your will,' said DI King, 'but you're safe now.'

'Who gave you this information?' said Gideon, shaking the police officer's hand off his arm.

'We're not at liberty to say,' said DS Penn.

'This is Margot,' he hissed.

'Mr Morris, we must ask you to come with us until we can ascertain your safety.'

'Gideon, go with them, I'll call Blanche, she'll sort this out—'

'You may make a call when you're at the police station, Miss Harvey. However, at present, there are other more pressing matters. We have a warrant for your arrest.'

'My arrest?' Caroline was unsure whether to laugh or feel scared. The entire situation was descending into farce.

'What's she supposed to have done?' said Gideon.

'Miss Harvey, we're arresting you for the unlawful imprisonment of Gideon Morris and the murder of Dexter Blake.'

31

CUMBERLAND LODGE, CARLTON, NOTTINGHAMSHIRE, JANUARY 1547

'Henry VIII is dead,' said Anne. 'Jane Seymour's son has been declared King Edward VI.'

An official messenger from the palace had arrived ten minutes earlier and as the most senior member of the household behind her younger half-sister, Lady Eleanor, Countess of Cumberland, who was indisposed, it was she who had received the news. When the man rode away, she had hurried straight to Eleanor who was resting in the grand solar of Cumberland Lodge, her favourite home.

'Would you like me to assemble your staff to pass on the news?' Anne asked.

'Yes, we must tell my steward, Appleton, he'll gather the household. Hurry, Annie, then return to me while we wait.'

Anne had arrived a week earlier and was shocked to see the deterioration in her younger half-sister's health. Eleanor had always been delicate but her skin held the hue of aged parchment and she moved with the caution of a woman of great age.

This morning she was stretched out on a chaise, her delicate frame propped against pillows, her legs swathed in warm blankets. Anne felt almost apologetic for her own robust health.

'It would be more in keeping with your status for you to read the decree,' said Anne, 'but I am happy to be your proxy.'

'Thank you, Annie,' she said. 'You are a great comfort. I wish my Henry were here, as the Earl of Cumberland he knows how these things should be done.'

Anne dropped into the chair in front of the roaring fire, staring at the missive in her hand. The wind outside was bitter and the bare trees surrounding the house sang a funeral dirge for the dead king with their eerie howling and sighing.

Who will truly mourn his loss? Anne wondered.

Henry had two wives surviving: Anne of Cleves who had escaped his clutches via divorce rather than the block thanks to her foreign royal blood and the current queen, Katheryn Parr. *Would they miss him or was their overriding emotion relief?*

And me, she thought, *do I grieve our lost monarch?* Her answer was strong and clear: no.

'We are cousins to the king,' said Eleanor and a pink tinge stained her cheek, a tremor of pride in her voice as the realisation struck her. 'Do you think we'll be summoned to court?'

'There will be no ladies-in-waiting required,' mused Anne. 'Not until the king marries and as he's nine years old, it might be several years before a match is decided upon.'

'But there will be a coronation,' said Eleanor excitement bubbling through her croaky voice. 'As his cousins, we shall be invited—' A violent coughing fit cut off her glee mid-sentence.

'What does your physician say about your health?' asked Anne as she poured Eleanor a glass of warm tisane containing camomile, honey and willow bark from the pewter jug on a trivet beside the fire.

'He suggests it is ague,' said Eleanor sipping the drink with gratitude, 'but I suspect jaundice.'

'When I travel to Norfolk next week, come with me,' said Anne, unable to bear the thought of leaving her frail sister. 'I can care for you, nurse you back to health. Let me talk to your husband and persuade him.'

'Oh, Annie, you've always wanted to mother us but I am loved and cared for here,' said Eleanor, giving her a wan smile. 'My daughter, Margaret, is a constant source of comfort, as are my loyal staff. I'm tended to with love and diligence; I want for nothing.'

She placed the glass on the small table inlaid with exotic fruitwoods that sat beside her. Anne noticed Eleanor's eyes had taken on a new determination and she did not know whether this was due to the tisane or the declaration from court.

'This news changes things,' Eleanor continued. 'There is no doubt my husband will attend the new king. Cousin Edward is a Protestant, as is my Henry, and it's imperative the earl is counted among those loyal to my cousin, the king.'

Anne stifled a giggle at Eleanor's repetition of the word 'cousin' with her desire to reinforce her close ties to royalty.

'The Protestants will wish to make their presence felt,' Anne agreed. 'This is a pivotal moment to seize power. The new king is but a boy. He will need loyal, trustworthy men to guide him.'

'There will be changes afoot and it's important to show we're ready to serve His Majesty,' said Eleanor. 'Despite my reluctance to let you go, Annie, perhaps it would be wise for you to continue on your journey earlier than planned.'

'You're right,' said Anne. 'This is a dangerous time and until the council of regents has been decided upon, there could be a coup to take control of the crown.'

'Go to Randall,' said Eleanor, as the implications of an

underage king filtered through their initial excitement. 'He may not hold a title but he has proved a better companion to you than your own husband. You will be safe in Norfolk until such times as we discover the nature of this new monarch and the regency. We shall see each other at Cousin Edward's coronation.'

* * *

The next morning Anne left Eleanor, her heart heavy as, despite Eleanor's belief of a family reunion at the coronation, she was sure this would be the last time she would see her sister alive. Eleanor struggled to rise from her chair to bid Anne farewell and the image scorched itself on Anne's mind as she and her entourage made their way from Nottinghamshire to Norfolk.

As they plodded through the wintry countryside, the trees bare, the roads rutted with slush, mud and puddles, Anne wondered what changes would be wrought by the new monarch. The Plantagenet, Henry VI, had been the last child to inherit the throne. He had been a baby of nine months old when his father, Henry V, had died in 1422. It had led to years of turmoil and brought challenges for the crown from his cousins who believed their claims to be monarch were stronger.

Her father had once told her the Brandons had seized their own power through wise choices and the wit to change their colours and loyalties as required. Her grandfather had been loyal to the Tudors, he had been Henry VII's standard bearer at Bosworth and from here the Brandon wealth and status had been assured.

Her own siblings were cousins to the new monarch, she thought, would they challenge his right to rule? Anne shuddered imagining prolonged wars, the country torn asunder and suddenly she was desperate to see Randall, to hug her children, to keep them all safe from harm.

The coach lurched over a pothole and Anne gripped the edge of her seat to stop herself sliding to the floor. Her mind cast towards her list of names and the plans she had made to cause irritation to the nobles, wondering whether she should continue with her petty revenge. As a woman it was impossible for her to wield power alone but her scheme with John Beaumont caused her huge amusement and a certain sense of self-satisfaction. She felt no qualms about stealing money from these nobles. It might be small amounts to them but to the women she helped with the money – the abandoned wives, the forgotten daughters and the desperate, penniless widows – she had saved lives.

In five of the six cases they had so far put into action, the unwitting nobleman had immediately paid. Each was horrified that the land they thought they owned was in dispute and were prompt with their thanks and payments to safeguard their reputations and estates.

The five whom had paid willingly were Edward Fiennes, Lord Clinton who had been stepfather to Henry Fitzroy, the king's only acknowledged illegitimate child; Thomas, Lord Wentworth, a cousin of Jane Seymour's on her maternal side; George Brooke, 9th Baron Cobham, the brother of Lizzie Brooke; Edward Courtenay, Marquess of Exeter with his distant claim to the throne and Ralph Neville, 4th Earl of Westmorland, a staunch ally of the king during his divorce from Katherine of Aragon.

The sixth, Henry Somerset, Earl of Worcester, was the only one who had chosen to challenge the document in court. However, when the case reached the bench, John Beaumont was the presiding judge and had found the document to be legal and binding. The case had cost the earl a great deal of money. Anne had been delighted but Randall had been uneasy.

'The Earl of Worcester is no fool, Annie,' he had said. 'Perhaps you and John should show more caution.'

'These men should be made to pay for what they did, sending an innocent woman to her death...' she had begun, but Randall had shaken his head.

'Nearly half of the jurors are dead from old age, illness and through their own foolishness,' he said. 'Leave them be, Annie, time and the angels will take care of the rest. I would also advise John Beaumont is less aggressive when dealing with your brother-in-law, Henry Grey, Marquess of Dorset.'

The previous year, John Beaumont and Henry Grey had fallen out to such an extent Beaumont reported the altercation to the Privy Council. Both men were summoned to London and to Anne's dismay, it was John who had been rebuked. His crime was showing lack of respect towards a peer. He was fined five hundred marks and bound over to keep the peace. Grey was also told to keep the peace but he was not fined. John had written to Anne in a fury and his determination to help her win the Warwickshire lands had intensified.

Randall had suggested they cool things down and with the upheaval of a new king and the changes this would create in the country, she realised his caution was to be heeded. Her claim for the Warwickshire lands continued its slow journey through the legal process but she was hopeful it would soon be heard and the matter resolved to her satisfaction.

This, she decided, will be enough. *I shall write to John and instruct him to wait before creating another fake land document.*

* * *

A week later, she and her entourage rode into the spotless courtyard of Randall's Norfolk home. The day had been fine and Anne, bored with being cooped up in her carriage, had chosen to ride the final ten miles. As she brought her horse to a stop, the groom helped her down but before her feet had touched the cobbles, he was there, his arms encircling her.

'I've missed you so much, my love,' Randall said, and they clung to each other. Anne felt as though they had been apart for months instead of a few weeks.

She took his hand and followed him through the large wooden doors to the solar. A fire roared and within seconds, their three children had descended upon her, squealing with excitement at her return. It was several hours before Anne and Randall were able to discuss the new king.

'I've heard from John Beaumont,' he said later that evening as they sat together in front of the fire, entwined on a chaise, a soft blanket over their legs.

'The Warwickshire land?'

'Yes, John is hopeful that under the new regime he may soon be promoted, which will enable him to hurry things along.'

'Good,' she said. 'What did he say about the court?'

'He claims the handover to King Edward has not been smooth. In the late king's will, Henry named sixteen executors who were to help his son rule until he was eighteen years old. However, Stephen Gardiner, Bishop of Winchester, who had been one of them was removed from the Privy Council in the weeks before the king's death. There's been much jostling for position with leading Protestants and Reformists making their presence felt, including Edward Seymour, Earl of Hertford; John Dudley, Viscount Lisle; Sir William Paget and Sir Anthony Denny who has charge of the dry seal.'

Anne's eyes widened.

'But the dry seal is used to sign the king's signature in his absence,' she said. 'I remember Papa was always wary of whomever wielded its power because it would make it possible for them to tamper with the law.'

'Exactly,' said Randall. 'There is also a rumour that before King Henry became bedridden a new clause was added to the will, creating an "unfulfilled gift's" clause.'

'A what?'

'It allows Henry's executors to distribute land and titles to themselves and others at court.'

'They can steal land?' asked Anne, aghast.

'And choose their own titles,' said Randall. 'Seymour, as the king's uncle, has claimed the title Duke of Somerset and made himself Lord Protector of the Realm and Governor of the King's Person.'

'But this makes Edward Seymour king in all but name.'

'Yes,' said Randall, his eyes dark with concern.

Anne shuddered. Seymour had been a guest at their table the terrible night Edward had tried to kill her.

'The new king is Protestant,' she said. 'There will no doubt be a move against the Catholics. Is there word of either of the princesses, Mary and Elizabeth?'

In his later years, Henry had repaired his relationships with his daughters restoring them to the line of succession.

'They're both at court but John has heard the Princess Elizabeth will be part of the household of the dowager queen at Hanworth Manor in west London. Your niece, Lady Jane Grey, will accompany her.'

'And my sister Frances?'

'At court already. Remember, she is cousin to the king,' said Randall. 'It wouldn't surprise me if we were summoned.'

'Eleanor believes the same,' said Anne, winding a long curl

around her finger as she thought. 'Her health is frail but she's confident her husband, Henry Clifford, as Earl of Cumberland will attend the new king.'

'And you, my love. If a request to join the court was sent, would you wish to return?'

She paused, staring into the fire. The flight from London all those years ago played out in a series of vivid images in her mind. Pembrokeshire had been their refuge but with Henry VIII dead, any threat he posed was gone; they were free to return.

'We could take a house,' said Randall. 'You'd be able to see your friends again. Perhaps Meg Roper could visit, it's been many years since you've seen her. The children could meet their extended family.'

'And you could see your friends,' said Anne, tracing her fingers around the palm of his hand. 'You've missed a great deal being stuck in Pembrokeshire with me.'

'There is nowhere else I want to be,' he said, pulling her even more tightly into his side. 'I was an orphan, you were my family, wherever you are is where my heart desires to be. There was no reason for me to remain in Norfolk on my family's estates. I don't remember my father, I was a babe in arms when he was killed falling from a horse. John Beaumont secured me a good price for the land I inherited from my uncle and this house and land from my father have earned us a valuable income over the years. John's wise financial advice has made us even wealthier and enabled us to build a happy, comfortable life. I have no regrets but I have long known you miss the glamour and mayhem of the court. Perhaps this is the time for us to return to the capital.'

Anne allowed his words to take hold. He was the most generous of men and this offer was tempting.

'What about Lord Powis?' she said.

'Powis is not popular at court. He has long exhausted the patience of the senior members of the nobility with his boasting and posturing. He spends a great deal of time either at Powis Castle or at Jane's family home in Ashwell in Hertfordshire.'

'And his children? I believe there are five and she is pregnant with a sixth.'

Randall nodded. Anne swallowed her frustration. Jane's fecundity was a matter she continued to find difficult to accept with equanimity.

'Will they be at court?'

'Perhaps but it's doubtful. Anyway, you'll be in the royal circle and they won't be able to reach you,' replied Randall.

The thought of returning to court, seeing her friends and being part of a new regime was an exciting prospect.

'If a summons arrives, then yes, it would be pleasurable to return to London,' she said but even as she spoke, she felt a strange sense of foreboding.

32

LONDON, DECEMBER 1551

Anne felt a fizz of excitement. John Beaumont had been created Master of the Rolls three months earlier and with the support of Sir Richard Rich it was possible he would soon be promoted to hear cases in Chancery. He had written:

> *This is it, Annie, we can present your case for the Warwickshire lands and if I'm presiding – which I shall be – there's no doubt we'll win. Henry Grey will wish he'd never challenged me.*

A scream of delight rose in Anne's throat, at last she could avenge herself on her father and her half-siblings, not to mention her husband.

'Randall,' she called hurrying along the corridor of their London home to Randall's office, 'John is to be made a Chancery judge.'

Randall looked up from the account book he was checking, a line creasing between his eyebrows as he frowned.

'Annie, no, please drop the case, there are rumours about John—' he began.

'But...' Anne interrupted, then she saw Randall's stern expression and she felt her excitement fade. 'What have you heard?'

'A letter arrived this morning from Sir Richard Ogle saying John is about to be called before the Privy Council. He's been accused of peculation when he was Receiver of the Court of Wards two years ago.'

'What's peculation?' she asked.

'It's the fraudulent appropriation of funds or property entrusted to your care but actually owned by someone else,' said Randall. 'The word is John has defrauded the crown of over £11,000.'

'No,' gasped Anne, sinking into the chair beside Randall. 'It can't be true.'

'We're both aware John bends the law to suit his purposes,' said Randall.

'But he's our friend...'

'Yes, but we're not without guilt, Annie. We've chosen to ignore his casual approach to legal matters as they often coincided with our own desires.'

Anne bit her lip in consternation. Randall was correct, John's slippery treatment of the law was an unspoken understanding between them all. John, like many of his fellow lawyers, felt he was able to manipulate the rules for his own ends. Anne had always found it thrilling, as though she were following in the footsteps of the past Brandons: the men who had dared to live near the edge of accepted behaviour in order to build a fortune. However, to hear John was suspected of embezzlement on such a grand scale was a shock and, for the first time, it made Anne question her behaviour.

'Will John be imprisoned?' she asked.

'Perhaps,' said Randall. 'I was hoping to discover more before telling you but in light of your news today, I realised it was important you should know. It's time for you to halt these proceedings against your father's will.'

'Even if I wanted to, it's impossible,' she said. 'John's been pushing it through the courts for years. He's obsessed with using my claim to revenge himself on Henry Grey and through him my husband, Edward.'

'Everyone is aware of John's feud with your brother-in-law,' said Randall. 'The question is, Annie, what is motivating you? Are you supporting this madness because you wish to challenge your husband and your brother-in-law? Or is it your Brandon pride?'

Anne hesitated, her words of defence freezing on her lips as she saw fury spark like an obsidian flame in Randall's eyes.

'I no longer care about having revenge on Edward or Henry,' she answered in a quiet voice.

'Are you sure?' Randall asked.

'Randall, we're so close to success but Edward isn't the reason I've allowed John to push this case so far. This is about my father...' she said but Randall threw his quill across the desk leaving a spray of ink and sprang to his feet.

'Throughout our time together, I've always supported you,' he said. 'We built a house on the edges of the world to protect each other after your father betrayed you, but when the call came to return to court, I followed. Whatever you have craved, it has always been my pleasure to create it for you because in your delight, I find my own joy.'

'Randall, I—' but he held up his hand to silence her.

'For years I've stood by and watched as you and John played games with the law. Each time he presented one of your forged documents I was convinced your subterfuge would be discovered. You have been fortunate, Annie, but this current court case is a fool's errand. You once promised me you would stop if there was a risk to our family and I implore you to realise we have reached that point. If you continue with this claim, it could destroy us. You might even be imprisoned. I love you, Annie, and if you love me, you will step away from this ridiculous quest to avenge yourself upon your father.'

'No,' she screamed as the pain of her father's betrayal ripped through her anew. 'He tried to force me into bed with the king. He should have protected me but he was prepared to sacrifice me to his friend's sick whims. The humiliation I felt when he disowned me in death by cutting me from his will remains here,' she pounded her chest, 'this is why I can't let it go. I must see it through to the end otherwise my heart will never be at peace.'

'Is a few hundred hectares of land worth more to you than me, than our love, our family?'

'No—'

'Your father is gone,' Randall shouted. 'He can never give you the forgiveness you crave. He can't take you in his arms and make this right, Annie.'

'I know,' she howled, tears streaming down her face, 'but I can take what is rightfully mine. I can win.'

They stared at each other in shocked silence, then Randall spoke in a voice of forced calm, 'I intend to return to Pembrokeshire in a few weeks when my business in London is complete. The children will accompany me and I hope you will be with us too. However, for the first time, your presence requires a promise.'

'Which is?'

'You will allow your father's will to stand. We don't need the Warwickshire lands but I do need you.'

Randall slammed the accounts book shut then stalked from the room. His voice echoed along the corridor as he requested his horse. Anne sat frozen in the chair. Outside she heard the clatter of hooves. There was a flash of chestnut as he passed the window, then she watched Randall gallop away into the morning mist.

33

THE OAK GROVE, PEMBROKESHIRE, APRIL 1552

Anne stood at the centre of trees in the oak grove. The wind ruffled the new leaves and she shivered. Despite the hints of spring all around her, the coolness of winter had not fully released its grip on the far-flung lands in the west. Daffodils bowed their golden heads in the gusting winds. The last of the snowdrops shivered as they scattered their fairy magic through the grove and at the far end was the standing stone. Its age and beauty stark against the softening green of the woodland surrounding it.

It was many months since she had seen Randall. Her heart ached to hear his voice, to feel his touch. Would it be white sails or black as the boat hurries towards the dying hero in the story of *Tristan and Iseult*?

'Randall, I've been a fool,' she whispered as though praying to the ancient gods of the oak grove. 'Will you forgive me, my love?'

The wind whispered through the trees and in the distance she heard the boom of the waves. He would either arrive for the rendezvous she had requested or he would not. If he spurned her, then she knew it would be a just punishment for her selfish behaviour.

After Randall had requested she withdraw from the court case over her father's will and she had again refused, events had moved quickly. For so many years the paperwork had crawled with snail-like slowness through the legal channels but as Beaumont took his position as Chancery Judge, her claim was swept to the bench with all haste. To the disgust of her half-sister, Lady Frances, Duchess of Suffolk, John found in Anne's favour.

Anne had been teaching their daughters, Elinor and Ursula, how to sew a cross stitch when Sir Richard Ogle arrived with the news she had been dreading.

'Henry Grey, Duke of Suffolk, has accused Beaumont of champerty,' Sir Richard Ogle announced when the two girls had been sent away with their nurse. 'The Duke and Duchess of Suffolk have requested an audience with the king to discuss the argument over Charles Brandon's will and His Majesty has insisted there is an investigation. Henry Grey also levelled allegations against you, Lady Powis.'

'Where is John?' Randall asked.

'He's been placed in solitary confinement in the Fleet prison,' Richard replied. 'Government interrogators are the only people allowed to see him.'

'What of Annie?'

'There's no warrant for her arrest at present but if Beaumont declares she was involved, she could face charges.'

'We must leave now,' Randall said when Richard departed with promises to keep them informed. 'The weather is not ideal but it's our best chance.'

Since their row over the court case, Anne and Randall had moved forward, polite around each other in the immediate aftermath and with an unspoken agreement never to mention

John Beaumont. Life had nearly returned to normal but with Richard Ogle's news, the true danger of Anne's predicament rose again, a black shadow in their world.

Anne stared at him in surprise.

'If a warrant for my arrest has been issued, it won't matter where we run,' she said. 'King Edward's guards will find me. We ran once before but this time, to flee would be an admission of guilt. I am the daughter of a duke, I shall not abscond again. John knew the risks and he made a solemn promise he would deny my involvement but I am no coward.'

'Coward?' Randall said, his voice harsh with fear. 'This is not about being a coward, it's about protecting ourselves. If you are imprisoned in the Tower. I have no title, no power, how would I rescue you?'

'You would find a way,' she said.

'And nothing I can say will persuade you to leave?' he asked.

'No.'

'Then my choice is clear,' he said. 'As soon as the weather permits, I shall take the children back to Hanworth Manor to keep them safe. You must do as you wish, Annie.'

'Randall, please try to understand—' but he walked away.

Three days later, he gathered up a sizeable section of the household and left. She had not heard from Randall nor her children since.

When news came of her estranged husband's death a month later, she felt the heavens were taunting her. She was free from the restrictions of her marriage, a widow, able to wed again, yet, the London house was empty and echoing without Randall and the children. It was then Anne realised the folly of her destructive path for revenge.

* * *

'Lady Powis,' said Miriam Richardson, her senior maid, bringing her back to the chilly clearing. 'Shall we continue to the manor?'

'You go ahead,' she said, waving to the small entourage with whom she had travelled. 'Take my horse, I shall join you soon.'

'Do you have a message for his lordship?' she asked.

Anne swallowed the unexpected lump in her throat and said, 'Please tell him the sails are white.'

Confusion flittered across Miriam's face.

'Very well,' she replied and led the way through the woodland to the extensive grounds of Hanworth Manor.

The clip-clop of the horses hooves faded away and Anne leaned on the ancient monolith. The plum-coloured sandstone was covered in lichen and she traced her fingers across the intricate patterns. Would he come? If he did, she knew there was a chance for them but if he sent a servant, then her stubbornness, her pride and her fool-hardiness would have cost the dearest part of her life.

The long and arduous journey had given Anne time to think about the past, the decisions she had made and the people whom she had loved and lost. The further from London she had travelled by boat, carriage and pony, the more her anger had abated. Her father was human, he had made mistakes but when she had needed him, he had always been there. On the night Edward had attacked her, the duke had given her and Randall refuge at Southwark Place, he had fought for her rights as her marriage collapsed and he had accepted her love for Randall.

She understood the pain he must have suffered when King Henry had made his terrible request. The difficulty of his position and, because she shared similar traits, the stubbornness and anger that had driven him to cut her from his will. As she placed both hands on the standing stone, she closed her eyes conjuring up her father's merry, handsome face rather than his desperation and bitterness during their final meeting. A warmth suffused her as she felt his love again, heard the echo of his laughter and remembered dancing with her feet on his as he guided her through the steps when she was a child.

'I forgive you, Papa,' she said into the cool green air. 'You were a mortal man, you made mistakes and I forgive you. I love you, Papa. Go well with God and rest in peace.'

A gentleness wrapped itself around Anne followed by a freeing sense of relief. Perhaps now, she would be able to save her relationship with Randall.

She felt his presence before she heard his gentle approach; his footsteps muted by the softness of the muddy paths in the grove.

'Annie?'

His voice was as familiar as her own heartbeat.

'Randall,' she said, turning to face him, tears streaming down her face. 'I'm sorry.'

He walked towards her, his arms outstretched, his face reflecting her own need to hold him.

'You're here now, my love,' he said.

'But you were right,' she said. 'I was a fool, thinking revenge on my father was more important than you, than our children. I failed you.'

'Annie, you could never fail me,' he said, wiping away her tears.

'I've talked to John Beaumont,' she said. 'I've told him to do what he must. If he wishes to implicate me, then so be it, but I shall never play such stupid games again. The loss of you, of the children, the things I care about beyond all others made me realise my behaviour was no better than my father's. He hurt people – my mother, my stepmother, Mary, me and countless others – with his double-dealings. I don't want to be like him.'

'You could never be like him,' said Randall.

'But I was and you tried to warn me,' she said. 'I've found it in my heart to forgive my father and now, I beg your forgiveness. If you will allow it, I would like to return home, to our simple life away from court.'

Randall released her, his eyes serious. 'There is one condition,' he said, and Anne swallowed her tears, ready to accede to whatever restrictions he chose to impose.

'I will do whatever you ask.'

Randall placed his hand beside hers on Mabe's Gate, their fingers almost touching.

'Marry me,' he said, his voice a whisper on the breeze.

Anne's eyes widened. 'Marry you?' she asked, her heart thumping in excitement.

'This is the condition I require,' he said, his fingers entwining with hers. 'If you wish to return then it must be as my wife. You will no longer have a title. You will be simply Mistress Hanworth but you will have all you desire.'

He looked up and Anne saw the love, the hope and the fear of her rejection in his eyes. She squeezed his hand.

'I accept your condition, Mr Hanworth,' she said, reaching forward to kiss him. 'I can think of nothing I want more than to be your wife at last.'

34

DEXTER'S PLACE, ST ISHMAELS, PEMBROKESHIRE, AUGUST, PRESENT DAY

Caroline wiped her eyes. Anne and Randall had been reunited. The strength of their love had saved them and, in finding forgiveness for her father, Anne had eschewed her yearning for revenge, returning to her home, family and lover.

Love, thought Caroline, the emotion we all crave, yet often it's a form of insanity. Her mind flickered towards Gideon and Margot's marriage, then away. She was in no position to judge and all she felt for them both was a terrible sadness.

It was early morning and she was sitting on the sofa staring out at the new day. The police had released her at midnight and she had returned home to seventy-nine missed calls from Gideon. After messaging him with the assurance she was safe and there were no charges, she had tumbled into bed and fallen into an uneasy sleep. For his part, Gideon replied telling her he had explained to the police it was a misunderstanding and he was not being held against his will, neither had he been threatened nor coerced by Caroline.

'I'll come over tomorrow,' he had messaged and she sent back a hug emoji.

She sipped from the cup of cooling tea by her side. Jonah was spending the day with Hywel and before his return, she was determined to end the lies. There was a slender possibility the truth would leak out after her lengthy interview with the stunned police officers but she suspected the calm and terrifying lecture given by her lawyer, Clinton Sova, who had worked with Blanche and Caroline for years had spelled out the level of legal retribution they would face if such a disclosure was ever traced back to them or the police station.

Yet with all she had learned about her accuser, Caroline felt sure some manner of garbled information might find its way to Gideon and this could not be allowed to happen. It was essential for Gideon to hear the truth from her. How else would he be able to comprehend the reasons behind her decisions: the fear, the love, the desperation that had driven her? The lies had grown out of control but if she explained, made him understand, she might earn his forgiveness.

She glanced at the clock; it was another hour before Gideon was due to arrive. In need of a distraction from her jittery nerves, she scrolled through her emails and saw one from Mark Llewellyn which he had sent several days earlier.

As she read the first line, she smiled. It was the final details of the Marquess House research into Anne and Randall's tale. When there was time, she would send Mark all the additional information she had discovered about Anne's story but for now she was happy to read what remained of the lovers' tale from the texts stored in libraries around the world.

There aren't many details,

Mark had written,

but thanks to The Diary of Henry Machyn, Citizen and Merchant-Taylor of London we do know that when Anne Brandon died in January 1558 she was married to Randall Hanworth. She was buried in Westminster in the parish of St Margaret's with a decent amount of pomp. There's an entry where he states she was interred with two white branches, thirteen torches, three great tapers and her coat of arms. Unfortunately, we've been unable to locate Randall's date of death or his burial place but they were clearly in London when Anne passed.

You mentioned Anne had been involved in dubious legal dealings with John Beaumont but despite extensive searching there don't appear to be any records of her ever being charged, fined or imprisoned. Although court documents do confirm her name was linked to the judge's champerty hearing. As for Beaumont, he was sacked from his position as Master of the Rolls and after giving a full confession, he was brought before the Star Chamber on 16 June 1552. He was treated with leniency and allowed to continue his legal practice but without his high-profile positions bringing in large amounts of money, he and his family struggled. He bounced back in April 1554 when he was made a Member of Parliament for Bossiney in Cornwall. He also sat for Liverpool and as a nominee for the Duchy of Lancaster. In 1556, he surrendered himself to the Fleet prison for a debt of £200. The last reference to him in the Inner Temple is on 16 January 1556, after this, the trail runs cold.

Caroline sighed, Anne's quest for revenge had been an illusion. No matter her actions, after his death, she had never have been able to receive her father's forgiveness or offer her own. Even Beaumont's desire to humiliate Edward Grey had failed, as

Powis had died before John could publicly humiliate him. Henry Grey, Duke of Suffolk was the one person who came away unscathed but he died a traitor's death in February 1554, beheaded at Tower Hill for his involvement in the Wyatt Rebellion.

Was it worth all the heartache? she wondered. All the scheming and plotting for the securing of land.

Her mind flickered to Travis. The endless threatening communications from Salter Holdings held a quality of the fantastical not dissimilar to Anne's games of revenge, especially when she considered the new information Blanche had sent overnight. She had emailed:

> The Arnolds are desperate, Caro. We can destroy them, Travis too. All you have to do is say the word.

But did she want to be as cruel or vindictive towards them? she thought. No, but she did want them to stop.

Without hesitating, she FaceTimed Travis. He answered on the second ring, wiping his hands across his three-day stubble in a gesture she had once found endearing but which now irritated her. Caroline wished he would either grow a beard or shave. He thought it gave him a rumpled, sexy, just-come-off-a-tough-case air, she thought it looked as though he had overslept. However, she buried her impatience with his contrived appearance and said in a calm voice.

'Talk to me.'

Travis was the man she had fallen in love with and who, for a long time, had loved her and Jonah. There was a good man inside him and she wanted to appeal to this side of his personality and hope he would do the right thing.

'About the flat?'

'Yes.'

'Blanche served us three months' notice in April,' he said, angrily.

'Which we extended for another month,' she said. 'Do you have any intention of honouring our request?'

'Where would we live, Caro?'

'You're an adult, Travis, find another place to live,' she said and he scowled. 'Why did you tell Lee Arnold about the cove?'

He was about to deny it but this was the reason she had wanted to see his face, for him to see her, for them to remember the feelings they had once shared. The silence grew between them and she wondered whether he would cut the connection, then his face crumpled.

'Oh, Caro, I'm sorry,' he said. 'I was showing off.'

Caroline resisted the urge to roll her eyes.

'What happened?' she prompted.

'One night, Lee and I were drinking while he outlined his plans for a string of small, exclusive holiday complexes. He wanted to highlight hidden areas and I told him about your beach.'

'Understandable,' she said forcing calm into her voice despite her frustration at his idiocy. 'We spent a huge amount of time there when Jonah was young. Did he seem interested?'

'Of course but we never discussed it again and I forgot about the conversation until the day he showed me a proposal for a series of luxury cabins with a path cutting through the woods and down to a beach. It took me a while to recognise it but when I realised he was trying to annexe Dexter's Place, I told him to find another site.'

'What did he say?'

'At first, he admitted it wasn't an ideal situation but he was sure you could be persuaded,' he said. 'I reiterated a firm "No" and he agreed to search for another location. As far as I was concerned, the matter was over.'

'Bella's dad lied to you, Trav,' she said. 'Salter Holdings, a division of Arnold Construction, has been hounding me with letters, each escalating in the level of threats. These missives, when combined with your and Bella's refusal to leave the flat, could make awkward reading if they were to be handed to your boss.'

'Please, Caro, don't,' Travis said. 'I'd be sacked, it'd be a disaster.'

'Why won't you do the decent thing and move out of the flat then?' she asked.

Travis dropped his gaze, his shoulders shuddered and Caroline realised there were tears in his eyes. He looked wretched.

'I told Bella,' his voice was so quiet, she almost missed his words.

'Told her what? Jonah?'

'Jonah, Dexter, all of it. Lee plans to blackmail you if you continue to resist his demands.'

Caroline felt fury rising. Her overriding emotion for Travis was disgust that he could remain involved with these duplicitous and ruthless people. The question was: did he know the truth about the Arnolds or were they lying to him too?

'Were you aware that Lee's company is in a desperate financial situation?' she asked.

'What? No, it isn't, Bella would have told me.'

'A large deal in the Baltics went wrong earlier this year and he's lost millions,' Caroline said.

'You're lying,' snapped Travis.

'Clinton Sova's team hired a forensic accountant to look into Lee Arnold's finances and they've concluded he has approximately three months until the receivers are called in,' she said.

'No doubt he thought if he could secure my flat it would be a useful asset to help him save his business. I'd guess he's decided using the Dexter Blake connection for the Pembrokeshire property will help him to sell the holiday homes for even more money and I assume his ultimatum will be that if I refuse to capitulate, he'll reveal the truth.'

Travis was silent, refusing to meet Caroline's eyes.

'Caro, what do you want me to do?' said Travis. He looked desperate but she felt no pity. 'Bella's pregnant, Lee is expecting me to propose but he refuses to help pay for an engagement ring or give us any money towards the wedding until the issue with the flat and your land is settled.'

Caroline was surprised how this news bounced off her without causing even the smallest wince of pain. Instead, she felt a wave of disgust at his weakness.

'Does Lee know you're legally bound by your NDA?'

'When the solicitor's letter arrived reminding me about it, Lee was furious. He knows it would be difficult to have a story printed in this country because of all Blanche's legal restrictions but he's threatening to print it abroad.'

'Not online?'

'No, he's old-fashioned, he wants a newspaper headline.'

Caroline felt a small thrill of dark pleasure at his misery.

'You're in a difficult situation,' she said, 'but it's not as simple as my giving you the flat. Have you forgotten it's in Jonah's name, too? Would you want to steal from a child?'

Caroline allowed the silence to grow, watching as Travis walked restlessly around the living room of the apartment over which they were arguing.

'When did you sign it over to Jonah?' asked Travis.

'Years ago, I did tell you but as usual, you weren't listening.'

Travis resumed his pacing.

'What about if I invested in Arnold Constructions?' Caroline said.

Travis gave a humourless laugh. 'Why would you give money to Lee Arnold?'

'Blanche's management company has evolved over the years. We've developed excellent business and investment contacts; this could be an interesting venture,' she paused, then added, 'Of course, there would be conditions.'

'Such as?'

'If I offered to bail out Arnold Constructions and Salter Holdings; you, Bella and Lee would have to sign new Non-Disclosures Agreements. You would also have to vacate the London flat with immediate effect.'

'Lee would never agree,' he said. 'Nor would Bella.'

'Are you sure? Once the word is out that Arnold Construction is about to go belly-up, the vultures will begin circling. Thanks to you, we've been forewarned about any potential blackmail threats or attempts to reveal the truth about Dexter. One call to Blanche and Clinton will have worldwide super-injunctions in place to thwart Lee Arnold. And, even if he did manage to publish something online instead, who would believe him? He's a desperate man making a last-ditch effort to save his business. It's pitiful. There isn't a newspaper anywhere that would go near him.'

Travis stared at her. 'Who suggested you make this call?' he asked, and the sneer was back in his voice.

'No one,' she replied. 'Travis, you've always thought you were the intelligent one in this relationship but you never were. You lived a millionaire's lifestyle on a police salary and when you were bored in the countryside, you found a woman in London. If Bella throws you out, you'll have to live on your own money until you find another wealthy woman to fall for your charms. It'll be a bit of a comedown.'

'You bitch.'

'No, I'm speaking the truth.'

'That makes a change,' he snorted.

Caroline curled her hands into fists but refused to allow him to rile her, instead she continued in a calm, cold tone.

'Are you going to approach Lee Arnold with my suggestion?' she said. 'If you do, Blanche and the business team will draw up the proposals, work out the funding and forward NDAs for you all to sign. This is your way out, Travis. You keep your easy lifestyle, marry the girl and have a child of your own. Everything you've always wanted. Except the penthouse flat, of course.'

Caroline was fighting to keep the bitterness in her voice to a minimum. She no longer loved Travis but helping to resolve his relationship problems so he could marry another woman was not an easy task.

'If I persuade Lee to accept, you won't ruin the business deliberately, will you? To spite me?'

'You've never known me, have you?' she said. 'Why would I risk my own money by ruining the company?'

'True,' Travis said. 'But why, Caro? If Lee's been threatening you, why not cut him loose?'

'Because in return, I want you and your in-laws to not only halt the threats to Dexter's Place and desist squatting in my flat, but I also want you to stop the cyberattacks and take down all the false accusations you've been posting about me murdering Dexter. Your accomplice has been caught, so the majority will be removed but don't even think about adding anything new.'

Travis looked confused. 'What accusations? What accomplice?'

'Stop lying, Travis,' she said, but he looked bemused. 'You don't know?'

'No, Lee doesn't like social media and Bella's dream is to become an influencer. She wouldn't risk her precious reputation by trolling anyone, not even you.'

Caroline considered him but her instincts told her Travis was telling the truth. 'Very well,' she said. 'As for the flat, we need to sort things out as soon as possible.'

'Do we have to move out?'

'Yes, unless you'd like to pay me rent at the full market price or buy it from me.'

He stared at her, his brown eyes softening. 'We were good together, Caro,' he said. 'It's a shame things fell apart.'

'Were we?' she asked, but there was no rancour in her tone. 'You hurt me, Travis, but I think we'd both been hanging on to a relationship that had run its course a long time ago.'

'I hear Jonah's in the new film,' he said.

'Yes, he won the part himself, no one knows about his connection to Dexter.'

'The new book's doing well,' he said.

'Yes, but it's the last one. No more Dexter.'

'No more Dexter,' he echoed. 'Give my love to Jonah. I'll call Lee, discuss your proposal.'

'Will you be able to persuade him?'

'If it's going to save his business, then yes. Bye, Caro.'

Caroline stared at the screen where his face had been, waiting for a flood of regret but none came, instead she was filled with relief. She scrolled to Blanche's number and as she walked to the standing stone, Mabe's Gate, on the edge of the wood where she had arranged to meet Gideon, she outlined her plan for Arnold Constructions and Salter Holdings. When she hung up, she felt as though Anne Brandon was walking beside her. One problematic man had been removed from her life. Now it was time to fight for the other, for true love and forgiveness.

35

He was waiting by Mabe's Gate, the ancient standing stone that had passed millennia staring out to sea on its lonely vigil. Gideon gazed towards Ramsey Island, its base lost in a hazy ethereal mist. Caroline's mind floated to the tale of Mabe's Gate with its legend claiming it was an entrance to another realm; on a day like this where nature was at her most mysterious Caroline could understand the origins of such a tale.

How had it looked when Anne and Randall stood here? she thought. Was there magic in the air then, too?

When she had suggested this place, its significance to Anne and Randall had been unknown to her, yet the Tudor couple had found love and forgiveness here. She hoped their lingering romance would help her and Gideon to discover their own path to happiness. A flicker of brightness caught her eye and a boat appeared, its sails blackened by shadows. She swallowed her sense of unease.

Earlier in the day, Caroline had left the entrance to the garden unlocked to allow him to make his way to their arranged meeting point. Gideon's eyes were following the boat too and he did not hear her approach. Ken was snuffling about in the long grass nearby and as she neared he ran towards her with an excited bark.

'Caro, you're all right?' said Gideon, turning, as he hurried in the golden retriever's wake, pulling her into an enormous hug.

Neither of them saw the sails glow white as sunlight hit the boat on its journey around the headland.

'Yes,' she said, returning his embrace. 'And you?'

'As soon as the officer explained they'd had a report from my distraught wife that I was missing, feared kidnapped, I knew we were dealing with another of Margot's tantrums. Connie's husband, Bart, has a friend who's a KC. I called her, explained the situation and she called Bart's friend, Duncan Rathbone to help. Once he'd made a few calls, everything was resolved.'

'What about Margot?' asked Caroline.

'I don't know,' he said. 'She won't answer her phone. Connie's left a message with Tubshaw but we assume Margot is lying low. Duncan threatened numerous counter charges we could bring if she tried this again.'

'Actually, Gideon, the reason Margot isn't answering her phone is because she's been arrested for wasting police time,' said Caroline.

It gave her no pleasure to deliver this piece of information. Gideon's mouth set in a grim line.

'Why? I don't intend to press charges,' he said.

'It isn't you or me bringing the charges,' said Caroline. 'She was the person behind the accusations of murder against me. She'd hired hackers to do the trolling but it was her insisting on the increasing aggression and violence in the messages. Margot made an official complaint to the police claiming to have information about the suspicious death of Dexter Blake.'

'What?' said Gideon, aghast.

'She told them there was no death certificate or grave for Dexter. Somehow, she even discovered there had been no funeral. When the police investigated further, they realised she was correct. Add to this her accusations that I was holding you against your will and the police were obliged to take her accusations seriously.'

'How did she know all this?'

'As well as hackers, she and her father hired a private detective to follow you, then me,' said Caroline.

Gideon stared at her and she knew he was trying to process all the information she had given him. As he worked through it, she saw realisation flicker in his eyes.

'But if there was no funeral?' he asked. 'Is Dexter Blake alive?'

'No,' said Caroline, and her heart broke at the devastation on Gideon's face as his momentary hope that his writing hero survived faded again. 'There is so much you don't know,' she continued, her words catching in her throat. 'A lifetime of decisions to unravel. Would you allow me the chance to explain?'

Caroline spread her fingers wide across the standing stone, feeling the roughness of the lichen. She imagined Anne and Randall pledging their love and asked them for strength as she took a deep breath and turned to face Gideon.

'Dexter is dead,' she said, 'and, in a way, Margot is correct in her claims.'

'What are you talking about?' he asked.

'I did murder Dexter Blake,' she said in a shaky voice.

'What?' Gideon's response was a mix of disbelief and nervous laughter.

'We spoke and I told him he would have to die after we'd finished the final book,' she said.

'Are you telling me you helped your grandfather to commit suicide?' he asked.

'No, it was my choice. I always knew he would have to go eventually. It was the only way for Jonah and me to move forward with our lives. None of us expected him to survive as long as he did.'

Gideon stared at her in horror.

'But, if you like, I can introduce you to him,' said Caroline, and she was aware of the strangeness of her words. 'Dexter can come back anytime he chooses.'

'Caro, are you feeling quite well?' asked Gideon.

'Come with me,' she said. 'There's something I have to show you.'

Caroline walked away, through the grove and back along the path to the garden where Dexter's wooden summer house waited, the door ajar. She glanced over her shoulder, wondering whether Gideon would follow. He had clipped Ken onto his lead and his phone was in his hand but he paced a few steps behind her, a wary expression on his face.

'Welcome to Dexter's office,' she said. 'Come in and I'll explain.'

Gideon did as she asked but he remained within easy reach of the doorway. Caroline walked over to the desk, which was positioned near the window. Beside it was a wing-backed leather armchair and matching footstool. Two bookcases held an assortment of old books, as well as a battered brass microscope, a telescope in a case and a sextant. On another shelf was a blackened pipe resting on a stand beside a leather pouch of tobacco and an old-fashioned cut-glass ashtray. On the desk was an electric typewriter and a neat pile of A4 paper.

In a row next to this were framed photographs of three men, all dressed in identical clothes. They each had grey hair, their lavish curls tamed by Brylcreem, hooded hazel eyes and high cheek-boned faces that held vestiges of the good looks of their youth. Each man wore a blue quilted smoking jacket with a silk burgundy cravat and they all glared at the camera as though it had personally offended them.

'Dexter Blake,' said Caroline pointing to the images. 'Except, it isn't.'

'Those are his publicity photographs,' said Gideon.

Caroline picked up the first frame and gave a sad smile as she passed it to Gideon.

'This is my maternal grandfather, George Harvey,' she said.

'You mean he used a pen name...?' said Gideon.

'No, he never wrote a word of the books,' she said. 'All he did was lend me his image and when he died in August 2012, my great-uncle Walter, Granddad's identical twin, stepped into the breach and pretended to be Dexter.'

She picked up the second photograph and showed it to Gideon.

'If you look closely, Granddad has a small scar on his lip and Walter doesn't,' she said. 'Granddad's death was the reason Dexter chose this moment to hide in Pembrokeshire and claim he was a recluse. It was also around then I realised I was pregnant with Jonah.'

'But...'

'Please, Gid, let me finish, then you'll understand,' she said as she reached for the third photograph. 'This is Cyril Paster, an actor, who walked around the garden with me and sat in here typing in the run up to the publication of the eighth book, *Ether Heracles and The Tropic of Pisces* because there were rumours that Dexter was being held against his will. Before then, this had been a summer house but to stage photographs we decorated the interior of this shed to make the myth of Dexter more tangible. Afterwards, I decided to leave it and quite often worked out here myself. We paid a photographer to take 'secret pap' shots of us which we leaked to the press ourselves. Uncle Walter had died the previous year and Cyril was the person Blanche found who most resembled my grandfather and Uncle Walter. Cyril was paid a great deal of money and compelled to sign a Non-Disclosure Agreement. Travis also signed one as did my family, although I didn't ask them to.'

'Caro, what's going on?'

Gideon was staring at her as though she was insane and she knew the moment had finally arrived. She took a deep breath and said, 'I am Dexter Blake.'

'What?'

She shivered at the admission; to say it aloud after years of lying and hiding behind her grandfather's photograph felt terrifying.

'I wrote the *Ether Heracles* books,' she said, 'and the reason you found them so familiar is because they were based on us. The crew of *The Oisin* was The Seven: you were Ether, I was Allegra, Nadine was Luna, Ben was Lucifer Transmere, Saz was Bylgja Opus, Jules was Taranis Locomute and Lizzie was Ken, the Egyptian goddess of love...'

'Because she wanted to be an archaeologist and study the Egyptian tombs,' finished Gideon.

'Yes,' said Caroline.

'Caro, how is this possible?' said Gideon.

'When Flavia ran me over a month after we'd finished our A-levels and broke my leg, I deferred my university place. To pass the time while I was stuck in a cast I entertained myself by writing a story based on the stupid things we'd done during college and our drama practical lessons,' she said. 'Those hours with everyone had been so special, all the laughter and love we shared, not to mention our kiss. To spend my days recreating us in another world where I had control was even more fun.'

'But you always claimed you wanted to write serious literature,' he said.

'True,' she agreed, 'but the sci-fi genre suited the ideas better and it was inspired by that old TV series your dad showed us, *Blake's Seven*. Once I'd begun, the story flowed out of me as though it had always been there. Dad read the first draft and showed it to his old school friend, Clinton Sova, who was in a relationship with Blanche. She read it and thought it was intriguing. When Blanche offered to represent me and the books, I suggested a pen name to leave me free to write grandiose fiction under my real name at a later date. She agreed but for different reasons; Blanche explained that sci-fi was a difficult genre for women to be taken seriously in and a man's name would make it easier to sell the books. I decided to use Blake as the surname, continuing the theme of our drama practical group—'

'And Dexter because of the lesson when we were given the exercise to march like soldiers and everyone else was shouting left, right, left right and I showed off to you with my GCSE Latin and began shouting sinister, dexter, sinister, dexter.'

'Because it was us, you were left-handed, I was right. The perfect pair. Sinister, dexter...' said Caroline.

'You were always Dexter,' he said in wonder.

'I thought you of all people might guess,' she said. 'The clues were hidden in plain sight.'

'Like the bookshop logo,' he said. 'It was my message of love to you. The clock, your boots which you always wore with ribbons instead of laces, the crash helmet. The kiss had meant so much but we both stepped back so as to protect other people from pain.'

'Imagine if we hadn't,' she said.

Gideon stared at her in amazement.

'Was Beau Ferris meant to be your ex, Travis?'

'He was,' said Caroline, 'and the reason I appeared to kill off Lucifer was because I was so angry with Ben for dumping me by text. When I'd forgiven him, Lucifer was allowed to return.'

'Luna was Nadine,' he said. 'You were jealous of my relationship with her, so you killed her in every book.'

Caroline looked shame-faced.

'Ether saved her every time though and in the final book, the crew worked as a team to bring her back to life.'

'And the others?'

'Saz was always so cool, I made her Bylgja, a rebel leader like you, but I was never sure how you felt about her. I created a relationship around you both that was complicated but not of your own making,' said Caroline. 'Jules always had an other-worldly air about him with his paisley jackets and patchouli oil, which was why I made him a Seer, a mystical person who was searching for their identity.'

'And the twist at the end of book ten when it was revealed why Allegra vanished for part of Book Four, *Race of Jupiter...*'

'To have Ether's baby and hide him from the Boucicauly.'

'It coincided with you having Jonah,' Gideon stated.

'Yes,' she said. 'The books have echoed my life for years.'

'But why did you go to such lengths to create a character for Dexter when you could have claimed the accolades for yourself?' asked Gideon.

'No one, especially me, ever expected the books to catch the public's imagination. When they did Blanche and the publishers were nervous that if the secret came out a girl in her early twenties was the real Dexter Blake, the bubble would burst. By then, Dexter had become a real person in my mind.

When I was writing, I'd have lengthy conversations with him, it was as though he was my invisible muse. It was my subconscious, my imagination, whatever you choose to call it but it began to speak with Dexter's voice and I felt me and my alter ego were in this together. Granddad was the one who suggested he be the face of Dexter but that was to stop people wanting to interview him, he would be an irascible recluse. It was the complete opposite to the real person. Granddad loved a party.'

'What about Dexter's life story?'

'All created by Blanche and me,' said Caroline. 'The trouble was, as Ether and the gang increased in popularity, it became impossible to tell the truth. It's why in the end, Dexter stepped back and named me as his representative. Of course I could discuss the books with authority, I'd written them, it was my world but throughout every interview it was imperative it was Dexter who was seen to be the driving force. By the fifth book, I was furious about the situation. In my heart, I knew it was my fault because I'd allowed the lie to grow and grow. Despite the fact it was my work, my story, my characters: Dexter was always lauded. It was frustrating but by then we'd signed the film contracts and part of the deal was to continue the myth of Dexter Blake.'

'I have no idea what to say,' said Gideon, staring down at her.

'When Jonah was born, I suggested to Blanche we come clean but she dissuaded me. It was around then I bought this house,' she said. 'It was a good place to hide, to raise Jonah and to continue writing. It also helped to heal my broken heart because by then you were married to Margot, although meeting Travis helped.'

Gideon's face was ashen. Even Ken had realised the serious nature of their conversation because he lay motionless beside Gideon, his tail touching his master's leg in a gesture of comfort.

'What fools we've been,' said Gideon. 'Margot trapped me into marriage and you were condemned by a foolish lie you told to protect yourself. How different our lives could have been...'

His voice trailed away and Caroline waited; unsure how to continue.

'Does Jonah know?' Gideon asked eventually.

'Yes, he knows the whole story,' she said. 'My life was ruined by the web my lies built around me, I was determined my son would never suffer in the same way.'

'Are you going to reveal the truth about Dexter?'

'Not yet but perhaps one day.'

'Will you make me sign a Non-Disclosure Agreement?'

'No,' she said. It was one of the many topics she had considered during her restless night. There would be no more secrets, no more lies and no more chaining people to her through legal agreements. 'Dexter is gone, the final book has been released, the story is over. If you choose to tell the world, then so be it.'

As soon as the words were spoken, Caroline saw the change in Gideon. His body tensed and his eyes flashed with fury.

'Is that what you think I'll do?' he said.

'No, of course not,' said Caroline in panic. 'All I meant was, the lies are over.'

'You think I'll run out of here and start shouting out your secrets? Why would you think I'd betray you again?' he said, and there was a bitterness in his voice she had never heard before.

'Gid, you've misunderstood—' she began, but he spoke over her in a voice of ice.

'Is that what this was all about? You lured me here in the hope I'd tell the world about Dexter and do your dirty work for you? You've just told me my hero has never existed. You've shattered my illusion of a man writing a magical world where I felt connected, where I'd found a place to belong away from all the difficulties of life, yet you're hinting you want me to be the one to break the news Dexter Blake was as much a fantasy as his hero, Ether Heracles.'

'No, Gid,' she gasped, horrified at his reaction. 'I didn't mean it like that—'

'You're as bad as Margot,' he said and there were tears in his eyes. 'You hide the fact you've given birth to my child, deny me the chance of being a father and a part of his life as he grows up. But, worse, you think you can manipulate me into revealing the biggest secret of all – Dexter Blake never existed – he was the imaginary friend of a woman too ambitious to risk using her own name on a sci-fi book. Caro, I've loved you for most of my life. I came here today to apologise for being foolish enough to marry Margot, to ask you to give me another chance but now, I don't know. You're not the person I always imagined you to be.'

'Gid, please, no, you've misunderstood...' she began but Gideon turned, Ken at his heel. 'Gid, please, come back.'

He marched away, vanishing from sight. A moment later, she heard his car start and roar off. Gideon had gone and in her heart she feared he would never return.

36

LONDON, DECEMBER, PRESENT DAY

'What do you mean he's coming with a different chaperone?' Caroline said into the phone, the hairs on the back of her neck prickling in panic.

She was in the back of a stretch limousine en route to the premiere of *Ether Heracles and The Elegua Crossroads*. Her hair fell in curls around her shoulders and her emerald-green evening dress made shooshing sounds as she sat further forward on the leather seats. Her knuckles were white around her phone as her demeanour switched from relaxed to horrified in a heartbeat.

'Wendy is taking Maddie Wells and Jonah is being accompanied by his father,' said Petunia Wallace, the head teacher at Jonah's stage school, Baddeley Manor.

'No, that's impossible,' replied Caroline. 'Jonah has no contact with his father. Mrs Wallace, this is a huge dereliction of duty. You've allowed my son into the company of a strange man pretending to be a relative. I hold you responsible for his safety and I'm going to hang up and call the police.'

'I can assure you, Ms Harvey, the man who collected Jonah

was known to him and has passed all our security checks,' Petunia Wallace snapped. 'Your son is perfectly safe.'

The car swept into Leicester Square where the screams of the crowds drowned out the telephone conversation. All around her people shouted, waving banners and copies of *Ether Heracles* books. Christmas lights twinkled and a drone version of *The Oisin* hovered above the crowd in the starry night sky giving London an alien appearance.

'Mrs Wallace—' Caroline shouted into the phone, but the line was dead. The headmistress had hung up.

Her car halted at the top of the red carpet and Caroline wondered whether to remain inside until she had located Jonah but the cheering outside from the *Ether Heracles* fans was deafening and sense told her this noise alone prohibited making calls. There was also the problem that if she did not alight, it would block the entrance for the next vehicle. It was with great reluctance Caroline accepted she would have to wait until she was inside before she could deal with this terrifying and unprecedented situation. She stuffed her phone into her evening bag and wished Flavia was by her side but her sister had a streaming cold so Caroline had come alone.

A clear crisp winter night had replaced the earlier rain and as Caroline gathered her cashmere wrap around her shoulders, she racked her brains whether she had missed an email or call concerning her son. She did not understand why Mrs Wallace had deviated from the arrangements that had been settled upon weeks earlier: Jonah, who had returned to school until the shoot for the next film began, would be brought to the event by his usual chaperone, Wendy Philips. This was a rule specified by the school. Why, then, had Mrs Wallace stated Jonah's father was accompanying him? Did she mean Travis? As far as Caroline was aware her ex-fiancé was on his honeymoon with his new wife, Bella.

Caroline called Jonah's number but it went straight to voicemail and before she could try Blanche, the car door was flung open. One of the black-tie wearing assistants proffered a hand and she had no choice but to climb out. A cheer deafened her as she emerged. Her fear was momentarily halted as she stared, overwhelmed, at the vast numbers of people who had arrived to celebrate the new *Ether Heracles* film.

'We still miss your granddad,' one woman shouted, waving a picture of Dexter Blake when Great-Uncle Walter had been playing the role.

'How are you coping without him?' another called.

'Love your tights!' a teenage girl screamed, pointing to Caroline's legs.

Caroline forced herself to smile, to play the part. Once again, the images of *Ether* book covers from around the world encased her legs but there was a new detail too.

'Look,' Caroline called to the girl. She turned, pulling her dress aside so the crowd could see her seams.

'What does it say?' the teenager shrieked in excitement, taking multiple photographs on her phone.

'It's the sentence that saved the Universe,' Caroline said.

'Where can I buy a pair?' shouted a chorus of voices in delight.

Caroline grinned, waved and moved away, pausing to reply to a few of the questions hurled at her by excited readers. Despite her smiles and her interactions, the entire time she was scanning the red carpet for Jonah. It was fruitless but it did not stop her searching. She was desperate to locate her son even though she knew the plan was for Jonah and Maddie to arrive last. Caroline allowed herself to be led up the red carpet by one of the ushers to where Joe Newman and Simon Keystone waited.

'Hey, Caro,' said Joe bending down to kiss her cheek. 'This is the biggest turnout yet.'

'It's unbelievable,' said Simon. 'Your grandfather created a true phenomenon with his books.'

'He did,' she agreed and in her mind she heard 'Dexter' laugh.

'This way please, Miss Harvey,' said a woman wearing a headset and clutching a clipboard. 'The two young stars will be arriving in a few minutes and we want clear shots of them before we go inside. There will also be the two short, pre-agreed interviews for British and US television. The meet and greets for the competition winners will be backstage afterwards but everyone other than the cast needs to be in the auditorium before they arrive.'

'They're here?' Caroline asked.

'We have confirmation both cars are five minutes away. If you'd like to make your way inside, please.'

Caroline resisted her impulse to shout at the woman, to insist on waiting for her son but as no one knew their true relationship, she could not publicly stake her claim. Instead, nerves jangling, she waved again to the crowd and walked into the foyer where Blanche hovered, her face alight with excitement.

'What the hell is going on?' Caroline snapped as her agent took her arm and dragged her away from the crowd of invited guests who were watching Caroline's entrance with interest. 'Who's chaperoning Jonah?'

'You'll see,' said Blanche. 'Come on, we have to take our seats.'

'Blanche, no—' she began.

'Trust me, Caro,' Blanche interrupted. 'Jonah is safe and will be here in a few minutes. He won't thank you for ruining his entrance.'

Aware people were watching their altercation and not wanting to create a scene Caroline allowed Blanche to march her into the cavernous auditorium. More smiling helpers, this time dressed in the uniforms of the crew of *The Oisin* ushered Caroline into one of the central seats near the front of the cinema. She glanced at her watch.

Blanche's phone pinged and a look of satisfaction flitted across her face.

'Don't move and stop panicking, Jonah's here,' Blanche said. 'I'll go and make sure all is well.'

Before Caroline could stop her, Blanche had pushed her way back into the milling crowd.

'The two kids have arrived…' she heard a woman say behind her before she moved out of earshot.

Caroline hesitated. Jonah was here which meant he was safe. He was also a professional and, Blanche was correct, he would be unimpressed if she flung herself at him while he was doing the two interviews they had agreed upon. If she held her nerve, she would discover the identity of this mysterious man claiming to be Jonah's father. She closed her eyes as a bizarre possibility occurred to her: *could it be Gideon?*

She had not heard from him since the day he had stormed away from Dexter's Place. For a week, she had waited for him to call, then she had tried his number to discover she had been blocked. Instead, she had contacted Ben and he suggested she give Gideon time.

'Did he tell you what we discussed?' she asked.

'No, he wouldn't say. I figured you'd had an almighty row,' Ben said. 'Leave him Caro, he'll come back. Despite what you think, he does love you.'

She hoped Ben was correct but as the weeks grew into months with no word from Gideon, she allowed her fragile dreams of a future with him to fade once again. When Eve told her she had seen neither Ben nor Gideon at the bookshop for months Caroline realised Gideon really had gone. She gathered her battered pride around her, nursed her broken heart and concentrated on Jonah, her family and her historical research. Her friendships with the team at Marquess House had blossomed and Caroline was working on the first draft of a non-fiction history book about Anne Brandon and Randall Hanworth.

The excited roar from outside dimmed and Caroline knew the doors had been shut which meant the cast was in the auditorium. She craned her neck for a glimpse of her son but could not see him. Instead, Connie waved, pointing to Maddie who was beside her, then to her relief Caroline saw Blanche leading Jonah down the stairs.

'Oh, thank goodness,' she muttered.

Blanche guided him along the row of seats to Caroline. Jonah was grinning, clearly having a wonderful evening and she had no intention of spoiling it but it took every ounce of her self-restraint not to drag her son into her arms and hug him.

'Who's chaperoning you?' she whispered as Jonah took his seat between Blanche and Caroline.

'I am,' said a familiar voice and Gideon dropped into the seat on her other side that should have been Flavia's. For the first time Caroline wondered about the validity of her sister's cold.

'You? How?'

Before he could answer, the film's producer, Marc Samuels, stepped onto the low stage in front of the screen, a microphone in his hand, and waved for attention.

'Good evening, ladies and gentlemen,' he called, pausing as he waited for the applause to end. 'Here we are again for another adventure with Ether Heracles and the gang...'

'Why are you here?' whispered Caroline to Gideon as the speech continued. 'You blocked me on your phone and have ignored me for six months.'

'I had a lot to think about,' said Gideon. 'A huge amount of research.'

'Into what?' she hissed.

'Anne Brandon and Randall Hanworth, they're a fascinating couple,' he said. 'I plan to do a series of documentaries on lost Tudor stories. They'll be the first people I investigate. Anne Brandon was an astonishing woman, even though she lived in what was effectively a world of illusion and lies, she managed to find true love.'

'What are you talking about?' snapped Caroline.

'No wonder you were drawn to her,' he said but there was no malice in his voice. 'Jonah tells me you're writing a book about Anne, perhaps we could collaborate?'

'Are you mad?' she whispered in fury but another part of her wanted to laugh.

This was such a Gideon response and, frustrating though he could be, she could see the seriousness in his eyes, his fear of her potential rejection.

'No,' he replied. 'I'm perfectly sane and no longer behaving like a stroppy teenager.'

'That makes a change,' she retorted but her heart was softening.

'I'm sorry for the way I behaved,' he murmured. 'What you told me was a shock but by the time I was back at the shop, I'd calmed down.'

'Why didn't you call?'

'I realised this time there was nothing to stop us being together and it scared me. We've spent most of our lives losing sight of each other and I knew, if things went wrong this time, I could lose you forever and I didn't want to take that risk.'

'Lose me?' she said. 'What makes you think I'll forgive you?'

'Because we love each other,' he said, 'we always have and we always will.'

'Mum, Dad, will you please stop talking,' said Jonah his voice stern, although his eyes twinkled with mischief, 'the film's about to start. This is my movie debut, a bit of attention would be welcomed.'

Caroline did a double-take at her son's use of the word 'Dad'. It felt strange, yet at the same time, there was a rightness to hearing it. And, he's correct, she thought, this evening is about him, not me and Gideon.

'Sorry,' she said, then hesitated before continuing because the words felt unexpectedly intimate, 'Your dad and I can talk later. Are you nervous?'

'No, I'm excited,' he replied.

'Here you are, son,' said Gideon passing a large tub of popcorn across her to Jonah. 'Let me know if you want anything else.'

'Sure thing, Dad,' Jonah replied.

'You're going to be incredible,' Caroline whispered and Jonah leaned briefly into her for reassurance before straightening up and applying himself to his popcorn.

* * *

The music began and as the story unfurled on the huge screen, Caroline's mind whirred. Gideon's presence was unnerving. Whenever she moved, her arm brushed his, her nose was filled with the subtle scent of his aftershave. She had never imagined they would be sitting side by side as their son made his movie debut. Jonah's eyes were fixed on the screen and she knew it was because he was about to appear for the first time.

Caroline reached for her son's hand and he wound his fingers into hers, squeezing them tight, a sure sign he was nervous. On her other side, Gideon did not appear to be breathing and Caroline wondered if Jonah had described the point in the film where he came on screen.

The screen flashed white and Jonah, ten metres tall, wielding a blaster, shouted: 'This way!' as Maddie raced into shot, her own weapon whining as it charged.

A huge cheer filled the cinema. Tears sprang into Caroline's eyes and she grinned at Jonah, then to her surprise, Gideon took her other hand.

'Our boy's looking good,' he whispered and she could hear the crack of emotion in his voice.

Caroline swallowed the lump in her throat and waited for Gideon to drop her hand but instead he wound his fingers around hers in the way he had when they were younger. Caroline lost track of the film as she tried to understand how she came to be sitting between the two men she loved best in the world, each holding her hand in the same finger-tangled way, rather than the usual palm-to-palm. Was it a Morris-family trait? she wondered as she allowed the warmth and familiarity of Gideon and Jonah's touches to envelope her.

The action moved on and when he was no longer on screen, Jonah dropped Caroline's hand and returned to his popcorn.

'I reread all the books,' Gideon whispered, his hand warm in hers.

'Why?'

'I had a theory and it was important to create a workable hypothesis.'

Caroline stifled her giggle. 'And your theory is...?' she murmured.

'The *Ether Heracles* books are a love story.'

Caroline rolled her eyes. 'Of course.'

'But it's a love story in disguise,' he said.

'Yes, it was deliberate but it's always been a story about finding true love.'

'I didn't understand, not until I read the magical sentence Ether and the crew have been chasing all over the Universe to find: *"The answer you seek that conquers all is true love"*,' he said.

'Had you not guessed?' she asked.

'No, I thought it was going to be "forgiveness",' he said. 'Some super-fan I turned out to be.'

'"Forgiveness",' she said in surprise. 'Where's the fun in forgiveness? I thought it was obvious the answer was love.'

They gazed at each as behind them the crew of *The Oisin* was ambushed by their mortal enemies The Wicked in the Abandoned City, and a battle began.

'I'm sorry, Caro,' said Gideon as the sound of laser fire filled the auditorium. 'You deserved better than my terrible behaviour. When you were at your most vulnerable, I failed you.'

'You had every right,' she whispered.

'Even worse, I compared you with my ex-wife,' he said. 'Can you forgive me?'

'Of course you're forgiven,' replied Caroline. 'There was no easy way of telling you the truth but I handled things badly.'

'Perhaps we both did.'

'Yes,' she agreed, 'but before we say any more, you have to watch the next scene.'

He gave her a curious look and turned back to the movie. She bit her lip, wondering if he would realise the depth of her feelings, her belief in their future together.

On the screen there was a huge explosion, the crew was sent into disarray. Ether was the first to his feet, hauling the others up, when a huge clock appeared, hanging in space.

'"The clock's striking ten-to-midnight, we have to return to the ship. Look, there it is, the white sails are flying…",' shouted Ether Heracles from the screen and Gideon turned to Caroline, his eyes wide in astonishment.

'My gift for you in the script,' she said. 'I added this extra scene especially. I hoped if you ever saw it, you'd realise how much I loved you and how the books were always about you, about us and our love.'

'I love you,' he said. 'If you'd be prepared to give me one more chance, I promise to love you for the rest of our lives.'

Caroline's breath caught in her throat at his words.

'I love you too.'

'"Forever this time?"' he asked and Caroline smothered a grin, it was one of the final lines in the last book of the series. The line Ether said to Allegra as they promised true love to each other.

'"Forever, Ether, until the stars have left the sky",' she replied.

As Gideon leaned over to kiss her, the screen showed an amethyst sky and the space ship *The Oisin* flying to its next adventure, followed by the words:

The End

THE REAL STORY OF ANNE BRANDON

The Tudor world was full of women – queens, queen consorts, princesses, duchesses, countesses, ladies and thousands without titles who toiled in the background. I first discovered Anne Brandon when I was researching a different book but the boldness of her behaviour stayed with me and a story formed in my mind with Anne at its centre.

She, like so many other forgotten women, was at the heart of the Tudor court during one of its most volatile periods. Anne witnessed all six of Henry VIII's wives be raised high then destroyed, she lived through the reign of Edward VI and Mary I, dying in the year when Elizabeth I took the crown.

Anne was a woman ahead of her time. She survived an abusive marriage before finding true love in the arms of a man with whom she lived openly while her husband remained alive. She was made even more fascinating by her brush with the wrong side of the law.

In *The House of Echoes*, I have tried to capture Anne's determined spirit and survival instinct. However, there are a number of places where I have used artistic license. Anne's husband did attack her and Randall but there are no records stating he tried to behead her, neither are there any documents suggesting she tried to revenge herself on the men who sat in judgement on Anne Boleyn. These are made up, as are the references connecting her to *Tristan and Iseult*. Mabe's Gate is a real standing stone in Pembrokeshire but the story Caroline tells is my own creation.

Anne was born in c.1507 and even before her birth, there was a taint of scandal surrounding her. Her mother, Anne Browne, who was the daughter of Sir Anthony Browne, governor of Queensborough Castle and Constable of Calais, and his wife Eleanor Ughtred of Kexby, North Yorkshire, had been abandoned by her betrothed: the philanderer, Sir Charles Brandon. He was always one to look out for himself and despite their engagement and the fact Anne was pregnant with his daughter, Charles eloped with wealthy widow, Margaret Neville.

Once Charles had helped himself to Margaret's money and land, this marriage was annulled and he returned to marry Anne Browne. Their daughter Anne was born, followed in 1510 by a second daughter, Mary. Anne Browne died during childbirth, leaving Charles Brandon a widower. For the next three years, Brandon rose through the ranks of Henry VIII's court and in 1513 he was betrothed to the eight-year-old Elizabeth Grey, Viscountess Lisle. Brandon was created Viscount Lisle and bought Elizabeth's wardship, making him a very wealthy man. Despite his adopting her title, this marriage was never to take place.

Charles Brandon's diplomatic missions took him frequently abroad and during one such trip in 1513 he met Margaret of Austria, Duchess of Savoy. Margaret was the daughter of Holy Roman Emperor, Maximilian I. Twice widowed when she first encountered Charles Brandon she had vowed never to marry again. She was the Governor of Habsburg Netherlands and a very well-educated and influential woman. It was therefore a shock when Henry VIII suggested a marriage between Margaret and his best friend, Charles Brandon, Viscount Lisle. A minor scandal blew up when Brandon requested a ring from Margaret and refused to return it until Henry intervened.

It is possible this was when Charles Brandon asked for a position for his eldest daughter, Anne, at Margaret's court; a much sought-after placement for the further education of young women. Margaret agreed and in 1514, when she was seven years old, Anne Brandon was sent to Mechelen, the court of Margaret of Austria, in the Netherlands. Among the other young ladies was Anne Boleyn, the daughter of rising diplomat, Thomas Boleyn. Whether the young women became friends is not recorded but they would have known each other and I created a close bond between the two Annes.

Anne Brandon remained in the Netherlands for two years, until she was summoned home to live with her father, now the Duke of Suffolk, and his new wife, Mary Tudor, youngest sister of Henry VIII and widow of the King of France. This marriage had caused a furore, as to marry a member of the royal family without permission was treason. However, Henry VIII was never able to remain angry with his favourite sister and his best friend for long and they were allowed to return to court. The huge fines imposed upon them as punishment for their marriage remained with Brandon for the rest of his life, leaving him forever short of money.

Over the next few years, the Brandon family grew to include Lady Frances, Lady Eleanor and Henry, Earl of Lincoln, in the laughter-filled home at Westhorpe Hall, Suffolk. Anne grew close to her new stepmother and enjoyed a happy childhood but with a father and stepmother at the heart of the court, it was not long before she was among the glamorous younger set.

When Anne Boleyn returned from the court of Margaret of Savoy in 1521, Anne Brandon would have been perfectly placed to watch as King Henry fell in love with the dark-haired beauty. This led to the upheaval of the King's Great Matter when he craved a divorce from Katherine of Aragon and changed the religion of England to marry Anne Boleyn.

Anne Brandon would have found herself caught between the divide forced upon her father and stepmother. Mary, Duchess of Suffolk had been sister-in-law to Katherine for the majority of her life, while Charles Brandon, as Henry's best friend had no choice but to help the king achieve his desire of marrying Anne Boleyn. We look back with knowledge, we know how the story unfolded but for Anne Brandon this would have been a difficult, possibly dangerous time, as allegiances shifted and the old world became the new.

In *The House of Echoes,* I created a friendship between Anne Brandon and Margaret (Meg) More, daughter of Sir Thomas More. Again there is no evidence the young women were friends but as their fathers were contemporaries and worked together for many years, I took the educated guess their daughters may have been friends, too.

In 1531, Anne Brandon married Edward Grey, Baron Powis, a rising star in Henry VIII's court. He had inherited his title as a baby and as I describe in the story, was in the unusual position of owning half of Powis Castle, while the remainder belonged to his Tiptoft cousins. It was an unhappy marriage with no children. Whether Anne never conceived or miscarried is unrecorded but in later life Edward would go on to have six illegitimate children with his lover Jane Orwell, suggesting Anne was unable to have children. After Edward's death, his eldest illegitimate son was granted his title.

It is not known when Anne met Randall Hanworth but in 1536 Anne and Edward were estranged and there are documents showing he accused Anne and Randall of plotting his death. The claim was that he caught them together in her bedroom and threw Randall out. However, this was not sustained and Charles Brandon petitioned the court to make Anne's husband pay her an annuity of £100 (approx. £30,000) per year. With Thomas Cromwell's help, Brandon was successful. Charles wanted Anne to follow Cromwell's advice and live quietly but she ignored him and continued to live with Randall.

By now, Charles Brandon had married the teenage Katherine Willoughby, 12th Baroness Willoughby de Eresby with whom he had two more sons. His sons with Princess Mary having died in childhood in 1522 and 1534. Lady Frances Brandon was married to Henry Grey, 3rd Marquess of Dorset, the parents of the future nine-day queen, Lady Jane Grey, and Lady Eleanor Brandon had married Henry Clifford, 2nd Earl of Cumberland. Anne's sister, Mary, was the wife of Thomas Stanley, 2nd Baron Monteagle.

When Anne was introduced to the Chancery Judge, John Beaumont, is not recorded but he was to become an important part of her story. At some point, Anne and her father fell out. My reasons in the story are without any basis but seemed an interesting guess. Until the row, Anne had very much been part of the court so whatever happened was huge. The estrangement resulted in Brandon changing his will and disinheriting Anne. He gave the Warwickshire lands he had promised Anne to her half-sister, Lady Frances. This was unknown to Anne until Brandon's death on 22 August 1545. Although there are no papers directly linked to Anne or official charges brought against her,

her name appears in court documents concerning John Beaumont, stating she was involved in a champerty scheme concerning the disputed lands.

Champerty is an illegal action where the plaintiff and the judge have an agreement before a lawsuit is brought. These cases usually involve land with the plaintiff suing for property they believe is theirs by right but beforehand making a deal with the judge agreeing to sell the plaintiff the land once it has been granted to them. In other words the judge finds for the plaintiff, he buys the land at a reasonable price and everyone benefits, except the person who really owns the land and is being sued.

Beaumont's career faltered, as Mark Llewellyn explains to Caroline in Chapter 34. There are no more records of him after 16 January 1556, so it is likely he died around this time.

There is very little other information about Anne, Randall or their life together but there is evidence that after the death of Edward Grey in 1555, Anne and Randall married. Sadly, where and when has been lost to time but there are surprising details of her funeral.

Thanks to *The Diary of Henry Machyn, Citizen and Merchant-Taylor of London* we do know Anne Brandon was married to Randall Hanworth when she died in January 1558. She was buried in Westminster in the parish of St Margaret's with a decent amount of pomp. There's an entry where he states she was interred with two white branches, thirteen torches, three great tapers and her coat of arms. Unfortunately, I have been unable to locate Randall's date of death or his burial place but they were clearly in London when Anne passed.

In writing Anne's story, I have used as many facts as possible and where there were gaps, I have tried to imagine myself into her world and what might have been. My guesses may be wrong but I hope Anne Brandon would approve. Anne was a determined, impetuous and brave woman. She, like her father, was an outsider in the glamorous world of the nobility, with no inherited title or fortune. All she had were her wits, guile, intelligence, looks and courage. In the end, she was successful: she married the man she loved and for a few years, they lived their happily ever after.

THE ETHER HERACLES BOOKS

The Ether Heracles books and Dexter Blake have always been integral to Caroline and Gideon's tale. From the beginning, I created the titles with very rough outlines of the stories but when I began writing *The House of Echoes*, I realised if the books were going to feel real, particularly as they were supposed to be world-famous, it was essential I knew what happened in each one.

Two weeks and a ten-thousand-word document later I had plotted all ten books complete with an imaginary publishing company and release dates. Here are brief outlines of each of Ether's adventures.

* * *

Book One – Ether Heracles and Andromeda's Sphere by Dexter Blake (Antrobus Publishing, March 2009)

Earth, Year 2095: The evil overlords, the Boucicauly, have ruled the known Universes for generations, few remember a time before they swept to power.

Yet, in every generation, a hero rises. One who is foretold in an ancient prophecy. One who will challenge the all-consuming darkness.

In Earth Barrack 894, Captain Ether Heracles and his best friend, Captain Lucifer Transmere, have been instructed to oversee the execution of three political prisoners – Luna, from the planet Stella Erratica in the Yoru galaxy, Taranis Locomute, a seer from Qing and, to Ether's horror, Bylgja Opus a soldier from their own ranks.

Ether has long been uneasy about his superiors' requests and to execute these prisoners is more than he is prepared to tolerate. With Lucifer and their trusted pilot and weapons expert, Allegra Cadwallader, they hatch a daring plan to free the hostages and escape in Ether's spaceship *The Oisin*.

Free at last, the crew is stunned to discover Taranis is the keeper of a long-held secret, a prophecy concerning the saviour of the known and unknown Universes. No one is named but Taranis believes the person destined to save them will soon be revealed. He explains there are a series of clues scattered around the Universe that will show how to defeat the Boucicauly. Taranis tells them the first clue is: '*Be definite about the article or all is lost.*'

Lucifer states trying to solve it is a fool's errand. He claims it is nonsense and this is proved by the rumours that there is a mythical creature called The OverRuler who is destined to join The Chosen One in the final battle. Ether is suspicious of Lucifer's outburst and suggests the crew vote on whether or not to continue with their quest to solve the mystery.

When everyone but Lucifer is in favour, they head for the planet of Rigil Kentaurus and the vast temple complex in its cerise desert wastelands where Taranis believes they will find the answer to this clue and the next in the sequence.

It is only when the dreaded assassins, The Wicked, materialise, Ether realises Lucifer has betrayed them in order to save himself. In a race against time to save the High Priestess of the temple, Ken Palanquis as well as his crew, a terrible tragedy befalls the crew of *The Oisin.*

* * *

Book Two – Ether Heracles and The Lake of Tawaret by Dexter Blake (Antrobus Publishing, November 2010)

The crew is reeling from Lucifer's betrayal and death. Ether suggests they seek refuge on Limni, a safe planet where the peace-loving inhabitants, the Wise Ones, are protected by a rainbow-coloured force field.

As Ether is appointed captain of *The Oisin*, with Allegra as second-in-command, they ask the Wise Ones for help with the next clue: *As a thing is done in reaction to a question, this will be the arrow that points you to the peaceful lake.*

To their surprise, the answer to the clue is on Limni and Bylgja wonders if they were drawn to the planet by another force. However, they must venture into the Deadly Wastes which is home to the evil Pig-Lizard, Despard. A scout from nearby Soutus Major offers to help them cross the barren wastes and lead them to the Crystal Cave where the answer to the clue and the next riddle can be found.

But as they reach their destination, the scout betrays them, leaving Ether and the crew to escape from the dread Maze of Doom and the fearsome Despard.

* * *

Book Three – Ether Heracles and Lugh's Hands by Dexter Blake (Antrobus Publishing, January 2012)

Aboard *The Oisin*, the crew realise the next part of their journey must take them to terrifying planet of Droxfo. Its capital, the City of Sages, is occupied by feral children ruled over by The Lugh.

The Oisin lands and the crew is taken to the current Lugh, Allegra's violent fourteen-year-old sister, Gordana.

As the eldest of seven daughters from high-ranking Boucicauly members, Allegra's decision to join the rebellion has caused a rift with her soldier sisters but when Gordana reveals that their sisters are leading double lives as rebels, Allegra feels safe in asking for help with their quest.

In the abandoned City of the Sages the feral children show them a manuscript containing the answer to the third clue and the curious fourth clue: '*As one who speaks, a seeker of knowledge, know the name of the person to reveal the next step.*'

But stumbling upon a hidden stronghold of the Boucicauly, the crew once more has to fight for their lives against the forces of evil.

* * *

Book Four – Ether Heracles and The Race of Jupiter by Dexter Blake (Antrobus Publishing, March 2013)

Ether is a man in turmoil. He has dark secrets and fears discovery would destroy the trust of his crew, particularly Allegra. The next clue seems to haunt him with its message: '*A need to obtain a heart's desire lies on the biggest planet with a secret of gold.*'

Luna deduces this means the silent gas giant of Jupiter. Fearing it could be a suicide mission, it is with trepidation Allegra flies *The Oisin* into the billowing clouds.

Below, they discover a golden planet of breathtaking beauty. However, the Jupiterians, led by Indraja, arrest the crew. Indraja takes Ether as a slave, transferring him to her harem while throwing the others in her dungeons.

Here they meet Beau Ferris, a handsome freedom fighter from the planet Ra. He offers to help them rescue Ether in exchange for safe passage home. Beau explains his mission is to obtain Nanoc, a metal unique to Jupiter, which is crucial to the creation of a weapon to defeat the Boucicauly.

Using their combined combat and psychic skills, the crew set out to rescue their leader but as they traverse the labyrinthine corridors at the heart of Jupiter, each is haunted by the truths of their past from which they have tried to hide. As Allegra discovers Ether's secret, she wonders whether her future is onboard *The Oisin* and takes drastic action.

* * *

Book Five – Ether Heracles and The Children of Ra by Dexter Blake (Antrobus Publishing, April 2014)

The crew is coming to terms with the revelation of Bylgja and Ether's childhood nuptials, followed by Allegra's knee-jerk marriage to Beau.

Ether sets the coordinates to Beau's home, the mysterious

planet of Ra. It is in the legendary Starburst Galaxy, a twin galaxy to the Milky Way. Beau assures them this is the place to find the answer to the clue: '*In the solar boat, the child steers as Ra. It shines forth in glory, to a subordinate who expresses a statement of fact and space.*'

Beau tells them of a secretive race who are the descendants of the sun God Ra. But as the crew search for answers in the underground pyramids, they realise that once again they have been betrayed...

* * *

Book Six – Ether Heracles and The Elegua Crossroads by Dexter Blake (Antrobus Publishing, June 2016)

Ken deduces the answer to the next clue: '*When there are decisions to make, the crossroads must be a place of caution or the elusive Elegua will cast his illusions in your mind,*' is on Luna's home planet of Stella Erratica in the Yoru galaxy. Ether and the crew believe this is a significant turning point in their travails.

The planet is known for being hostile so the crew is surprised by the absence of guards and the apparent peace. Luna is reunited with her family but when she explains their mission, her parents are terrified and try to stop them. This is when Ether notices the subtle signs of underlying tension.

With so much resting on the success of their search, Ether has no choice but to ignore the warnings and set out for the Abandoned City and the Blue Lapis Dome.

But when they arrive, The Wicked are waiting and the crew face their toughest battle yet.

* * *

Book Seven – Ether Heracles and Nareau's Curse by Dexter Blake (Antrobus Publishing, June 2018)

After their narrow escape on Stella Erratica, Taranis reveals the next clue which he discovered as they fled.

It states: '*In the lair of Nareau, the seeker who is pure of heart will be shown the truth.*' Taranis explains it is on the inhospitable planet of Arach which is ruled by the spider warrior Nareau and his companions, Na Kika the Octopus and Eel the eel.

They are legendary in their loathing of outsiders but thanks to a Taranis and Nareau's shared past, he assures Ether they will be welcomed.

Tales of Ether and the crew's adventures have spread far and wide and when *The Oisin* is pulled in by a tracking beam Nareau greets them personally, delivering the joyous news the Boucicauly's rule is weakening around the Universe.

Nareau offers his finest warriors to Ether and they set off to the lair of the Cursed Ghost where there are dangers they have never imagined.

* * *

Book Eight – Ether Heracles and The Tropic of Pisces by Dexter Blake (Antrobus Publishing, June 2020)

Ether is a worried man. The next clue: '*In the heart of the fish, the third person is singular and only the true-hearted soul of destiny will break the evil.*' Allegra's calculations point to the solution waiting on the enigmatic Tropic of Pisces, a place from which no explorer has ever returned. Ether offers the crew the chance to turn back but they tell him they are with him to the end.

The amphibious inhabitants of the Tropic of Pisces welcome

Ether as a god. Everywhere there are creepy statues of Ether and Allegra but despite being asked to rule, Ether explains his mission and the Pisceans agree to help.

Allegra has long wondered how the questions have been scattered across the Universe. The Pisceans explain The Over-Ruler laid the trail and the identity of this ethereal being will be revealed in the final battle.

As Ether leads his crew and a battalion of Pisces soldiers towards the Sacred Oak Grove and its purple pool, the terrifying Frog People ambush them and they find themselves in a deadly fight for survival.

* * *

Book Nine – Ether Heracles and The Space Sirens by Dexter Blake (Antrobus Publishing, June 2022)

In the troughs of millennia-old sound waves at the edge of the Universe dwell the Space Sirens; a race for whom Ether harbours a personal hatred.

When Bylgja deciphers the clue: '*In accordance with reality, the journey is nearing its end and the power of the Voices of the Dark must be harnessed,*' she realises their next destination is the deadly DarkZone at the edge of time, which nestles in the first sound waves. Ether knows they are at a point of no return.

Beau reveals his twin sister, Zeau, was taken by the Space Sirens and as the crew approach, the truth about the Space Sirens is revealed. Ether finally finds peace with this race of light beings.

With hope of a successful mission, Ether and the crew set out for the fearsome Obsidian Mountain on the planet of

Diamond Light, said to be both the Universe's origin and its end, as well as the resting place of the final clue.

When terrible creatures appear, a new fear arises in the shape of a familiar face and the prospect of another battle to the death.

* * *

Book Ten – Ether Heracles and Ishtar's Legacy by Dexter Blake (Antrobus Publishing, June 2024 [posthumously])

It is the most powerful force in the Universe, the feeling of that drives us through the seven doors to the seven judges to secure our sacred destiny.

The unexpected distress call from Lucifer Transmere has shocked the crew. He is trapped on the slave planet Ereshkigal, where the temple related to their quest is located. Ether knows their only choice is to risk saving their former friend and hoping the trust he promises is genuine.

Upon arrival, they are greeted by Ishtar, the Babylonian goddess of love and war who was summoned to Ereshkigal by a vision of the OverRuler. Ishtar insists Ether accompany her alone through a maze of doors to find the final clue. The rest of the crew teams up with Ishtar's generals, Ingmar and Arishna, to rescue Lucifer and free the slaves.

As Ether finds the answer to the final clue and Allegra frees the slaves from the Boucicauly guards with their giant venom-spitting peacocks, a wave of white light suffuses the Universe. The prophecy has been resolved and the final battle between good and evil has begun.

Who will win? Will Ether triumph? And who is the OverRuler?

In the final, most spectacular of Blake's books all the secrets are finally revealed.

* * *

For those of you who are curious, the sentence the crew has been uncovering is mentioned by Gideon in Chapter 36 but in case you missed it: '*The answer you seek that conquers all is true love.*'

SELECT BIBLIOGRAPHY

If you're interested in discovering more about this period of history, then some of the books I found useful were:

Sarah Bryson, *The Brandon Men, In the Shadow of Kings* (Amberley Publishing, Stroud, 2021)

Mike Dixon-Kennedy, *A Companion to Arthurian and Celtic Myths and Legends* (Sutton Publishing, London, 2004)

Jennifer Kewley Draskau, *The Tudor Rose, Princess Mary, Henry VIII's Sister* (STA Books, 2015)

Kathy Lynn Emerson, *Who's Who of Tudor Women* (Kathy Lynn Emerson Books, 2020)

Eric Ives, *The Life and Death of Anne Boleyn* (Blackwell Publishing, Oxford, 2005)

Sandra Lawrence, *Witch's Forest, Trees in Magic, Folklore and Traditional Remedies* (Welbeck, London, 2023)

Lauren Mackay, *Among the Wolves of Court, The Untold Story of Thomas and George Boleyn* (I. B. Tauris & Co Ltd, London, 2018)

Sir Thomas Malory, Edited, Stephen H A Shepherd, *Le Morte D'Arthur* (W W Norton Publishing, New York, 2004)

Sir Thomas More, *Utopia* (CenterSpace, 2022)
Beverley A Murphy, *Bastard Prince, Henry VIII's Lost Son* (The History Press, Stroud, 2001)
Elizabeth Norton, *The Lives of Tudor Women* (Head of Zeus, UK, 2016)
Mary Perry, *Sisters of the King, The tumultuous lives of Henry VIII's sisters – Margaret of Scotland and Mary of France* (Andre Deutsch, London 1998)
Melita Thomas, *The House of Grey, Friends and Foes of Kings* (Amberley Publishing, Stroud, 2019)
Alison Weir, *Mary Boleyn* (Vintage Books, London, 2012)
Peter Wohlleben, *The Hidden Life of Trees, What they Feel, How they Communicate, Discoveries from a Secret World* (William Collins, London, 2007)
Jill Young, *Pembrokeshire Standing Stones* (Gwasg Carreg Gwalch, Llanrwst, 2015)

Other sources:
Godchecker.com
Dictionary of National Biography
History of Parliament Online
British History Online
Wikipedia

ACKNOWLEDGEMENTS

Thank you for reading *The House of Echoes,* I hope you enjoyed meeting Caroline, Anne, Gideon and Randall with their friends and families as they traversed the unknown paths and galaxies of true love.

This has been a challenging book to write for many personal reasons and my thanks for all the help, love and support along the way is even more heartfelt than usual. Thank you again to my wonderful agent, Sara Keane, with her kindness, humour and understanding. Thank you to Sarah Ritherdon for her patience, consideration and care while she waited for me to deliver the manuscript. A huge thank you to the wider team at Boldwood Books too: Amanda, Nia, Marcela, Ben, Sue, Shirley, Mills and the marvellous group responsible for the cover, copy-editing, proofreading and marketing. You made a difficult time far easier to manage.

Thank you to all the people who are always there to offer support, advice and wine. Deborah Black, Gemma Turner, Alison, Katy (God-daughter extraordinaire), Martha and Richard Miles, Shaun Rose, Kathryn, Simon, Daisy and Nelly Bennett, David Cottrell, Ian Connell, Emma Gregory, Jo Walker, Viv Bishton, Suzi Judd, Kate Richardson, Colena Abosh, Jane Cable, Carol McGrath and Bijou Mgbojikwe. Also, a huge thank you to Juliet and Bob with their extended families and the perfect day in Polzeath.

Most importantly, thank you to you for reading this book, without you, none of this would be possible.

If you would like to know more about Anne Brandon and her extraordinary life, then read on.

ABOUT THE AUTHOR

Alexandra Walsh is the bestselling author of dual timeline historical mysteries. Her books range from the fifteenth century to the Victorian era and are inspired by the hidden voices of women that have been lost over the centuries. Formerly a journalist, writing for national newspapers, magazines and TV.

Sign up to Alexandra Walsh's mailing list here for news, competitions and updates on future books.

Visit Alexandra's website: http://www.alexandrawalsh.com/

Follow Alexandra on social media:

facebook.com/themarquesshousetrilogy
x.com/purplemermaid25
instagram.com/purplemermaid25
tiktok.com/@alexandracwalsh

ALSO BY ALEXANDRA WALSH

The Forgotten Palace

The Secrets of Crestwell Hall

The House of Echoes

www.ingramcontent.com/pod-product-compliance
Ingram Content Group UK Ltd.
Pitfield, Milton Keynes, MK11 3LW, UK
UKHW020327170125
4139UKWH00086B/1767

9 781804 159651